Elyana whirled, arrow nocked to her bow. "It's here!"

Drelm ripped one of his throwing axes free and perceived the sway of branches where there was no wind, just to the left of the tracks Elyana had been examining.

Elyana launched an arrow into the emptiness beside the bending branches. A second and third winged after as Illidian's sentries came running.

But the arrows only clattered from the side of some huge unseen object. Elyana cursed and shouted for blades.

Drelm launched his axe, his teeth bared in a grin that displayed his lower canines. For all that he strove for balance, Drelm never questioned a righteous battle, and this was surely one of them.

His axe stuck in something at roughly head height, and then blood sprayed forth to dye scales hung in midair a deep scarlet. Whatever the invisible beast was came on swift feet. The thing's tread was silent, but the ground rocked as its bulk raced forward.

Drelm slapped Charger's haunch to send him galloping to safety, then took up his battleaxe and rushed the monster with a savage cry. He was awash with the joy of battle, and he grinned to find Melloc beside him with bared sword.

He kept track of the monster's approach by his axe, which seemed to be floating above the bloody scales. Just as the axe drew within striking range, a great weight slammed into his side and sent him flying . . .

The Pathfinder Tales Library

Called to Darkness by Richard Lee Byers
Winter Witch by Elaine Cunningham
The Wizard's Mask by Ed Greenwood
Prince of Wolves by Dave Gross
Master of Devils by Dave Gross
Queen of Thorns by Dave Gross
King of Chaos by Dave Gross
Pirate's Honor by Chris A. Jackson
Plague of Shadows by Howard Andrew Jones
Stalking the Beast by Howard Andrew Jones
The Worldwound Gambit by Robin D. Laws
Blood of the City by Robin D. Laws
Song of the Serpent by Hugh Matthews
Nightglass by Liane Merciel
City of the Fallen Sky by Tim Pratt
Liar's Blade by Tim Pratt
Death's Heretic by James L. Sutter
The Dagger of Trust by Chris Willrich

Stalking the Beast

Howard Andrew Jones

Cover art by Sam Burley.
Cover design by Andrew Vallas.
Map by Crystal Frasier.

Paizo Publishing, LLC
7120 185th Ave NE, Ste 120
Redmond, WA 98052
paizo.com

ISBN 978-1-60125-572-3 (mass market paperback)
ISBN 978-1-60125-573-0 (ebook)

Publisher's Cataloging-In-Publication Data
(Prepared by The Donohue Group, Inc.)

Jones, Howard A.
Stalking the beast / Howard Andrew Jones.

p. : map ; cm. -- (Pathfinder tales)

Set in the world of the role-playing game, Pathfinder.
Issued also as an ebook.
ISBN: 978-1-60125-572-3 (mass market pbk.)

1. Monsters--Fiction. 2. Imaginary places--Fiction. 3. Good and evil--Fiction. 4. Pathfinder (Game)--Fiction. 5. Fantasy fiction. 6. Adventure stories. I. Title. II. Series: Pathfinder tales library.

PS3610.O62535 .S73 2013
813/.6

First printing October 2013.

Printed in the United States of America.

To the memory of my father, Victor Howard Jones, for the gift of story and so much more. I wish you were here to hold this book.

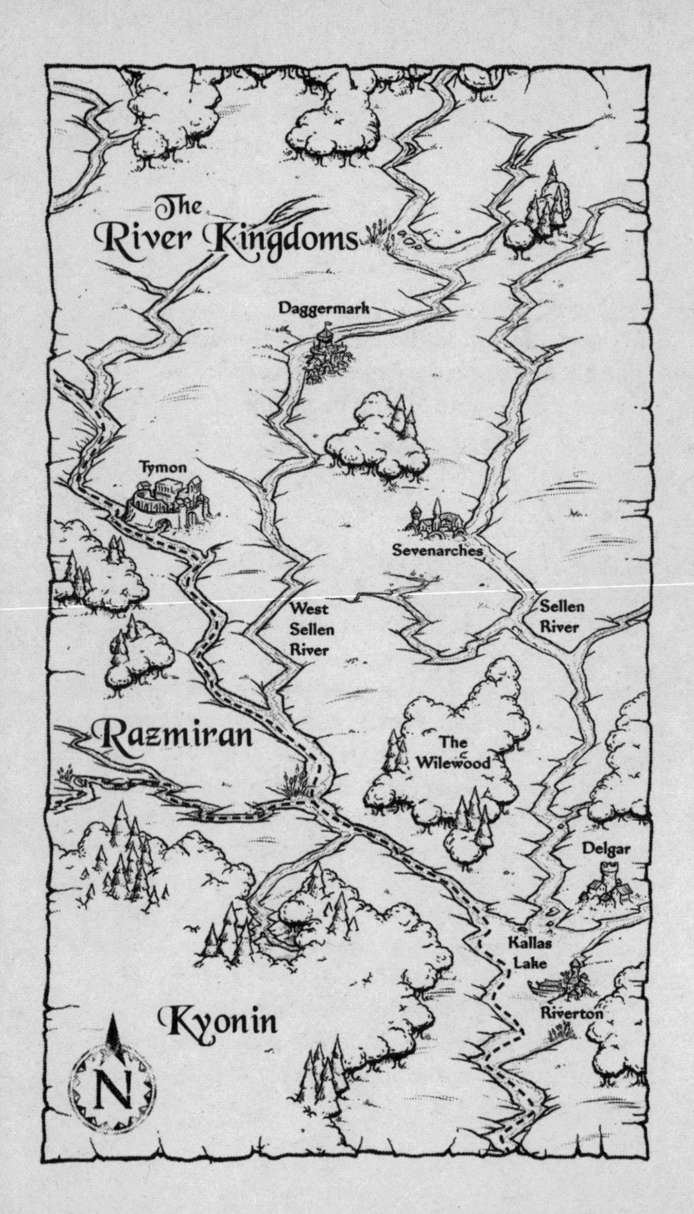
The River Kingdoms
Daggermark
Tymon
Sevenarches
West Sellen River
Sellen River
Razmiran
The Wilewood
Delgar
Kallas Lake
Riverton
Kyonin
N

Chapter One

The Sorcerer's Wand

Elyana

Melloc screamed in terror as the emerald bolt splattered his bright blue tabard. He stumbled for cover.

Elyana dropped, sliced the nearside straps that buckled the leather armor sizzling beneath his ruined tabard. The cackle of the sorcerer who'd thrown the spell was a distant irritation

"Stay down," Elyana hissed to the young guardsman. His panicked struggles threatened to expose him to more fire. There was precious little room behind the rounded brown stone where he and Elyana had raced for protection. It didn't stretch a full horse length, and if either of them were to rise into a crouch, Onderan could target their heads.

While Melloc fumbled with his other buckle, Elyana heard a loud pop from atop the boulder, like grease in a frying pan. Her gaze whipped up. A green glow burned along the stone's rim.

Nothing to worry about there . . . yet. She reached over Melloc to slash his other strap, then rolled to snatch her bow and sent arrows winging across the distance between them and the mad sorcerer. Three shafts arced out over the sunlit meadow, disappearing behind the dappled sienna boulder a hundred yards distant.

She fired three more and then, as the arrows were still airborne, dropped the bow and grabbed the shoulders of Melloc's armor to aid the young man as he wrestled out of the boiling, popping ruin. Once free, Melloc lay panting, his bright eyes intent upon the nacreous green edges of the fist-sized hole in his armor. Steam snaked upward, bringing with it the scent of scorched padding.

"Gods," he whispered. "Thank you, Elyana.

Elyana clapped his shoulder. "You alright?"

"Fine." Melloc's answer was a little too swift to be true. He felt the white tunic he'd been wearing beneath the armor, then lifted it to inspect the muscled torso beneath.

The ends of his blond mustache trembled as he breathed deeply. "Can he burn through the whole rock? The one we're hiding behind, I mean?"

"Maybe," Elyana answered, "but I don't think he will. That would drain the magic in his wand. He was probably aiming for your heart."

Melloc paled.

"Relax. We have him pinned." She offered a reassuring smile.

Grace and beauty tended to be the bywords for elves in human societies, and Elyana was like them in that regard, from slender tapering ears to long limbs. Yet she was far from some primped, high-society diplomat. Elyana was a warrior woman, with weathered gear that included the worn black sheath that held her longsword, the battered but sturdy quiver slung over her shoulders, and the finely fashioned recurved bow of bone and yew. Loose black breeks tucked into heavy cavalry boots, and brown sleeved armor of interlocking leather plates draped her from neck to thigh, covering all but a hint of the beige cuffs and collar of her shirt. If the sword belt cinching it all off defined her waist and hinted at curves beneath, it was no concern of Elyana's. Armor was for staying alive, not attracting suitors.

Though her garb was all but colorless, Elyana herself was crowned by auburn hair pulled tightly back from her forehead. Her eyes were a violet so vivid they seemed almost to glow. Those eyes now left consideration of Melloc as she peered at the distant boulder where Onderan had taken refuge.

No one could hope to survive in the River Kingdoms for long without some wildlands knowledge, and Onderan was no novice. But he was not nearly as crafty as he supposed, for he'd managed to be chased into a narrow, steep-sided valley with a dead end.

With its lovely wildflowers, colorful red-brown cliff side, and abundant greenery, the area seemed an incongruous site for a battle to the death.

The sorcerer's voice was a dry rasp, yet deceptively light. "You missed me again, elf!" he shouted. "But I didn't miss your friend. Did I kill him?"

One of several things Elyana liked about Melloc was his composure, remarkable in someone still under the age of twenty. But the young man's brush with death had apparently shattered his good judgment, and he couldn't resist an answer.

"Still alive, madman!"

Elyana held a hand up to him, shaking her head. Melloc's cheeks flushed a little in embarrassment.

"Well," Onderan responded mockingly, "I thank you for guiding me to such a highly defensible position. You did fine!" He laughed. "I have a better shot at you than you do at me!"

"Stupid bastard," Melloc muttered. His eyes narrowed. "I'd trade a lot for a good shot at him."

"You nearly traded everything," Elyana reminded him. Melloc's gaze locked with her own and she saw his jaw shake in rage. "We've got him in a dead end, remember?"

Melloc nodded reluctantly.

"There's nothing he can do unless he gets *you* angry enough to make a mistake."

"Right."

"If you get killed on my watch, your father will have my head."

Melloc grinned at that. "Father's too fond of you to take your head."

The lord mayor had, politely enough, indicated his interest, and she acknowledged this with a faint quirk of her lips. "True or not, I don't intend to lose you because of an old fool's taunts. We just have to keep Onderan occupied until Drelm's in position."

At mention of the captain of Delgar's guard force, Melloc glanced at the steep cliff overlooking the east side of the sorcerer's hiding place.

There was yet no sign of the big half-orc. Drelm was not especially nimble, but he was an experienced climber. Elyana expected him to arrive at the summit at any moment. Onderan would be unable to see him from his hiding place.

"If you want to trade insults, go ahead," Elyana continued, softly. "Just remember why you're doing it."

Melloc brushed the ends of his mustache with grass-stained hands. They shook a little, she saw, reminding her this kind of opposition was new to the young man. A year on the guard force had seen him chase off a few wretched river pirates and break up some brawls, but he'd never faced a sorcerer out to kill him.

Melloc stared into the blue sky above their boulder. "What finally made you snap?" the young man called. "You get tired of living in the wastelands, old man?"

"I got tired of your father!" the sorcerer called back. "Lording it over everyone on the river like some prancy Taldan duke! Course, there ain't any Taldan dukes who'd want an orc in their family tree!"

Melloc's brows furrowed.

"How you feel about that, boy? A green pitchfork in your sister's hay patch?" Onderan cackled gleefully.

Melloc fumed and fumbled at his sword.

"What are you planning?" Elyana whispered tightly.

Melloc pointed at the boulder, in Onderan's general direction. "He insulted my sister *and* the captain."

Elyana stared at him. "Melloc," she said, "when Drelm and Daylah marry, they're going to be having sex. A lot. You do realize that?"

"Of course I do!" The boy exclaimed, then immediately lowered his voice, and his head. "But it's no one else's business! Least of all his!"

"You'll be hearing about it for the rest of your life," she told him. "And so will they. Best get used to it.

"It's no one's business but theirs," Melloc repeated.

"Do you plan to trim the head off every gossip or old prig you ever meet?"

Melloc frowned.

"Tell me, Elyana," Onderan called to them. "You're good with animals! You ever ride on the orc's green saddle!" He dissolved into titters.

"He goes too far!" Melloc snapped.

"Your sense of honor will get you killed." Elyana liked the boy, but she was losing patience with him. If she'd known they'd end up hunting a fugitive on today's patrol she would have brought Demid or Gered. She raised her voice. "What is it you want, Onderan?"

The madman laughed. At the same moment, Elyana caught sight of Drelm crawling forward to the height of the overhang sixty feet above the sorcerer.

Her friend was broad and thick, and his skin indeed held a faint greenish tint. As he was on duty, the half-orc would normally have worn the same sort of metal helm still shielding Melloc. This he'd put aside so sunlight wouldn't reflect and reveal his position. The blue tabard of Delgar, too, had been removed, and Elyana supposed that was because her fastidious friend didn't want to mar the cloth with mud or grass. Drelm possessed a fine chainmail shirt, but today he was garbed only in the same light leather byrnie formerly worn by Melloc, well browned and matched almost to the color of his hair. A chameleon would have been hard pressed to blend into its surroundings so well.

"What do I want, elf?" Onderan asked. "I already have what I want!"

Drelm's head turned toward Elyana, and she knew he was awaiting her signal. He was no great marksman with a bow, but he had a good eye with his throwing axe, and Elyana was sure Onderan would already be dead if she'd commanded it.

But she didn't want the sorcerer dead. Not yet. She wanted answers.

Why had Onderan, a cantankerous but pliable old hermit, suddenly launched into a killing spree against every living thing at Hamdan's farm? And when had he ever commanded the kind of power he displayed now?

Drelm had wanted to bring Onderan down like the mad dog he was, and, seeing her friend's precarious situation, she was starting to wish she'd let him. Drelm could easily scale down the face of the cliff, but he'd be well exposed doing so.

Elyana signaled to him to move forward on his own call. He raised a hand in acknowledgment, then waited.

She'd have to keep Onderan talking. "There's got to be something you want, Onderan!"

Once more he laughed. "Are you offering yourself? All this talk of fornication get you excited, Elyana?"

"He's disgusting," Melloc said softly.

Elyana's lips twisted in agreement that was not revealed in the tone of her reply. "I'm not up for negotiation."

Drelm must have judged the moment right, for he was lowering himself over the side, seeking footholds. She saw he'd removed his usual gauntlets, but retained his heavy boots. She hoped they had good traction.

"Too bad," Onderan's voice came back. "I've had my fill of wine. And the best food that godsforsaken, puffed-up, filthy village can manufacture. Your father ain't lord of much, Melloc!"

"There's gold," Elyana suggested.

"What do you mean?" Onderan shouted back. "You're offering me gold?" Again came that cackling laugh. "You'll pay me to expose myself to your arrows? How stupid do you think I am?"

Elyana's response was immediate. "That's not what I'm suggesting."

Drelm inched a little farther down the cliff, then slipped out of her sight behind an outthrust rock.

There was a sudden silence, and Elyana felt a stab of fear. If Onderan were to turn his head he'd spot Drelm, and that wand would make short work of him.

She steeled herself to hear a sudden cry of triumph and to see the heavy body of her best friend plummeting through the air, half-dissolved by a sorcerous blast.

But the silence continued. Finally, Onderan asked a question. "What *are* you suggesting?"

Melloc's smile was wry. "I was wondering the same thing," he whispered.

She ignored the boy and raised her voice once more. "You know I don't care about backwoods farm rats, Onderan! What I need is a sorcerer. One who can do a lot of damage!"

There was still no sign of Drelm. Where had he gone?

Onderan's laugh was shorter this time, not mocking so much as incredulous. "You want to work with me?"

"It's not about *wanting*, Onderan. The River Kingdoms aren't exactly swimming in competent sorcerers. I had no idea how dangerous you could be."

Elyana knelt, head low so that it didn't rise higher than her cover, then lifted three arrows from her quiver and set one to her string.

"Hah! I'm full of surprises!" Onderan shouted back. "What do you want, and what will it pay?"

She waited until she saw Drelm's foot and leg extend from behind the outcrop that blocked him. Fifteen feet lay between him and the ground now.

"Answers," Elyana shouted. "And there are—"

Onderan's voice rose in a strangled cry of fear and surprise.

A green bolt of energy soared through the air toward the figure on the cliff. Drelm's body stiffened on impact. There was the briefest delay, and then he dropped feetfirst.

Elyana was already launching arrows, seized by cold dread. It was no easy thing to shoot a hidden target, so she was thankful for Onderan's screams of outrage. Each time he shouted impossible things about Elyana's ancestry she had a better chance of homing in on his exact location.

Beside her, Melloc was chattering some worry about Drelm, and asking if it were alright to charge, and how she knew she wasn't hitting the captain. She was too busy firing arrows skyward in rapid succession to answer him. Ten were airborne in as many seconds. The moment the last one left the string she whistled for her horse.

Calda galloped up from where she'd been hidden in the thicket behind them. Elyana vaulted into the mare's saddle without touching the stirrups. At the same moment, she heard a scream of pain. Onderan, not Drelm.

A single touch to her horse's flank set the animal galloping forward.

"He might be faking it!" Melloc called.

Elyana's answer was only a mutter. "Not for long."

The dun mare raced across the meadow at full speed, but it felt impossibly slow to Elyana until she'd rounded the large boulder and saw an armorless Drelm standing over the prone, motionless body leaking blood from a gruesome head wound. A hand axe, the proximal cause of all the blood, was buried deep in the sorcerer's forehead. One of her own shafts was stuck through his thigh.

Elyana grinned in relief, and her keen sight caught the smoking armor a few paces beyond Drelm, discarded by the half-orc. Arrow shafts sprouted like strange plants in the vicinity of Onderan's hiding place.

"Nice work," Drelm said in his low, deep voice. "He was too busy with the arrows to spell me again."

Calda let out a long snort as Elyana swung down. The mare danced lightly with ears erect.

"It looks like you and Melloc are both going to need armor repair," Elyana said. "Any serious injuries? You could have broken your legs."

Drelm patted his left shoulder. "A little scorched. Nothing serious."

Elyana knew better than to ask if he wanted her to take a look.

There was a thunder of hoofbeats as Melloc rode into view, his eyes brightening in relief as he reined in his gray gelding and dropped down. "Are you alright, Captain?"

Drelm grunted, and his small eyes looked briefly over Melloc. He must have satisfied his own curiosity about the young man's health, for he didn't speak.

Melloc then joined Elyana in looking down at the body. He let out a low whistle. "I thought we were going to catch him alive."

"I planned to." Drelm pointed to the axe. "That would have hit him in the arm, but he ducked."

Elyana looked over the body. Onderan didn't look so much like a sorcerer as he did a trapper who'd survived in the wild alone for long years. He wore a furred hat, leather pants, a filthy white shirt, and a threadbare blue vest that seemed mostly fashioned from patches and mud. His beard was wild and thick, its gray shot through with a little brown.

Elyana bent to the long, rather elegant black wand that lay beside the dead man's gnarled fingertips.

"Is that safe to touch?" Melloc asked her.

"Likely so," Elyana told him, although she was scanning it now without laying a hand to it.

Melloc's mouth twisted sourly. "I know you're not supposed to search sorcerers because they trap their clothes. But I'm not sure we'd want to touch him anyway."

"I've never met a spellcaster who trapped his or her clothes," Elyana answered. She didn't add that she'd searched her fair share of dead shadow wizards. Her old friend Arcil had once snorted in contempt at the idea that wizards and sorcerers would booby-trap their belongings, as they'd constantly be triggering the traps themselves.

"Check the horse." Drelm pointed to where a black gelding was tethered by its reins to a spindly elm a good arrow flight toward the end of the gorge. Onderan's mount stood in a bed of clover, munching contentedly.

The horse had been stolen from Hamdan's farm, and, judging from their worn but cared-for look, so had the saddle and saddlebags.

Melloc hesitated. "Do you think the saddlebags are trapped?"

Now the boy was being cautious? Elyana answered without looking up, and kept the rebuke from her voice. "Onderan didn't seem to be much of a planner. They're probably fine."

While the boy stepped away, she crouched and considered the blood-smeared face with its slack, gap-toothed jaw. The protruding haft of Drelm's throwing axe was distractingly just a finger span off true center.

She began the grisly business of searching the corpse by putting her right hand to first his arms, then his chest, then his legs. The battered dwarven bracelet she wore around her bicep was ugly enough that she always hid it beneath her sleeve, but it had served her well for many years. In addition to lending a small enhancement to her physical prowess, the bracelet, by accident or design, thrummed whenever she made contact with any other enchanted item, or a limb favored by one.

Onderan proved remarkably free of any sort of magic, apart from the wand. That and the gold in his coin purse were the only clean things in his possession, unless you counted the stolen food and wine in his saddlebags.

She stood puzzling over the matter with Drelm while Melloc brought up the horses and retrieved the half-orc's gear.

Drelm had grown accustomed to Elyana's methods over the years, yet couldn't seem to leave off pacing as he waited. He didn't push her to speak until she'd been staring down at the gold she'd dumped in the grass for a long time.

Drelm's explanation was simple. "Sometimes," he said in his low rumble, "people are just born wrong. They can fake it for years, and then something breaks inside them. All the hate and crazy comes out at once."

"Yes," Elyana acknowledged. "There's an awful lot of gold here, though, Drelm."

"Surely. Stolen from the farmers."

"I don't think so. For starters, Onderan went on a spending spree in Delgar a few nights ago. Remember? Demid told us about it last night. And I'm pretty sure that was before Onderan killed Hamdan and his family. You saw how recent the kills were."

Drelm grunted at that. "Maybe he killed someone else, first."

"Who? A tax collector from Daggermark? This is Livondar's coinage, and it's freshly minted. How'd he get it? Everyone says Onderan's been living alone in that nasty shack since before Delgar's founding."

Drelm frowned, and Elyana could almost see him working through the possible conclusions. "Do you think someone paid him to kill Hamdan and his family?"

She shook her head. "Not unless Hamdan was a lot more important than we realized."

Drelm scratched his jaw. "Well, Hamdan wasn't any kind of warrior or wizard in disguise, but I suppose there might have been a bounty on him."

There were a lot of bounties on Riverfolk—part of the region's draw was how far it lay from civilized lands, so it attracted its fair share of those with prices on their heads. "Even if that's true," she answered, "why pay someone who's not a bounty hunter to go kill him instead of killing Hamdan yourself?"

Possibly because someone didn't want to get his hands dirty, she thought to herself. She didn't believe that, though.

Melloc returned with Drelm's horse, Charger, and stepped slowly over, clearing his throat to announce himself.

"What if Onderan here got paid to do something else, but needed a horse and some supplies to get there?" the young man asked. "It was just his bad luck we stopped at Hamdan's place to water our horses this morning."

"Maybe." Elyana frowned. "We'll let your father decide what to do with the money. If Hamdan has any relatives, I suppose they should get a cut of it."

"That sounds fair," Melloc agreed.

Drelm grunted appreciatively. As a devout follower of Abadar, god of laws and civilization, Drelm was ever concerned with fairness, though he applied the principles rather bluntly.

"Let's gather up the gold." Elyana reached down to gingerly touch the wand beside the dead man's fingers.

Its surface was mostly smooth, and cool to the touch. Her bracelet hummed gently against her upper arm, as she'd expected.

A set of decorative rings was set a thumb-width from the wand's slimmer end. There was an unfamiliar sigil carved on its lower haft, but no obvious activation word. "This seems a little odd too, doesn't it?" she asked.

Drelm just looked at her, so she explained further. "If he'd ever had a wand like this before, we would have heard about it."

"That's a fair point," Melloc agreed. "There's a lot about this whole thing that's strange."

That was an understatement. From the horrifying moment they'd come upon the massacre of man, woman, child, and beast at the farm, through the moment they'd tracked the horse and rider into the wilderness, Elyana had been puzzling over the explanation. Melloc, though, was being groomed for an officer's post, so she wanted to see what he would make of it. "What do you think should be done?"

The young man required little time to reach his conclusion. "We should look at Onderan's shack. And we should approach carefully."

"Why?"

"In case there's been a visitor. Someone who paid him. We don't want to ruin the tracks."

Elyana smiled. "Well reasoned. A visitor would almost surely have arrived by horse, particularly one who came with gold."

Drelm grunted agreement. "Smart as his old man," the orc said.

Elyana wasn't quite as impressed, but said nothing as Melloc flushed a little at praise from the half-orc. It was easy to see how much the boy looked up to his father, Avelis. He practically lived for hope of a good word from him.

Melloc cleared his throat and feigned composure. "What do we do with the body?"

"Leave it," Elyana said.

"For carrion?" Melloc sounded horrified.

"We'll bury his victims. He can rot."

Melloc looked to Drelm for reassurance, but the half-orc was already climbing onto his great warhorse.

Elyana slid the black wand into her pack and swung into her saddle. In a few moments they were moving at a good clip over the rolling grasslands toward the Sellen River.

They were halfway to Onderan's wretched shack when the screaming started.

Chapter Two
The Thing by the River
Drelm

It was easy to see why some people acted without regard—they lacked balance. Drelm understood the struggle for balance because he fought for it every day. Achieving it was no simple matter, and, being a warrior, he even allowed that not every battle could be won. What mystified him were men like Onderan who'd so clearly decided to give up fighting their baser instincts. If the old wizard had but followed the teachings of Abadar, he wouldn't now be worm food. Such power as he'd wielded with that wand might have been put to some useful purpose.

Drelm was a practical man, and usually put as little thought into the death of bad men as he did the end of mad dogs. Yet he'd not been able to shake the memory of Hamdan's two dead boys, one with his face melted away. The same horrors had been visited upon a half-dozen geese, a donkey, and two draft horses.

Drelm's lips curled in anger as he rode out from the site of Onderan's end. He was proud to have killed the wizard. But if what Elyana said was true—and what Elyana said was usually true, for she was very clever—then there was some greater danger. And it was Drelm's goal to make the village of Delgar and its surrounding environs as free from danger as he could.

Yet it did no good to worry about what one didn't know, and a warrior was always better served to focus on his surroundings, so Drelm put his concerns aside.

It was good to be in the saddle, after all, astride his great black Charger. He'd never owned a finer animal. The horse was almost tireless. Some horses seemed to live for eating, but Charger lived to move, growing impatient if too many days passed without new sights. Like many of the best things in his life, Charger had come to him through Elyana, who had personally trained the horse.

It was good to sit so fine an animal, and to ride with his best friend. It was good to have a home where they both belonged. Elyana was not the outsider she'd been in Lord Stelan's village, loved by some and mistrusted by others. Here, in Delgar, she and Drelm were equally valued. Drelm had known respect under the great Lord Stelan, and he thanked Abadar every evening that he had served so fine a man. Yet Delgar was even a better place.

Someone screamed.

The sound had been forced from a male voice. Drelm's hand went instantly to the haft of one of his throwing axes.

Elyana gestured for them to halt and cocked her head to one side as the horses stopped and shifted restlessly. She pointed southeast as the scream trailed off, then nudged Calda. The light brown mare sprang into a gallop.

Drelm and Melloc quickly followed, and Drelm had to restrain Charger so he did not race past the elf's horse. The animal was fiercely competitive.

Elyana looked over at him as they galloped. Her auburn hair, tied off behind her, thudded against her back and the top of her quiver with each hoof fall. "That was an elven voice," she called.

Drelm didn't question how she knew—when Elyana said a thing, it was true.

The scream resumed at a higher level. At the same moment a clear horn call pierced the air, sweet and plaintive.

A strange fire blossomed in those violet eyes, and Elyana kneed her mare forward to greater speed as they rode past a copse of willows.

Drelm never thought of his friend in a romantic way—she was his sister warrior, and his heart belonged to another—but he admired her easy grace. Elyana was like a hunting cat, sleek, agile, a beautiful predator. He had never met anyone quite like her, even other elves. Oh, she might resemble them physically, but she never projected that weary, aloof superiority. And she didn't waste her time with pointless talking, which annoyed him even though he didn't understand a word of the elven language.

He and Melloc followed Elyana through the roughened upland that gave way to rolling grass. After almost two years patrolling outside Delgar, he'd learned the countryside well enough to recognize the thick stand of trees that lay ahead. He knew that as soon as they reached them they'd be on a hill looking down toward the eastern run of the Sellen.

Elyana signed for Drelm and Melloc to go left while she circled in from the right.

Drelm motioned Melloc after him, then reined in the eager Charger so he trotted in along the edge of the trees.

Much of the woodland of the River Kingdoms was old-growth forest—towering oak and ash. Drelm always liked the crisp, clean smell of the stately old trees, but this day the air was marred by the scent of blood. His horse caught the scent and snorted in warning, ears swiveling back. Drelm shot a glance to Melloc, but the boy was sharp and already had one hand to his sword hilt.

They saw the bodies the moment they cleared the woodland. Midway between the trees and the two long boats drawn up neatly on the sandy shore were the remnants of an elven hunting party.

Two of the corpses lay scattered near the blood-smeared grass north of the boats, but two more were crumpled by ash trees at the forest's edge. One of them held a hunting horn.

Drelm rode into the midst of the massacre and dismounted heavily, battleaxe to hand. Melloc was there a moment later, and both were bending down over the body clasping the hunting horn when they heard the cold, crisp words of command behind them.

"Throw down your weapons! Press your faces to the dirt!"

The speaker was male. Drelm was fairly sure he was an elf just by the musical quality of his voice. What he didn't understand was how the elves had managed to sneak up behind him.

He and Melloc turned their heads slowly, discovering at the same moment that three elves had stepped from the woods. They were garbed like their dead brethren, in forest greens and browns, their long straight hair tied back from their foreheads. If it hadn't been already clear from the commands, their expressions left no doubt that their anger was barely held in check. Drelm was used to seeing a sort of permanent condescension stamped on elven features, but the eyes of these three were narrowed in fury.

"You heard me, orc! Drop or die!"

The speaker was unusually brief for an elf. Drelm didn't like taking orders from those outside the chain of his command. He was still weighing his choices when Melloc spoke out.

"This is no orc," the youth declared, "but a man, the captain of the Delgar city guard. He is pledged to the daughter of the lord mayor, my sister."

Drelm was pleased with the boy's courage. A lot of veterans didn't have the stones to face hostile warriors with leveled arrows, and those that did might have sounded a little more worried.

The leader's amber-flecked brown eyes flicked briefly to Drelm, then back to the boy. Neither he nor his companions looked likely to lower their weapons, and the one on the right pulled his bowstring further back.

To Drelm, most male elves looked fairly similar. Upon closer scrutiny, though, he observed that the one who addressed them had a slim scar along the edge of his nose.

"We came to help," Melloc insisted. "But if you slay us, you kill the heir to Delgar and his future brother."

"Kyonin cares nothing about anyone in your festering dungheap of a village," the elf said, icily. "Drop, or die. I will bandy no more words with you."

"Kyonin may not care, but I do." Elyana's voice came calmly from behind the rank of elves. "Do not turn," she said swiftly, then lapsed into the elven tongue.

Scar Nose, all but gnashing his teeth, held a quick, sharp speech with the woman he could not see, then lowered his weapon and, saying something to his companions, stepped to the side. Each of them kept their arrows nocked, though the weapons were no longer trained upon Drelm and Melloc.

Elyana strode out from the trees, her own bow held almost carelessly. When the lead elf addressed her, she cut him off abruptly.

"Speak Taldane. The boy wears no tabard because it was destroyed in a fight with a sorcerer. And you can see Captain Drelm's. Surely elves of the Kyonin border patrol know of the half-orc in Delgar's service." It was not so much a question as an insult.

The leader's head rose; slim nostrils flared, and then he returned his arrow to its quiver in one swift motion.

"You must be Elyana Sadrastis," he said, coolly. "I have heard tales of you, and the . . . half-orc with whom you ride. I am Captain Illidian. You must pardon our manner, cousin. We did not return in time to aid our friends, and found these two bent over their bodies."

Elyana didn't look as if she felt particularly like pardoning anyone. She whistled, and Calda trotted around the trees, ears high. "Don't stand talking," Elyana told Illidian. "Don't you want to find what did this?"

Illidian turned to his companions and, after a few rapid-fire elven words, they deployed to left and right and took up posts. At a few more phrases, Elyana's brows rose in stunned disbelief. "What of tracks near the bodies?"

Drelm was wondering the same thing. He again bent down beside the blood-spattered warrior at his feet. There was no missing the huge, splay-foot lizardlike tracks, complete with clawed toes. "Whatever did it can't have gone far."

Illidian's mouth tightened as he returned to speaking a formally accented Taldane. "We aren't fools. The beast seems capable of appearing and disappearing at will. It may be miles away at this time."

Drelm directed Melloc to examine the bodies closer to the boats, and the young man hurried to comply. His horse was jittery around the smell of blood, and resisted as Melloc led him by the reins.

Drelm stared down at the bugler. The lower third of the elf's body had been pressed down by a great weight, and his clothes were saturated with internal juices. Insects already swarmed over him, attracted by the foul smell. Drelm's stomach was practically iron, but even he found the sight disquieting. He turned to Illidian before tracing out another large depression in the grass. Was this the sign of a long, heavy tail? "What kind of beast is it?"

"No one's ever seen it," Illidian replied, "because it seems to be invisible. It does leave tracks, almost as if it wants to be followed, and then disappears."

"And it doesn't eat," Drelm pointed out. He turned from his consideration of the corpse with the horn and looked around at all the dead elves. None of the four had been so much as nibbled. The bugler looked as though his chest had been seared with something not too dissimilar from the effects of Onderan's magical wand, just a little larger.

Down by the boats, Melloc stared at a body that had been torn nearly in half.

"You tracked it here?" Elyana asked Illidian.

"I can't believe you haven't heard of the thing. It's been raiding up and down the River Kingdoms lands for the last weeks. We found its fresh tracks near the riverbank on the Kyonin side, then searched the north bank until we saw where it had come out."

Elyana paced away from him, then knelt by one of the ash trees on the edge of the small line of woods.

"What is it?" Drelm joined her.

Elyana pointed to the ground, where the half-orc saw the passage of something weighty into the woods via smashed tree limbs and squashed bushes. In the detritus were a muddle of marks, two or three of them showing a reptilian print wider across than a good-sized ale barrel.

"The thing's moving slowly east," Illidian went on. "It's been seen in Tymon, and there have been attacks in Lambreth and the Sevenarches as well, and a bold assault against one of our patrol outposts. If it keeps moving west, Riverton or your Delgar are next. It tends to level structures in its path."

Drelm turned back to the elf. "What do you mean by 'level?'"

"It brings down buildings and kills everyone inside," Illidian replied curtly. "It's mostly impervious to damage, although sometimes a lucky arrow or blade can find a mark. When it returns, it always seems completely recovered."

Drelm frowned at the thought of this. "And you think it's moving toward Delgar? How do you know?"

"I can't know, for certain." The elf's jaw tightened grimly. "But the line of its wanton ruin runs in that direction." Illidian turned away, and Drelm understood suddenly that the elf was troubled by the bodies of his men. With that realization, he knew a sudden pang of sympathy.

"I do not have a shovel," Drelm told him, "but if you have extras, I'll help you dig."

Illidian eyed him in surprise. "That is kind of you." His voice was strained. "But we will transport their bodies to Kyonin for our funeral rites."

Elyana was still bent over the marks, and called back to them. "It looks as though it has a tail."

Illidian nodded once. "It has four feet, with clawed toes, and a long, tapering tail that it doesn't always drag behind it. I estimate that it must stretch at least five horse lengths. Its maw is huge—it can cut a man, or a horse, in half with a single bite. And it has two grasping appendages in front. I spoke with a survivor of an attack who described snakelike movements."

Drelm was confused by his meaning. "It sounds more like a lizard. A big lizard. Not a snake."

"I refer to the fore appendages," Illidian's tone was curt, as though he were explaining matters to a simpleton. "They may be tentacles. It is hard to say, since no one's actually seen the thing."

"So it's no kind of natural beast then," Melloc volunteered.

Illidian's look was scathing, and Melloc's cheeks flushed. "It's invisible," Illidian repeated.

"It kills for sport," Drelm added. Few natural animals killed for sport, even those with a taint of sorcery.

"Is it some kind of dragon?" Melloc asked quietly.

"No." Elyana stood at last. "It is no dragon." She took in the ground to the right, then left. "Drelm," she said, "if what Illidian's saying is true—"

"You think I would lie?" Illidian's eyes narrowed. "My kinsman are slain, and you think—"

Elyana cut him off. "If his account is accurate the thing must still be close."

"I told you," Illidian insisted, "it comes and goes as it pleases."

"But how far does it go, Captain?" Elyana asked. "You said you followed it. It lured some of you away, am I correct?"

"You are."

"And then attacked, here, when half of you were deep into this stand of woods. It deliberately separated you, then vanished once more. Suppose that it's watching now? It was surely watching before."

"That's why my soldiers stand watch."

"It sounds as though this thing's a threat to all of us," Melloc ventured quietly. "Has anyone thought we might do better if we were to join forces? Hunt it down?"

Illidian looked at Melloc as if noticing him for the first time. "It's easier to herd fish than to loose the River Kingdoms at the same quarry."

"But you do think it worthy of consideration?" Melloc asked. "My father is a man of reason. I'm sure he would welcome—"

Melloc was saying more, but at Calda's whinny Drelm turned to the woods.

Elyana whirled, arrow nocked to her bow. "It's here!"

Drelm ripped one of his throwing axes free and perceived the sway of branches where there was no wind, just to the left of the tracks Elyana had been examining.

Elyana launched an arrow into the emptiness beside the bending branches. A second and third winged after as Illidian's sentries came running.

But the arrows only clattered from the side of some huge unseen object. Elyana cursed and shouted for blades.

Drelm launched his axe, his teeth bared in a grin that displayed his lower canines. For all that he strove for balance, Drelm never questioned a righteous battle, and this was surely one of them.

His axe stuck in something at roughly head height, and then blood sprayed forth to dye scales hung in midair a deep scarlet. Whatever the invisible beast was came on swift feet. The thing's tread was silent, but the ground rocked as its bulk raced forward.

Drelm slapped Charger's haunch to send him galloping to safety, then took up his battleaxe and rushed the monster with a savage cry. He was awash with the joy of battle, and he grinned to find Melloc beside him with bared sword.

He kept track of the monster's approach by his axe, which seemed to be floating above the bloody scales. Just as the axe drew within striking range, a great weight slammed into his side and sent him flying. When he landed on his back it did not feel terribly different from the time he'd hit the street from two stories up.

He immediately pushed up on his arms, though his head reeled. The battle continued, with three of the elves firing. Elyana was in the saddle and galloping forward, blade raised.

The creature had moved out from the foliage, a fact evident from the axe and bloody spot still suspended in the air. Of Melloc there was no sign, but Illidian, enraged or a little crazy, chopped at some invisible force lifting a struggling elf into the air. Another elf, just to the right of Elyana's mount, was sheared suddenly in half so that his legs and an arm holding a bow went one way and the rest of him hung momentarily suspended—within the great, invisible mouth, Drelm, supposed—then was expelled onto the grassy sward.

Elyana's sword carved a long line of blood along the thing's flank as Calda galloped under her.

Still staggered, Drelm climbed to his feet. His battleaxe lay three yards distant, but he laid hands to his second throwing axe and let fly, only to see it sail harmlessly into space.

The beast appeared to be moving, and though the ground was shifting under something weighty, Drelm had no idea where it moved until Illidian shouted in pain and dropped, writhing, his right arm severed just below the elbow.

"Abadar preserve us," Drelm said. He charged forward, passing under the struggling form still held aloft by some unseen force, thinking that he could at least drag the elven officer out of the way.

Then, suddenly, the elf before him dropped. So too did the axe suspended in midair. The bloody line in its side, sketched by the galloping Elyana, disappeared.

The beast was gone.

Elyana curveted Calda, spun her around and flung herself off the animal to tend to Illidian. The elf captain had clambered to his feet, and was paling rapidly as he stared at the ruined, bloody stump of his arm and the blood-drenched garments that clothed it.

Drelm knew Elyana's healing could save the captain, so he gathered his axe in case the thing came back, then looked over the elf that had dropped nearby.

He wasn't moving, and Drelm saw why the moment he bent to investigate. The beast had pulped the elf's rib cage.

Drelm rose with a prayer to Abadar on his lips, and searched the battle site for Melloc.

He found him a few moments later, staring sightlessly at the sky.

Drelm let out a long, slow breath. Now that was something he had hoped not to see. What would he say to the boy's father? To Daylah?

Drelm lowered his battleaxe and leaned against it, staring down at the young man. True, Melloc had spoken before he thought sometimes, and not always reasoned things through, but even a fool could have seen that the boy was meant for big things. He'd been brave, and clever, and horse and weapon skills had come as naturally to him as they had to Drelm. You couldn't say that about every man.

Melloc looked almost lifelike lying there, except that his neck was a little looser than it should ever be on a living body. The half-orc decided that the same invisible limb that had knocked him flat must have struck Melloc a little higher.

It was very sad. Still, Melloc had died on the field of battle, with a sword in his hand. Drelm felt certain the boy's father would be proud.

Chapter Three
Too Good to Miss
Lisette

Most of Delgar's buildings were fashioned from rough-hewn timber, lacking exterior plaster or even a second story. Unless you enjoyed the smell of fish scales and muddy water, there was little to recommend the place, although Lisette appreciated the community's nod toward organization. A lot of river communities couldn't be bothered to fashion straight roads—or straight houses, for that matter. Delgar at least had been built on a grid plan, and as she and Karag climbed out of the barge that afternoon, she was able to take quick stock of the little town.

For the last week of her journey she'd heard rumors about a hunting expedition jointly sponsored by several of the famously uncooperative River Kingdoms. Delgar was to be its launching point, which was probably what had drawn her bounty so far north. Apparently, experienced hunters were to be paid good coin, and the old rogue probably hoped he could pass off as one.

She and Karag blended in fairly well with the crowds thronging the little village, for no one could guess by looking at their gear that they earned their coin hunting men, not beasts.

She scanned the faces they passed, taking the place in, ignoring the return appraisals from knots of varied martial types who wound their way through the muddy streets.

Dark of eye and dark of hair, which she'd cut to the nape of her neck, Lisette had the pale complexion of a Chelaxian. Her pants were dark, loose, comfortable, and tucked into well-worn, calf-high boots sewn from lizard hide. A pair of pistol butts stood out from the sash tied at her waist, weapons of fine iron and dark, highly polished wood. Her single mark of flamboyance was the slim red feather thrust into the side of her brimmed cloth hat.

As Karag finished unloading their gear, he handed a matching flintlock rifle up to her. She shouldered the weapon without remark, the brown strap sliding across the long black sleeve of her shirt and the rim of her black vest.

The burly dwarf hefted a second rifle on his own shoulder, the long muzzle poking three feet above his blond locks. He then lifted a huge leather bag as thick around as himself and propped it on the other shoulder.

"Let's get this over with," she said, and they started forward.

The two made an odd pair. Karag was Lisette's physical opposite in nearly every way, for he was blond and pale and sturdy. Where she strode with pantherish grace, he swaggered. If passersby even recognized the rifle he carried for what it was, they would probably have assumed it was his, but it belonged to Lisette just as much as the powder bag slung across Karag's back, the rifle over her own shoulder, or the brace of flintlock pistols thrust through her belt.

"You ever hear what they're really supposed to be hunting?" Lisette asked him. She ignored the appreciative whistle of a leather-clad barbarian leaning against the side of a building.

"It's some monster the elves drove out of Kyonin," Karag answered in his low rumble. "If the long-ears can't be bothered, they'll just chase a beast out and let everyone else . . ."

Karag's voice trailed off, and Lisette's gaze swung to follow his own.

A thickset man with a full beard had just stepped from the sprawling, two-story building ahead of them and stood now under a hanging placard carved with a leaping fish. The hood of his light traveling cloak was cast back to reveal a balding pate peppered with red hair. Beside him were two younger men of similar build, their receding hair heavy with grease.

Lisette cursed in disbelief. It was never, ever this easy. She'd tracked the man for the better part of two months, always staying just behind him. And now he was there before her within a few moments of reaching Delgar.

"Velmik," Karag whispered.

Even as her hand swept toward her right pistol, Velmik spotted her. With a deep-throated shout he dove back through the doorway. His sons hurried after.

Lisette wasted no breath cursing. "Back entrance," she ordered Karag, then leapt to the wooden porch to push into the throng of men Velmik and his sons had stumbled through.

The fugitives left a wake through the middle of the tavern's crowded common room, a wide space crammed with long wooden tables and broad-shouldered men and women, many of whom were now cursing, their heads turned toward Velmik. The murderer ploughed toward a closed door beside the stairs to the private rooms. One of his boys was ahead of him; the other was looking back at Lisette. His hand went to his belt, and fastened not around the sword hilt, but an axe haft. Lisette knew then that she faced Gern, who had a reputation with his throwing axe. That meant the one starting up the stairs ahead of Velmik had to be the eldest, Hadek, against whom there was a minor bounty. Not half the size of the one on Velmik, and it wouldn't have brought her out to the wilds, but with him so close by she wouldn't dream of passing up the opportunity.

Gern charged up the creaking steps after the others. "Hurry, Dad!"

A man and woman at the top of the stairs froze at sight of Hadek and backed off.

Lisette elbowed a gawking servant girl out of the way and pulled her pistol free, cocking the hammer with her off hand. As she brought the muzzle in line with Velmik's broad, retreating back, Gern sent the axe flying at her head.

She sidestepped, firing as she felt the passage of the haft brush her hat brim. She missed by only a little, hitting Hadek instead. The man dropped with a girlish scream and his father whirled. Behind Lisette, the axe smashed into a row of glasses at the bar, and there was an uproar from the bartender and any number of patrons. She thrust the smoking pistol through her belt and drew its twin even as Gern pulled a second axe.

Velmik crouched by his firstborn, who whimpered on the stairs. The older man bared teeth as he faced her, drawing steel.

She notched back the hammer of her second pistol and snapped off a shot. She grinned through the swirl of black gun smoke—she'd known even as the weapon kicked in her hand that it had been true. Gern staggered and jerked as a leaking red hole materialized in the center of his forehead. He sprawled.

The thunderous pistol shot set women screaming and men shouting in terror. Many dove for cover or rushed the door. Lisette calmly shoved the smoking pistol back through her sash and drew her short sword.

Velmik charged down the stairs, eyes mad and rolling, lips peeled back to show stained and crooked teeth. He brandished his long notched sword like a cleaver.

"You killed my boys, you bitch!"

Lisette snatched a tankard from the abandoned bar and hurled it at Velmik's head. Her aim was not as accurate with her off hand, but the bald man swerved. The tankard banked off the stair rail, spraying sour-smelling ale. The instant's distraction was all Lisette desired. She lunged forward, slicing rather than thrusting, and cut Velmik across his neck and upper chest. The old fool was wearing leather armor but no neck guard.

It was not a deep strike, but it was enough to spoil Velmik's own and set him clawing instinctively for his throat. He looked down, wide-eyed, as she drove the sword through his hand and out the back of his neck.

Blood spurted forth, and Velmik gurgled a bit as he wobbled, then sank, finally flopping onto the floorboards like a fish. His sword struck the stained planks a second later with a dull clang.

There came a brief silence, over which she heard the labored breathing of Hadek, collapsed with glassy eyes upon the stairs.

She wiped her blade on the back of Velmik's shirt.

Karag burst in through the back doorway, panting, and suddenly found every pair of eyes in the whole tavern staring at him and the musket he carried in two hands.

The silence lasted only a moment longer, and then the buck-toothed bartender demanded to know who she was, how she dared, and, most loudly, who would pay for the damages.

"I am a bounty hunter," Lisette told him calmly, "and two of these men are wanted in Andoran, Druma, and Isger. Karag will pay the damages." At this the dwarf stepped to her side, a little red-faced.

"They never came out," he explained swiftly, softly, "and I heard gunshots."

She had surmised that. "There was no real trouble," she told him so his dwarven pride would remain uninjured. "Bag these two up, and pay this gentleman for his trouble. Your pardon, sir," she said to the proprietor with her prettiest smile. "I'm afraid I must leave your fine company."

The bartender and the others gawped. She didn't mind the attention at all; it might make her stay in the place a little simpler.

The crowd broke into low murmurs, talking among themselves and staring darkly. A few were even moving back toward their tables, though they were cautious about it. The bartender was actually scowling.

"This is Delgar," he said with a drawl. "You can't just wander into the town and kill people in my bar! We have laws!"

Karag stepped up to the counter, his head just clearing its edge. "Lisette has full authority—"

"This is my inn!" The barkeep's face reddened. Lisette heard angry murmurs from the crowd behind her. Curious. She hadn't anticipated this at all. Quietly, methodically, she took up one of her pistols and cleaned the inside of the muzzle with a rag she pulled from a vest pocket.

From behind came a loud clump of steps, and a lull in the mutters as a deep, male voice demanded silence.

Lisette paused in the loading of her pistol and turned.

A peculiar figure strode through the doorway. At first glance he was just another broad, powerful man-at-arms. And then she saw so many incongruities that she was not sure which to consider first.

It was not so remarkable that she faced a thickly built member of the city guard bearing a sheathed sword. What *was* remarkable was that he was a half- or at least quarter-blood orc. Even out here in the uncivilized wilds, most folk didn't trust their kind, and there was no missing the greenish hue or the foreword thrust of the thick jaw and upward-pointing teeth. Yet here was no coarse brute, either, for his garb was immaculate, from polished helm to the glimpse of leather armor she perceived beneath the spotless blue tabard with its black, crenelated tower. Her eyes shifted briefly to the tall figure striding in behind him, likewise immaculate, likewise wearing leather armor and a white-and-blue tabard with a stone tower, but his long mustaches and slanted eyes were merely peculiar as opposed to extraordinary.

"What has happened here?" the half-orc growled.

"Captain," the barkeep began, and once again Lisette started. *Captain*? The barkeep pointed at her. "This woman just killed those three men on the stairs with some kind of magic."

The bright, rather small eyes in the half-orc's face shifted immediately to her, then to the gun.

"You need to set that down," the captain growled.

Karag stomped over from the bar to stand at Lisette's side. He glowered up at the orc, who seemed careless of the dark look, for he gave the dwarf little attention before focusing again upon the gun.

"Who are you?" Karag growled.

The tall, mustached guardsman had stepped to the half-orc's side, and it was he who answered in a mellow voice with the faint trace of a Brevic accent. "You are addressing Drelm, captain of the Delgar guard. And he has given your . . . associate a command. Put aside the strange wand. Immediately."

Lisette's smile did nothing to change Drelm's expression; it remained grim even as she passed the still unloaded pistol on to Karag. "I am a bounty hunter," she said, "fully licensed in five separate countries, and at least as many municipalities, including Tymon. Two of those men were known bandits and murderers; the other was a relative. I was not after him, but he attacked."

"Proof?" Drelm asked.

Lisette was used to thinking on her feet, but it took a moment longer to decipher the captain's short command.

"I have posters for them here," she said, "in my vest pocket."

"Pull them slowly," Drelm told her.

"Of course."

The captain's eyes never left her hand as she produced two quarter-folded pieces of parchment. They crinkled as she passed them across to one large, greenish hand.

The knuckle on his first finger was scarred with a long, slightly paler line.

She watched as his eyes tracked across the likenesses of Velmik and Gern—not perfect, but fair enough—and then the words beneath. And she kept the smile upon her lips, knowing that he would demand some sort of fine, or impose some other penalty to enrich himself. She knew better than to object. Here was a "man" clearly used to getting his own way by physical intimidation. The curious thing was how the barkeep and two barmaids were both focused upon the "captain" expectantly. She would have thought they would view any interaction with him with fawning politeness, as you had to do in larger cities when the gangs shook you for protection money.

Drelm finished what must have been a somewhat labored examination of the words, for he was long about it, and handed the papers off to the Brevan. "Compare them."

"Yes, Captain." The Brevan stepped around Karag, walking with a horseman's swagger. His boot heels, she noticed, were silver.

"They did a lot of damage." The barkeep pointed to a row of smashed glasses sitting on a dark shelf behind him. Lisette glanced over the bar top and saw a trio of broken bottles lying on the dark floorboards amid a spreading pool of sweet-smelling wine.

"We will gladly pay for the damages," Lisette told them. "Although all of this was because Velmik's son threw an axe."

That didn't hold any sway with the barkeep. "He wouldn't have thrown an axe if you hadn't followed him into my inn!"

The Brevan had climbed the first two stairs and was glancing back and forth between the two pieces of paper and the bodies. "Captain," he called, "two of these look just about right. And the third must be a son of the older one."

Drelm's small eyes flicked to the barkeep's. "What will repairs cost?"

Lisette could see conflicting emotions warring on the barkeep's face. He looked down at the damage, then back to the orc.

"Five gold sails."

"Three at best," the Brevan said as he wandered over. "I can smell that wine from here. Not exactly high elven vintage."

The Brevan was right, but Lisette knew better than to offer any opinion.

"Three," Drelm said to Lisette. "Pay him. Demid, collect the coins."

"Yes, Captain."

Lisette couldn't believe she was getting off that lucky. Drelm glanced once more at the dwarf, who still watched with suspicion, and faced the rest of the tavern's occupants.

"Many of you are new faces," Drelm said as he drew himself up. "This is not how we do things here." He tapped his chest. "Those who kill, face me. Those who steal, face me. Those who hurt an innocent, face me. I give this one"—he pointed to Lisette—"this one chance. She is new. She is a bounty hunter. She has taken her chance, and yours. Next time, you face me. Am I understood?"

He snapped this last. A few of the folk—locals, probably—were direct with their reply: "Yes, Captain!"

The others looked away and mumbled.

Drelm's lips pulled back in a snarl, and he roared. "Do you understand me? You will answer, 'Yes, Captain!'"

"Yes, Captain!" the customers called back.

"Again!"

This time the tavern timbers seemed to shake a little with the noise. "Yes, Captain!"

Drelm grunted, then glanced back at Lisette. "No more bounties before speaking with me."

"Of course." Lisette tried a smile, and produced a gleaming cold coin. She lobbed it twirling into the air between the half-orc and herself. "For your trouble."

Drelm caught it without looking in one massive fist, then addressed the Brevan while staring at her. "Lieutenant Demid, she is new. Speak to her."

"Only the mayor pays the city guard, little sparrow," the Brevan said from behind her.

Drelm then pitched the coin, without once considering it, toward the barkeep. "I levy fines for bribery," he said. "There, keep it. Now you profit from the mess."

Stranger and stranger. Lisette couldn't quite figure the captain's angle. Only some wet-behind-the-ears Eagle Knight would be so honest. Certainly no half-orc in a village no one had heard of.

"Do you have more targets in Delgar?" he asked her.

"Probably not," Lisette answered. There was always the possibility she'd bump into someone else.

"'Probably not.'" Drelm grunted, a low, almost thoughtful sound. "If it becomes 'probably yes,' see me before you spill more blood, or you and I will have a problem."

At last he acknowledged the dwarf, who muttered under his breath. Something dwarven, from the sound, and an insult, from his dark look.

"I don't speak dwarf," the half-orc said, then his eyes tracked back to Lisette's. "Tell him threats to me when I'm in uniform are threats to the guard."

Lisette's hand tightened on Karag's shoulder. He tensed under her fingers. She did not leave off smiling. "I'll make sure he knows."

Drelm grunted.

The Brevan strode past then, coin purses in hand. "They had thirty-two silvers, Captain, and a handful of coppers."

"For the treasury," Drelm said.

"Yes, Captain."

Her first thought was that the half-orc was an idiot and meant to have the lieutenant turn the money over to the city coffers. Then she realized they were saying that solely for the benefit of listeners and would surely cut themselves in for a nice percentage of the money, for Demid had certainly announced fewer funds than he'd actually found on the bodies.

Drelm surveyed the room a final time, then turned heel and strode away.

"Karag," Lisette forced almost sickly sweet kindness into her voice. "Make the rest of the arrangements. And keep the captain's warning in mind. I do think," she added, "we'll be better welcome at some other inn for the night."

"I suppose you're right," Karag said, and turned to consider the bodies, and the barkeep, who still watched them. Everyone, actually, was still staring at them, although some had returned to their meals.

"My pistol?" Lisette asked. It was evidence of how peculiar the encounter had been that Karag had not instantly returned it to her. He did so now with an apologetic look, then strode toward the bar. In this place she didn't imagine he'd be able to drag the bodies to an alley and cut off their heads. One way or another, though, the dwarf would have to decapitate the corpses and drop the heads in salt. It didn't matter to her how he did it, so long as they stayed on the right side of the law—and, more importantly, so long as the evidence of the kill was preserved long enough to collect the bounty.

She walked out past Demid and stepped to the edge of the raised platform, leaning against the warm building shingles while she checked over the pistol bore and fished around for her pellet and powder. She was not at all surprised to find the Brevan guard following her out, black eyes afire with interest.

"You have strange talons," he said, "but are a deadly bird. The dwarf didn't slay any of them, did he?"

"No."

She pulled out a powder packet and bit off the end with her teeth, then spat it to the side.

Demid's lips turned up in a slight smile.

"Is there something funny, Lieutenant?"

"Demid," he said. "I assure you that I take you quite seriously."

She wasn't sure what to make of that, but decided not to press further. "So what are a Brevan and a half-orc doing on the guard force in a nowhere village in the River Kingdoms? It almost sounds like a joke."

He repeated the word doubtfully. "A joke?"

"Sure." She pulled free a bullet from another pocket and held it up to the sun. "A Brevan and a half-orc walk into a bar. But I don't know the punch line."

"The punch line. Oh, yes. No, it's no joke, Lady . . ." He waited expectantly.

"Lisette."

"Lisette. How lovely. I might begin such a joke myself. An angry dwarf and a beautiful marksman—marks-woman—enter a bar. But I also don't know the . . ." He paused to make a rolling motion with his hand, then finished: "punch line."

"There isn't one." Lisette put home the bullet, and, satisfied, tamped it down. "What is it you want, Lieutenant?"

"I am curious about you. Part of my duties as a guardsman of Delgar, you understand."

Was he flirting, or was he actually searching for information? The more time she spent in this place, the more unsure she became. She could read men, though, and even though Demid clearly found her attractive, there was a coolness in his gaze. "Of course."

"For instance, I've never seen wands with handle grips before."

"You mean these?" As she tapped the muzzle of her pistol, he nodded. "These aren't wands, they're guns. No magic's involved."

"Ah," he said. "I've never seen one before."

"But you've heard of them?"

"Alchemical, aren't they?"

Clearly he wished to hold one, but she wasn't feeling charitable. "Something like that."

"I see. And where is it that you're going?"

"I wish only to find lodging for the night. Somewhere where I might obtain a warm bath."

"Ah." Demid clicked his tongue. "That's more challenging than usual, owing to the hunt. Are you planning to participate?"

"I'm only here for Velmik. I just want a warm bath, a night in a real bed, and then I'll be on the next boat out."

Demid listened with interest, then provided directions to a home near the walled city center. "Madame Celene has expensive rooms, and is careful to whom she rents them. Most of these would not be welcome there. Your friend," he continued, "would have to be . . ."

"Gentlemanly?"

"Polite," Demid said with a nod.

"He can manage that. I thank you, Demid."

"Of course." He executed a smart half bow, turned on his heel, and retreated to the inn.

Interesting. He had not been looking for a bribe, or romance, but inspecting her, almost as though he were a guardsman in Almas. A real professional. Well, the River Kingdoms attracted fugitives. Likely the Brevan had some sort of complicated backstory, and probably one less interesting than she supposed. Curious as she was, she decided she was thankful neither Demid nor Drelm were the types who liked to brag about their past.

Lisette slipped her gun back through her belt, readied her second, then tucked her supplies away. She checked her appearance in a small glass mirror, finding a few blood flecks, which she wiped from her cheeks.

Demid's directions and information proved accurate. Madame Celene, a beanpole-thin woman with a personality dry as day-old bread, could have done with some of the Brevan's politeness. Elyana rented a room for a silver wolf—a criminal rate out here in the middle of nowhere—but it came with a warm bath, and privacy, and Celene told her the latter was not likely anywhere else in the village this week.

The outrageous fee soured Lisette's mood even after a long hot soak in a sparkling clean iron tub off Madame Celene's kitchen. She was upstairs in the tiny bedroom allotted her, methodically checking over her gear, when a loud rap rang against her door.

Lisette reached immediately for one pistol, which she put close to hand. She was partially dressed, in shirt and pants, although she was uncorseted and barefoot, and her wet hair hung wild about her shoulders.

"Who is it?"

She expected an answer from Karag. Still, you could never be too cautious in her line of work. She glanced over her shoulder at the narrow, shuttered window overlooking the street. The afternoon sun cast lines of light through which dust motes drifted, highlighting the polish on the old floor planks. Madame Celene kept a tidy inn.

"I have a message for you, miss."

The voice was that of a young man's. Lisette lifted the pistol and pulled back the hammer with a faint click. "From whom?"

"Someone from the court, miss."

That struck her as more than a little curious. "You don't know?"

Apparently the message boy thought so too. "I'm sorry, I don't," he admitted. "I was just supposed to find the lady who'd . . ." There was a brief pause. "Killed those men at the tavern. You're her, aren't you?"

Lisette was still wondering how to answer that when the boy spoke on.

"I'll just slide this message under the door. No need to pay me. My fee's already handled."

The floorboards creaked outside then, probably from the boy shifting weight, and a small envelope slid slowly under the door.

Lisette stared at it from a distance.

"I'll be going now," the young man's voice said, nervously, and then his footsteps receded hurriedly.

Lisette slowly lowered the hammer, put the gun aside, and stepped to the envelope, though long years in the field made her cautious even with this simple act. The letter might be poisoned or trapped, or the letter might be a distraction while something else was underway.

In the end, though, it proved just a letter, sealed with wax that lacked the mark of any kind of seal. The message within promised twenty gold sails for a brief discussion with the lord mayor, so long as she understood she that was to be completely discrete about the summons, both before and after the meeting.

An unexpected development, and a profitable one. Probably the man was looking to drop a criminal the local guard force hadn't been able to kill. Someone too clever for, say, a half-orc. The discretion was peculiar, but compared to some of the requests she'd heard over the years, it didn't amount to much. Likely Lord Avelis didn't want anyone knowing his guard force couldn't handle the matter.

Lisette readied herself in short order, pleased that she'd kept one blouse clean just for these sorts of emergencies.

One street over, the wooden buildings gave way to a handful of stone homes immediately outside the walled enclosure that surrounded the seat of government. The ten-foot wall wouldn't hold off an army for long, but it would keep back the kind of bandit forces that usually assaulted River Kingdoms settlements.

She passed through the open gates and tried not to stare too long at the two spear-bearing guardsmen. It was odd enough that they should look so competent, odder still that their helms matched, and that their hair and faces were well-groomed, but beyond that, they were actually wearing clean tabards. One simply didn't encounter that level of organization in River Kingdoms villages, which tended to rise and fall every generation. So far as she knew, Delgar was only a few years old. It had no business being so well run.

She understood now that the symbol she'd seen on all the guards' tabards—a small tower with an arrow slit and four merlons—was a fair likeness of the tower of the keep ahead of her.

Beyond the gate was about what she'd expected—an expanse of rich black dirt and scrubby grass with various outbuildings and storage sheds. A stable stood along the wall directly west of the gate. All of this, too, seemed finely ordered. There were no sagging roofs or rotting joists, no mismatched roof thatching.

How did the lord of this little burg manage such order in the midst of such chaos? He might not be the simple hayseed with delusions of grandeur she'd anticipated. Lisette supposed it didn't really matter, so long as the money was good.

As she crossed the compound, the keep's metal-banded door opened wide, and out walked three tall, splendid figures. One was dressed in black traveling clothes, like herself, and the others in green and brown forest gear.

Elves. She'd seen her share of them in various cities, but these were no ordinary citizens. They walked with a warrior's confidence, shoulders wide. Their eyes had a veteran's look, measuring all that they took in.

Each gauged her as they walked for the stables, and as one adjusted the strap of his quiver, she realized with a start that his left hand was nothing more than a hook. He was the shortest of the lot, though still half a head taller than herself, and one of the most beautiful creatures she had ever seen, even for an elf. His coppery brown hair was long, straight, and thick, and his dark eyes were dotted with luminous amber flecks. Many elven males struck her as youthful or effeminate, but not this one, whose fine-featured face seemed grimly competent, and was marred by a small scar along his nose. She was shocked to find that her breath actually caught in her throat a bit as his eyes met hers. Worse, he seemed to see or hear it, for his gaze fastened on her a moment longer. Then he glanced at the hook upon his arm. His expression hardened, and he strode after his companions.

Lisette wasn't used to feeling regret, but she had a mad impulse to follow and tell him that it wasn't the hook she'd gasped at. But what should she care about what an elf thought of her feelings?

She found someone else watching: a lean, bearded man in the tower doorway. She returned his scrutiny as she walked closer.

The stranger stood perhaps six feet tall, with a full head of brown hair. That and his beard were lined with distinguished bands of silver. His face was weathered but handsome, and she guessed him to be somewhere in his late thirties or early forties. His breeks were brown, his cuffed and collared shirt white and tight over thick shoulders. He had a swordsman's build, she thought, though she saw no blade upon him.

Lisette halted before him.

"Welcome," the man said in a subdued baritone. "I think you may have come to see me."

"Lord Avelis?"

"Avelis will do," he replied. "And you are?"

"Lisette Demonde. Of Cheliax."

He didn't quite manage to hold in his surprise. One eyebrow twitched. Somehow, she was not quite what he'd expected. But he didn't let it stop him. "It was good of you to come so quickly. Please, follow me." He turned on one boot heel and addressed someone out of sight within the building, telling them to bring refreshments.

Lisette followed the mayor through a common room, then a deep doorway—almost a short tunnel—and into a long, narrow office. Apart from a small, high window, the room lacked natural light, which explained the lanterns hung from dark joists over the desk.

There was just barely room for Avelis to slide around the desk, and this he did before turning to face her and gesturing to the chairs.

As they took their seats, she noted the well-crafted wooden cabinet under the window behind him. The elm desk was simply but finely made, and the papers on its surface neatly stacked.

"Your arrival was fortuitous," Avelis told her. "I've made inquiries about . . . those in your line of profession, but none of them have come."

Lisette smiled thinly. "The River Kingdoms is a long way to come for twenty gold sails. I assume you don't want someone local."

"You assume correctly."

A chubby servant girl knocked upon the door behind them and hurried forward with a platter holding a wine bottle and two glasses.

"Just set it on the desk, Syra. Thank you. Please close the door behind you."

"Yes, Mayor," she said, curtsying to him before she departed. The door shut with a heavy thud.

"Please, have a drink." The mayor's hand indicated the platter.

"You're very kind. After we discuss our business, perhaps."

Avelis nodded once, sharply. "I'll cut to the point." He reached under the desk, and Lisette tensed as she heard a drawer being opened. A moment later, Avelis set a cloth bag upon the wood, where it jangled with a heavy thud. He pushed it toward her. "Twenty gold sails. That's for hearing me out and keeping your mouth shut. Even if you don't like what I offer you."

"That's right."

She loosened the leather tie cord and peered within, then lifted one of the coins to the sunlight. It was Andoren currency, with a shine so clear it must be virtually unhandled. She tested one between her back teeth, found it appropriately soft and pure, and dropped it back in with its fellows before cinching the bag and dropping it into the pack she'd slung over the chair back.

"Don't you want to count it?" Avelis sounded amused.

"I did," she said, which wasn't entirely true, but she could tell there were at least fifteen sails in there, which was good enough for her. "Alright, Avelis, I can see you're serious about this. What do you want me for?"

Avelis steepled his fingers. "I need you to kill an orc."

She laughed. "Any decent mercenary can do that job, Mayor. And your town is crawling with them. Your guard force looks surprisingly capable."

"Oh, it is. But it's the captain of my guard I want you to kill."

The expression upon his face was so strange, what with his twitching smile and the burning gleam in his eyes, that she thought at first that he joked.

She realized he was serious as he spoke on. "I suppose I should explain that he's partly human."

She cleared her throat. He probably wasn't going to handle this well. Avelis seemed like a man who was used to having his way. "I'm a bounty hunter, Mayor, not an assassin."

Avelis shrugged. "Is there a difference? I'm putting a private bounty on him."

She wanted to ask how large that bounty was, but she was already treading on thin ice. "Has he broken the laws of your community?"

"No."

Lisette shook her head. "Then that's an assassination. That's not my line."

"Oh, you haven't yet heard my price."

Now the trick was leaving the meeting gracefully. She offered a few alternative suggestions. "If you want him killed, hire some guards to attack him. Hire some bravos. Poison him."

"My guards are fiercely loyal to him. They would sooner betray me. And he would kill any warriors sent against him. Poison . . . would be too suspicious. I want you. And I will pay you very well."

Again she saw that strange gleam in his eyes, and the peculiar shifting smile. She felt a dawning curiosity about the money. "How well?"

Avelis reached slowly into an inside pocket to produce a small red silk bag. He undid the drawstrings, cupped his left hand, and poured out a stream of small gems, each the size of her thumbnail. Lisette recognized bloodstone and carnelian, moonstone and onyx.

"Every one of them is worth at least fifty gold sails. A fortune that transports well."

It was far more than what Lisette would have guessed. She had many questions, but thought to keep him talking while she considered the matter. "Pardon my asking, but if you have all of these, what are you doing . . . here?"

Avelis's eyes narrowed. "That's not really your concern, is it? Do the job well and all this is yours." He extended the palm of his hands, strewn with gems, and Lisette reached out to select one. She held it up between thumb and forefinger, and directed it into a mote-filled sunbeam.

"That's more than four thousand sails for what's likely to be a week's work."

Lisette had been paid in gemstones often enough that she knew a real one when she saw it. She dropped that one back into his palm and chose another at random. It, too, was finely cut, glimmering with color.

She'd had good reasons for walking away from her earlier profession, and even finer reasons for permanently keeping her distance. Yet this was good money—absurdly good, given the circumstances—and if she played things right, no one would ever know. How would the Black Coil ever hear about the death of a half-orc in the River Kingdoms?

With this kind of money she might finally have the funds to set up permanent residence in Triela in one of those rambling old Chelish-style mansions. There were any number of them sinking slowly into disrepair. Between this and the funds she'd stashed in Almas, she might just be able to lay claim to one and afford the upkeep.

The real question might have been why the mayor wasn't doing the same thing. But then, as he said, that really wasn't her business. Maybe he was one of those driven to command. Or maybe he'd done something terrible under his real name and had fled to the frontier to start afresh.

She considered the mayor as she dropped the gem back into his palm. "Why do you want him dead?"

His smile widened, showing teeth, and he gathered in the gems. "He killed my son, and is marrying my daughter. He will rule after me . . . unless I kill him."

Had he missed the obvious? Some, blinded by desire for vengeance, were too quick to dismiss easier methods. "Wouldn't it be easy to forbid the marriage and bring him to trial?"

"It's not so simple." Avelis's lip curled in a savage sneer before he regained composure. "It was no blade that killed my Melloc, but negligence. My son was on patrol with the orc, who didn't have the brains to safeguard him. Most of the village doesn't even think it's the orc's fault." The mayor's eyes burned. "He's got all of them fooled."

"What do you mean?"

"They like him. They trust him."

"A half-orc?"

Avelis nodded once. "Two years ago this community was on the brink of ruin. Bandits and river raiders were a constant threat. Despite my best efforts, the town was lawless and violent."

"And Drelm fixed all this for you?"

"The orc and his friend. An elven woman named Elyana. They were just passing through, but with their help things quickly turned around. I was grateful, understand. He's been my guard captain now for the last year and a half, and Elyana remains a sort of informal advisor. She's very, very good."

Lisette managed not to smirk at the open lust in the man's tone. So Avelis had a thing for pointed ears. Then again, given her reaction in the courtyard, who was she to talk?

"The town has embraced them," Avelis went on. "They've even embraced the idea of him . . . courting my daughter.

But the thought of his blood mingling with mine . . ." The fingers on the mayor's left hand slowly curled inward, and he stared down at the clenched fist, almost in surprise. It began to shake. "I should have seen it," he said through gritted teeth. "He means to rule after me!"

Lisette thought she had a handle on the matter now, but she summarized for clarity. Before discussing contracts, she always made sure expectations were clear between her and her employer. "You want him dead, but not in an obvious way. And you don't want to anger the village, or his friend the elf?"

"Exactly."

"How is it that a half-orc and an elf are friends?"

Avelis snorted. "They served together over in Taldor. I thought they were lovers for the longest time, or I'd have been more worried when Drelm was near my daughter. He's so . . . proper . . . I didn't even realize what was happening until it was too late."

"Well, I don't have any love for orcs. But my reputation is as a bounty hunter. I take on legal cases. I'd like an official contract."

Avelis favored her with a long look, then set his elbows on the desk and steepled his fingers. "I think the money's good enough that we don't need a contract. Don't you? Papers can fall into the wrong hands."

"Maybe you should think about hiring someone else then. As I said, I'm not an assassin." Not anymore. And by her covenant, she could not work as one. She shouldn't even be sitting here.

"Well, I'm the ruler here, and I'll pay a large bounty. I can even turn the paper over to you, if you wish, once you succeed."

"I always come through on a contract," Lisette said.

"I've no doubt. You managed to impress Lieutenant Demid, which is no mean feat. He said that you felled three men, and that you used strange weapons that launch metal balls, but aren't magic."

He was doing his best to change the subject. "That's true enough. I want the contract with me."

"That's really not possible."

She thought about walking out. Yet . . . "Then I want half, now."

"Half?" he spluttered.

"Unless you give me a contract that will hold up in court."

Avelis frowned, and his good looks soured. The eyes narrowed, lines curled about his mouth, and she saw what he would look like in ten or fifteen more years. A bitter, angry old man.

Avelis let out a pent-up breath. "Very well. But there is one more condition. Drelm must die, but it can't be done in a way that alerts anyone—especially not Elyana, whom I would rather remain to serve the town. Her counsel is quite valuable to me."

I'll bet it is, Lisette thought, but Avelis seemed oblivious to how much he was revealing about himself. "And it can't be done promptly," he continued. "You've probably noted the influx of warriors."

"It was hard to miss."

"A deadly beast's killing people up and down the river."

"One beast?"

"We think so. It was my son's last wish that we band together to launch an expedition to hunt the thing down. I've joined forces with Kyonin, Tymon, Riverton, and Sevenarches, and we've scraped enough together to reward those who kill it. Drelm and Elyana are heading the expedition. It must succeed—it was the beast that killed my boy, and I will see it go down. Which means Drelm can't be killed until the thing is dead. He's too good a warrior. Do you understand?"

More complications. She should have known it would have more complications. "So you want me to go on the expedition with them through the wilderness and pretend to hunt for this thing with them. What sort of beast is it?"

"No one's really seen it." Avelis turned over an empty palm. "What we do know is that it likes to kill. It's smashed into homes and outposts and hunting camps up and down the river for the last six months. It comes and goes as it likes, vanishing right in front of witnesses."

Better and better. She kept the disgust from her voice. "I see."

"Some of the best trackers in the River Kingdoms will be along," Avelis said. "I can't imagine it taking more than a week. And at some point, while you're trying to shoot the beast with one of your alchemical wands, Drelm will just get in the way. And he *will* get in the way—he'll be in the forefront to kill the thing, I guarantee it. And you, with your ranged weapons, will be standing back. Easy."

Somehow she doubted it would be as easy as he supposed. And then Avelis opened the bag once more. "Hold out your hand, and we'll count out your advance. That is, if you're in."

She hesitated only a moment. "I'm in."

Chapter Four
The Expedition
Elyana

Dawn had come to the little village. Light filtering through the trees clustered along the riverbank painted the dusty streets in tawny rose. A cool morning breeze stirred the leaves.

As was normal on such a day, Delgar's people were already up, moving off toward shops or running errands. Normally the children would be running to start their morning chores, but today dozens gathered to stare at the men and women waiting expectantly in the town square south of Delgar's keep.

Elyana watched them from her doorway vantage point. The throngs that had come to apply for the expedition were even more diverse than she'd expected. The majority were a mix of human Riverfolk, seasoned warrior types with sturdy if battered armor and weapons. But there were dwarves too, and halflings, and a mix of other races. She could guess that many were mercenaries, come to hunt the beast and collect the coin. Others, she knew, sought vengeance, for she had overheard talk from Delgar villagers in the last week and saw their grim faces mixed in with those of strangers.

The professionals chatted among themselves with bored disinterest, trading an occasional dark smile if they recognized one another. Those who had lost loved ones or friends to the creature shifted with nervous energy.

"None of them look frightened enough," she said quietly to Drelm, who only grunted.

The two waited just inside the dry goods shop, he in his armor and tabard, she in her weathered brown traveling gear, her hair pinned back.

Lieutenant Demid and two other guardsmen were posted at the crowd's edges. Elyana didn't expect any trouble—not yet—but only a fool took unnecessary risks.

Only two clerics had established homes in Delgar. The matronly priestess of Calistria walked now with her single acolyte along the edge of the gathering, calmly offering a kiss and the touch of her three-pointed holy symbol to any who desired the blessing of her god.

Her competition, the most recent addition to Delgar's priestly population, strode back and forth on the east side of the street in his black robe and iron mask, imploring the crowd to seek protection not from the arms of men, but within the arms of Razmir.

"I'll give him a point for cleverness on that one," Elyana admitted grudgingly.

"We need a priest of Abadar," Drelm said gruffly. He'd been repeating that for at least a year. He'd written multiple letters to the temple to the God of the First Vault in Riverton, but the head priest of the order continued to politely relay that no one could be spared. Likely none of the priesthood wished to leave the larger settlement, whose civilized comforts were meager enough, for this outpost in the wilderness. Last spring the villagers had taken pity upon the half-orc and helped construct a small stone shrine dedicated to the deity Drelm worshiped so devoutly. None of them, however, had joined him in prayer to a deity they privately viewed as a god for rich men and cities.

"How much longer do you want to give them?" Drelm asked her.

"Another few moments." As Elyana spoke, a tall, thick figure in untanned leather strode in from a side street, trailed by what at first seemed a pack of wolves. Elyana smiled at sight of the rawboned powerful woman she knew for Cyrelle the huntress.

"I wasn't sure she'd come," she said to Drelm.

The crowd gave back, warily eyeing the big woman and her pack. Cyrelle halted a few feet from them and brought her hand down crisply, and all seven of her animals dropped instantly to their haunches.

"It will be good to have her with us," Drelm said, which was almost glowing praise from the half-orc.

A native of Riverton, Cyrelle had helped them a few months back when they'd trailed another murderer into the forest depths. Her command of her dogs, and her woodcraft, were remarkable.

"And here's an Oaksteward," Drelm said.

"I wasn't sure they were really coming."

There was no missing the tall figure near the back of the crowd, or the ornately carved staff he leaned against.

"Sevenarches has been having its own trouble with the beast," Drelm remarked. "I'm surprised they didn't send more."

"I hope he passes muster," Elyana said. "It will be good to have a healer. You can go a little easier on him, I suppose, so long as he can defend himself and has the stamina."

"You mean to test even a druid from Sevenarches?"

"Everyone," Elyana said. "Even Cyrelle and Illidian." Her eyes shifted to the crippled figure in the shadows of a tree at the very back of the crowd. Even from a distance he seemed to brood.

"Why test Illidian?" Drelm asked. "You know he can fight. And he's the one who pushed hardest for this."

"The rest of the expedition needs to know he's skilled, even with only one good arm. He insisted."

Drelm grunted. "Is that for their sake, or Illidian's?"

It was a fair question. Sometimes, even after the last few years, Drelm's astuteness surprised her. "Those who come with us must see what we all can do if we're to rely on one another."

Drelm nodded in agreement.

"There, I think that's about it," Elyana said as the final two hurried in from a tavern. These stood out like pups near a wolf den; a young man and woman, scarcely past their fifteenth or sixteenth birthdays. He was fair-haired and gangly and carried a sword a little too big for him. She was dark-haired, her pale face freckled, and wore a beautiful scarlet cloak a little too long for her. Its hem trailed into the street's dust.

"The young ones," she said, "are always in the biggest hurry to die."

Drelm did not answer this, but she could guess his thoughts. Those who were too weak to win had no business fighting, and deserved what they got.

"Let's go meet them."

One by one, the members of the crowd turned toward her as she stepped onto the long porch of the merchant's shop, watching as she moved with long strides, one hand steadying the sword at her hip.

Closing on two centuries, much of it spent fighting, Elyana could assess a man or woman's fighting prowess with minimal scrutiny. She could gauge that the short, dark-haired fellow was more dangerous than the big man beside him in the polished armor. Even after all these years, though, she still couldn't always tell by looking which of the professionals lived for the thrill, which for the love of killing, and which had secret death wishes.

Of course, some were obvious. Her eyes shifted back to Illidian, watching stonily from beside his full cousin, both of them in forest green. She had met his like before: an individual so single-minded he would hazard his life and all those he led to quench his bloodlust.

She planted her feet before setting hand to sword pommel. Drelm stepped out beside her and stood at her right side.

She lifted her chin and raised her voice. "I am Elyana Sadrastis, and this is Captain Drelm. We will lead the expedition." She paused, as though considering the assembly for the first time. "We are the final arbiters of who joins it. We intend to take sixteen of you and no more—eighteen total. It's not enough that you know your weapons or your spells. We will be living wild. The beast we hunt is wily. It's deadly. We'll have to depend upon one another to survive."

"Is it true about the money?" someone shouted from the back.

Elyana found him—one of two red-haired dwarves armored in leather. She paused and stared at him before surveying the crowd once more. "Something else I wish to impress upon you is that the captain and I command. For the duration of this expedition, you will think of yourselves as our army, and us as your officers. You will obey our orders without question." She paused to let that sink in. "This monster's vicious, and some of us are going to die. If you listen to us, we think those numbers will be fewer. As to the money, the governments of the nearest River Kingdoms have pooled their funds. Enough to pay each one of you who signs on five hundred sails. No more, no less."

There were audible groans, even some muttered complaints that they should risk their lives for so little, although others in the crowd chattered excitedly. Most of those watching must already have known this was true, for they showed no change of expression.

"Should you perish," she went on, "whomever you claim as your dependent will still receive that money. The lord mayor has pledged that they will be paid, and he is a man of his word. So. Should we ask you to sign on, be clear about who your next of kin is, and where they can be found." She fell silent for a time. They still watched, expectantly. The young cloaked woman had her hand in the air.

"I'll take questions from any of you who qualify. Now it's time to see what you can do. Drelm?"

The half-orc stepped to her side and spoke succinctly. The applicants were divided into two groups to start with, Drelm studying their melee skills and the ever polite Lieutenant Demid directing the ranged weapon tests.

Elyana observed both groups from the porch, and found few surprises. The dwarves proved deadly with their axes at close range, but they weren't very fast. She had judged them woodsmen, not warriors, and they were swiftly outfought in a mock combat. The young man with the overly large sword proved unskilled beyond a few basic cuts and parries. A huntsman with a bad limp was disqualified despite his excellent bow work, for he would not be able to keep up if they were forced to dismount. He protested loudly that he would come without guarantee of pay, and Demid had to have him ushered off by the guardsmen Gered and Tern.

Then there were the applicants whose testing was only a formality, like Illidian, his cousin Galarias, and the dark-haired Aladel. The elves outshot everyone without breaking a sweat, and parried every strike with ease. She would have expected nothing less from them.

A few had to have special circumstances accounted for, such as the bounty hunter. Elyana had been unimpressed by guns the one time she'd seen them in action, but she quickly saw just how useful Lisette could be, so long as she had the backing of her dwarf assistant to reload weapons for her. She proved more than sufficient with her sword work.

The huntswoman Cyrelle was another for whom she made special allowances. She was only a fair shot and a passable swordswoman, but her command of her hounds was deservedly legendary in the southern River Kingdoms. Each of the hundred-pound killing machines wheeled, lunged, and halted on the instant. But it was not Cyrelle's fighting prowess, or even that of her animals, that Elyana most valued. In all the River Kingdoms, few could equal Cyrelle's pack in their ability to track and find prey, and Elyana knew of none who could surpass her.

After she confirmed Cyrelle's admittance, Elyana moved over to watch Drelm put the Oaksteward through his paces, hoping the half-orc would recall that she'd stressed a healer need only be able to keep up and defend himself.

When the druid pulled down the hood of his brown robe, Elyana saw he was older than she'd imagined, with a bald pate surrounded by a fringe of wispy brown and gray hair. His leathered face was seamed with lines. Yet for all the look of age, his shoulders were broad, if slightly hunched, and the hands clutching his staff were large, knotted, and discolored with scars. Any worries she had as to the man's fitness for travel were put to the test the moment Drelm narrowly sidestepped a vicious whack to his head. The watching applicants gasped, but Drelm let out a harsh bark that was approving laughter.

The druid stepped back, lowered his staff hesitantly, then returned Drelm's laugh with a gap-toothed grin of pleasure.

"Elf," said a gruff voice beside her.

She had to look down to find the speaker, the red-haired dwarf who'd asked her about money. He and his near twin stood frowning. Was it chance that they stood on her left, or were they warriors enough to know it would be harder for her to draw her sword and defend from that side? Unintentional or not, the approach struck her as aggressive, and her eyes narrowed in disapproval. "Elyana will do."

Drelm called for the next applicant, and she glanced over to see the advance of the wiry, dangerous-looking fellow with dark hair she'd noted beside the big man in armor.

"That beast killed our cousins," the dwarf said. The knuckles gripping the haft of the axe slung over his shoulder were white. "Me and Ragnar mean to go on this expedition and take vengeance."

"You didn't pass the test," Elyana said simply.

The other dwarf, presumably Ragnar, spoke up. His nose had been broken, and the long scar through his beard gave him a fierce countenance. Yet he was more deferential than his relative, bowing his head respectfully. "Your pardon. We don't feel we were given a fair trial. We know we're not fast. But we know the woods, and we know how to fight."

"I'm sure you're right," Elyana told him.

"We want another chance," the first speaker insisted.

Elyana nodded slowly. "What are your names?"

"I am Ragnar, Lady," said the more polite one, "and this is my brother, Larak."

Elyana bowed her head respectfully. "I'm pleased to meet you."

"Likewise." Ragnar bowed his head to her, and Larak echoed the gesture less deeply.

She almost hated to do what must come next. She maintained her politely formal tone. "Do you suppose you would perform better, given another chance?"

"I am sure we would." Hope shone now in Ragnar's eyes, which cut sharply. The coming demonstration would be much easier on her conscience if the fellow were an ass.

She tried to warn him. "If I allow you to try again, shouldn't I allow all of those who failed a second chance?"

"This is different," Larak said, almost in a snarl. "We were fighting against an orc-blood. Everyone knows they hate dwarves."

Drelm was above such things, though they were unlikely to believe it. She tried telling them anyway. "Captain Drelm cares only about bringing the monster's head. He doesn't care if you're dwarf, gnome, or halfling, so long as you can fight."

"With due respect, Lady, my brother and I can surely fight."

"Can you move swiftly when the time demands? Can you obey on the instant? Can you be ready for attack at any moment?"

"Yes," Ragnar assured her with another head bow. "I assure you—"

She drew her sword in a flash of steel. Larak, more wary, pulled up his axe, sending his brother stumbling back with his off hand. Had he put both hands to the haft he might have been a threat, but Elyana had already tapped him on the side of his head with the flat of her blade.

"Dead," she said.

Larak raised one hand up to the side of his face. "You cheated—and that blow wouldn't have killed me!"

"It could have," Elyana told him.

Larak scowled. She saw his hand shaking on his axe haft and knew he was tempted to lash out.

It was Ragnar who charged. He came in swinging wildly, foam flecking his lips and beard.

Elyana leapt aside from one blow, then another, and when she struck him in the side of the head with her flat she hit with full strength.

Enraged as he was, Ragnar seemed to feel nothing, and pressed on, swinging again and again. Around her she sensed the testing had halted. She heard the mutters of the crowd and the shouts of Larak for Ragnar to stop.

Elyana had fought beside and against berserkers and knew that Ragnar wouldn't halt until he was stunned or dead. She'd heard the telltale creak of a strung bow being readied. Illidian, probably, readying to loose an arrow.

"He's mine," she shouted. She didn't want the loss of prestige in the moment before she assumed command, and she didn't mean to kill today. There would be deaths soon enough. All she'd really intended was a lesson, partly for the dwarves but mostly for any onlookers.

The metal band she wore about her upper arm enhanced her strength, but even with its magic, she was unlikely to win a battle of might with a dwarven warrior, so she didn't try to parry, a tricky enough technique against an axe in any case. She sidestepped a terrific blow that would have cut halfway through her, then darted in to smack her blade flat against the right hand gripping the axe. Even in his berserk state Ragnar winced, and his grip loosened. She slipped behind him then, kicking hard at the back of his right leg as he pivoted to follow.

This set him stumbling, and she sprang forward on his right, slammed her hilt onto the knuckles of his other hand. Eyes burning with hatred, he still tried to cast his weapon. It sailed past her nose and slammed into the ground perhaps a fingernail's breadth from her boot.

She stepped back as Larak and two other dwarves—one of them the markswoman's assistant—rushed Ragnar and forced him down.

She found Drelm beside her, chuckling. "Nicely done."

Elyana said nothing. She'd miscalculated just how fine a warrior Ragnar truly was. It was luck, not skill, that had saved her toes from being cut off by his final assault. Privately, she wondered if Drelm had made a mistake with the fellow. For the sake of discipline, though, the dwarf would have to remain behind.

She sheathed her sword and stepped apart, her demeanor calm. "Get back to it," she instructed Drelm.

The other dwarves wrestled Ragnar into submission and led him away. She knew an inward pang as she realized that deep choking sound was the sound of him weeping.

"That was needlessly brave of you," said a familiar tenor behind her. Illidian, speaking Elven. Elyana turned to face him.

He stood with strung bow braced in the clasp mechanism attached to the stump of his left arm. He looked relaxed now, but she had no doubt he and his companions had stood with arrows knocked through most of the fight. "A berserker's almost as bad as a mother bear," Illidian went on.

"I provoked him."

"I heard the whole thing. You but tested him to prove to him, his brother, and all those who watched that the captain's judgment had not been in error. That I understand. What I don't understand is why you didn't simply step aside. We could have shot to wound, and there are enough healers here that he would have been mended soon enough."

"It was an illustration of command. Some here know me only by reputation. They saw me hold my own."

One of Illidian's high eyebrows cocked. "That's interesting. So they would not follow your orders the instant you take command?"

"You know it doesn't work like that."

"In Kyonin it does."

"Yes, well, this isn't Kyonin."

"That's abundantly clear." He eyed her for a moment. "You promised me an officer's position. But you did not announce it."

For all that she remained uncertain about Illidian, she at least liked that he was far more direct than many of the elves she'd known. "Because," she said, "by your own admission, you wished to demonstrate your ability first."

"That's true," Illidian conceded. His gaze darkened. "I wish my people had heard me out. I could have brought a true force here, Elyana. A regiment of archers, backed by wizards."

"Why didn't they?"

He laughed shortly, bitterly. "Because the beast has left Kyonin. The humans are right when they call us cowards."

"Another elf would simply say you're cautious."

"A convenient lie," Illidian said tersely.

He had hinted at all of this before, but she did not remind him. Illidian seemed capable of only two lines of conversation: this one, and the other about vengeance against the beast that had killed his soldiers and taken his arm. She wondered if he had always been so single-minded.

Elyana nodded a farewell and walked back to the porch she used as her speaking platform. Illidian did not take the hint, and followed.

He stopped at her side as she looked over the combatants once more. "How is it that you got involved?"

That struck her as an odd question. "It needs to be done."

"I'm not referring to the hunt for the monster." With a sweep of his good arm he took in Delgar's square and figures assembled within, and the roughhewn timber buildings beyond. "I mean this town, and these people. How could you possibly be invested in their long-term future?"

"I'm not sure that's your business."

"Isn't it, cousin? Your temperament is well suited for service in Kyonin's border rangers. I'm told you even briefly served among them."

"You would think," she said. "But Kyonin's rangers have no place for my best friend."

That struck Illidian silent, but only for a short time. "Are you referring to the half-orc? You name him your best friend?"

She was long since ready for this conversation to be finished. Yet she managed a thin smile. "You're a warrior, Illidian. You've risked your life beside comrades who would give their life for you. Haven't you?"

"You are correct."

"Then you know the greatest test of loyalty comes from those who stand with you in battle. I trust Drelm with my life. He has never failed me."

"That's very interesting," Illidian said. She wasn't entirely sure what he meant by the comment. "That I can understand, then, Elyana," he went on. "But why have loyalty to this place? You can see humans changing year to year. In ten or twenty more, the lord mayor might be dead, and then who can say what will happen to Delgar? Without another strong hand it will go the way of all the wilderness towns. Incompetents will run it into the ground, or bandits will pillage the place, and soon there will be nothing left of it but the ruined keep the mayor found, unmourned and forgotten."

"I'm not really doing this for Delgar."

He cocked his head to one side, with his strange arm momentarily bringing to mind a bird with a broken wing. "Why, then?"

"I'm fond of many here," she said, thinking of Demid, and the mayor, and many of the folk she interacted with each day. Elyana looked over to Drelm. "And this is Drelm's chance to have a home. A wife. I mean to help him secure it before I leave."

"You're leaving?"

She wondered why she had told him that. She'd said nothing of her decision to anyone else.

Another familiar male figure was making his way toward the platform. Avelis, spare, well manicured, simply dressed. As usual, he had ignored her standing recommendation and ventured forth without a guard of his own. With all these strangers in the city, he still insisted he would keep no barriers between himself and the community.

He raised a hand in greeting, then paused to watch a grizzled archer let fly at a distant target.

"That is between the two of us," Elyana said. "Neither the mayor nor Drelm have heard a word of the matter. I wish them to hear it first from me."

"It shall be as you wish." Illidian followed the direction of her gaze. "I must admit that this particular man seems a cut above the ordinary. I think I understand your . . . appreciation of him as well."

"I am glad," she said. "Illidian, you're going to have to command humans if you serve with me."

"If?"

"A commander's responsible for all the lives under his command. Elf, human, or whatever else."

His lips thinned; his tone grew clipped. "I take my command seriously."

"I know you do. But I wonder if you'll value all lives equally. Even short ones."

His head rose indignantly. "I don't like what you imply."

"I'm not implying, Illidian. I'm telling you that you're prejudiced. If you mean to command soldiers that I've selected, you'll treat them just like your elves, or you'll answer to me."

The elf's expression darkened further, but the mayor's arrival silenced him.

The mayor smiled, favoring her with a head bow. "Good morning, Elyana. And to you, Captain Illidian." Avelis rested one hand on his belt buckle and shielded his eyes from the sun, now rising over the treetops. "How are the candidates looking?"

"I think a number are promising," she answered.

"A few of the applicants asked to see me personally," Avelis said casually. "Either out of politeness," at this he nodded to Illidian, "or because they wished special treatment, or because they wanted to sign on as officers."

Elyana nodded.

"Apart from the captain here, the only interesting one was the markswoman. Have you seen her use her strange weapon?"

"I have," Illidian answered. "She's remarkable."

"I thought she might be. I was hoping to see her do it, though. Did she make the cut?"

"So far," Elyana replied. "I'll speak with all the candidates before I make my final decisions."

"Of course." Avelis faced Illidian. "Captain, is there anything else you require? Were your quarters satisfactory yesterday evening?"

"You are very kind to ask, Mayor." Illidian imitated Avelis's own head bob. The mayor's polite formality seemed to engender it in response. "My men were as comfortable as if we rested in our own beds."

Elyana doubted that, for she had occasionally slept on fine elven linens, so soft she could rub her finger along one and feel no fibers.

The mayor brightened at the compliment. "That's good to hear. I'm so glad you're along. Elyana is never as cautious of her own welfare as might be nice. A good general commands from the rear, not from the front, but she and Captain Drelm constantly risk themselves in the heat of battle. Knowing you'll be accompanying her reassures me she'll be coming back alive."

"I will do my best to ensure her welfare," Illidian answered.

Elyana frowned. "All I need from you is to carry out my commands."

The elven captain's smile was icy. "But of course."

Chapter Five
Blood and Bullets
Drelm

The tower's banquet hall seemed a lot smaller now. Light lanced in from arrow slit windows high along the walls, piercingly bright, but it was the candelabra that painted the shadows on the walls. It was blunt and heavy, suspended by thick chains, and Drelm himself had seen it lowered and hoisted many times as the candles were readied before one of the lord mayor's important gatherings.

Today that wagon-wheel candelabra hung over an odd and mismatched assortment of men and women. He and Elyana and the crippled elf, Illidian, stood at one end of the table, and the grim and grizzled veterans they'd selected sat on the wooden benches that flanked it.

Drelm had been taught by Lord Stelan to know the soldiers under his command, and so he had already committed their names to memory. He was already acquainted with the slim woman in the blue feathered hat with the dangerous eyes—Lisette. Next to her was the dwarf, Karag, who always returned his scrutiny with a glower. He'd bear watching, because dwarves often made it a point to manufacture grudges.

Next to them were two sellswords from Tymon: Marika, dressed in furs and boasting a terrific scar along one half of her face, and Grellen, a heavy-lidded blond with a frontiersman's fringed leathers. Drelm himself had picked these two, and even if he had not learned something of their history, from the way they'd yelled encouragement to each other during the trials and were always found no more than a few paces apart, it was easy to guess they worked together.

At their side was a small lean fellow with short dark hair, all deadly speed and sharp knives. Venic, he called himself, and Drelm had thought him a city creature until he'd seen how softly he moved through the undergrowth in the wilderness trial.

There were also the two elves. Galarias was blood cousin to Illidian, with gold hair and flawless skin, both deadly accurate and self-possessed. He had yet to speak a word, but Drelm knew he understood the common tongue, for Galarias had followed all instructions without hesitation. Aladel was dark of hair and eye, and if he was not quite as fine a shot as Galarias, he was a better blade. He wore blacks rather than the Kyonin border patrol's brown and green, and he was different from both Illidian and Galarias in the comfortable way he mixed with non-elves.

The next member of their group stood only the size of a half-grown child. Drutha the halfling was dressed fully in forester's green from hat to boots, in an outfit hung with satchels and pockets and holders for vials and globes. She didn't have that merry, friendly, insipid look Drelm had glimpsed on the faces of many halflings, but Drelm still wondered as to her utility, no matter that Demid and Elyana had chosen her.

Then there was a rangy human, Calvonis, who identified himself as a farmer, though he'd worn a tarnished helmet and old leathers when he'd fought. There was no missing the martial past in his bearing, or the way he wielded his sword. He said that he'd been farming until the monster had destroyed his home near Riverton and killed his wife. Drelm understood the need for vengeance, and how it could knock a man off his stride, and he respected the man's incredible focus during every trial.

Next to him were the two magic-workers: flame-haired Vatok, the smiling, paunchy wizard dressed in comfortable traveling clothes; and the old Oaksteward, anchored to his staff and looking dour and serious, in part because of the graying eyebrows that shaded his eyes.

Finally, there was Cyrelle the huntress, a sturdy woman of broad shoulders, tall or taller than any man at the table. For all that her hair was short and coarse, and the fact that she was easily twice as wide around as Elyana, she somehow reminded Drelm of his friend.

"So here you are," Elyana said. "Congratulations. Take a look around the table, and know that some of us here are going to die."

Drelm almost smiled at the startled reactions that spread through the group. Elyana had guaranteed their attention, although a few reacted differently than he would have anticipated. Galarias seemed unfazed, which might simply have been that cultivated elven aloofness, and Venic reacted with all the passion of a lizard. Karag actually looked angry, and Lisette smiled thinly, as though Elyana had shared a private joke that only she was clever enough to comprehend.

"We'll raise our odds if you remember who's in charge," Elyana continued, "and follow orders. The three of us"—at this she raised a hand to Illidian and Drelm—"will be leading. If you don't obey, you're out. If you feel like you can't obey, you're out. I hope there're no questions on that score." Elyana paused, scanned the group, and continued. "We'll divide into squads in a moment. Right now, I mean to get to business." Elyana put palms down on the table and leaned toward them. "The monster. Over the last weeks we've gathered all the information we could find on the thing. That's meant sorting through the ridiculous and the exaggerations to get to the truth of what we'll be facing."

"Is the thing really invisible?" Drutha asked. Her voice was bright and high, but not guileless.

Elyana did not take exception to the question. "It is," she said, nodding slowly. "But we still have a fair idea of its size and abilities. Illidian?"

With his one hand, the elf pulled a long roll of parchment and set it on the table. He held it in place with his palm while he unrolled it by pushing with his hook.

"Hold that, please," he instructed Calvonis, the nearest to the far corner, and then looked over to Galarias at the other. "Cousin, if you don't mind?"

Galarias grasped the paper, and Illidian then glanced to Drelm.

The half-orc didn't want to be bothered with holding a corner throughout what was likely to be a long-winded talk, so he drove his knife through the border, affixing it to the table.

Illidian blinked at him in mild disapproval, then apparently decided Drelm's action was unworthy of comment. He put his crippled arm behind his back.

"From its tracks, we estimate the beast at least four horse lengths long. There is evidence of a tail that likely stretches almost that length. The feet are wide around as a decent-sized tree bole, though a shade smaller than Captain Drelm's waist."

The halfling down the table chuckled. Drelm frowned, for he had not seen humor in the remark.

Illidian continued. "It has claws upon these feet, and we have seen scales when blood ran from them." The elf's eyes burned. "We have drawn its blood; we can bring it down."

Illidian used a charcoal pencil to sketch a vaguely lizardlike form on the paper, complete with tail. "We can't say with any certainty what its height is. There are other challenges in addition to its tough hide. It is capable of spraying corrosive venom."

"Corrosive?" The mercenary Grellen asked.

"It could melt your face," Drelm answered. He had asked the same question when Illidian had used the term earlier. Grellen's eyes widened, and he exchanged a concerned glance with Marika beside him.

"It does not do so continually," Illidian went on, "which suggests to me that it may take a while for the accretion to build, or that it requires concentration or aim. What it does use, repeatedly, are two long grasping appendages." Illidian sketched out two snakelike tendrils extended from the beast's shoulders.

"As we have not seen it, we cannot be sure as to where these tentacles are attached, or, indeed, their true reach. But the monster deploys them with great speed and strength. They don't seem to be able to extend more than half again the length of the monster itself." Illidian set down the pencil. "They are capable of squeezing a full-grown warrior to death in a matter of moments. Are there any questions so far?"

Someone down the table laughed in disbelief.

"You say that you've drawn blood," Karag, the dwarf, interjected. "With what? I've heard arrows just bounce off its hide."

"Scales, not hide," Illidian corrected.

"I have drawn blood," Drelm told the dwarf. "With my axe. A good blade, solidly delivered, can slice through."

"But doesn't the thing just vanish?" the wizard Votek asked. "And then return, fully healed? What's the point in attacking it at all?"

"We will attack to kill," Elyana said. "And we'll move onto the how of that in a moment. Right now we want to stay focused on what the beast can do. Illidian?"

The elf resumed his lecture. "It can vanish, seemingly on the instant. It doesn't seem to return right away once it's wounded even a little. I must also point out that it is almost completely silent. You cannot hear its tread, heavy as it is, although you can feel the ground shake."

"How is that even possible?" Marika demanded. Her voice rose in wonder.

"Magic," Votek answered, and the scarred mercenary woman looked down the table at the wizard.

Votek rested his hands on his plump belly. "It's likely some wizard's experiment gone wrong, or else a monster wandered in from another plane. It's clearly no natural creature."

"The wizard's got to be right," Karag agreed. "But how will we fight it if we can't even see it? And the wizard's right about another thing—if it just disappears, how will we ever kill it?"

Elyana's eyes glittered, and Drelm knew a sense of satisfaction, for Elyana had told him the answer before the meeting.

"The moment we know we're in the presence of the beast, Cyrelle will deploy her hounds." Elyana leaned out across the table to indicate the sides of the drawing. "Even if we can't see the beast ourselves, its location will be defined by the animals that smell it. From there, Drutha and Votek will deploy spells that both stain and harm it. In moments we'll have a better idea of its location and anatomy. Our friend Jorn"—she looked down the table at the Oaksteward—"will use his influence over the natural world to slow the beast."

"That's all well and good," Calvonis said, "but what about harming the thing? How do we get close to it if it's whipping around tentacles that we can't even see?"

Illidian answered. "We damage it as much as we can from a distance, first. We've taken steps already as far as arrows." He bent down beside him and set a long feathered shaft upon the parchment paper. "All the arrows carried by archers in this group will be affixed with stone heads." He lifted the weapon so that it caught the sunlight. "They penetrate more deeply and have more stopping power. And these have been enchanted by an elven spellcaster."

Votek leaned back in his chair. "It sounds as though you've given this matter a lot of thought."

"Yes." Illidian's answer was clipped. "You might say that."

"The plan," Elyana said, "is for the dogs and magic wielders to 'paint' the thing's location and for arrows to keep it busy. We've acquired toxins to apply to sword and axe blades for those of you who have to get in close. That will include me," she added. "Even if the thing vanishes,

I hope we can count on its wounds and poison finishing the thing off."

Marika cleared her throat and stretched huge arms, finally cracking a knuckle. She looked to her side, as if searching for someplace to spit, then seemed to think better of it. "That's all well and good," she said finally, her voice betraying a faint, rolling accent that Drelm hadn't been able to place. "But this is a battle plan for perfect conditions. There's no telling where we'll face this thing. Battles are chaotic. The odds of us being able to rally to meet it are . . . well, I'd think it more likely I'd end up in bed with a Taldan duke."

Her friend Grellen chuckled.

Drelm was about to object to the comment, then saw Elyana's smile, wickedly confident.

"Spoken like a veteran. Good. I'm glad you have no illusions. None of us should have. I have seen your skills at work, and I've consulted with those of you with additional talents. And I've been formulating some plans."

What then followed was an in-depth discussion of the sort of details that pleased Drelm most: tactics. After only a short while it was clear even to Marika and Karag that Elyana knew her business, and for the next hour and a half she introduced various situations and how best they could deploy their forces in those circumstances. Whenever one of the others, like Calvonis or Marika, would suggest something Elyana seemed not to have considered, she would immediately suggest a counter, or a slightly different arrangement of squads, so that Drelm could not be certain whether she had already thought of the matter or was just incredibly quick on her feet. Knowing her as well as he did, he knew both were possible.

Finally Elyana dismissed them to find lunch and stretch their legs, ordering them to meet again at the keep come afternoon to practice working together.

Drelm turned down an invitation to join Grellen and Marika for lunch, but pointed them toward the best inn in town, then left the keep in good spirits.

Immediately outside the wall, though, he found the young man and the woman in the scarlet robe he'd disqualified that morning. Both crowded forward.

"Captain Drelm," the young man said with a bow. "I hope you will indulge me. I would like another word with you."

Drelm frowned. "You're not ready for this kind of venture. Neither of you." He started past.

"Won't you at least listen?" the girl demanded shrilly.

"I have already judged," Drelm said, simply. "It's too dangerous for you."

"But we've got to come with you!" The girl tugged at his arm and Drelm struggled against baring his teeth in a full scowl.

Her face was twisted in anguish. "My brother and I swore we'd kill the monster! It killed our parents, and our uncle, and our baby brother. I know my brother's not that practiced, but he's very quick, and he's a fine woodsman. And I know magic. You have but the one wizard!"

"No," Drelm told her.

The girl still clung to his arm. Her brother watched behind her, pimply face mournful in despair.

"We'll do anything," she insisted. "You need people to help carry things, don't you? And don't you need people to cook? I can cook. And my brother knows the woods, he can hunt—"

"No." Drelm showed more teeth as he repeated the word again. He didn't understand why that word was so unclear.

She raised shaking hands just shy of Drelm's chest, as if she were resisting an impulse to grab and shake him.

Drelm sighed. "You didn't qualify. You would die. Your brother would die. Or get in the way so more of us die." Drelm deplored weakness, although a sad woman always engendered a protective spark with him, so he added just a little more. "We will kill the thing," he promised. "Don't worry. Stay safe, and pray for us."

He ignored the final sob and strode off down the street. Rejected applicants and the curious looked out from storefront porches.

People needed to better understand their destined roles. The boy might make a decent warrior, but now was not the time, and this was not a campaign for seasoning the green. Only veterans would return. And the girl needed to go set up a potions shop or work magic in the farm fields. She was no huntswoman.

As he rounded the corner Drelm discovered a small crowd had gathered about a black-robed figure on the steps of Delgar's largest inn, the Rambling Badger. Drelm frowned, slowing his step to look over the situation.

Ten people were arranged in an arc below the wooden porch now serving as an impromptu stage, staring fixedly at the robed figure in its iron mask.

Drelm knew by sight that the fellow was the new Razmiri priest. They always wore iron masks. Usually they wore gray robes, but this one, for some reason, was in black.

Drelm halted to learn whether the man was trying to incite trouble or violence. Like a lot of priests, though, he was preaching the opposite.

"... is not the answer," he was saying in a high, piercing voice. "You can no more kill this kind of monster than you can wield a sword against a flood, or wrestle the winter wind. No!" The figure raised one pale hand toward the overhang above him. "If you desire safety, you must pledge your heart to Razmir, the living god. He who walks still upon Golarion!"

There was considerably more in this vein, but Drelm had already lost interest. He lingered just long enough to decide that no one was apt to start throwing rocks or fighting as a result of anything the Razmiri said, which was all he really cared about.

He'd heard of Razmir—it was hard not to have heard of the living god, because his priests were all over the River Kingdoms, and had even built a temple in Delgar—but Drelm had no real interest in any god but Abadar. He was willing to accord most gods his respect, but any god that preached fearful, bovine obedience rather than right-minded balance, which Drelm took to mean appropriate steps at the appropriate time, struck him as unworthy of attention. Anyone who thought their god would personally protect them against the beast was a fool, but that was their lookout, not Drelm's. He could protect the people of Delgar from a lot of things, but not from being stupid.

He moved off.

Drelm hadn't encountered the beast personally since it had killed Melloc, but he had come upon its massacres twice—the torn and mangled bodies, the smashed homes, the scattered limbs. Grown men had died with their swords unbloodied. Only a handful reported ever laying a blow against the thing, or witnessing one, and only one other apart from Illidian and Elyana and himself had seen blood.

But then, mostly the creature attacked at night, and most survivors only relayed that it was invisible.

Now, though, they would have their force, and put the monster down, and then he would be free to marry the woman Abadar had placed within his path and filled with love for him. Daylah. She was almost through her mourning for Melloc. He would kill the beast, avenge his friend, and then take the woman to wife.

Even now she waited for him with a meal she would have insisted upon preparing, for she took special pleasure in readying his food. She would understand that his duties had delayed him. He did not know how he had become so blessed—

His attackers timed their movement perfectly, for at the same time that he heard a scuff behind him, he saw two figures slide into the side street ahead. No bandit would be foolish enough to assault him in this town; it was obvious even to him that these men were after something else.

Drelm slipped quickly to the left, drawing his throwing axe as the crossbow bolt intended for his throat struck his armored shoulder. He scarcely felt its bite.

The two in front loped forward, cloaks spilling open as they pulled short swords. The one on the right had a near lipless mouth that formed a ring of surprise in the moment before Drelm's axe embedded in his face. He dropped like a stone even as Drelm whirled with his second throwing axe. One of the two assailants who'd come from behind led slightly, and it was this one who caught the axe in his chest and doubled up, his sprawl setting his companion stumbling. Drelm spun forward once more, pulling up his largest axe.

But that attack came to a sudden end with a single crack of thunder. A red and bloody hole appeared just above the man's nose, and he sank to the ground.

Drelm grunted. Abadar be praised—it was the markswoman's work. He'd seen her shooting and knew the sound and the kind of holes her attacks left. Where she was now he could not see and did not care.

He spun to face the final assailant.

Robe belling behind him, the wiry fellow rushed forward with twin swords, eyes slitted.

Drelm showed his fangs in a roar. He didn't wait for the attack, for an axe is a poor defensive weapon and Drelm lacked patience. He came forward swinging.

The human ducked his first blow and stabbed furtively. The sword glanced off Drelm's armor. The captain caught the second strike on the haft of his axe, where it scored the leather beside his thumb.

Drelm kicked out, but the swordsman sidestepped and came in low. Drelm took the strike on an armored elbow, then crashed through a weak guard. The axe bit through the man's shoulder blade and neck. Blood rained. His opponent sagged, vomiting blood and screaming until Drelm finished him with a blow to the head.

The battle had been invigorating, and Drelm smiled in satisfaction. It was only after that he frowned, realizing he'd have to delay his visit to Daylah until he'd cleaned up. Only a little of the blood had stained his clothing, but it wouldn't do to show up with droplets of it on his gauntlets, arms, and tabard. He'd discovered high-society women didn't approve of that sort of thing. After Melloc's death, Daylah had been unduly worried every time he rode out on patrol. What would she say if he wandered in to eat with her looking like this?

As he scanned the street for further opponents he saw the markswoman, walking slowly down the side street while reloading her rifle.

"Friends of yours?" she asked.

Drelm bent and wiped his axe blade on the cloak of the man at his feet. He then kicked the body over and considered the fellow's face. "Never saw this one before."

He walked back and forth between them, the markswoman keeping pace, and considered each. None looked familiar. It wasn't the first time someone he didn't know had tried to kill him. "Galtans, probably. They send someone after me or Elyana every few months." He bent to retrieve his throwing axes, cleaning each in turn on the dead men.

The woman looked puzzled, then bent over the man Drelm had axed in the face. She seemed untroubled by the gruesome wound. "They don't look Galtan."

"The Galtans probably hired them," he said, then added: "That was a good shot. It saved me some time." He hadn't really needed the help, but he thought it would be polite to voice his appreciation.

Her answer was careless. "I was in the area. We need to get used to watching out for each other. What'd you do to anger the Galtans?"

"Long story," Drelm said. "And I'm already late. I'll have to change, now."

"Do you think there will be more of them?"

"Someday," Drelm answered. "They'll need better luck." He took note but withheld comment as the woman looted the men's coin purses. He grunted in appreciation when she turned them over to him.

"For the city coffers?" she asked.

"Always." He raised a hand in farewell, then trotted out of the alley. He'd send a patrol back to do something about the bodies.

By the time he'd told one of his men about the corpses and changed clothes, another half-hour had fled. He found Daylah waiting in the walled garden outside the wood-and-brick house where she lived with the lord mayor, just beside the keep.

She brightened as she rose from the bench, and Drelm was reminded anew how unreliable his memory was. When he was away, he recalled that she was beautiful, but whenever he was once more in her presence, it was as though he looked upon her again for the first time, like a man brought forth from a darkened cave into dazzling sunlight.

Daylah was small and lush, broad across the shoulders and hips, narrow through the waist. She was no fragile city-bred girl, but a buxom country lady with an unruly bob of blonde hair that she was constantly pushing from bright blue eyes. He forced a tight smile, because he knew he was intimidating when he showed all his teeth.

"I had started to worry," she told him. Daylah's voice was husky, though not at all unfeminine. She stepped forward and held his hands as he looked down at her, drinking her beauty in. She tossed her hair out of her eyes. "Is everything alright?"

"Just a little trouble in town. Nothing to worry about. We've weeded out the worst applicants. What is there to eat?"

She laughed. "The only details you like to hear are about food." She released his left hand and indicated the bench. She'd covered it over with a blue blanket, and a basket with wrapped foodstuffs sat on the other end. "Have a seat."

He chuckled a little at her. He preferred to hear about weapons and battles, but he liked that she took such pleasure in making his meals, so he indulged her while she displayed each item—the bread, the boiled eggs, the jams, the broiled fish. She was excited, too, about the Galtan wine she'd gotten from some river trader. Drelm had pretty much given up on all things Galtan, and disliked sweets, but he grunted in appreciation because he knew it would make her happy.

Once he was munching, she grew more reflective. "Did you find some good people?"

Drelm nodded. "I think they'll do."

"How long do you think it will take?"

He swallowed. "I can't say. But I will come back to you as soon as I can."

"For the food?" she asked with a faint smile.

"For your company. And the food," he added, to which she laughed gently. "Now tell me about the dress. Did you sort things out?"

"I'm surprised you're interested. I'd rather hear about the people you'll be hunting with."

He waved that away. "I would rather hear you talk."

"So you can eat?" she chided.

"So that I can remember your voice while I'm away."

Her expression softened then, and she touched his hand.

In truth, the details about her wedding dress were eye-glazing. Apparently there had been some kind of trouble about the cuffs and collar. There were three kinds of lace that would have suited, but the local dressmaker had used a fourth that Daylah thought the worst possible choice. Also she was thinking about redoing the neckline. It was very dull, but she was so pretty that he enjoyed watching her in motion as she spoke even about such things as this, for her face lit, and her hair moved, and she was pleasant to look upon from so many angles. It was a good life.

Chapter Six
New Friends
Lisette

The courtship was as boring as everything else about the half-orc. At the keep, Lisette had seen Drelm speak briefly with a man at the gate before unceremoniously turning over the coin purses she'd lifted off the assassins. She was positive Drelm hadn't put a stubby finger on a single one of the coins, which led her to believe he might really be as stupid as he seemed.

After that, Drelm had disappeared briefly into the keep to emerge in another clean tabard, the blood washed from his arms, hands, and face. He'd strode forth stiff-backed once more (no one could accuse him of bad posture), this time knocking at the wooden gate set in a high stone wall of one of the town's nicest homes—which really wasn't saying much.

Finding a good way to look in on his doings there had been tricky until Lisette realized there was a barn loft with a decent vantage point only a few hundred feet off. She was planted there now beside a hay bale, the loft door below the roof winch open just far enough for her to watch events.

And Drelm was as dull and respectable as dirt. Almost any other man she'd ever met would have had that plump and bosomy peaches-and-cream piece bent over a bench and moaning the moment the garden door shut, but Drelm was taking his lunch with her like a country squire.

Apparently the only important thing Lisette was going to learn about her quarry was that he was good in a fight, which she'd already guessed. Drelm probably hadn't needed her help in the side street, even outnumbered four to one. He had heard, seen, or smelled those four coming. She couldn't quite remember if half-orcs had a superior or inferior sense of smell. However he'd been alerted, he'd dispatched them with blazing efficiency—presumably by instinct, because there was little intellect or curiosity on display once he'd done the killing. He was like one of those trained monkeys people dressed up in clothes in the south. Someone had taught him civility, and so he went through all the motions, whether it be turning gold over to the authorities, slicing up your food, or—and this part amused her the most—keeping your wick dry until you reached the marriage bed. He hadn't even tried kissing the girl.

The galling thing had been shooting the Razmiri rather than the half-orc. It would have been an easy shot into Drelm's back, and she could have been out of the town before anyone asked any questions. But Avelis had hired her to carry out the job a certain way, and she meant to earn the rest of those gems, so she was resigned to carrying out his wishes. She hoped protecting Drelm from other assassins wouldn't be a regular part of the affair. Almost she had asked him why a Razmiri might want him dead, but after he'd dismissed the discussion of Galtans she didn't think she'd get anywhere with that line of questioning either. She'd found the little golden mask symbol around the neck of the one Drelm had axed in the face. Were Razmiri now sending assassins, or had an assassin simply taken up the faith?

The mayor might be able to tell her, but she wasn't about to approach him again. Bad enough that so many had seen her speak with him. The two had an explanation ready for that, should there be future inquiries. A second conversation would be more challenging to credulity if suspicion were ever raised that the mayor had hired her.

She would just have to handle it on her own.

That afternoon, the expedition members trained together and grew familiar with one another's capabilities. Lord Avelis watched much of the proceedings, and Lisette was amused to observe how close he stayed to Elyana. She couldn't tell if the attraction was mutual. The elf seemed all business, though she was unfailingly cordial with the mayor.

Elyana set the group working through tactics for well over three hours, long past the time for dinner, then had them sit down at a table with the Calistrian priestess, her acolyte, and a whole lot of papers. A larger settlement would have had bureaucrats on the payroll, but Delgar had only one, so the aging but still rather saucy priestess donated her time, being more educated than most. One by one the expedition members sat down to identify their next of kin so their earnings would be sent on if they failed to return.

Lisette invented a relative in Absalom that the expedition reward money could be sent to and put her name to the form.

Once everyone was through with the paperwork, Elyana spoke briefly about what she expected come the morning, and the mayor spoke a little longer about honor and pride and the pursuit of vengeance in a noble cause and interspecies cooperation and other rot like that. Lisette tried not to let her eyes roll. Half of the expedition folk hung on his words like he was a newly anointed saint come back from Heaven.

Afterward, she and Karag retired to an inn close to Madame Celene's and sat at a table in the back of the common room, slowly nursing a decent homebrewed ale. There were plenty of seats due to the locals having some big celebration outside—a farewell and good-luck party, near as she could tell. The idiots could stay up late drinking if they wished. She knew there would be hard days ahead, and she meant to spend a final night lying on a comfortable mattress.

Karag dined with her. He'd been in a sour mood ever since he'd returned from mixing the preservative for the heads last night, now stored in a chest in Madame Celene's cellar sealed with one of their locks.

It wasn't the head-chopping or body-dumping that had angered the dwarf, but the thought of having to take any kind of orders from a half-orc. Karag had been going on about how his brother and some of his uncles had been killed by orcs ever since. She'd never seen Karag so emotionally invested in something apart from dog races.

After Karag was through with the pile of greasy sausages and the salty cabbage, he pushed his plate aside and took a long swig from his third mug of ale. Then, finally, he cast a sidelong glance her way and took an awkward stab toward dinner conversation. "So, who'd you sign to have your money sent off too?"

Lisette smirked. "My dear sister, in Absalom."

That got his full attention, and his eyebrows rose. "I didn't know you had a sister."

"I don't."

His brow wrinkled.

"I lied," she said softly, then sipped from her own mug.

Karag shifted uncomfortably in his chair, then frowned. "I don't know why you'd do that. I signed up my cousin Otrek."

What had gotten into Karag? Usually he'd be chuckling at this. She stared at him, hard, to make sure he hadn't suddenly developed a dry sense of humor. He hadn't. "First," she said, "I don't plan on dying. Second, do you think these country rubes will actually get Otrek the money if you end up dead?"

"I think they might," Karag said defensively. "And Otrek could use the money. He's on the outs with the rest of the family."

She leaned back against her chair and took another long sip. "You're just full of all kinds of private details this week. First you went on about the orcs jumping your family, now it's all about your hardscrabble cousin."

Karag's look was baleful.

"I don't know what you're worried about," she said. "But if you plan on kicking off, I can make sure the money gets to him."

"My cut for the other job, too," he said darkly. His eyes locked onto hers. "Some of my family's got magic. I expect I'd have ghost powers to haunt you if you didn't keep your word."

Her laugh dropped short as she realized he was deadly serious. "Sure, Karag." She took another swig.

Karag set down his mug. "I'm going to go listen to the music."

"If you like," she said, and the dwarf hopped down from the chair and stomped away. There was a brief rise in the sounds outside as he pushed the door open. Some low-voiced man was leading a number of others in a sing-along about Darvin the hero. Lisette thought she could live the rest of her life without hearing another song about the plucky young man and his adopted halfling brother, but everyone up and down the Sellen seemed to be requesting the tales these days. The sound dulled once more as the door swung shut.

She ordered another ale, for she liked the taste, and she wanted something to keep her throat wet while she dined on the local fare. It wasn't especially good, but she didn't really care. She was dead tired of fish, which seemed to be served with most meals here along the Sellen.

She was finishing her food when Venic, the little wiry fellow from the expedition force, wandered over with a bottle of wine and two glasses.

There'd been no missing him all through the competition. Venic had professional killer written all over him. He was small and dressed in drab colors, with a plain face and a shock of black hair. Apart from the good shave and the well-trimmed nails, there wasn't much memorable about him. Just the way a good assassin would want things.

"Do you mind if I join you?" he asked. Even his voice was nondescript. He had a plain, mild tenor, with no regional accent.

"Why not?" she answered.

He hooked a foot under one chair leg to pull it out and sat down beside her. He watched as she worked another helping of stewed cabbage onto her fork, then drove a knife into the cork and worked it free of the bottle. He sucked in a sniff and a smile passed briefly over his face. He poured a drink into one of the glasses, pushed it toward her, and poured himself another.

"I've had enough already."

He flashed a toothy smile. "Indulge me. We two are some of the chosen. Let us drink to our success."

"I don't like Galtan wine."

That brought him pause. He shrugged, then raised his own glass to her. "Then I will drink to the beauty of my dinner companion."

He raised it a modicum higher, then brought the glass to his lips and sipped.

"I know who you are," he said softly, leaning a little toward her.

"Of course you do. I am Lisette Demonde."

He smiled. "Everyone in Delgar knows that. I mean I know who you *really* are. Your reputation precedes you. For instance." He pointed at the right sleeve of her jacket. "I know that if I were privileged enough to glimpse the flesh along your wrist, I would find the tattoo of a small black snake."

"A snake?" she said, feigning amusement. What she felt instead was a cold, blind rage. Who was this man?

"They say you're the only one who ever left the Black Coil alive."

This was very bad news. How could he possibly know so much? "I'm a bounty hunter, not an assassin."

He smiled thinly. "You need not be coy. Only an idiot would be going on this journey to actually kill the beast.

And you and I aren't idiots. I thought, given our shared profession and likely . . . overlap of goals, that we might provide each other a certain professional courtesy." He swirled the wine in his glass and leaned forward conspiratorially. His voice was low. "This is not, as they say, a target-rich environment. For instance, I'll get paid if my targets drop. It does not matter, really, who strikes the bull's-eye. So there's no need for competition between us."

Inwardly, Lisette groaned. Outwardly, she pretended to consider his words before looking up at him through her lashes. "This isn't the place for this kind of talk."

"Of course."

"Perhaps we should retire to my room at Madame Celene's, down the street. Bring your wine. And see if there's anything for dessert."

"In this place? It's possible, I suppose. You take the wine, and the glasses. I'll follow shortly."

Complications. She didn't need complications. She'd hear him out and decide what course to take, although she was inclined to simply kill him and have Karag drop another body in the Sellen later in the evening. It astounded her sometimes how discrete the dwarf could be about such things.

Madame Celene's was but a short walk away, and she told the woman's nephew, lounging in the front hall, that she was expecting a male guest. The young man fought down a smirk, managed a nod, and promised to send him up.

Only a few strands of weak evening light filtered in through the window of her room now, casting the meager furnishings in shadow. There was a single bed, a bedroll for Karag, and the small chest with its grisly contents.

Apart from a worn dresser, a chipped bowl for washing hands, and a tarnished metal plate that served as a mirror, there was only the lantern. This she lit.

She then slid one of her pistols under the pillow, divested herself of her gun belt, and undid the top button of her blouse. She was not especially well endowed, but she had curves, and a flash of that flesh was enough to distract many men. She took a moment to fluff her hair. Women always strove so hard to get every hair into its perfect place, but she'd learned men preferred a wilder look. Surely it had always worked on Kerrigan, whose dark eyes had lit with desire when she thought herself at her most ill-kept.

She worked through the sudden pang deep in her chest at thought of those strong brown hands. She had loved his hands, no matter that they were perpetually powder-stained, just as her own were now. She'd thought him plain, at first . . .

She frowned at herself and pinched some red into her cheeks. *Stay on task.* She poured a little of the wine into a glass and set the bottle and the other glass on the floor beside her.

The knock came on her door, and she called for the man to enter, then lowered the wine as if she had just taken a sip. She hadn't detected the scent of anything in the wine, but why not have him thinking she'd consumed some?

Venic flung the door wide and considered the room carefully before striding inside.

"Were you expecting a surprise?" Lisette asked.

"In our line, shouldn't I always?" Venic glanced behind the door as he shut it, then returned his attention to her. "I thought you didn't like Galtan wine."

"Sometimes I like different things."

He stepped to the dresser and set down a chipped platter supporting a round pastry. "Pie," he explained. "It looked fresh."

"I noticed. Blackberry pie. But what I don't know is your own name. Your real one."

He smiled wryly. "I am Devin Mervil."

She didn't know him at all, but she allowed a twitch of one eyebrow, as if she had recognized the name and tried not to show her true reaction.

"So you've heard of me."

"You seem clearly to have heard of me."

"Oh, I surely have. Did you really kill an Alkenstar marksman after you made him your lover?"

People were saying she killed Kerrigan? She worked hard not to let her anger show. "Is that what they say?"

"That's what they guess." He moved forward and sat down on the bed, leaning close, but setting his hand beside her knee rather than upon it. "They say that you have no loyalty but to money."

What a little bastard. "No good bounty hunter does."

"Assassin. And you're supposed to have been one of the best."

"I'm flattered people think so. I'd prefer they think of me as a bounty hunter. It comes with fewer complications."

"Does it?"

"Why don't we get down to it, Devin. Who're your targets?"

"The elf and the half-orc. Of course."

"Both of them?"

"They have enemies."

"What sort of enemies?"

"Does it matter? What of you?"

"Just the half-orc."

Devin's eyebrows lowered. "That's strange."

"Why do you say that?"

"The elf is the smart one. Kill her and he's just another warrior."

"Oh, he's more than that. I saw him fight today. You didn't mastermind some other attempt on him, did you?"

His surprised look seemed genuine. She paused, lifted up goblet and bottle, and poured him a drink.

"You're not playing with me?" he asked. "There're three of us after them?"

"There were four of them," Lisette said. "Galtans, I think."

"Galtans?" At that, his nostrils flared. Good. She'd pegged him right. He'd been bought and paid for by the Galtans, and was incensed that his masters had dispatched someone else after his quarry.

"He killed all four of them in a trice." She snapped her fingers.

His eyes flicked alertly up to study her own. "How close a look did you get at them?"

"Very close. I was following."

"You were following him, but didn't slay him while he was distracted?"

"I have very specific instructions," she admitted slowly. "Then was not the time to act."

"Very interesting. And what are those instructions?"

Her smile was coy. "What of you? Why haven't you acted yet?"

"Obviously, it will be far simpler to kill them on this expedition and have it look like an accident."

"Obviously."

"Is that what you're waiting for?"

"Somewhat." She pushed at her hair, showing off her slender neck as she adjusted her posture. "And you're saying that you get paid regardless of who does the killing?"

"So long as they end up dead, and I am in the vicinity. And you?"

"I think my contract would be honored if the beast managed to kill him off."

"What do you think about the monster we're to go hunt?"

"I don't much care."

"You don't?" Devin snorted. "Haven't you listened to the gossip?"

"Talk is free. And I don't care enough about the matter to learn the truth."

Once more he studied her. "You're planning to kill him as soon as possible, aren't you. Maybe the first night?"

"No. You?"

"I'd just as soon get it over with. The beast, whatever it is—and I think it's probably some kind of demon—kills indiscriminately. You did hear about that entire river hamlet it demolished, didn't you, on the East Sellen?"

"No."

"How incurious of you. Well, I think it would be good if we could arrange to kill them at the same time. You please your employer, I please mine, and we both get paid. I just need to make sure they're both dead."

"Hmm." Lisette tapped her lip, blinked at him. "That might suit. I've got to know, Devin. However did you hear about my past?"

Devin laughed, a short, sharp sound. "Did you think you'd completely erased your past with a name change? You're too memorable. It would be better for you if you were plain. But you're a beautiful woman, and your weapons are too distinctive."

"They are. They ensure I'm remembered as a bounty hunter. Not an assassin. One works within the law, the other without." Kerrigan's words, and she could almost hear his voice as she said them. She was surprised at herself for speaking them—she didn't need to justify herself to this man.

He took a long sip, then swirled the wine in his glass. He seemed to think that an essential action while drinking. "The weapons merely ensure you're distinctive. They always told us not to stick out, didn't they? I wonder if the reason you 'switched' careers is that you got tired of *not* standing out. Understandable, I suppose, if somebody looks like you."

He was wrong again. Whatever his name might truly be, he was blunt and obvious. "I've lost count of the number of compliments you've given," she told him. "Compliments are one thing. But if you really want to please a woman . . ." she paused to cross her legs, leaning just a little toward him, "you should learn to give her what she wants."

"Which is?" She saw his eyes slide involuntarily down toward the gap in her shirt.

"I took special pains to erase my past in Cheliax," she told him. "I would very much like to know how you knew my name, and the order I served."

He chuckled. "If I told you, I'd reveal my employers."

"That's no secret. It's the Galtans. What do they want with me?"

"How did you—"

She smiled fetchingly. "Don't worry. Your secret is safe."

It was that moment that her hand came up with the pistol. He was accomplished enough that he batted her hand aside. With a flick of his other wrist a blade slid into his hand, but Lisette was already rolling off the bed and avoided his knife thrust.

He cursed at her and came off the mattress. Lisette spun and crouched now, catlike, pistol extended. But when she pulled the trigger the weapon clicked. Misfire!

Devin drove in quickly. Lisette was no stranger to knife fights, but neither was Devin, who wielded his blade like an extension of his own arm. She thrust the hand aside as it jabbed at her rising form, then rabbit-punched him and stepped to his left.

Devin grunted and stumbled, and she reached for her weapons belt. Her hand closed on the pie plate instead. Her master had hammered home the lesson that you use the weapon you have, not the one you wish for, so she didn't grab again for the haft of the other pistol. Devin had recovered and was advancing until the berry pie plate hurtled at him. Nimble though he was, half the dessert caught him on cheek and jowl, and the plate slammed against his forehead. Not a fatal blow by any means, but a fine distraction. He struck a half second later than he might've, partially blinded by warm berries and their juices.

He missed. Lisette had dropped, bracing herself with one hand while her leg swept him. He fell, cracking his head on the bed frame before he slammed into the floor. He was still lying there, partially stunned, when she came to stand over him with her second pistol.

She cocked it. "Last chance. How did you know who I was? My hair is changed. My weapons have changed. My dress has changed. I have left the west. No one should know."

Lisette put her boot on Devin's dropped knife and dragged it closer to her. While he moaned and felt his head, she crouched for the knife and rose with it in her left hand.

"I'll count to three," she told him.

"That gunshot would bring attention," he replied weakly.

"You'll be too dead to care. One."

"You won't risk controversy."

"You were trying to rape me. Two."

"You'll shoot me anyway!"

"No. On that you have my oath. Tell me what I wish to know. Three."

"Okay! Okay!"

Lisette's finger did not tighten on the trigger. "Speak, then."

"My order has word of you. I think all assassin's guilds have word of you. From the Black Coil."

"I left with their blessing." Why would he dare lie, now? Lisette's lips twitched up in a near snarl despite herself.

"I don't think your old master sees it that way. Your description and your choice of arms have gone out to all of us. We're to report any sighting back to the Black Coil, for payment."

Lisette almost hated to ask. "Why?"

Devin's eyes met her own, reluctantly. "I don't know. But I do know that if you are seen to be acting as an assassin and not a bounty hunter, it's to be carefully noted."

"And rewarded?"

"No—just noted."

Lisette puzzled over the information only briefly. Of course. They only reason they wouldn't reward for word of her working as an assassin is that her old masters wouldn't want lies. Just information. And she knew, likewise, why they'd care. If she practiced her old trade she'd face a bounty of her own. Before, she'd been playing it safe. Of course they were actively watching her.

The smart thing to do would be to find Karag and disappear into the night.

But Avelis had half a fortune left to hand over, and Lisette meant to earn it. Besides. Lisette despised anyone telling her what to do.

"Well?" Devin asked. "Did you learn what you needed?"

"I did." She lowered the gun.

Devin smiled in relief. "I wasn't sure I believed you."

"Oh, I keep my word," she told him, then dropped on him with the knife.

Chapter Seven
A Final Word
Elyana

Elyana was grooming Calda in the stables in the hour before dawn when the guardsman Stefan came to see her with a young man in tow.

She stepped out of the stall, bringing the lantern with her. She hung it from a nail, set her brushes on an overturned bucket, and brushed the horsehair from her hands. "Good morning, Stefan."

Gray-haired Stefan always looked tired, but was dependably to be found at the postern gate every night. He preferred the hours. "And good morning to you, Lady Elyana."

Elyana didn't particularly care for the title, but Drelm had insisted upon it. She held no formal rank in Delgar, and the half-orc thought it undignified for the guards to address her by her first name. She had tried that for a while, but the soldiers seemed generally more comfortable addressing her with an honorific.

"You have a visitor." Stefan indicated the boy behind him, then moved aside.

The young man stepped forward and Elyana's eyes tracked to the folded paper he carried in one hand. "Your pardon, Lady." He sounded as nervous as he would addressing a real noblewoman.

Elyana smiled as gently as she could, then knelt so she might greet the boy eye to eye. Men of all ages seemed intimidated by her appearance. She understood they found her attractive and knew too well how ardor made fools of those who desired her. She had long cultivated a distant manner toward most men, but was kinder to youngsters. It was hardly their fault she looked like their ideal, and she didn't wish to seem cruel.

"Do you have something for me?"

"A letter." He met her eyes, then looked down. "From the gentlemen known as Mr. Venic, um, milady." Belatedly he extended the paper toward her.

She took it, curious, and studied the wax seal. The stamp lacked any kind of sigil—it was just a round pattern to smash the wax. Carefully penned lettering addressed the note to her, Lady Elyana Sadrastis.

It must be a farewell note. Probably Venic had decided to resign via this method rather than face the more pronounced shame of a face-to-face meeting. What else could it be?

"You've delivered your note," Stefan said behind the boy. "Best be on your way."

"There's something more," the boy said as Elyana fished a couple of coppers from her coin purse.

"Oh?" Elyana arched an eyebrow and held back from giving the tip.

The young man nodded briefly. "I wasn't supposed to hand that to you unless he didn't come back last night. To the inn, I mean."

Elyana studied the boy. He couldn't be more than ten, lean and sun-browned, with a band of freckles across his nose. He seemed uncomfortable in the scrutiny and shifted a little.

"So he didn't return?" Elyana asked.

"No."

Strange. "Did he say where he was going?"

The boy shook his head. "All he said to me was that he'd be going out, and if he didn't return I was to give this to you before dawn. He paid me before he left."

"I see. And you're sure he didn't make it back last night? He might have checked into his room while you were sleeping."

"No, ma'am. I looked at his room this morning. Very carefully."

Elyana smiled wryly at the last. "I'm sure you did. Alright, young man. Thank you for doing as you were told." She dropped a handful of coppers into his hand and nodded to Stefan, who led the boy out of the stables.

Elyana broke the seal and stepped closer to the light.

Venic's hand was even and unremarkable, rather as he was.

To Elyana Sadrastis,

I go this evening to speak with a member of our expedition about her past. My sources inform me that the woman presenting herself as Lisette Demonde, the bounty hunter, was once a member of the Chelish guild known as the Black Coil. If you have not heard of them, it is because their activities are usually confined to Cheliax. They are murderers for hire. It is my fear that Ms. Demonde is targeting someone within our expedition, and I urge the utmost caution. I strongly suggest you ask her about my whereabouts this morning if I do not arrive to speak with you before departure time.

Venic of Gralton

"Marvelous," Elyana said to Calda, who had her head down as she contentedly munched some hay.

Venic's cool manner had troubled her from the outset, but she'd put that aside when she saw just how competent he was with his blade. Who was she to turn talented help away? He wouldn't be the first or last River Kingdoms dweller with a dark past, or the first washed-up warrior looking for a chance to earn some gold.

Yet his letter stretched credulity. If Venic had been worried about Lisette's identity, why confront her by himself rather than coming to Elyana beforehand? Especially if he thought her some kind of elite assassin. And who, exactly, were his sources?

If Venic were here now, he might claim he'd wanted to give Lisette an honorable way out, but that explanation didn't wash. And so Elyana was left with an ugly little mystery and the seed of discord. There were several possibilities. The first was that Venic was simply looking to trouble the expedition. The second was that someone else was looking to trouble the expedition and had played an elaborate scheme with Venic as a pawn. Either of those options suggested there were some who wanted the expedition to fail, which made no sense unless the beast's rampages had a purpose, which required a great deal of conjecture.

The third possibility was that Venic had written the truth about Lisette's profession.

Yet Lisette Demonde was a bounty hunter, come to Delgar in search of another quarry entirely before throwing in with the expedition when she learned of it. Why would an assassin pretend to be a bounty hunter? Assassins survived by remaining hidden, and Lisette was hardly that.

The more Elyana turned the problem, the more she became certain someone was out to jeopardize the expedition. Lisette's marksmanship was phenomenal, and at close range her guns had better stopping power than arrows. Moreover, she was a seasoned veteran. To lose her would weaken the group, and the more Elyana thought about the matter, the more she thought that must be what Venic wanted.

Why he sought to bring trouble was a question she didn't understand.

Come dawn she was sitting saddle upon Calda as the expedition members filed into the keep's walls. Drelm, Demid, Illidian, and the elves were performing a final check of the foodstuffs. Only a faint trace of light colored the sky, but it was enough for elven sight.

As Cyrelle sorted the gear in her saddlebags, her dog pack lay at ease, lolling with deceptive calm beside her horse, each with its head on its front paws. The Oaksteward was quietly performing a dawn prayer near the eastern wall, and the red-haired wizard, Votek, was in a quiet but animated discussion with the halfling. Drutha's dog sat beside her, white-and-brown-spotted fur hung with packs and storage gear. Calvonis, Grellen, and Marika were looking carefully over their stock of arrows.

Lisette and her dwarf were adjusting the saddles on the horse and the donkey they'd been loaned by the mayor. Neither looked any more suspicious than anyone else, but she supposed that if Lisette were a trained assassin she wouldn't have any tells.

Venic made no appearance.

At a sudden thought, she called out for the wizard. "Votek!"

The man heard his name and turned, then walked quickly over. He smiled affably up at her. "Good morning!"

Elyana noticed for the first time that the haft of a lute poked up over the wizard's right shoulder, tied somehow to his large shoulder bag. He must be strong, for all his paunch, for she had noted earlier that it bulged with gear.

"And to you, Votek. Tell me, do you know any spells for learning the truth?"

Votek rubbed at his wild shock of red hair, looking chagrined. "I'm afraid that's outside my line of specialty. Why do you ask?"

Disappointing. But then, she'd never found magic the easy answer promised in stories. "Just curious. Tell me about this." She reached behind her, rifled through her saddlebag, and brought forth Onderan's wand. She handed it down, being careful not to direct it at him.

Votek grasped it cautiously. "What's this?"

"A man used it to murder every man, woman, child, and farm animal he could shoot a few weeks ago."

Votek's eyebrows rose. "What does it do?"

"It fires some kind of acid. But I have no idea how to activate it. It would be of great use against the monster we hunt."

"It certainly sounds like it. Do you know the trigger word?"

"No. I was hoping you could help me with that."

Votek scratched at his hair again. "This is a matter that requires study. Maybe when we stop this evening?" He turned it over. "I don't recognize the make," he admitted. "But maybe if I examine the magical signatures on the thing." He turned it over once more and ran a hand over the banding. "Do you mind if I hold onto it? I might be able to try a few things whenever we stop for a break."

"By all means. Just be careful."

He bowed his head with a theatrical hand flourish. "Fear not, my fair Captain. I know what I'm about."

She nodded to him, then scanned over the assembled folk once more and glanced to the closed postern gate. Roosters crowed outside the wall. From somewhere near at hand she heard the bleat of sheep.

There was still no sign of Venic. Elyana straightened in her saddle and called for attention. Gradually, everyone ceased their activities and turned to face her.

"Have any of you seen Venic since yesterday evening?"

Lisette answered almost immediately. "He had a drink with me, last night." She smirked. "He tried to follow me to my room."

Elyana hadn't expected such an easy answer but let no surprise show on her face. "Had he been drinking?"

"Oh yes."

"He's probably still lying in the gutter," Marika said, then laughed slowly. "Or under some fat whore."

"None of that talk," Drelm growled from behind Elyana. "There are ladies present."

Lisette grinned at this; Marika traded a startled glance with her friend Grellen.

Elyana raised her voice to address them all. "Has anyone seen him, at all?"

The expedition members looked back and forth among themselves. Finally, the halfling piped up. "Should we send someone out to look for him?"

"I'll go, if you wish," Demid volunteered.

But the Brevan was too useful to send on an errand boy's outing. She looked down to the attentive officer, speaking quietly. "No, thank you, Demid. This is Venic's lookout. If he doesn't turn up, he doesn't go. And if he doesn't go, he doesn't get paid." She faced the others once more. "Finish checking over your gear. We'll leave in a quarter-hour."

Shortly thereafter, Drelm called for everyone to form up and began handing out the supply packs, assisted by Aladel. Elyana wasn't quite sure how that had happened, or why, but the dark-haired elf had taken over the clipboard as Drelm turned over the bags and wine sacs. He still wore his own gear rather than the traditional garb of the forest rangers, though Illidian had told her he'd served on the border decades ago. He seemed to have a good head for organization, so she let him be.

The expedition members moved swiftly through the line, then carried their belongings to their mounts. Elyana watched every one of them with great care, trying not to make her scrutiny of Lisette too obvious.

Damn Venic and his stupid letter.

Demid drew up beside her stirrup and cleared his throat. "Elyana?"

She found the handsome Brevan smiling confidently at her.

"You're a man short," he observed. "Although he was a short man to begin with."

Elyana acknowledged the cleverness with a faint smile. "We will make do without him."

"Allow me to volunteer my services." Demid brought his heels together and straightened, clearing his expression.

Elyana shook her head. "No, Demid. You're in command of the city guard until Drelm returns."

"Gered will handle things just fine."

"Gered will manage things." Elyana dropped her voice and leaned out toward Demid. "But he will not lead. The gods forbid it, but if something awful should happen, the guards need a leader."

Demid nodded reluctantly.

"I thank you, though," she added. "It was noble of you to volunteer."

He dismissed the compliment with an easy wave and a broad smile. "These walls are no place for a cavalryman. Someday . . . someday I'll have that money saved up."

"I'm sure you will." More than once the Brevan had wistfully discussed his wish for land in his native country, where he meant to raise horses, but had disclosed little else about his past. The longer she knew him, the more certain she was that he had once been an officer in some army, and probably a nobleman to boot. If Demid wanted her to know the details, though, he would tell her. There were far more pressing matters to worry over.

Finally, everyone was mounted, the halfling on her dog, Karag on a mule, and everyone else on horses.

With the barest nudge of her knee, Elyana set Calda forward along the line of them. "The beast was sighted west of town two days ago. First thing, we're all looking at the tracks." She resisted a sudden impulse to set Calda curveting. No need to show off. "Fall out."

She led them down the central street past the long lines of homes and shops. Many of Delgar's residents turned out to wish them well, and the priestess of Calistria shouted blessings upon them as they passed. So too did the masked priest of Razmir, in his way, calling that if they took succor in the faith of the living god no harm would befall them.

The lord mayor and his daughter waited at the very end of the road. Avelis raised a hand and told them to go with the blessings of all the gods of justice and mercy. Daylah stared forlornly at Drelm, but if she looked for a final acknowledgment of love or tenderness, she searched in vain, for Elyana knew that the half-orc believed showing such things while on duty reduced his dignity. He allowed himself only a raised hand in farewell before he faced forward.

At this, Daylah reached up to wipe tears from her eyes. The half-orc, Elyana thought, had much to learn about women.

After a half-hour, the sun was fully risen and filtering through the trees by the riverside. Much of the River Kingdoms woodland was old growth, so there was enough space between the trees for riding. The shade beneath the boughs of oak and pine gave everything a false twilight.

She didn't have to remind anyone in her group that they needed to be on guard: she had picked only the best. She set her squad of five on point, with Drelm's group flanking to her right and Illidian's squad a quarter mile to the left, nearer the river. With the elven captain was the Oaksteward, who she assumed would be treated with respect even by Kyonin elves, and Calvonis. Riding with Elyana were Cyrelle the huntswoman, Votek, Lisette, and Karag. Cyrelle's hounds ranged ahead.

Elyana and Cyrelle rode point. In addition to the hounds, the thickset huntswoman had loosed her hawk, Balok, as they left the town, and Elyana knew from their previous venture that Cyrelle's distant look was her communing with the mind of the animal, a power granted her by a ring passed down from her grandfather.

Elyana's squad arrived at the most recent tracks in just under an hour. A half-dozen hounds milled about the site, their noses to the ground. Elyana raised the horn and gave three swift bleats—the prearranged call for the other groups to hold position—then slid down to examine the area once more. Votek joined her, his eyes settling apprehensively upon the shadowy woodlands. Cyrelle walked with her hounds.

"You two, keep watch," Elyana called to Lisette and the dwarf, then stepped over to Cyrelle, now bent beside one well-defined imprint. Her lead hound, a gray-black beast named Scouter, stood nearby with his ears cocked to attention. His immense head reached Elyana's thigh.

"Have you ever seen a print like it?" Elyana asked.

"No." The huntswoman shook her head, bemused. Her voice was a low alto and bore a faint, rolling accent of the far northwest. "It's even larger than I imagined."

Elyana had seen three sets of tracks in the weeks she'd spent stalking the beast, and these were among the clearest. They were as large as a wyvern's print, and similar in that five pads were clawed. But this monster seemed heavier, displacing more ground as it walked.

She broke off the examination to eye the surroundings, surreptitiously checking on Lisette and her dwarf. Both were faced away, and shifting appropriately to take in their surroundings. Votek finished with a complicated set of hand movements, then dropped his eyes from out of the magical world so that they met Elyana's own.

"There's nothing magical here." The wizard sounded almost embarrassed. "No residue, no nothing."

As she expected.

"It's interesting." Cyrelle stood and peered off into the woodland, shading her eyes with one large hand. "There are no signs of droppings anywhere."

"I've never found any," Elyana agreed. "Any idea when these tracks were made?

"I'd say four days old," Cyrelle continued, which jibed with Elyana's assessment. "Probably . . ."

Cyrelle fell silent in mid-speech, stilling utterly as she listened. A dog barked, and she looked over to Elyana. "Barten's found something." She headed east at a quick trot, doubling back to parallel the route by which they'd entered the little woodland.

Elyana snatched her bow and followed, motioning the others to remain where they were. "Keep track of your horse," she snapped at the paunchy wizard, for Votek's animal had wandered off to nibble at a mulberry bush.

Two of Cyrelle's hounds came with her, loping to either side of Elyana and Cyrelle. A hundred feet out Elyana saw a third, presumably Barten, with his head lowered beside a juniper bush.

Elyana kept watch while the huntress examined the site. "Horse tracks," Cyrelle relayed to Elyana. "Unshod. From about the same time as the beast's prints."

"Probably another victim," Elyana said glumly.

"Let's be sure, and find out."

Elyana assumed they'd find a body, or a skeleton picked clean by scavengers. But after they'd trailed the horse prints east for some twenty minutes, they learned the prints paralleled those of the beast's. For several leagues the tracks lay very close to one another, up until the ruins of a dead forester's fortified home. Here the unshod horse seemed to have waited in the distance while the monster rampaged. Elyana and Drelm had searched the ground thoroughly a few days ago, and buried the poor forester and his wife. But Elyana had not looked far enough out to find the hoofprints.

A careful examination of the situation took more than an hour, and Elyana was none too pleased with what she learned. She stood contemplating the nearest run of trampled dirt, where she'd located the beast's prints. A few hundred yards away those same prints disappeared into a bog. She stood with the others, studying the unwelcoming terrain.

Insects whined and frogs croaked. A dragonfly flitted past and settled onto a rotted stump. Elyana had seen enough to shatter her earlier suppositions about the beast's nature, and she wasn't liking the directions those lines of thought led her.

"What's troubling you?" Lisette asked. "This is good news, isn't it? The more we learn about our enemy, the better our chances."

Cyrelle answered. "There're some weird bits about all this." She scratched a spot of dried mud off her cheek. "Elyana, you notice that there aren't any horse droppings?"

"I did."

"And the horse wasn't shod," Cyrelle continued.

"Even I can see that," Lisette admitted. "But a lot of frontier horses don't have horseshoes."

"It's a ghost steed," Votek said softly, and Elyana looked over at him.

"A ghost? What are you talking about?" Cyrelle sounded both troubled and confused.

"It's not really a ghost," Votek said, a little apologetically, "but a spell. An old spell, and a useful one. A wizard—or a sorcerer, or a witch, I suppose—can call up a magical animal and ride it."

"Like conjuring a demon," Lisette offered.

"Well, not really," Votek said, then waggled his hand a little. "I suppose it's a little similar. The horse isn't a demon, though, it's just a . . . spell that functions like a horse. Anyway, an illusory steed would leave prints, but it surely wouldn't leave droppings, because it's not alive and doesn't need to eat." The wizard shifted his pack, then eyed Elyana. "I think you guessed this the moment you saw the horse tracks."

Elyana shook her head. "Not until we saw the horse tracks alongside those of the beast. But I've been wondering for a while whether or not the beast had a reason."

"A reason?" Lisette prompted.

Elyana frowned. "Somebody has a reason for making it attack. It has a handler, or a wizard. Maybe it really is some kind of demon. I'm wondering now how many other times there were horse tracks near one of the attacks that I just didn't see. I wasn't focused on looking for horse prints, and there usually are horse prints near settlements . . ."

"In this line of work," Cyrelle said, "you've got to look at what's there rather than what you expect."

Elyana nodded. "Well said." And something that Elyana should have known, given her own long years in the wild. Until recently she'd been assuming they tracked some kind of sorcerous abomination, out on its own and killing. Like a rogue bear or dog. "So it's probably being guided."

"The question is why," Votek said. "Why would anyone want to do . . . this?" He turned a pudgy hand toward the splintered logs of the cabin.

Elyana didn't answer. She was thinking back to the horse tracks they'd found when she finally got back to the sorcerer Onderan's miserable shack, a day after Melloc's funeral. Many days had passed since Drelm had axed Onderan by then, but she'd discovered the trace of an unshod horse's prints in some of the loose soil a few yards from the weed patch that passed as the sorcerer's vegetable garden. Could those, too, have been made by a ghost steed?

Cyrelle shook her head in disgust. "So assume someone *is* commanding the attacks. It seems like an awful lot of effort to kill a bunch of folks that don't own anything worth taking."

"Some people get a real thrill from killing." Lisette's lips were downturned. Elyana eyed her keenly, wondering if she spoke from experience. "I've seen all kinds of bastards over the years," Lisette went on. "Oh, some of the men I hunt, they just got real angry one day and took it out on someone. But some of them, they get a taste for it. I suppose wizards can be like that, too."

Karag had been standing silently at watch for the whole of the conversation. He hadn't said a word since before dawn, and the only sounds from the dwarf had been him occasionally shifting his foot in the undergrowth as he watched the distance. Now, though, he turned, put a leg up on a log, and declared, "It's a summoner."

"A summoner?" Cyrelle repeated.

Elyana had heard the term, although she had no personal experience with any practitioners from that branch of magical study.

Lisette looked just as surprised as Elyana to hear an opinion from the dwarf. Either the bounty hunter was a fine actress, or the dwarf's words had caught her off guard. Might that mean she was somehow involved in the beast's attacks and didn't want Karag revealing anything? Or just that Karag didn't normally know much about magic?

Once again she cursed the added complication of Venic and his letter. She had enough to trouble her without constantly having to worry about Lisette's true motives. She turned to Vatok. "Is Karag right?"

The wizard folded his hands over his protruding belly and tapped it rhythmically. "He has a point," he said, then added sheepishly, "I should have recognized that personality earlier. It makes a kind of sense—absent motive, of course. Summoners have to stay close to the creature they call, which would explain the tracks."

"It's the only good answer," Karag declared truculently.

"What's a summoner?" Cyrelle asked.

"A magic-worker who's linked to a creature," Votek explained in that same amiable tone. "Like you are to your animals." "Except a summoner calls something up from the pits of hell," Karag said with a snarl.

"You sound as though you speak from experience," Votek said to the dwarf, not unkindly.

The dwarf's expression grew even more sour. "My uncles had to face down this bastard who could conjure up a leaping, fiery thing that looked like a skeleton horse with a scorpion sting. Except that it put out waves of heat, and fear. He was extorting a silver mine. Almost twenty warriors died fighting him before it was all over."

While Elyana listened, she caught sight of Lisette's intent expression. She wondered if the bounty hunter had heard the tale from the dwarf before.

"Is there anything we need to know to fight a summoner?" Cyrelle asked.

Karag pressed his lips together in thought for a long moment, then nodded. "The summoner will hide, but you have to remember if you kill him—like any wizard—the spells stop."

"That's not necessarily true—" Votek started to object.

Karag looked as though he were about to explode.

"Certainly a dead magic-user can't cast any new spells," Elyana said quickly. "When we attack, we need to make fighting the summoner as much of a priority as the beast, if not more so."

"Which will be tricky," Votek added, "especially if he's invisible. Which seems likely to be the case."

"How do you figure that?" Cyrelle asked.

"It only stands to reason." There was a note of pride in Votek's voice as he spoke on. "No one has ever reported seeing a steed during any of the attacks, have they?" He looked to Elyana for verification.

"No," she admitted.

"So, there you are. He can make himself invisible, he can make the monster invisible, and he can make his magical steed invisible."

"A summoner can call his beast to him, too, whenever he wants," Karag said. "Or make it vanish. The summoner's been toying with you, then calling it back to him."

Votek cleared his throat. "I still want to point out that this is conjecture, not certainty. It takes an inordinate amount of effort each day to prepare spells like those I use. I'm not a summoner, but I'm sure the training is similar. Why spend years honing your craft just to go hunting people in the River Kingdoms? We lack a reason."

"You haven't seen what I've seen," Lisette said darkly. "Where are you from, wizard?"

"Gralton."

"I'm from Cheliax," Lisette pressed on. "And believe me, there're people there who put a whole lot of thought into just how people should be killed. And have you ever heard of the priests of Zon-Kuthon?"

Elyana winced a little at that. She'd never faced one directly, but she'd dealt with the traps they left behind.

There was a nervous quaver in Cyrelle's voice. "You think we're dealing with some of them?"

"No," Elyana and Lisette said as one. They then looked at each other.

"They'd be a lot more obvious about it," Lisette explained.

"And there'd be a lot more blood," Elyana went on.

Lisette nodded. "Sounds like you've dealt with them."

"Once or twice. Once was enough."

"That's the truth," Lisette agreed. She might have meant to reassure Cyrelle as she addressed her. "If this was the work of those rat-humpers, you'd find their victims staked out, half skinned. They would have lived for days in excruciating pain. The people the monster kills die too fast to make the Kuthite priests happy."

Cyrelle shook her head in disgust, then spat and muttered a prayer to Calistria.

Elyana decided a subject change was in order. "It's not them. And I don't think we're going to find an explanation right now."

"There aren't any stories of anything . . . important going missing from the attacks, are there?" Votek asked. "Do you think this summoner—if that's what he is—might be looking for something?"

"Nothing's ever missing," Elyana said. "Not even the people, or the houses. They're just shredded."

"Maybe that's why he keeps doing it," Votek suggested. "He's looking for something and hasn't found it yet."

Even if Votek remained doubtful, Elyana was convinced they faced a summoner, and supposed he'd been watching, perhaps even listening, as she and Drelm and Illidian met that first time beside the bodies of Illidian's patrol. Where would the summoner have been, though? "When Drelm and I fought the monster," she said, "the summoner would have seen how outclassed we were. We'd hurt his monster, but I don't think we'd done any serious damage. It could have kept on killing. Why did he stop?"

"If he, or she," Lisette said, "gets his jollies killing and frightening, it helps to have a few survivors now and then. So people can hear just how scary the monster is."

"Maybe you hurt it more than you realized," Cyrelle said, "or he was afraid you had."

They rendezvoused with the other squads and, after updating them about their findings, spent the rest of the day searching for any sign of tracks that had exited the bog from another direction. They found none. The last sign of either beast or horse was a large hanging bough that had been bent to one side. No backtracking turned up anything more, except leeches that Grellen acquired while dropping into an especially deep waterhole.

Elyana was in a dour mood that evening as they set up camp. One day was gone, and while she now had a better idea about the nature of their enemy, she had no idea how to find him.

So she decided on a different course. She led them to dry ground in a small hilltop clearing, surrounded on three sides by trees. Her thought was they could better see if something came toward them, for the monster would set tree limbs swaying. She set Drelm and the mercenaries to arranging wooden spikes in the gentle slope that made up the fourth side.

She sent Illidian, Galarias, and Aladel out on a long-range patrol to search for tracks and paths, and appointed sentries while the rest of the expedition prepared the camp. She then pulled Votek aside.

"I see you have a lute," she said.

"I do. I'm a fair player." He smiled slyly.

"Play for us, then."

"For morale?"

"Something like that."

Votek looked surprised. "Wouldn't you rather I look over the wand?"

She shook her head. "Not just yet. I want you to play."

Elyana had never yet met a musician truly reluctant to demonstrate his gifts, and Votek proved no different. But he likewise proved better than Elyana would have guessed, with a low, sweet voice. Soon he was strumming one of the ballads of Fife and Darvin, and Cyrelle, Drutha, and the old Oaksteward, who were overseeing the cooking, joined in happily with each chorus.

There was no missing Drelm's thin-lipped disapproval. He rose from his work with Marika, Grellen, and Calvonis, and was striding directly toward the wizard when Elyana called to him.

The half-orc's large head swung slowly, then his eyes widened into almost comical surprise as she motioned him over. By the time he'd reached where she stood brushing Calda, he'd regained his composure.

"I want him playing," Elyana said softly.

Drelm cleared his throat. "Shouldn't we make smokeless fires, and silence the music?"

"No."

She waited for the half-orc to work through it. His jaw moved, almost as if he were chewing over the possibilities. After a long moment, his expression cleared.

"You mean to draw the beast to us."

"Yes."

He chuckled, then smacked her shoulder in delight. Elyana pretended it hadn't hurt.

"Brave Elyana." Drelm chuckled once more. "I should have guessed. Baron Stelan always said you should make the ground fight for you."

"A lot of people say that," Elyana pointed out. It was basic tactical doctrine, and, much as she was fond of Stelan, Drelm should know the motto had not originated with him any more than "prepare for the morrow by planning today" had come from the mayor. The half-orc cherished wise maxims, but always seemed to think they originated with the person speaking them.

"The baron said it a lot," Drelm countered, then strode back to his work, whistling the same tune Votek played.

At the footfall behind her Elyana turned slowly, hand dropped to her knife. She'd set Karag up to watch ten paces back, but this wasn't Karag. It was Lisette, polishing the end of one of her muskets with a gray rag. The markswoman kept the wood so clean it could bear reflection, and the metal portions of her weapons gleamed.

Elyana had only ever seen guns in use one time before, in a siege, and hadn't been especially impressed. Until she'd seen Lisette they hadn't seemed particularly useful in combat. She'd dismissed them as a way for normal men and women to simulate the powerful attacks of wizards, with less accuracy and more complexity, and didn't expect them to last. Lisette's skill had her questioning her earlier judgment.

"You're really trying to lure it in?" the bounty hunter asked.

Elyana returned to brushing Calda's flank. "Never let your enemy choose your battleground."

Lisette stepped to her side and smiled knowingly. "And you're not sure which way to go anyway, are you?"

"That's right. So I'm presenting a target. A juicy one."

Lisette gestured to the encircling trees. "Suppose he's out there watching, right now?"

"Let him."

"But won't he know what you're doing?"

Elyana returned the brush to Calda's saddlebag and patted the side of her nose. The animal snorted in response, lowering her head and tilting it. Elyana chuckled and scratched behind the offered ear.

"Aren't you afraid he'll know what you're doing?" Lisette pressed.

"We're facing someone very arrogant. Even if he sees our preparations, he'll think us overconfident. I'm hoping he'll be tempted to show us his power. He can see us making these spikes and setting our sentinels, and think that we feel perfectly prepared. Especially if we put on a show."

"And then you'll hit him with the plans we've laid."

"Exactly."

Lisette shouldered her weapon. "Suppose our fat wizard is right and we've got an invisible summoner. What's to have kept him from sneaking in and hearing all the plans you told us back in Delgar?"

It was a fair question. She doubted someone could have done it—not with guards and wizards and dogs so close—but that was the problem with wizardry: it defied normal limits. Perhaps more interesting, though, was Lisette's manner. If she really was an assassin, what better time to attack than during a monstrous assault? It would be easy to claim she'd shot her target accidentally. Why, then, make it so obvious she was thinking about the tactical situation?

Possibly because Lisette wasn't in league with the summoner, and because she wasn't really an assassin. Yet she'd identified herself as hailing from Cheliax, just as Venic's letter claimed. But as Elyana's foster father had once told her, the best lies were always grown with a sprinkling of truth.

"You're the bounty hunter," Elyana said at last, finally ending Calda's long scratch. "What do you think?"

"I think killing a wizard's harder work than you think."

"So you've killed some before?"

"Maybe I have. A few more than you, I wager."

Elyana smiled grimly. "I think you'd be surprised."

"Maybe I would, at that," Lisette said after a moment. "I have a hard time getting a read on you."

"A read?"

"I can't usually tell what you're thinking."

"That's what humans always say about elves when we're not doing what they want."

Lisette allowed a faint smile and reached over to pat Calda's side. "So what is it you want out of this, Elyana? Seems pretty clear the mayor has something for you . . . but you don't return it. And I don't believe any of that talk about you and the half-orc."

"What talk?"

"You know very well. But I don't think he's ever been your lover. So what is it that keeps you in the middle of nowhere?"

Elyana wasn't really interested in a personal dialogue with Lisette, but didn't want to seem unfriendly, either. So she kept her answer simple. "Sometimes a thing just needs doing, and you're the only one who can do it."

"You strike me as smarter than that."

"Do I? Maybe I'm just lucky."

"No—I think you're like me. You make your own luck. You make your plans, surround yourself with the best, and wait for your enemy to slip. When they do, you're ready to spring.

"That might be."

"There you go, being mysterious."

Illidian's voice rang from the woodlands. "Elyana!"

It was not a cry of alarm, but a warning that the patrol returned. In a few moments, the elves were leading their horses uphill, and they hadn't come alone.

Lisette cursed softly. Elyana merely frowned as she caught sight of the young sorcerer and her brother who had failed the expedition trials. They, too, led horses, and both humans and mounts were splattered with mud. The boy tried to look resolute and stolid. The girl's lips were pursed in anger. Her fine scarlet cloak was hardly recognizable, so thick was the dirt and filth.

Illidian called to Elyana in Elven as he neared. "I found them skulking a few leagues to our rear."

"You can't make us not hunt the beast." The girl tugged her drooping mount forward. Her eyes blazed defiantly as she stopped before Elyana and Lisette. "Don't think you can make us stop!"

"I didn't say I would."

Illidian halted to her left, an amused and contemptuous smile flitting at the corners of his mouth.

"Then tell them"—the girl looked fiercely over to Illidian—"to release us, and our weapons."

"That would be a death sentence," Elyana replied. Especially, she thought, given that the summoner and his monster have almost surely honed in on the expedition by now. She felt certain the summoner would not allow the expedition to advance much further without demonstrating his murderous powers. But she didn't say this to the girl or the young man. "If you're out there on your own, you're liable to be killed. Even a strong hunting party's in danger from the beast."

"Then we will join you," the girl told her. "Free of charge."

Lisette laughed. "Oh, that's rich. We can't be distracted looking out for people that barely remember to wash behind their ears."

"I'm a trained warrior," the boy objected. "Your captain saw me. He knows I can handle my blade."

"You two can barely handle a mud bath," Lisette said.

Elyana held up a hand. Lisette fell silent, but this merely left an opening for the boy to continue his pleas.

"We don't wish to be paid," he continued. "We just want to help. That thing has to be stopped."

"Most of the applicants agreed with you," Elyana reminded him. "But they had the sense not to follow. Tonight you'll bed down with us, and help keep watch. First thing in the morning, you must return."

"We won't," the girl said. "We'll still follow you."

Elyana frowned. "We'll see." She looked to Illidian. "Give them back their weapons and find them a spot out of the way."

The elf's reply was laconic. "As you command."

Elyana addressed the brother. "You, what's your name?"

"Poul."

"And your sister?"

"I am Melias."

"Well, Poul, Melias, you'll have to take care of your own horses, and eat from your own supplies."

"We expected to carry our weight," Poul insisted. "We're just asking you to give us a chance to prove we can do it."

"I'm giving you a chance to sleep in as safe a place as we have out here." Almost she spoke on about how she was certain the beast and its master were aware of them, and might even be seeking them, but she held her tongue. If the beast had a human master, mightn't the master have human informants?

Suppose the boy or the girl *was* the summoner? Either was too young to have mastered the level of proficiency this kind of magic surely required, but she well knew that powerful spellcasters could alter their appearance.

She sighed to herself. "Go on. Illidian, get them out of here."

"Leave your horses here with ours," Illidian instructed. Galarias walked with him, shooing Poul and Melias away almost as though they were lambs. Aladel lingered, though.

"Would you like me to picket their mounts?" the dark-haired elf asked.

"Kind of you," Elyana replied.

Aladel bobbed his head. "The boy and girl are exhausted," he said. "I thought I'd save them the time."

"Was there anything . . . strange about them, Aladel?" Elyana regretted the question almost the moment she said it.

The black-cloaked elf arched an eyebrow. "How do you mean?"

"She's wondering if they really are who they seem to be, I expect," Lisette explained. "We're chasing a magic-worker."

"Of course," Aladel answered, then gave Elyana a brief nod. "I didn't see any surprising sign of competency, if that's what you mean. They were astonishingly simple to ambush. And even if you were pretending incompetence, why make yourself miserable by backtracking into the bog?"

"Maybe if you're working hard on your part," Lisette suggested.

"It may be," Aladel allowed, politely. "But I think they're nothing more than they seem to be. A boy and a girl, driven by vengeance and grief."

"Thank you, Aladel," Elyana said. She considered him with a little more care, for his judgment had impressed her.

He offered a brief smile, bowed his head, then clicked his tongue and led the horses off to where the others were hobbled, a few paces back. She watched him retreat.

Lisette smirked. "I can guess what you're thinking now."

It took a moment for Elyana to change the track of her thought. Of course—Lisette assumed she was admiring Aladel's physique, despite the fact that his cloak obscured it. Humans had such one-track minds. "Do you mean I'm thinking that, if someone had to follow, I wish it had been that berserker dwarf?"

Lisette laughed and stepped away.

Chapter Eight

An Unexpected Guest

Drelm

Drelm hadn't said a word of complaint, but Marika had teased him good-naturedly as they finished their work, for his stomach had been growling for the last quarter-hour. If Marika had been under his direct chain of command, he would have reprimanded her, but seeing as the woman was working hard with the planting of spikes, he let the matter lie.

Still, when supper was ready he didn't join Marika and Grellen, sitting instead by the huntswoman, Cyrelle. It wasn't that Drelm didn't mind a good joke; he just didn't enjoy being a target. Through most of his life all jests aimed toward him had been malicious.

Those on first watch had already eaten, and the cool twilight of the woods gathered around them like a cloak, bringing with it the fresh scent of pine, unfortunately seasoned with a hint of wet decay from the nearby bog. Already he heard the hoot of an owl and the chirruping of insects. The croaking of frogs had grown into a cacophony.

The bread had been freshly baked this morning and was a welcome treat, even if the bakers of Delgar routinely baked chewy rather than crisp loaves. Drelm wondered if he could have Daylah make him crisp loaves when they were married. He preferred the solid crunch of them when he bit down.

He was tearing into a strip of dried venison when the halfling sat down near him.

Drutha gave him a polite good evening and then dug into her pack to remove an elaborate assortment of individually wrapped ingredients—slices of mushroom and tomato, a flaky-looking bread and a sort of grayish-green paste that she spread over its top with a small black knife, some crisp young chard, and several slices of mutton. Drelm couldn't help staring. Finally, Drutha sat everything upon the bread, then folded it in upon itself and took a bite.

It was only then that the halfling noticed she'd gained an audience, and stared by turns at Drelm, Cyrelle, and the grim-looking Calvonis, who had just taken a seat on the grass at the halfling's right.

"I didn't plan on being the evening's entertainment," she said lightly, then took a small, neat bite.

Drutha was a creature of browns. Curling brown hair, large brown eyes, brown vest over a whitish brown shirt, brown leggings. Her feet were likewise topped with curling brown hair so thick it almost seemed fur. Now that he considered her in detail, it occurred to Drelm that he didn't usually see halflings looking so prosperous. Surely they rarely ate so well.

Cyrelle laughed. "It's good to see someone who appreciates a decent meal. You look as hungry as I am.

I wish I'd packed a sandwich that looked so good!" Cyrelle, like Drelm, was eating the expedition fare.

Drutha chewed and swallowed. "Well. I thought I might not come back from this one, so I splurged a bit. I've had enough dry meat." The good humor faded slightly from her eyes. "And gone without too many times."

"I hear you there, halfling," Calvonis said gruffly. The lanky former soldier still wore his battered helmet and armor. "Wish I'd planned that well."

For all that he said he was twenty-five, Calvonis looked as if he were in his late thirties, for his frame was gaunt, his skin leathery. He'd handled both sword and bow well, but been reluctant to say where he'd seen service. So said many in the River Kingdoms.

"What brings you along?" Cyrelle asked.

Calvonis's dark eyes flicked up. "The beast killed my wife," he answered tonelessly. He was fingering a little silver necklace that Drelm recognized with a start as a Razmiri mask. He'd thought Razmir only attracted cowards and fools.

"Did you see it?" Drutha asked, taking another nibble before continuing. "The beast, I mean?"

"No one can 'see it,'" Calvonis returned. He ceased rubbing the mask and let it hang loose in front of his armor. "But no. I just found the evidence. I returned from hunting, and . . ." He fell silent and savagely tore off a hunk of dried meat.

"It needs to be stopped, friend," Drutha said into the awkward silence. "I don't mind the pay, at all. I assure you." The halfling woman offered a brief smile. "But I'm for the cause myself."

"I'm with you, Drutha," Cyrelle assented. "Where do you hail from, anyway? You don't hear tell of too many halfling woodswomen. Woodhalflings. You know what I mean."

"I rode from Mivon. We have a small community south of Jovvox." Her eyes took on a dangerous light. "We're not all wee little city folk begging for work."

"I never said you were," Cyrelle replied amiably. She took a long swallow from a large wine sac at her side, then wiped her lips with the back of her hand and offered the drink to the halfling.

Drutha brightened, gave a nod in thanks, and transferred her sandwich to one hand so she can take a quick bolt. "Wow—quite a kick there! You're from Riverton?"

"I come from there now, if that's what you mean." Cyrelle received the wine sac and the halfling resumed work on her sandwich.

"I hear you've a way with all beasts," Calvonis said to Cyrelle, his voice sounding lonely and remote. "That you can tame anything that comes your way."

Cyrelle chuckled. "People do talk, don't they? I'm good, but I'm not that good. It's not just a matter of snapping fingers. It takes years to train an animal up right, even if you do have the touch."

Drelm found himself nodding in agreement. Elyana surely had the touch, but it took her long months to ready one of her horses for the saddle and longer still to ready it for battle.

"I was just wondering," Calvonis said, "whether your powers could control or confuse the beast."

Cyrelle shook her head. "No, lad. I've got no delusion about mastering it, or even distracting the thing."

Calvonis had been staring at her wine sac. "Is that corn whiskey?"

"It is. You want a swig?" Cyrelle offered her wineskin.

"I do."

She passed it over and Calvonis took a belt. Drelm saw a cold smile spread over his face as he closed his eyes. For a brief moment he seemed at peace. He then returned it.

"You must have a stomach on you," Cyrelle said. "That's a pretty potent mix."

"Just right, I think."

Drelm finished up his own meal and stood to wipe bread crumbs from his clothes.

"What of you, Captain Drelm?" Drutha asked

"What of me?"

"How did a tiny little spot like Delgar rate you and Elyana?"

Drelm wasn't sure how to answer that.

"Don't be modest," Cyrelle said. "A lot of folk around here have heard about Elyana's feud with a pack of shadow wizards in Taldor. And how you rode into a Gray Gardener stronghold in Galt to save one of your friends."

"I haven't," Calvonis said.

"I have things to do," Drelm said, and moved away, ignoring Drutha's plea to tell the stories in his own words. It wasn't becoming to speak of oneself like that, and Elyana's past wasn't their business unless she wished to speak of it. Drelm was pretty certain that she didn't.

Drelm knelt down near where the horses were picketed and made his nightly prayer to Abadar. As was lately his habit, after bowing his head and reciting the

Prayer of Balance, taught to him by Baron Stelan, he thanked the god for leading him to so many opportunities, and strengthening his will so he might better find balance. Lately he'd added a new innovation, for the matter of Abadar's worship in Delgar, or lack thereof, nettled him. "I'm no great speaker, Lord," Drelm said. "But if you guide me, I'll show the folk of Delgar that you're more than the god of rich men. I would lead them to you, and share your teachings, if I could find a way to be a better man."

Abadar was the lord of civilization, and that meant patience and balance. It also meant laws. Drelm put great stock in laws, for without guidance society would descend into chaos, just as he himself would.

So far as Drelm understood, Abadar held sway over nearly everything that was good in life, and Drelm remained grateful to him. It continually saddened him that Drelm hadn't been able to bring the lord mayor to Abadar's worship, for Avelis reminded him, in many ways, of Baron Stelan, the man who had first introduced him to Elyana. Both men led by example. And both loved wise words, the mayor even more than the baron.

Drelm closed with a final request. "If you but steady my hand, I will slay the beast in your name, and bring you even greater glory. Amen."

After his prayer, Drelm appraised the spots where he and Elyana had posted sentries, then relocated Grellen to one of the lower branches, because without a stronger light source a human was fairly blind up there. After that he walked a circuit a quarter mile around the camp with Cyrelle and two of her hounds, looking for spoor. They found many signs of wildlife, but nothing that seemed related to the summoner or his ghostly horse.

"Maybe he's steering clear of us," Cyrelle suggested as they made their way back to camp.

"Maybe he's waiting," Drelm responded.

And wait he did, until the dead low hours of the morning, near two bells.

Drelm was on watch when the monster came, along with Drutha, Calvonis, and Aladel the elf.

The dim glow of the firelight showed him the sign of the beast's passage as it dashed up from the trees, for it set limbs swaying and trampled the undergrowth. The ground shook as the beast charged up the grassy slope. It knew, by scent or some magical sense, where they'd concealed the spikes and the shallow pits, and bypassed them all.

Drelm shouted the alarm and sent one throwing axe flying before dropping from the tree. He was glad for the fight. "Cyrelle! Send out the hounds!"

The hounds were already barking, of course, but the huntswoman was supposed to dispatch them to seek the summoner, sure to be lurking somewhere just beyond the campsite.

Elyana was awake and shouting for a volley. And that was good, because it meant Drelm need no longer worry about the overall conflict, and could focus on the battle. That's what he preferred. He had a score to settle with the beast. With Abadar's grace, he would avenge young Melloc.

A flight of arrows came streaming overhead, and he heard them sink into the beast's side. Two of the three shafts stuck quivering in what seemed midair. A third sailed past it on the right.

As Drelm's second axe tumbled forward, Votek dashed up beside Drelm and threw his hands out while shouting an incantation. The wizard's red beard and hair were matted to the left and he wore no shirt, but he looked far from ridiculous when his fingers glowed and energy streamed forth from both palms to strike the oncoming beast. In moments, the wizard's spell had defined the left side of a large, lizard-shaped skull and much of a huge, turtle-like body behind it sparkled with golden dust.

"Good!" he heard Illidian's distinct voice shouting. "Fire at will!"

The rest of their group was up and moving in the dim firelight, and as Drelm lifted his battleaxe he heard war whoops from Grellen and Marika. Cyrelle's hounds raced into the woods to the east, barking furiously.

The beast lumbered on. The Oaksteward stepped up to Drelm's left and swept his staff around as he sonorously expounded a spell of his own.

Before he could finish, a gout of burning liquid sprayed from a space out ahead of the sparkling dust—presumably where the thing's mouth was.

"Down!" Drelm shouted. He and the wizard dropped. The Oaksteward did not, and his spell was disrupted by an agonized scream. Drelm scrambled quickly to his feet even as he heard the distinctive pop of gunfire and the dull twang of additional bowstrings.

The Oaksteward went down in a smoldering heap. Drelm spared him no time; he would either use magic to recover, or he'd die. Nothing the half-orc could do would change any of that.

And then, beside him, something flamed into existence. Drelm spun, axe raised, and found himself staring at the back of an immense horned ape, half again his size. The creature's fur glowed red and fire rolled along its edges. Votek screamed in agony as the beast's massive hands clutched his chest and face. The sound of sizzling flesh rose into the air, along with an awful stench.

Drelm's axe cut deep into the muscles of the thing's back and it roared and spun, wielding the limp wizard like a whip. Drelm sidestepped as the sizzling, screaming wizard's legs flailed into the ground beside him. Drelm swung again, but the monster was nimble and leapt back. It bared gleaming black fangs and roared at him, then flung the wizard to the earth and jumped on him, caving in his chest. Poor Votek let out a final cry of pain and then fell silent as his clothes caught fire from the monster's burning feet.

The half-orc had never seen a burning monster like this before, but he wasn't afraid. The line of dripping blackness that crossed the creature's torso showed he had hurt the thing, and if he could hurt it, he could kill it.

When the creature pushed off hind legs to charge on all fours, Drelm timed his swing against the moment its left hand touched ground. He took the limb off at the elbow.

The thing screeched and tumbled. Drelm dodged too late and was bowled aside by the creature's smoldering body. Calvonis was beside him then, waving a sword and shouting something about the heat.

Lisette was braver. She screamed at the monster as it searched for footing. "Look up here, goat-rutter!"

It showed black fangs as she fired both pistols, one a split second after the other. Both bullets hit, and one eye socket disintegrated into red ruin. The other bullet blew out the back of the monster's blazing head. Still it surged forward, screaming and reaching with both its clawlike hand and its smoking stump. Drelm knocked Lisette clear and brought the axe down across its shoulders. There was a spray of black ichor, and then the thing vanished in a flood of black smoke before it struck the ground. Only the trail of burning grass and the broken, blackened body of the wizard testified as to its existence.

Cyrelle's hounds had come back up the slope and now harried the larger beast's back legs. One invisible tentacle had snatched up the little sorcerer's brother, Poul, who stabbed weakly at the limb he could not see with a dagger.

Drelm hefted his axe and charged.

He sliced his axe into what the wizard's glowing dust showed as a thick neck and was rewarded with a spray of blood. Partly blinded, he nonetheless swung again, for the ichor had defined a larger patch of the monster's scaled flesh.

The half-defined lizard face turned, and he smelled a fetid reek. Drelm leapt to the right as another gout of smoking acid sprayed, but was unprepared for the heavy object that collided with him. It was the other tentacle. He'd almost forgotten about them. A thick, serpentine mass suddenly constricted his waist even as it lifted him bodily into the air. His angle was bad, but Drelm twisted and struck deeply, and there was a satisfying gush of foul-smelling blood. He was raising his axe for a second blow when the thing whipped him free, and he sailed helplessly through the air.

Drelm released the axe and threw his hands in front of him, thinking he might catch himself and roll. But he found he had no control while airborne, and in a moment he was upon the ground, stunned and groaning. He could not be entirely sure where he hurt, because everything was in pain. He heard the barking of dogs and screaming, but it all seemed to be from far, far away.

He wasn't sure how long he lay there, his vision going in and out. It seemed a very long while before someone with a weak grip raised his head to pour something down his throat. Drelm drank without hesitation, and immediately felt renewed vigor. He sat up, blinking, and found himself regarding the curly-haired halfling.

"I thought that might bring you around," Drutha said.

Drelm reached for his axe, then remembered he'd let it go. His eyes now working properly, he searched the darkness for sign of the monster.

But he didn't see anything. Votek's spell must have faded, or the monster had vanished.

He staggered to his feet and ripped his knife from his belt. There was the pile of rags that was the druid, still smoking. Nearby, a shirtless red-haired form lay twisted on its side, licked by flame. The girl who'd claimed to be a sorcerer was weeping over the twisted corpse of her brother a little farther off.

But no one was fighting anymore. He turned to the halfling. "Where's the monster?"

"Vanished," Drutha reported quickly. "It just up and vanished, right in the middle of taking a bite out of Marika. It seemed to be taking some real damage, finally."

Drelm then realized a number from their troop were missing. "Where's Elyana?"

"She's out looking for the summoner, along with Cyrelle and Aladel."

"Casualties?"

"Our healer and wizard are dead. So are Marika, and Poul. Illidian and Galarias are wounded."

The half orc grunted and sheathed his knife.

It was worse than the halfling had told him. Of the wounded, Illidian's cousin Galarias was best off. A bloody bandage wrapped his forehead. He was tending to Illidian, who lay on the forest floor near the fire, breathing raggedly. The captain's shirt was heavy with blood.

Lisette and Calvonis were on guard, watching the distance.

Drelm had no personal regard for Illidian, but he respected the elf's fighting prowess. They'd need all the swords they could get to take the thing down. He stepped up to Galarias to get a report. "How bad is he?"

Galarias glanced up. "I have successfully stopped the bleeding," he said, his accent rather thick. "But I am not a true healer. He is very weak, and there is little I can do for him."

Drelm frowned. "Drutha, you have any more of that stuff you had me drink?"

The halfling trotted up. "I gave you all I had," she said, adding, "You looked worse than he did."

That was saying something, because Illidian looked pretty bad.

"Drelm has a penchant," Illidian said weakly, "for getting knocked down by the beast. We share that much, don't we, Captain?" The elf offered a death's-head's grin.

Drelm nodded. He respected a warrior who could take a few blows and keep fighting.

"Who's watching the perimeter?" he asked.

Lisette spoke up quietly from beside him. "Karag, Calvonis, and Grellen. You're welcome, incidentally."

Drelm really didn't understand why warriors needed to hear thanks, but now, after the battle, was a time for praise. "Nice shot with the monster."

Illidian tried to prop himself up on one arm, wincing. "The summoner targeted those he thought were the most dangerous. The wizard. You. The druid. He toys with us, to show his power."

"I didn't know he could call up other monsters," Drelm said.

"Now you do." Illidian gritted his teeth and sank slowly back against the grasses. "Let's hope he doesn't have any more . . . surprises."

"Elyana had best return shortly," Galarias looked up at Drelm. "You should sound your horn for her. Illidian's heartbeat weakens."

The half-orc lifted the horn to his lips and let out a blast. He noticed then that his own breath seemed a little short.

As if he himself had conjured her, Drelm heard the clomp of hooves, and Elyana rode in, trailed by Cyrelle, Aladel, and a pack of hounds. Three of the dogs, Drelm noticed suddenly, were missing.

"Illidian needs you," Drelm said as Elyana dropped down beside him.

Elyana was splattered in dirt and gore. Her brow wrinkled as her gaze swept over Drelm. "Gods, you look terrible."

Drelm grunted.

"I'll see to you next," Elyana said, then bent down beside the one-armed elf. Galarias spoke rapidly to her in Elven, and so too did Illidian, though his voice was so low Drelm wondered if he was understandable even to his fellow elves.

Drelm had seen Elyana work her healing magic before, and it was often interesting to watch. She knelt over Illidian, closed her eyes, then rolled up the blood-soaked shirt and set hands to the naked flesh of the captain's chest. Drelm suddenly realized what he'd assumed was a bunch in the bloody fabric was a spot where one of Illidian's ribs had poked up the shirt.

As Drelm watched, the bone sank into its proper place. A muscle wound itself around the bone, and then skin grew suddenly across the rents and tears in the captain's chest.

Elyana sat back, gathering her own breath.

Illidian's eyes focused upon her own. He spat out a question, in Elven, and Elyana answered curtly. Whatever she said sent his eyebrows arcing up his high forehead. Quickly, though, he mastered himself and answered with a short phrase of his own.

Elyana then rose and turned to the others. "We will bury our dead, and rest, then move out at dawn."

"Move out where?" Drutha asked. "What if it comes back right now?"

"It's wounded," Elyana replied, "and its summoner is a magic-user like any other. I've fought wizards before. They don't have unlimited reservoirs. They need rest, and time, to prepare new spells. I don't intend to give this one time. Drelm, come with me."

She then led Drelm away over by the edge of the circle, several paces apart from where Grellen kept watch in a tree. That odd hiccupping noise, Drelm realized, was the sound of Cyrelle sobbing as she dug a hole for one of her hounds. The rest of her animals assisted with the hole by concentrated effort with their front paws.

Elyana made Drelm sit and then gingerly removed his helmet before tossing it down. He didn't remember it being so tight.

"I don't think you'll be wearing that thing again," she observed.

There was only a slim trickle of light from the campfire this far from it, but there was no missing the huge dent in the back of the helm. "Drutha gave me a healing draught."

"A good thing." Elyana laid cool hands to the side of his face. He watched her close her eyes and the thought of Daylah came unbidden to him as her expression relaxed. There were significant differences between the elf's high cheekbones and Daylah's round softness, but they were both pleasing to look upon.

Other aches he'd barely noticed were gone then, as well as a ringing head pain. Elyana sat back, breathed out. "You'd fractured your skull. And here I always thought it was rock hard."

Drelm grunted. "Why bring me here?" he asked softly.

There'd been no reason to perform her healing anywhere in particular, but she had deliberately brought them as far from any other member of the expedition as possible. What with the sound of digging and the calls of night animals, they were effectively out of hearing range of anyone so long as they whispered.

"We circled the campground for a half-mile out," Elyana said. "Aladel, Cyrelle, and her hounds. It's possible one of us missed spoor in the darkness, but Aladel and I are pretty old hands at this, and Cyrelle's hounds turned up no interesting scents."

Drelm thought he understood, but he wanted to hear her explain to make sure he hadn't missed something. "So the summoner wasn't there? Maybe he was up in a tree."

"Possibly. But wouldn't the dogs have caught scent of him? There would have been tracks up to a tree."

"He's a wizard, right? Couldn't he fly?"

"Karag says he—or she—is a summoner, and it seems true. I've never fought one, but from what I've heard most of a summoner's spells are about conjuring monsters. Like that flaming thing you fought. It didn't occur to me that he could summon more than one thing at a time, but I won't make that mistake again."

Drelm nodded. "He might know some other spells, too."

"He surely does. Remember how close the tracks of his steed were to the monster? I think he must have some kind of control range or communication limit. Or maybe he just wants to stick around and watch."

"Alright." That sounded reasonable to Drelm.

"Think on this. The summoner's beast knew its way up through our spike traps. He or she targeted our wizard, who was probably our best chance against the monster, and killed our healer so we'd remain weak. I can keep us going, but I'm easily tapped out. The summoner knew exactly where to strike. And there were no tracks outside the camp showing where he commanded from." She paused then, watching him, and he knew that was a hint to puzzle things out.

Her meaning came to Drelm in a flash. "It's someone inside our group," he growled.

Chapter Nine
Fallen Friends
Lisette

The job just kept getting worse.

Lisette had crept silently up on Illidian's tent. She'd understood the Elven words passed between the captain and Elyana while Illidian lay wounded, knew that when he'd asked for tracks she'd answered they must talk, and understood that Elyana was worried about something new.

Illidian and his underlings were the only expedition members who slept in tents. Galarias and Aladel shared one, but Illidian slept alone. That made creeping up to listen in on the conversation a little simpler.

Once Lisette had heard Elyana's speculations about the summoner's location, she wondered why she hadn't thought of the issue herself. Of course the summoner would infiltrate their group. It wasn't as though the expedition organizers had been secretive. They'd apparently advertised for it up and down the Sellen's run through the River Kingdoms.

Lisette lay there in the darkness as the elves debated the likely suspects. Both Elyana and Illidian were able to concede to the other that neither of them was the summoner, and Illidian agreed it couldn't be Drelm, but Elyana refused to be dead certain about Galarias or Aladel.

Lisette had never thought of herself as charitable, but she was willing to believe the other elves were free and clear. A good commander knew her, or his, operatives. So she could discount Elyana, Drelm, all three elves, and herself and Karag. Seven eliminated and three dead left her with few suspects: the halfling Drutha; the huntswoman Cyrelle; the warriors Calvonis and Grellen; and the girl, Melias.

Lisette, like the elves, had seen almost every one of those five involved in some aspect of the combat, whether it was Calvonis screaming as he swung at the monster's flank, or Drutha peppering the creature's side with flasks that broke to scatter smoking blue fire, or Grellen dragging his dying friend to safety. She supposed one of them might have been faking. It might be that the summoner was planning to slowly thin their ranks, and to sow more fear. If nothing else, with both the wizard and the healer dead, the expedition had been fairly well crippled.

The girl hadn't managed much of anything besides launching some sort of ineffective dart spell while her brother died. How could it be her, though? Surely no one but a teenager could be as naively self-centered and stubborn as Melias has been so far.

The summoner's identity as a mole was an unpleasant knot, and Lisette was cursing herself for being so foolish as to get involved in unraveling it. It was bad enough that, once again, she'd helped her eventual target. Avelis didn't want Drelm dead until the monster was finished, and she was holding to that both because she honored her contract and because she was starting to suspect they needed every hand possible against the monster.

She lay silent, then felt a cold chill as Elyana revealed something completely new. The Galtan assassin Lisette had killed had arranged for a note to be sent to the elf in case of his disappearance, and it had exposed her background as an assassin. Lisette's mind spun with her possible courses of action even as she wondered why Elyana hadn't already acted against her.

She then realized that naturally Devin hadn't known Lisette's target when he'd written the note—how could he, seeing as how she'd killed him shortly after he'd learned? So Elyana didn't know who Lisette was after and, as she told Illidian, wasn't convinced the accusation was true. Elyana was inclined to believe the letter had been meant only to cause trouble.

"You should have said something to me about this earlier," Lisette heard Illidian reply to Elyana.

"I had no opportunity, and I wished to observe her."

Lisette used an old breathing exercise to force her racing heart down to a normal speed. It was not yet time for flight, or fighting.

"I have observed Lisette," Illidian said, "and she's had ample opportunity to attack one of us. She hasn't taken it."

Lisette smiled at that. The mayor's complicated instructions had at least bought her a little more time. How could anyone think she was after Drelm when she'd risked her life to defend him?

Elyana seemed inclined to agree with Illidian's opinion, and in the end both she and the elven captain decided that while Lisette might bear watching, she was not likely to be the summoner, or in league with him.

Eventually they too turned their conversation to Melias. Like Lisette, they doubted she could be the culprit. Illidian, though, was wondering if she might be rendered useful.

"Let's see how capable she is," Illidian suggested.

Elyana sounded doubtful. "You've seen her spellwork. She's a rank beginner."

"Even a rank beginner can work a wand. I saw you give that one you told me about to Votek. Did he learn how to work it?"

"Not that he mentioned to me."

"Show it to her."

"I doubt she'll make any headway with it."

"You're probably correct, but what harm will come of it?"

Elyana was quiet for a long time, and Lisette strained to listen in, wondering if she were whispering. Finally, though, she heard the woman sigh. "Very well. It will do no one any good if it's just tucked into the wizard's rucksack."

They then fell into a long discussion about the wand, and the mad sorcerer who'd wielded it, and Elyana's pet theory that the summoner and the sorcerer's efforts might be related. Illidian then relayed tales he'd heard of other killing sprees within the River Kingdoms and condescendingly suggested that because humans frequently murdered each other, there need not be any connection whatsoever.

Lisette would have had a hard time arguing his point, but she couldn't help wondering if Elyana was on to something. Almost she shook her head. She really shouldn't have gotten involved in this one. What was it Elyana had said just a few hours ago? Ensuring that you chose the ground of your battle? Lisette hadn't done a very fine job of that.

Lisette crept back to her bedroll as she sensed them finishing up. Karag was asleep near the fire embers, and she slipped out of the darkness to lie beside him on her own bedroll.

Karag had always been a little touchy when it came to dwarven matters, but Lisette didn't quite understand what had set him off this week. He hadn't really minded at all when she'd told him they were going to target Drelm—it was only over dinner last night that he'd started acting strange.

She was just closing her eyes when she heard his voice.

"You learn anything good?" he whispered. He then rolled to face her. With his back to the fire, she could see very little of his expression. His breath smelled sour, as of ale. He had a limitless capacity for the stuff, and had probably packed several wineskins of it on the side of his mule.

Lisette checked to either side. Drutha was closest, about five feet over, and snoring loudly.

"They think the summoner's part of our band," she told Karag softly.

The dwarf shook his head. "This is a helluva thing you've gotten us involved with."

"I know."

His eyes flicked up. "Seems to me maybe you should have talked with me before taking this job."

It didn't matter that she herself was regretting the job; she was the one who paid him, and he had no right to question her. It was time to remind him of that. "You work for me, Karag."

"Aye, for the bounty hunter Lisette." He jabbed at her with one thick finger, then lowered his voice. "Not for Lisette the assassin. Or whatever else you sign on to be."

She sneered. "Two years we've worked together. It's a damned inconvenient time to grow scruples."

Karag was a long time answering. He rolled over to stare up at the canopy of leaves above. His voice was pitched so low she could barely understand him. "I've been thinking maybe all the money I want out of this is what I get out of that beast's hide. From the mayor. But then I think, much as I hate orcs, maybe what I want is an even split. It's not like I'm doing a third of the work now. I should get half."

Lisette kept her tone light, not revealing her boiling anger. "You figure?"

"That thing can tear either of us apart. There's no telling with magic. Or monsters. I'm not just your backup on this one."

"It's bad form," she reminded him, "to renegotiate in the midst of a mission."

"I figured you'd say that. I say it's bad form to take on a job that's so different without bothering to consult me."

"Sixty-forty," Lisette offered.

"I'll think on it."

"Think on it fast," she hissed, and sat up. She stuffed both pistols through her belt and left the dwarf brooding near their blankets.

She had never expected this from Karag. They'd never been friends, exactly, but she and the dwarf enjoyed a certain morbid camaraderie. She was realizing now just how much she'd begun to depend on him, which made her even more angry. He'd become an expert with the loading and priming of weapons. As good as she was herself, though not as fast as Kerrigan. Of course, it would have been hard to be as fast as Kerrigan. Those big, powder-stained hands of his had been remarkably capable.

At thought of those fine hands her frown deepened, and she found herself striding away, off toward the tree line. The figure moving on her left she identified as Elyana, just now leaving Illidian's tent. The elven woman didn't walk for her bedroll, but to where the horses were picketed. She was always doing something with the damned horses. She was worse about them than Lisette was about her powder and guns.

A second figure had stepped forward from Illidian's tent as well: one who, by his profile, watched the elven woman drift gracefully away before raising his face to consider the stars shining high above the clearing, framed by the dark treetops that surrounded them on three sides.

Even by darkness, Illidian was beautiful. As she stepped closer she could not help noticing he didn't reek of man-stink and boots, even after a long day in the saddle. He smelled of leather, and blood, and the sweet musk that was elven sweat.

His head turned to her as she drew near. She was not sure, really, what she intended, but even as she questioned her own motives she halted before him.

"Don't you need rest?" Illidian asked gently.

"Don't you?"

"I have trouble sleeping." His hand fell to the elbow above the empty sleeve, for he had removed his hook. "I frequently do. But it's no struggle for an elf to go without sleep."

"Sometimes a woman can go without sleep."

She felt his gaze settle keenly on her then, and he faced her more fully.

"You're not so blunt in your speech as many humans," he said.

"Do you find that interesting?" Lisette stepped boldly closer to him.

"I find you interesting," he said softly. "Very interesting."

"And why is that?"

He touched the curls of her hair. "I can sense that it is the hunt that fires you, and that you thrill to a good chase. You are deadly and seasoned . . . Yet you are beautiful."

"Beautiful for a human?"

"Beautiful by any standard," he said, and, not missing the hint of her upturned lips, he kissed her.

She returned that kiss without revealing the burning turmoil she felt within. With a man, this union would be folly. But with an elf . . . No, there was no good reasoning about it. She was in a foul mood, and knew two ways to relieve it. She wasn't about to get drunk. Illidian, though . . . She had wanted him from the first moment she'd caught sight of him, so she took his hand and led him through the canvas flap to his own bedroll.

Soon she knew him very well, forgetting her anger and loosing her desire in one swift and glorious flood. As she rode him he muttered nonsense words in Elven, praising her beauty and wishing, in a forlorn way, that such beauty would not fade so swiftly, because he did not think she understood him. Something uncoiled within her as he spoke, and she told him how beautiful he was, though she kept from saying that sight of him had brought her heart to her throat. She was no little girl to say such things, even if she felt them.

After, she lay with her head upon his shoulder and he stroked her bare arm and traced fingers along the surface of her naked skin.

"How did you come to be a bounty hunter?"

His question was so casual she didn't think she would have been suspicious if she hadn't just overheard his talk with Elyana. Her preference would have been to say as little as possible, but she meant to allay his fears.

"I used to have a different line of work. In Cheliax. I didn't have any choice in the matter," she added. "I was sold into service, and worked my way up."

"What kind of service?"

"I killed things," she said. She wanted him to understand that she wasn't in *another* old profession.

"If you're saying what I think you're saying," he said, delicately, "then those sorts of careers aren't easy to leave. How did you do it?"

"I had a series of assignments with a marksman from Alkenstar. A kind of noble, if you will. We . . . became close." Was she saying too much? She'd just wanted to hint that she used to be an assassin so it would seem she hid nothing. Why, then, did she feel compelled to keep talking? "And he had the pull, with my organization, to help see me clear. He told me I had too much conscience to do what I was doing, but suggested we join forces to do similar work. So we did."

"I'm sorry," he said, and kissed her gently on the cheek.

She did not understand, at that moment, why the action touched her so. "What was that for?" she asked quietly. Her heart trembled a little even as she scoffed.

"He's dead," he said simply, "and you cared for him very deeply. I heard it in your voice."

She pressed closer to him then, and kissed him, and he kissed her back, and before long they took greater time to explore one another until they lay exhausted together.

She did not creep back to her own bedroll until shortly before dawn. She fell swiftly asleep once more. When there came a touch at her shoulder she smiled at first, her dream self recalling the touch of her elven lover. It was a rude shock to find Karag's hairy face frowning at her. The sky over his shoulder was touched with a hint of amber.

"Elyana means to move out in the next quarter-hour. Best grab some food. I let you sleep as long as I dared."

"Why didn't you wake me sooner?"

"I saw you had a late night of it."

Lisette scowled and sat up.

Karag spoke on as the rest of the camp bustled to life. "I've decided I want fifty-five, forty-five, on account of you not telling me the game was different this time."

"You push your luck," she snapped.

"You push yours, without me. We're partners. Hell, the elf treats her orc better than you treat me."

Lisette didn't know how to respond to that.

"You can see the way he talks to her," Karag continued. "They're real friends, Lisette."

"Friends? I thought we were business partners, not spit-swappers. You stupid dwarf." She rolled out of her blankets. "You remember that time I dragged you out of Druma with blood running into your beard? Or the time I swung back to shoot those bastards when your mule went lame?"

Karag only frowned.

"Did I need to hold your hand when I did that?" She jabbed at him with one finger. "If I can't count on you, I'm dead. But I tell you what. If I think we're outnumbered and going down, I'll save a bullet for you. Because we're close."

She ran through a string of curses in her head as she methodically checked her gear once more, then stepped away to the fire, where the stupid half-orc was bent over a bowl of oats. He saw her and passed up a wooden bowl, indicating the cooking pot slung over the fire.

She snatched it away, instantly regretting that she revealed her emotions, but the rudeness of the gesture didn't seem to register with the half-orc. She served herself, then crouched down on a rock beside Melias, who looked like she'd just come through another crying jag. She sniffled so much Lisette found herself wishing she'd taken a seat beside Drelm

Halfway through the meal, Elyana and Illidian paced into view, chattering at each other in the musical language of the elves. Elyana and Aladel had been out on an early patrol and discovered tracks of a horse heading west, and she and Illidian debated now whether those tracks were recent, or if they'd been in place the night before. She caught Illidian looking over at her, and she felt herself brighten a little at his attention even though she kept her expression bland.

Soon they were in the saddle and riding west, split once again into three groups. Melias rode with the central party, presumably so Elyana could watch her.

Drelm had been placed in charge of Lisette's squad with Karag and Calvonis. Elyana and Illidian, having decided she was no threat to Drelm, had made it that much easier for Lisette to get close to him.

She was looking right at Calvonis's helmeted head when the fanged, long-armed thing swung down from the trees and grabbed hold of his horse's skull. The mount screamed in terror while the hairy monster showed fangs in a roar. The creature wrenched, there was a loud snap, and the horse dropped.

Lisette's horse reared in fright, and Karag's mule shied backward. Drelm spun his great warhorse with an elegant curvet and drove in, swinging his axe one-handed.

Lisette fought for control of her animal. Cursing her mount, kicking it, wrestling its head to the left all did no good—the stink from the beast was too much for the animal. She calmed it long enough to leap down, and then she was rushing forward with her rifle for a clear shot.

Calvonis struggled to push the horse's carcass out of the way to free his trapped leg. The thing roared at Drelm, who'd just cut a broad slice into its furred chest. It raised one titanic paw and clouted him in the head, staggering him.

Lisette shot the animal through the chest, where its heart should have been. This set it spinning but didn't drop it. Once more it roared, swinging again at Drelm, who ducked.

Karag ran up with her second rifle. Just as she was drawing a bead on the creature a second one dropped from the trees behind Drelm, and she shifted targets. It was damnable bad luck she was supposed to ensure the half-orc lived until the summoned beast was dead, for she might have shot him "accidentally" at any point in the exchange.

"It wasn't there a moment ago," Karag said as he rapidly readied her first rifle. "It just popped out of nowhere! It's the damned summoner!"

"That's magic for you," Lisette snapped, and dropped the second rifle beside him. She pulled a pistol from her sash.

Calvonis freed himself from his dead horse at last, cursing. Drelm dropped his axe into the second ape's shoulder. Lisette fired, missed as the thing drove suddenly forward. She tossed down the pistol as she drew its replacement, fired again, caught the beast in its shoulder blade. It was in mid-roar as Drelm split its skull in half lengthwise. Blood and brains splattered out in a wide arc, flying far enough even to catch Lisette's shirtsleeve. The monster slumped to the ground, twitching, and Drelm lowered his bloody axe. A moment later the creature vanished in a puff of smoke, though its blood still coated their clothing and gear.

A limping Calvonis joined them, his sword dripping blood to the hilt.

"Finished the other one off," he said, panting.

The sounds of barking, snarling dogs and the shouts of battle rose from the right, where the other squads were hidden by the trees.

Calvonis raised his sword. "Follow!" He dashed off at a good clip, still limping. Drelm ran after.

Lisette grabbed both rifles from Karag, handed off her pistols, and followed.

She had just caught up to Drelm when the ground gave way beneath them and they tumbled into darkness.

Lisette landed heavily on Drelm's shoulder, knocking the breath from her lungs. The half-orc had hit the dirt floor of the pit trap only a heartbeat before. Lisette slammed her head and elbow into the wall and briefly saw stars. It took a moment before she realized the cracking noise she'd heard was not her aching arm, but the bore of her best rifle, which had broken off.

"You alright?" Drelm asked gruffly. One huge hand steadied her as she struggled to her feet.

She glared at him in answer; he only blinked back and looked up out of the hole. The rim, perfectly rectangular, lay some eighteen feet overhead. She expected to see

Karag leaning down with a rope, but there was no sign of him, only the tinny clack of weapons and distant shouting.

"Lisette!" Calvonis was there, leaning over the edge, weakly defined against the white square of light he now blocked.

"We're alright," Lisette shouted up. At the same moment Drelm roared to grab a rope, Calvonis pulled back his head.

"Hang on," he called. "I'll get help!"

"A rope, not help!" Lisette shouted back, then cursed to herself. "Idiot."

"The summoner planned this well," Drelm said. "He must have called beasts to dig traps and lured us here with the tracks."

"He's toying with us," Lisette agreed.

"Can you climb to my shoulders?"

"I could. But it wouldn't get us far." Lisette looked up to the hole above. "How could he have dug this in a single night?"

"I don't think he did," Drelm told her. "These have been here a while. Look at the sides."

Lisette put her hand to the flat side of the wall and found it dry to her touch.

"Abadar watches over us," Drelm said. "We're lucky the summoner planted no spears."

Lisette sourly regarded her ruined rifle. "The next time you see Abadar, tell him to luck us out of the hole entirely."

At that moment, something large tumbled into the hole, blocking light in the brief moment before it slammed into them. Something hard and cold and metallic bashed her face, spraying her with warm liquid. Blood. She spat it out in horror as she heard laughter from above.

Karag. It was Karag who'd fallen on them, limp, bloody—and dead. The light shaft caught on one of his blank, staring eyes.

Someone had pushed a very dead Karag into the hole. Drelm helped Lisette wrestle her comrade off her, and she fought down a surge of fear as she looked up to find the source of laughter.

Once again, the rectangle of light framed the figure so that she couldn't see features, only the limned outline of his head. But there was no mistaking the man looking down at them. Calvonis.

"I'll bring more help," he said, "just as soon as I can."

He laughed again and was gone.

Chapter Ten
The Wilewood
Elyana

Elyana happened to be looking at Cyrelle when the ape swung out of the trees and knocked the huntswoman from the saddle.

The creature landed heavily beside the groaning Cyrelle and was reaching for her head when Elyana's sword stroke left a deep red furrow along the black fur of its back. It spun, showed its fangs, and roared, only to take a kick to the face as Calda reared and lashed out with two heavy hooves.

The ape staggered. Cyrelle rose to one knee and jammed a thick-bladed knife deep into its side.

There was no missing a second cry of alarm to the north and another simian roar from farther off. Closer at hand, Melias shouted something that was a mix of scream and incantation, and Elyana heard a thud as of something heavy falling just behind her.

Cyrelle's dogs came running back, barking furiously. They'd ranged right past the tree the ape had dropped from only a few moments before. She didn't think they'd missed it—it hadn't been there. The apes had to be the summoner's work. The creatures were hardly native to the woodlands of the River Kingdoms.

The ape was not yet dead. It clawed at Cyrelle, who rolled, taking only a glancing blow to her shoulder. Elyana leaned out to drive her sword through the back of the creature's throat. Blood spewed twice; once with the thrust and twice as it roared.

The mercenary Grellen arrived at a sprint and then cut the thing almost in half with one mighty cleave of his gleaming longsword. As the body dropped, it vanished in a puff of smoke. Grellen leapt back in astonishment.

"Glad you could make it," Elyana said, though on voicing the words, they sounded harsher than intended.

"I'm not much on horseback," the mercenary said, panting, "or I'd have gotten here faster."

"See to Cyrelle." Elyana started after where she'd heard the second ape.

Melias's mount had fled into the deeper woods, and the girl was crawling backward through leafy detritus when Elyana reached her. Another ape stalked the girl on hairy knuckles. Elyana ducked a low tree branch and goaded Calda to speed, but two hounds beat her there, shooting forward to latch onto the monster's legs.

The beast roared, swatting at them. They danced back, snarling, and the monster stomped after, swinging heavy arms.

Elyana dropped her sword point-first into the forest floor, where it stood quivering as she whipped up her bow and nocked an arrow. The first shaft thrust through the monster's cheek. The next two ended up in its chest, and it wailed for a moment before it dissolved into black smoke.

A quick scan revealed her own squad was mostly unharmed, but there were still sounds of shouting from the others. In response to her assessing look, Cyrelle managed a breathless, "I'm fine," even though she was wiping blood from her mouth onto the back of her hand.

"Get the girl's horse," Elyana commanded Grellen, "and get yourselves mounted, fast." She snatched her sword and rode north.

Calda easily threaded around the wide tree boles, and within moments Elyana was in sight of a second battle. Drutha warily sat her dog, watching while Illidian knelt upon the ground holding a rope. It was a strange sight until Elyana realized that the rope hung into a square pit in front of the elf, and she halted Calda in mid-step, for she saw that one of the horses lay contorted nearby. Aladel's gelding had been too large to plummet into a second pit, but when the ground had given way the horse must have broken its neck, for it lay motionless with its rear haunches pointed toward the trees and its front end rammed into the pit's far side. Darkness gaped below. She felt a sudden stab of regret. Was Aladel dead? She'd rather begun to like the competent, well-spoken elf.

She showed no emotion in her orders. "Round up the others," she told Drutha, "and check on Drelm."

Drutha nodded once and with but a light touch her dog turned and ran south.

Illidian glanced up at her. Clearly he was having some difficulty holding a rope with a hand and a hook, but he was too proud to ask for aid. Wordless, she stepped to his side and took up the rope, which he had anchored around a nearby tree bole.

"What happened?"

"Those monsters popped into those trees at the same moment we hit the pit traps. Galarias and his horse dropped into one. Aladel managed to dive clear of the one he triggered. We killed the monsters, and Aladel climbed down to check on Galarias."

"I'm coming up," Aladel's voice echoed hollowly from below.

She tried to show no relief in her posture or voice. As a leader it was bad form to show favoritism, especially when Illidian's own blood cousin, Galarias, might be dead.

Elven vision was adept at piercing darkness, but there was little to be seen apart from a mass beneath the elf now climbing up via the rope and handholds in the pit. When he reached the edge he nimbly pulled himself clear, then undid the rope from his waist. The gaze of the dark-haired, black-garbed elf was sober. "Galarias is on the bottom, under his horse," Aladel said quietly. "They will not be coming up. I'm sorry, Illidian." He eased saddlebags off his shoulder and set them heavily upon the ground. He traded a quick glance with Elyana, smiled grimly.

Illidian loosed the rope and stood stiffly, then stepped to the very edge of the pit and stared inside.

For a moment Elyana was afraid he meant to pitch himself after.

"I grieve with you, cousin," Elyana told him.

Drelm's horn call split the air from somewhere to the south, and Elyana cursed.

" Walk lightly," she said. "There may be more of these damned traps. Ride double, and follow my tracks."

Elyana wished she might have trodden more carefully herself, but the best she could do was lean slightly to the left so she could eye the terrain as she guided Calda.

Could they really have missed the summoner last night? Or might he still be a part of one of their squads, sending forth a summoned horse to lead them to these pits?

Cyrelle's hounds were baying somewhere south, ferociously, as though they had a strong scent and meant to chase it to the ends of the earth. Swiftly the sounds ebbed westward.

Elyana arrived at the site of their first battle with Cyrelle's ape, then followed the tracks of her companions to where they were hunkered around another pit. Grellen was steadying the rope while Drutha kept guard and Melias stood nervously clutching the black wand. She was wide-eyed, almost dazed, and Elyana wondered how she could possibly survive much longer. The hazards of the expedition were far beyond her level of capability. Of Cyrelle there was no sign.

"Who's in the pit?" Elyana asked. Could all four of Drelm's squad have been walking so close that they'd plunged in together?

"Calvonis is the summoner," Drutha reported, her eyes bright and a little mad. The halfling's dog, sensing her mood, growled. "Drelm and Lisette are down there, and they're not hurt too bad. But Karag's dead."

"Calvonis?" Elyana repeated.

Drutha's voice was low, bitter. "He's a fine actor, isn't he? Lisette said he dropped Karag's body into the pit after them."

Elyana's mind cycled back to the moments when she had seen Calvonis in action. Had there been some moment that she'd missed, some statement that she should better have understood?

Lisette was scowling as she clambered from the pit. A large bruise stood out along one cheek, and her face was blood-spattered. She glared at Elyana then at the surroundings in general.

Drelm came up more slowly, the dead dwarf slung over his shoulders. Elyana and Drutha stepped closer to drag the blood-drenched corpse from him.

"He's heavier than he looks," Drutha said, then added, quickly: "No offense meant to the poor fellow."

Elyana had a hard time believing anyone had ever called Karag a poor fellow before that moment. Even in death he looked mean. Judging from the bone- and brain-splattered back of the dwarf's skull, Calvonis had struck from behind.

Drelm pulled himself up, fastidiously brushed some dirt off his tabard, then reported the sequence of events in more detail. As he finished, Cyrelle returned, her horse snorting in greeting at the others.

"My hounds are still after him," she said, breathless, "but can't outpace his spectral horse. I've got Balok watching him from above."

Elyana nodded. She pushed through the shock and anger; there was no time to wonder what might have been done differently. "His horse spell has to wear out eventually," she observed. "Casters need their rest to work their spells, and he's gotten no more than the rest of us. We must keep after him."

"But why is he doing it?" Melias asked. "It makes no sense. He was sitting next to me just this morning at breakfast, and handed me some bread . . ."

"He's cracked, girl," Grellen told her. "I wish I had a better answer. He needs killing."

"We're in complete agreement there," Drutha replied. "Why would he reveal himself now, though? It doesn't make sense."

Now wasn't the time for debate. Elyana turned to Illidian. "We must pursue. If you'd like to remain behind to bury Galarias—"

"No." Illidian cut her off with a short chopping motion, made with his remaining hand. "Galarias would want us to hunt this man down." He slipped into Elven. "All that he was in our world is gone, now, and anything I do for him is more for me than him."

Aladel had come up behind the grieving captain and put a hand to his shoulder, but Illidian shrugged it off. "Let us be on with it."

Lisette waved off any suggestion that Karag needed burial, though judging by the scowl etched across her face, the dwarf apparently had meant more to her than Elyana realized.

The markswoman rummaged through the dwarf's gear and added what she wished to her own saddlebags, then Drelm eased his body back into the pit, where it landed with a sodden thump. Lisette claimed not to know what god the dwarf worshiped, saying only that he took a lot of their names in vain.

"I will ask Abadar to guide him, then," Drelm said, and bowed his head at the side of the pit.

Elyana would not have thought Lisette could look more angry until she glowered at the offer. Drelm, though, seemed oblivious. Like most of the half-orc's prayers, it didn't take long.

Elyana sent Aladel and Cyrelle ahead with Grellen. While Drutha and Drelm oversaw the consolidation of their remaining supplies she took Melias aside.

"You're stuck with us now, girl. You claimed to be a sorcerer, but I haven't seen you manage much. What spells can you handle?"

The girl met her eyes only briefly before looking shamefacedly down at the forest floor. "I can conjure some magic bolts," she said softly. "And slicken up the forest floor, like. And I can start fires, and do a few other little things that probably aren't that useful right now."

That was about what Elyana had expected. Demid had rejected her, declaring her an amateur, and the girl's self-assessment bore that out.

"Are you having any luck with the wand?"

Lips tight, the girl shook her head. "I can sort of see the . . . number of syllables the incantation needs to work, but I haven't been able to find them yet."

"You keep trying," Elyana said. "That might be the only thing standing between you and a monster. But make sure you keep it pointed away from us while you practice." She wished she hadn't had to add that caveat, but there was no telling what a rank novice would do.

Weakly, the girl nodded her assent.

A few moments later they were mounted on the remaining horses, and within half an hour they'd completely left the tree cover to venture across open and rolling hills. They caught up to Cyrelle and her hounds, and the huntswoman reported that her hawk still followed the summoner, headed north and west.

"He's on a coal-black, glowing mount," the huntswoman reported. "I don't know how we'll catch him. It doesn't ever slow." She leaned down to pet the side of her foam-flecked mount.

Elyana looked over her shoulder. What she wouldn't give for a real wizard. "Melias. Any idea how long this kind of spell can last?"

The girl shook her head, slowly, her eyes down.

"It will depend upon how skilled the caster is," Illidian said.

"But even a skilled caster can't ready more spells when he's in the saddle, can he?" Elyana asked.

No one seemed to know for sure, but all agreed that was likely true. "Then we keep pushing him," she said.

Illidian's teeth showed in a savage smile.

"What if we're just doing what he planned, though?" Drutha asked. "What if he wants us to chase him?"

Elyana looked down at her. The halfling could not help but look faintly comical perched there atop her dog.

"What are you saying?" Grellen asked gruffly.

The halfling looked up at the graying mercenary, who'd stopped at her other side. "Elyana and Drelm think Calvonis set those traps a while ago," she said, "and the only way he could have done that is if he planned to lure people here."

"I'm tired of debating this," Illidian called from ahead of them. "He toys with us. He thinks this is a game." The elf nearly spat the last word.

"We follow," Elyana said to Drutha's searching look. "We push until he breaks."

"What if we break first?" Drutha muttered.

Elyana pretended she didn't hear.

Come late afternoon, Cyrelle reported that her hawk had seen Calvonis cross a wide river, then dismount before a forest on its far side. The summoner's horse had vanished, and then he had walked into the woods. So thick was the canopy that the hawk could find no sign of him below. Drutha pointed out that Calvonis surely knew they would be following, and might even have known that Cyrelle's hawk would see exactly where he entered.

"It's probably another trap," she added, as if that weren't already clear.

They reached a hill overlooking that river, the Sellen on its southward run toward Kallas Lake, by early evening. Illidian cursed in Elven the moment he looked down upon it and the forest on its other side. Elyana understood his fury. The river was wide and the ferry lay on the far shore, so they'd be obliged to swim. The trees on the far side were thick with foliage. They would be hard pressed to lead horses through that tangled mess. Still, they could track Calvonis easily through the woods, and the large beast he summoned would have a hard time maneuvering where the trees were so thick. To her questioning look, Illidian showed his teeth.

"Don't you see?" he asked. "That's the Wilewood. We've reached Sevenarches."

"So?" Lisette prompted.

Aladel's reply was serenely calm. "The druids forbid all elves from entering Sevenarches."

"And there's nasty things said to be in the Wilewood, lass," Grellen added.

"Can't get much nastier than what we've seen already," Lisette snapped.

Grellen only shook his head. "You'd be surprised."

"Damn the druids." Illidian kneed his animal forward.

"Wait a moment." As Elyana held up her hand she worried briefly that Illidian wouldn't obey, but he slowed his horse a few meters down the slope and turned to look up at her expectantly.

"I'm new to the area myself," she admitted. "Why do the druids ban elves from Sevenarches?"

"They will not say," Aladel answered quietly.

"And what," she asked, "do they do with elves that trespass?"

"Some get escorted to the border," Aladel answered. "And others are never seen again. It's a point of contention between Kyonin and the druids, but they won't divulge whatever secret they keep."

"A pox upon them," Illidian snapped. "My blood cousin lies rotting in a pit, and my patrol lies sleeping in border soil. Let the druids stop me if they dare. If the rest of you will not ride, I go alone."

"We will go," Elyana said grimly. More and more she worried that Drutha was right and that their pursuit but acted out a plan Calvonis desired.

It took far longer than Elyana would have preferred to find a narrower point along the riverbank, and even then it was a long swim over, each holding to the saddle of his or her mount, or, in Drutha's case, a pack horse. Grellen confessed he didn't swim very well, but it was Lisette who seemed most nervous. Even though she said her powder was stored in watertight oilskin bags, she nervously held the packs on the height of her saddle, out of the water.

Once all dogs, horses, and expedition members finally crossed, Elyana had little trouble locating the improbably perfect hoofprints of Calvonis's magical steed, and she took careful note of his own bootprints. Might he wait just beyond the thick line of trees, as Drutha feared, beside more traps? Or did he lair more deeply?

She cast her eyes skyward. Out in the open, she'd be calling to set up camp in another hour or so. And they were all tired. They would have to leave their horses outside the trees, which meant they'd have to shoulder all their supplies.

Yet how could they dare stop, now? Calvonis was surely tiring. And from what Aladel had said about the Wilewood, no human was likely to have allies within.

She commanded them to ready for a march, then stepped aside and cleared her mind of worries so she might communicate fully with Calda. While she had a special bond with the animal, aided by her magic, conveying complex ideas was far from simple.

The mare didn't like this strange place with its disquieting woods, and was pleased to learn she might return to that cool hill with the long sweet grass across the river. She promised she would shepherd the herd—the other horses—and wait for Elyana. Harder to explain was the passage of time, but Elyana felt fairly sure Calda understood that if the expedition didn't come from the woods by the time of high sun she was to lead the herd back to the feed grounds. She rubbed Calda's nose, gave her a final sliver of dried apple, then left her.

Elyana took careful note of the point where Calvonis had entered the woods, then led the expedition a third of a mile south. She'd be damned if she followed his track precisely into the timber this time. Surely he couldn't have arranged traps along the whole line of trees.

The others followed, quiet. The space beneath the canopy in this forest was close, and strangely ominous. Elyana tried to shake off the sense they were watched, and couldn't quite do it.

She advanced with Cyrelle and the elves, leaving the louder group to manage a few hundred paces behind them. The huntswoman's hounds slid silently ahead through the undergrowth, their coats rendered black in the sketchy light.

"It's not right in here," Cyrelle told her quietly.

"I share your sentiment," Aladel agreed.

Cyrelle spoke on; she seemed uncharacteristically nervous. "I've heard folk say these woods are haunted, but I always thought that was just the druids trying to scare people off. Now I'm not so sure."

A rich, thick voice rang out from the trees on their left. It sounded amused. "The Oakstewards?"

Elyana whirled, only to find nothing there. The man's voice then came from behind them.

"I wouldn't be so worried about the Oakstewards," it said. "I think, instead, you should be concerned about yourselves. For you have trespassed into the Wilewood, and it belongs to me."

The hounds came creeping back to Cyrelle, whimpering, their tails between their legs. The big huntswoman had to shush them before they quieted their whining, but they insisted on huddling as close as they could beside her.

Elyana put her hand to her blade. "Back to back," she ordered. "One of you face each direction." She then raised her voice and addressed the air. "Who are you?"

It was not her imagination—the shadows beneath the trees were deepening, as though the darkness were a living thing, clutching at them with eager fingers.

"I am Lord of the Wilewood," the voice called to them, though she still could see no speaker. "And you are trespassers. Outsiders are not welcome here."

At that very moment Drelm and Drutha, Lisette, Grellen, and Melias came hurrying forward, ahead of something that laughed eerily behind them. They fled into the dim light that remained in a circle about Elyana and the others. All else was darkness.

Elyana pointed them into defensive positions.

The voice had taken on a deep, echoing quality, and Elyana was no longer sure from which direction it came.

Darkness fell completely, as if a theater curtain had dropped and all the stage lights were down. Even Elyana's sight couldn't pierce it.

"Stand fast," she told the rest of her forces. "Form a ring."

"Spread out," came a voice from her left. *Her own voice.* "If we separate they can't get us all."

"That's not me!" Elyana shouted. "Stand fast, form a ring!"

"You heard her," Drelm barked from close at hand.

"That voice is not me," called a voice like Drelm's, from Elyana's right. "You heard the elf! Run for it!"

"Split up," the duplicate to Elyana's voice called again, and then as her people babbled among themselves, echoes of their own voices and worries rang all about them.

"Come with me," one that sounded like Drutha urged.

"Elyana!" She heard Cyrelle cry from somewhere to the north. "They've got me!"

"I'm going after her," she heard Grellen shout.

"Stand!" Elyana cried. "Melias, can you dispel this magic?"

"I'm trying," the girl answered timidly.

"Dispel my magic?" the voice demanded from outside their circle. "Here, in the very heart of my power?"

Laughter rang from every direction. It wasn't just the one voice, either, but a whole host of them. It sounded like there were thousands upon thousands of folk watching from the darkness.

Elyana suddenly perceived countless pairs of eyes, glowing in a circle some ten yards out—red eyes, green eyes, blue eyes, all at different heights. Some were small and set low, as if they were rodents. Others were wide apart, at the height of trees.

"Illusions and trickery," Illidian said beside her. "Had we a real sorcerer, we would better know the reality of what we face."

Melias actually sounded indignant, though her voice was touched with fear. "I'm doing the best I can."

"We should never have come in here," Drutha said, and her own dog whined.

"Should never have come," shouted a wheezing voice from behind, and then the words were tossed from high voice to low everywhere about them, growing gradually into a chant spoken by voices in every timbre, so loud that it set Elyana's bones to vibrating.

"We did not come to harm you!" Elyana shouted, though her words were lost in the blizzard of noise rising from behind those glowing eyes. "Listen!"

Still the chanting continued.

"Listen to me! We pursue a summoner and his monster. When we find him, we will leave!"

"Leave!" The voices cried. "Leave!" Again and again the words were repeated.

Elyana drew her sword. It glowed dully, a shining silver even in the impenetrable gloom. Nearby she saw another blade rise into the air. Grellen's, she thought. It too had a faint magical sheen.

The chanting dulled, faded. Still the eyes watched.

"You draw your blade here, elf?" The first voice asked, mockingly. "Whom do you mean to strike with it?"

"We are after only the summoner," Elyana replied. "His magic has ravaged our homes. Killed our people. Slain an Oaksteward."

There was no immediate response, and the shimmering orbs regarded them, unblinking.

"I have felt a human's passage through our lands," the voice said finally. "A human worker of magics. He is the summoner you seek?"

"Yes," Elyana answered.

One by one the eyes winked away until there was only one set left, a green pair a few yards before her. The darkness, too, began to ebb, so that she perceived that her group remained about her in its entirety. From out of the gloom stepped the owner of the luminous eyes, a humanoid form fashioned solely of dead leaves and branches and rotting forest detritus. Brown-gold leaves shaped a cruel smile as it advanced within striking distance and raised a hand with sticks for fingers.

"Sheathe your sword, elf," it told her.

This Elyana did, telling her people to hold position. One of the dogs whined furtively.

"We bring war only to the man we chase," Elyana said. "If you grant us passage, we will leave your woods as we found them."

"You have already disturbed my woods," the entity told her. "Offering to leave is no gift to me, for I could arrange your death in one of your heartbeats and be done with you."

"You could try."

The fey thing, whatever it was, considered her through the glowing green circles set into its leafy face. Elyana realized that the movement she saw along its brow was a crawling caterpillar.

"It may be that I can use you, elf," the thing decided, "and we may both be pleased. Serve me, and I will give you the summoner."

"Make no bargain with the fey," Illidian warned her.

She heard a low murmur from Lisette. "I thought that's what folk said about elves."

"We want the summoner, and safe passage out," Elyana said. "For all of us. And we mean to return to our own time, and land."

The fey laughed. "How great a wizard do you think me? Do you suppose I can transport you to some far off realm?"

"One hears tales," Elyana replied.

"Make no bargain, Elyana," Aladel cautioned, "until you know what it wishes in return."

"I grow weary of interruptions," the creature snapped. "Do I speak with one, or all of you?"

"You speak with me," Elyana declared. "I lead them. What do you ask in return for this bargain?"

"Your aid. An hour's march into the Wilewood is a threat I cannot face. Something evil has taken root there. If you destroy it, I will let you go free and turn your quarry over to you for disposal."

"What sort of 'evil' do you mean?" Elyana asked.

"You're hunters, are you not? Think of them as your quarry."

"Why can't you kill them?" Drelm asked.

The thing smiled at them. "It is beyond the duties of my office."

Stranger and stranger. "What is your name?" Elyana asked.

"You may call me Snowlock, if you wish. My people name me king, but I am no king of yours, and I do not wish you to be my subjects."

"Snowlock, I must consult with my people."

"You do not lead them?"

"They chose to join me on a hunt for the summoner, not for a hunt into the Wilewood for something else entirely. We must speak. Privately."

"If you wish. I will give you a quarter-hour. If you have not decided before then . . . well. You are not the only hunters in the woods." Snowlock smiled. Then, as they stared at him, the sticks and leaves collapsed into their component pieces, the leaves fluttering, the sticks thudding into the soft ground. The glowing green points of light that were his eyes flew swiftly off, winding into the distance as though they were winged beetles.

"What the hell is that thing?" Grellen demanded.

"One of the fey," Aladel answered with certainty. "Likely from the First World, the old realm where nature still rules. I have long heard it said that that plane intersected with the Wilewood. The fey's presence here may be tied to the reason the Oakstewards want all elves kept from their lands."

Lisette shook her head. "It doesn't seem like we have much choice. Really. I mean, we either go hunt his monsters, or he hunts us."

The little sorcerer cleared her throat, and then, when all eyes went to her, she cleared it again and nervously licked her lips.

"Speak up," Elyana said. "You're a member of the expedition now."

"Well," she said, then hesitated briefly. "I think a lot of what he's doing is tricks. I don't really think we were surrounded by thousands of fey. I think that was an illusion. Now, he must be a powerful caster if he can do so much to us, but . . . he's not as powerful as he seems."

"So you think we should kill him?" Drelm asked.

The girl blanched. "I'm not saying that. I'm just saying that maybe we shouldn't be as afraid of him as . . . maybe some of you are."

Cyrelle chuckled and shook her head of dark hair. "You at all serious about fighting the fey?"

"I'm not sure we can take him down," Elyana said. "I'm not sure I *want* to take him down. I just want Calvonis."

"It'd be easier to make a choice," Grellen said, "if we had some better sense of what we faced."

"I don't think we're going to get that," Elyana said. "We must decide if we want to fight him or take his offer."

"Then I say we take his offer," Lisette said darkly. "And if he betrays us, we kill him. I'm tired of talk."

"Well said," Drelm agreed. But then, he would. Elyana valued many things about Drelm, but complex decision-making was not his strong suit.

Elyana made her choice and considered her charges once more. After this, how many would be left? "I'll call him back. If there are any of you who disagree, speak now, and I'll make your freedom a condition of our bargain. You need feel no shame."

Drelm grunted skeptically.

Illidian and Aladel returned her look with ones of dour conviction.

Grellen patted his sword hilt. "We've nearly got him, now. I aim to finish the job." He glanced at Melias, standing at his shoulder, and she nodded quickly.

Cyrelle bobbed her head resignedly, and one of her hounds whimpered a little.

Drutha piped up: "I don't quit when things get challenging."

"Well," Lisette said with a tight smile. "It looks like we're all equally stupid."

"I guess so," Elyana agreed. She turned from them and called Snowlock's name.

Chapter Eleven
Champions of the Court
Drelm

Drelm didn't like the bargain they'd made with Snowlock, and while he understood its necessity, that didn't mean he enjoyed the trek deeper into the forest's dark recesses.

They followed the strange green entity into the twilight timber, where the shadows were thick. The smell of the vegetation had changed—it was wilder, fresher, *greener* somehow. Drelm really wasn't one for deep thought, or superstitions. The first he respected a little, particularly when its utility was demonstrated to him. The second merely irritated him. Some superstitions he knew to be true, but none of them changed the fact that if something was bad you should kill it. He was especially annoyed by creatures that deliberately tried to scare him. While many of his comrades grew more and more nervous about the strange sounds and the glowing eyes that appeared and disappeared along their route, Drelm just grew more and more angry.

The brown human-shaped thing that pranced ahead of Elyana claimed it was the same entity who'd spoken with them in the first place, even though it had a different smell. The voice and the manner were the same, at least.

From off to the west came a gibbering noise and a growl, then a crash of brush receding from them. Drelm showed fangs in a scowl. "What was that?"

The leafy head of their new ally turned almost completely around to look at him even as the body moved forward.

"There are many wonderful beings out there in the woods," it said, as though there were nothing at all remarkable in striding unerringly forward while you were looking to your rear. "Not all of them are my subjects."

"Were those your subjects?" Drelm asked.

"It's hard to say," the creature answered lightly, "since I did not see them." And then it turned its impossible head forward again and continued to lead the way through the dark trees.

Cyrelle sidled up beside Drelm. Her remaining six hounds slunk close beside, ears back, tails cast low.

"Does your friend know what she's doing?" Cyrelle asked quietly. Her glance toward Elyana made her meaning clear, though her words had been clear enough.

Drelm only grunted. "Always."

"Does she know the fey?"

Drelm wasn't sure what was meant by that question. "Elyana's clever."

"The fey aren't exactly known to be kind. They've got a sense of humor. They might be leading us deep into the wood to play some kind of joke. One funny to them, not to us."

"You think they plan an ambush?" Drelm asked. "They could have ambushed us back there."

"Maybe. Maybe that was all bluff, and the really dangerous forces are further in. Or maybe, like I said, it's some kind of joke."

Drelm thought briefly about that. "Suppose it is. Then what?"

"We should be careful. That's all I'm saying."

"We're ready for attacks," Drelm said, wondering why she wasted her air with the obvious. Of course they should be careful. Why wouldn't they be?

This apparently wasn't what Cyrelle wanted, for the big woman frowned and moved off. That was women, though. They always wanted more than what they told you. They might say they just wanted your opinion on dress fabric, but near as Drelm could tell, they didn't actually want an opinion. They just wanted to share their feelings.

"She's right, you know," came a gruff voice from behind. It was Grellen, with the sorcerer walking at his side. She seemed to have latched on to him as a protector. The man looked up at Drelm from under heavy eyelids. "It's some kind of trap."

"Then we'll kill some fey," Drelm said after only brief consideration.

The warrior's expression didn't really change, nor did the girl's. But then, Melias always seemed to be nervous. Drelm supposed he would be as well if he were completely useless when he wandered into a battle, hard as that was to imagine.

From the east came a long growl, then, nearer at hand, something in the shadows answered it with the strange, gibbering cry he'd heard earlier. He wondered what kind of animal was making it.

All too soon he found out. A horde of dark shapes erupted from the woods. Each was roughly humanoid, possessed of arms and legs and a torso, but all of these were wizened and warped and brown, as though they were roughly carved from tree bark.

None of them had a head.

Cyrelle's dogs barked savagely. Elyana shouted to form a circle and the front of the line fell back while the rear of the column advanced.

It was a good place for neither attack nor defense. The boles were thick and close and light was poor. Yet Drelm loved a good fight, and nothing brightened his mood like a little action. He grinned as he readied his battleaxe and stepped out to meet the mewling thing that clawed at him with misshapen limbs.

When his axe whistled down it cleaved through a dried and bony arm and sent a clawed hand spinning. His strike kept on and drove deep into the central body. The thing was not wood as he had thought, but some kind of pulpy substance and filled with foul-smelling brown ichor, like a rotten gourd. It erupted, geyserlike, and emitted a mournful hooting noise as it fell.

The things were coming from both directions. He heard the distinctive sound of a rifle shot and saw a hole blown through the one nearest him, but it didn't slow. Drelm took one of those clawed swipes against his breastplate so he could move in close, then sliced deep through the creature's body, sending it sliding apart in halves. The monster's internal fluids burst forth and spilled onto Drelm's boots.

The half-orc pivoted, for he'd heard the sound of more footfalls crushing through the underbrush. Elyana, off to the right, shouted to close ranks.

Grellen was beside him and swinging his dully glowing sword to tremendous effect. The useless sorcerer advanced behind him, brandishing the black wand and shouting different phrases. Nothing happened when she did so. Farther off, Cyrelle's hounds loped to latch onto the sticklike legs of one of their adversaries. Somewhere out of sight he heard the high-pitched shouts of Drutha in battle fury, and the explosions of her alchemical warfare.

It ended as swiftly as it had begun. The few remaining monsters faded into the woods.

Elyana gathered her people together. Cyrelle was bandaging a long scratch down one arm, and one of the dogs had a gash down her back, but that was the extent of real injuries. More than half of them had been sprayed with the beasts' blood. Fortunately, no one seemed to be suffering from any kind of ill effects, despite the smell.

While the others traded off sentinel duty and weapons checks, Drelm strode up to where Elyana stood talking with Snowlock.

"What were those?" Drelm demanded.

"I was just asking our guide the same thing," Elyana replied. Her sword hung loose in her hand, directed away from Snowlock, but Drelm knew how deceptive that stance was.

"As I said," Snowlock said in that cheery voice, "there are many beings in the Wilewood."

"Wonderful beings," Elyana corrected.

Snowlock laughed. "Those are velells. They're very agile, aren't they? But no real threat to warriors such as yourselves."

Elyana sounded unamused. "I've never heard of them. Is there anything else we should be looking for?"

"I cannot say, exactly, what you should be looking for, but I can guess that you will meet with further opposition the closer we come to the center of the wood. Where the evil dwells."

"And what will this evil be like?"

Snowlock raised a misshapen hand to his leafy face, plucked a small beetle from it, and tossed the bug away. "No one knows. The evil can command any forest creature it desires. Just as I can."

"If you can command creatures from the Wilewood," Elyana said, "why didn't you command those?"

There was no guessing what the thing's expression meant, or if it even had one. Its voice, matched roughly to moving lips, laughed nervously. "I am king, I assure you. But it is a challenge to rule such a chaotic land."

"Yet you can give us a powerful summoner?" Elyana asked.

"Oh, that's easy. Monster-fighting is hard, though. Trust me"

"Alright, Snowlock," Elyana agreed skeptically. "How much further?"

"Only a little while," he said. "Just a little while."

In another quarter-hour there was a second attack, this one from writhing plants with leafy maws. These proved simpler to drive off than the creatures Snowlock had called velells. Shortly after that, when the darkness was almost complete, they faced off against three boars that were close to the size of bears, and Lisette proved her mettle by killing one and grievously wounding another before any of them closed.

A short while later Snowlock slowed, then turned that head completely around once more. The rest of his body followed, shifting rather than turning, and he waved them forward with jointless arms that moments before had seemed to hang the other direction.

"We are nearly there," the king told them in a hushed voice. "The clearing lies before us. It's there you must do battle."

"Why there?" Elyana asked.

Snowlock sounded as though the truth were ludicrously obvious. "Because that is the place for all battles. Now you must wait, so that I may announce you."

The head started to turn.

"Wait," Elyana said. "No one needed to announce to us for the last three battles."

"That's because I was merely testing to see whether you were as mighty as I thought. I am quite pleased with your performance. Your next battle will be official."

Drelm was still sorting through the meaning of that particular statement as Snowlock started forward.

Elyana cursed through her teeth and followed, though the elf stopped at the tree line. Drelm and Illidian both came up beside her, and the rest of the group waited behind.

Snowlock stepped forward into a misty clearing that was roughly circular, where the trees ended abruptly and gave way to ankle-high grasses, intermittently visible beneath the drifting mist. Drelm had not remembered a full moon, yet it shone high and silver and especially large, filling the clearing with its light so that the ancient oak in its center seemed large around as a house, lush and green. The tree and clearing both spoke of high summer rather than the coming fall.

"The bastard sent his own men to attack us," Lisette said. She had come up alongside Drelm, although it was Elyana she addressed.

"It seems so," Elyana answered.

"Then he can't be trusted," Lisette hissed. "I say we shoot him."

"I don't think a bullet can kill him," Elyana replied. "We keep up our end."

Lisette looked none too pleased, but Drelm's eyes left her as he heard Snowlock address the empty air in front of the oak tree.

"King Woodlock, it is I, King Snowlock. I have come with my challengers. We will best your champion, for my warriors are better than your own."

Something awoke within the mist and swirled upward to face Snowlock. In moments, their strange guide faced a twisted version of himself, one whose legs and feet disappeared within the mist beneath him. As he grew more and more substantial, the mist itself faded, and the creature's body took on a green, leafy sheen. Where Snowlock was fashioned with dying and dead forest detritus, this one was formed of bright greenery and flowering vines.

"What is your wager?" Woodlock asked.

"Why, when I win, I want to begin my rule at the waning of this moon."

Woodlock laughed, his leaves shaking with the sound. "You are arrogant to believe you can win another moon's worth of days. I shall defeat you utterly and your own people will mock your misfortune."

Woodlock and Snowlock continued their exchange of insults.

Aladel sucked in a breath through his teeth. "I should have seen this."

Elyana immediately turned to him, eyes burning. "What do you know?"

"We're nearing the change of a season. The fey are intimately connected with the natural world."

"So?"

Aladel turned up his palms in a helpless gesture. "The fey may be strange, but they still follow traditions. Some of them, anyway."

"Get to the point," Elyana snapped.

Drelm agreed with her. Elves were long-winded. He sniffed the air. Woodlock and Snowlock were still debating, but things were stirring on the edges of the circle—creatures with glowing eyes that set the greenery shaking as they touched it.

Aladel grew more intent. "I've heard that, in some fey societies, when each season ends, the summer and winter courts battle to see who will rule, so that summer might last a little longer, or winter might come a little sooner."

Drelm wrinkled his brow. "The fey make the weather?"

"No," Aladel answered, "though they can sometimes affect the local climate—what I'm saying is that we're walking into something other than what we were told."

Drelm grunted. He might have said that sooner. "Snowlock lied?"

Elyana looked at the back of the strange creature fifteen feet ahead of them, then to Drelm. "*He* probably thinks the other side is evil. I don't know that this changes anything," she said to Aladel, then added, "though it clarifies the situation."

Drelm puzzled over her conclusion, for he didn't feel like the situation was clear at all. "Should we be in this fight, then? How would Abadar view this?"

Elyana's look was grave. "I can't pretend to know what any god might think. But the fey are wild creatures, like those boars. Neither good nor evil, in the strict sense. If you fear that we'll be fighting the innocent, or the just, rest easy."

This made sense to Drelm, but he muttered a prayer to Abadar to give him guidance anyway.

Snowlock and Woodlock, meanwhile, seemed to have finished their posturing.

"You will see," Snowlock raged. "Summon your people. Mine await outside the clearing."

The greener creature laughed. "Do they? Have you forgotten that they are not inviolate until they *enter* the clearing?"

Elyana cursed, and in the same breath shouted: "Forward into the clearing! Everyone—go!"

From the left rose a shrill hooting noise, and then a high-pitched scream of agony. Drelm whirled and raised his axe, already moving toward the sound.

Aladel was down. Standing over him was a hulking bearlike shape lifting blood-soaked claws. Its head was that of an immense bird, and turned sharply and machinelike to eye them before opening its maw to let out another shrieking hoot.

Grellen charged the thing, sword outstretched, and Illidian drew his own weapon.

Drelm rushed toward the beast, teeth bared in a grin. Curiously, though the monster was bearlike, feathers sheathed it. He'd never seen it's like.

The elf was down but not dead, for he moved feebly. The monster leaned over to peck savagely at Illidian, who sidestepped before landing a blow against its arm.

Drelm arrived, and his blade sliced deep through the creature's feathered flesh. He came near to slicing one arm completely through, and there was a fountain of blood. There was also another shrill blast of avian rage, and then the beak swept toward him. It slammed into his armor with the force of a sledgehammer, and he staggered back. Dully he was aware of Elyana shouting to retreat, and of a higher-pitched scream of indignation from what had to have been Snowlock, decrying that the attack wasn't fair.

The monster was apparently unconcerned with fairness, and followed Drelm as he backed away. Grellen darted in to slice the thing's leg, but the creature was so tightly focused upon Drelm it seemed not to notice.

"There's more coming!" Melias cried behind him. He also heard the now-familiar thunder of one of Lisette's muskets. The beak in front of him splintered, fully a third of it blown away.

If anything, this enraged the monster further, and Drelm was still its victim of choice. It advanced, shrilling, razor claws shining in the leaf-filtered moonlight.

And then one arrow appeared through its eye as if by magic, and a second a fraction to the right. Two more thunderous gun pops followed and the creature staggered. Drelm felt cool fingers on his arm even as Elyana bounded past, avoiding a disemboweling swipe with the ease of a dancer before driving her blade deep through the creature's vitals. She spun away from a returning blow.

Drelm saw that another of the things had indeed appeared behind the first, and was advancing on Drutha, who shouted for her dog to run.

Elyana struck again, and the beast went down. Drelm grabbed his axe and Cyrelle darted forward with Illidian to put arms under Aladel.

"Fall back," Elyana ordered.

Drelm retreated with Grellen and the sorcerer. The oncoming creature stamped after them, reaching up with one great feathered arm, but just as Drelm was readying to swing, the beast lowered the limb. The half-orc realized he'd put a foot into the clearing, and glanced right and left before baring his fangs a final time.

The thing didn't see, for it had turned its monstrous back upon him and was retreating into the woods.

Drelm quickly took stock of their new surroundings.

It looked like everyone had made it into the clearing. Elyana was bent over Aladel. Cyrelle was arranging her hounds in a line before her, and had drawn her blade. Drutha sat on her dog, a sling in one hand.

"My champions!" Snowlock stood at the clearing's center, waving impossibly elongated hands. "You must stand to present yourselves! The champion of the evil one comes!"

Snowlock indicated the tree beside him with an expansive gesture, and Drelm wondered for a moment if the tree itself were the enemy.

But then a familiar figure stepped forth from the shadow of the tree. Under the brilliant moonlight there was no mistaking the broad-shouldered, lanky form and dark gleam of the helmet he wore.

Calvonis.

Chapter Twelve
First Blood
Lisette

Calvonis held his head high and thrust back his shoulders, smirking at them.

Lisette wished that the stupid fey would announce the start of the battle, or sound a horn, or whatever it was they were going to do, because she had her rifle loaded and could raise it to her shoulder in half a breath. The problem of Calvonis would then be over, and Drelm would surely be dead shortly thereafter. From what Lisette had seen, if she hadn't been there to save the half-orc, he'd have been dead or critically wounded two or three times during the journey already.

"That's your champion?" Snowlock capered back and forth upon two spindly branchlike legs. "You will see no more of this moon, let alone one to follow!"

"But this is not my champion," Woodlock cried, exultant. "This is my servant. As I have told you. None in the woods must harm him lest they face my wrath. He commands my champion. Your champions must fight the creature that he conjures, not him." Woodlock actually giggled a little, as if he were a child playing a trick. He waved his leafy hands and his voice rolled down to them.

"This is how it is done, champions of Snowlock. I shall conjure a mist, a curtain. While you make your preparations for a hundred count, the other champion does so as well. The moment the curtain drops, the battle begins. Any champion who leaves the circle, dies. Any champion who attacks someone outside the circle, dies. Whoever is left standing at the end, lives. The rules are simple."

Grellen cursed a blue streak.

"Are there any questions?" Woodlock asked.

"I have one." Calvonis's voice was smooth. Amused. Lisette wished dearly that she could blast him immediately.

"Speak then, my servant."

Calvonis bowed his head to the fey lord. "I was wondering, noble king: If any of Snowlock's champions wish to swear allegiance to me and pray to the glory of Razmir, the living god, might they fight at my side?"

"That's perfectly fine with me," Woodlock said amiably. "Do any of you wish to switch your allegiance?"

The curses that rose from Lisette's side didn't entirely surprise her, although she was astonished by the colorful wording of the halfling's declaration. From everything she'd seen of the little alchemist so far, she was nearly as polite as the half-orc.

Lisette didn't reply herself because she knew Calvonis meant only to amuse himself. She didn't understand the whole Razmir angle, but didn't really care, for she had an idea.

"Your pardon, King Woodlock." Lisette's voice was pure sweetness and light. "I have a question of clarification."

"Speak, then," Woodlock commanded with great aplomb.

"None of you had best contemplate betrayal!" Snowlock's head had swiveled around to face them, eyes aglow. "I will be very, very angry."

Lisette ignored him. "I have two questions, King Woodlock. First, are only champions bound by the laws of this match?"

"Champions and kings are bound by the laws, and must keep this space inviolate."

"My second question, O King, is this: if we are still free to switch our allegiance, does that mean we are not yet champions?"

This seemed to puzzle Woodlock, whose reply was hesitant. "I do not completely follow you."

"Well, surely a champion could not switch allegiance once the battle began. So we must not be champions yet, until the battle starts."

"I suppose," Woodlock admitted, "that you are correct, because while some have switched sides in the past before a battle, it is forbidden to do so once the curtain has gone up."

"Interesting," said Lisette, and snapped her rifle to her shoulder.

Calvonis's eyes bugged, and she had the satisfaction of seeing him frantically leap to the left.

The bullet that should have taken the summoner in the chest took him in the shoulder instead, and he spun and dropped. Lisette brought up her pistol as she started forward at a run.

"She cheated!" Woodlock cried. "She cheated!"

But Snowlock crowed in victory. "She did not! She was not yet champion, and you said he wasn't a champion at all! Oh, the cleverness!"

Before Lisette could cross the distance a thick curtain of mist rose before her. She paused in mid-stride and stepped back, fearful of coming upon the beast all on her own.

"Get back!" Elyana warned.

And Lisette did so, wondering when the hundred count would start. She passed where Snowlock had stood and saw only a few leaves drifting down beside a little pile of sticks.

Drelm came up and patted her shoulder, laughing as she reloaded her rifle. That just incensed her further.

"That should slow him down," the half-orc said.

"I meant to slow him down forever."

Elyana, meanwhile, arranged her troops, barking orders like a mercenary sergeant.

Aladel was up and moving, if stiffly, and had his bow ready. The moonlight rendered everything in blacks and grays, but even so he seemed a little wan.

Elyana spoke quickly about Drelm and Grellen attacking on different flanks, but Lisette wondered if it would amount to anything. The summoner was whittling them down, and he had certainly carried himself like someone well rested. If only she'd had her second rifle ready! Karag would have handed it right up and she could have blown the summoner's head off even as the mist dropped.

But that rifle was ruined now, impossibly expensive to replace. And Karag was dead. He'd grown into an incredible pain in the ass, but he'd gotten so efficient with his reloads she'd begun to take for granted her ability to fire in rapid succession. He'd been so very good at disposing of bodies, and preserving the evidence, as he'd always preferred to describe keeping heads or other body parts stored for clients.

Calvonis had taken something very important to her, and she meant to make him pay.

As Lisette finished checking over her weapons, she loosed her longsword. She remained a good blade, though she had no intention of going shoulder to shoulder with that hulking invisible monster.

Once she was through with her weapons she fell back beside Illidian and Aladel, who'd taken position on the best high ground available, a little mound. Both knelt amid arrow shafts thrust into the earth, as though praying in a peculiar garden. Lisette took her space to the right of Illidian and lay down her powder horn, musket balls, and rammer one after the other, just below her pistols.

Illidian's eyes were narrowed, cruel, but his mouth ticked up slightly as he looked her direction.

"Now we both have blood to avenge," he told her. "Let it be that we both find satisfaction this day."

"I'm leaving prayer to the orc," she replied.

"Half-orc," Aladel corrected quietly. He did not seem to notice the frown she gave in response.

Lisette adjusted her hat and surveyed the field. All was quiet, save for the girl, Melias. Elyana had finally found something useful for the sorcerer to do; the girl was counting down from one hundred, slowly. She had reached thirty. From the surrounding trees, thousands upon thousands of eyes shone in the moonlight. A fair number of them glowed.

She tried to ignore them. "What's your plan?" Lisette asked Illidian.

"I mean to drive arrows through every inch of the thing's face."

"Then pray," Aladel said, quietly, "that the halfling's strikes do the trick this time. Or ask it of Drelm."

Melias arrived at fifteen.

"I gave up on prayer," Lisette said. "It's up to me to keep my powder dry, isn't it?"

The dark-garbed elf favored her with a sad smile. "Any control is temporary, or illusory, save that over your own state of mind."

Damned elves. Illidian was the only one she really understood.

Melias arrived at ten.

The warriors crept forward, Grellen to right, Drelm to left. Elyana stood at the side of Drutha, still seated on her dog, the halfling's sling heavy with one of her three remaining glass containers. She'd told them earlier in the day that the beast's attack had shattered almost half her supply.

Elyana's arrow was nocked but not quite raised, and a flaming brand was driven into the ground beside her. With but a dip of her hand she would be able to light the cloth tied about the shaft of the arrow, or reach for the other two likewise banded with cloth, which she'd planted in the ground beside her.

Melias reached five.

Cyrelle stood a little forward of Elyana, her dogs arranged in a spearpoint before her. No longer did they seem frightened. Their ears were erect, their noses pointed toward the mist. The hounds' woman shushed two of them as they began to growl.

Melias reached one, then zero, and stopped her count.

Yet the mist remained. Unintentionally, Lisette found herself counting forward, wondering if the fey folk had a different counting scale. She reached up to seat her hat more firmly on the crown of her head.

"What are they playing at?" Illidian asked.

Lisette wondered at the peculiar grating noise, then saw it was Illidian's hook rubbing against his bow.

At that moment the mist dropped. Lisette saw nothing that lay beyond it, but she snapped up her rifle as both elves raised their bows.

"Hunt!" Cyrelle shouted, and her dogs were off like a bowshot. They ran to the left barking, and the pattern they formed around the target showed the shape of the beast as it advanced on the circle's far edge.

Lisette and the elves swung their aim north toward the invisible creature. An unseen limb lashed out and sent one dog broken through the air. It landed, whimpering, with a thud, but the monster's path was revealed, and Drutha was already launching her first glass globe into the center of the space defined by Cyrelle's dog pack. It splashed out against a scaly hide, burning and smoking, and Elyana sent a burning arrow into the discolored midst.

Her aim was precise, and soon an entire horse-sized section of the creature was a visible, flaming red mass.

"Fire at will!" Elyana screamed.

The red wall of fire turned even as the halfling flung a second globe. This one missed, sending up a cloud of hissing steam to the creature's left. Lisette heard the halfling curse as she readied a final globe. Elyana and Aladel fired steadily but Illidian, like Lisette, waited.

"I want to see its face," Illidian told her.

The ground was shaking, and the flaming portion of the monster's side closed to fifteen yards as it stamped toward their position.

Drutha's third globe soared into the air and splashed across a long, broad, snakelike head, and Elyana's following arrow set that face aflame. The beast slowed, shaking its head from side to side, and Illidian launched his attack, arrow after arrow flying forward. Each one sank near the scaly maw, now twisting madly from right to left.

Lisette frowned. This was fine and well if you were just trying to hit the beast, but she needed it to stand still so she could shoot it through its eye.

"Now!" Drelm cried, and, axe raised, charged out and away from the beast. Grellen mirrored his course on the left, swinging wide before driving back in to avoid the thing's unseen tentacles.

It would be very easy to fire now, take Drelm in the back of the head, and claim it was an accident. But Lisette was veteran enough to know the battle was not yet won, and that Drelm was a tremendous asset so long as they were in the thick of the fight. She aimed her barrel toward the flaming head, saw it rising. The beast was opening its mouth to spray.

Illidian called out a warning to Elyana, and the elf and Drutha dashed to the right, Elyana throwing herself to the ground in advance of the halfling's racing mount. The spray seared the ground only a yard from Aladel, who returned a gleaming arrow that lodged in the creature's jaw. As the monster roared, Lisette finally saw the outline of an eye socket betrayed by Drutha's chemical attack. She fired.

The monster's roar choked off, and Lisette let out a little cry of victory. Rather than race forward to wield either pistol, she bent to reload the gun.

Drelm, meanwhile, chopped repeatedly into the monster's side with his axe. Grellen, a few steps behind, was whipped aside by something—the monster's tail, perhaps—and tumbled out into the moonlight.

Another unseen force buffeted Elyana aside, then whisked Drutha and her dog into the air, the pair screaming and whining as they hurtled to the right. They bounced with a cracking of bones and gear.

Through this all, Illidian and Aladel kept up a steady flight of arrows. Cyrelle's dogs had fastened on one stumplike leg and sent blood streaming, and Cyrelle herself was hacking at that forelimb with her sword. Grellen had pulled himself back up and joined her.

Melias seemed content with waving her wand and shouting odd phrases, like a child playacting.

They'd done a lot of damage, and fire continued to eat away at the beast's side and head. The creature was stamping frantically to left and right, perhaps in an effort to put out the flames, and Lisette put off waiting for the perfect shot and fired any time she was certain she'd strike the head.

Beside her, Illidian muttered low under his breath. He and Aladel were down to a handful of arrows. Elyana might have been completely out, for she was dashing forward, sword drawn.

That's when a blinding flash of light burned on the right. Lisette cursed foully and shielded her eyes.

"Stop this at once!" a bold, male voice demanded. "Kings of the Wilewood! Step forth!"

Still Lisette could barely see, but through slitted lids she could make out three robed figures amid the glare, each holding a staff.

The command continued to ring out, echoing as if it reflected from cavern walls.

"It's the Oakstewards," Aladel said, voice dulled in wonder.

"No elves are permitted within the Wilewood," announced a female voice, just as stern. "You know this, yet you have permitted their presence!"

Lisette's vision cleared at last. She now saw why the rest of her group wasn't still beating on the monster: the damned thing had vanished completely, along with the flame that had engulfed it. Arrows that had stood out from its body now littered the forest floor.

Woodlock and Snowlock rose in a swirl of plants and leaves littering the clearing and stepped up to the three robed interlopers standing near the oak.

Elyana shouted for Cyrelle and Illidian to check Drutha and hurried to where Grellen struggled to rise.

The glare faded, and as Illidian rushed toward the dead or dying halfling, Lisette studied the three figures. Their voices were no longer being cast wide for all to hear, but sounds of outrage rose from the fey kings. Muttering and calls could be heard likewise from the dark of the surrounding trees. Lisette picked up the words "exception" and "trespass" and "sacred" among the complaints.

"What's going on?" Lisette worked quickly to reload, starting with her rifle.

"Those are almost assuredly Oakstewards," Aladel answered, his gaze focused on the strange trio. "The druids who rule Sevenarches. I didn't know they held so much sway with the folk of the Wilewood."

"Does this mean the challenge is over? Can I shoot Calvonis?"

"We'd best not leave the ring to look for him," Aladel warned.

Lisette finished loading her rifle, then strode up to join the conversation.

There were three Oakstewards: a matronly woman with red hair; a younger, pudgy bald man with a thick rust-brown beard; and their leader, tall and stern with a short gray beard.

Both of the fey kings were aghast that anyone would interfere with their competition, but the Oakstewards were adamant that a sacred trust had been broken the moment the fey permitted an elf within their lands.

"What about us, then?" Lisette asked, one hand on her pistol butt. "We agreed to fight for this king, and we were winning. How are you going to square that?"

The tall leader shifted his gaze to take in Lisette.

"Who are you, who does not know that elves are forbidden within any portion of Sevenarches?"

"We're what's left of the group chasing the beast murdering folks across the River Kingdoms. And you Oakstewards should know all about it, because you sent one of yours along with us."

All three of the Oakstewards were staring at her now, and the two fey kings had fallen completely silent.

"You are of the group stalking the beast?" the leader asked. "Where is our brother, then?"

"He's dead." Lisette felt a surge of pleasure at the dismay that spread over the faces of the three she faced.

Elyana stepped up to her side, her hair unbound and windblown, a bloodied hand resting on the pommel of her sword. The moon reflected in her eyes, and in its light she looked carved of silver and shadows.

"I am Elyana Sadrastis," she said with a queen's dignity, "and I speak for us. Who are you?"

The elder druid answered her haughtily. "I am Kilvor Edegren, head steward of the Eastern Reach. Do you know what you've done?"

Lisette saw the elven woman's eyes narrow. "I have led a team of warriors after the summoner behind the attacks upon the River Kingdoms. It's you who fail to see what you've done."

"And what is that?" Kilvor demanded.

"The champion of King Woodlock is the summoner who controls the beast. We were winning the fight with him."

The redhead indicated Lisette with a bob of the staff she carried. "This woman says one of ours was slain by the summoner."

"Yes," Elyana replied. "We were betrayed from within before we crossed the border."

Kilvor's frown deepened. "Elves are forbidden in these lands. All know it."

"So I've heard," Elyana snapped. "But the monster's summoner is here, now. Have these fey turn him over, that we may have justice."

"That I will not do!" Woodlock said, and his eerie head pivoted, neckless, to regard Elyana with burning eyes. "He controls my champion, and is inviolate except upon the field of combat!"

"We weren't inviolate until we reached the field of combat," Lisette pointed out. She forced a smile when the glowing eyes turned upon her, for it seemed then she could feel their burning malevolence.

Kilvor addressed her, his voice a modicum less stern. "You cannot trust the bargains of those from the First World. Their understanding is . . . different from our own."

"We bargained in good faith." Elyana pointed to Kilvor. "If you wish us to leave the Wilewood, we shall do so. But so too should the summoner, so that both kings must find a new champion."

Lisette thought that a clever point. It set both fey kings arguing with one another so that they seemed once again more like children than deadly and capricious monsters.

"You admit you knew you weren't welcome here," the redheaded Oaksteward said to Elyana. "And yet you came."

Elyana's jaw clenched, and it took a moment for her to answer. "I know you don't mean to sound thick, so maybe you don't understand. I've lost six members of my expedition to that bastard, and scores of innocents have perished because of him. He was heading into the Wilewood, so I followed."

"What's so special about the border anyway?" Lisette asked.

"That's none of your concern," Kilvor snapped. "And your interference in this matter has made things worse. I will speak to the kings. Please await me apart from us."

Lisette looked to Elyana, who sketched a half-formal bow and retreated. Lisette followed.

"That bit about both champions being released was a fine point," Lisette told her.

"We'll see if it makes any difference."

The rest of their group waited for them. Three bodies lay in a row on the sward; two more of Cyrelle's hounds, and Drutha. Lisette was surprised to feel a cold shock at sight of her body. She supposed that she'd liked the halfling woman.

"I managed to save her dog," Elyana said coolly, "and another of Cyrelle's. But there was nothing I could do for her." Though there was no change of expression, her voice softened. "I liked her."

Illidian all but gnashed his teeth in fury as Elyana caught him up on events. Lisette kept her eyes on the three Oakstewards and the two fey kings, deep in talk.

This, she thought, was a damnable job. One of the worst she'd ever signed on for. The kind of job that had inspired her to leave the Black Coil to start with. She'd been a damned fool to take it on.

Kilvor remained in conversation with the two fey kings, but the other Oakstewards walked down from the tree to join the expedition, the hems of their long dark robes trailing after.

The pudgy druid set his staff into the ground, then bowed his head in turn at Elyana, Lisette, and Illidian. "We are making arrangements," he told them. "But negotiations with the fey are difficult."

His companion, the redheaded woman, just couldn't hold off saying more. "You should not have come here. You should immediately have consulted with the Oakstewards."

"Shut up, woman," Lisette snapped.

Elyana shushed her as the woman's expression soured further.

"There was no time to waste finding you," Elyana explained coolly.

"You should have made the time," the woman insisted. "And what possessed you to make any kind of agreement with the fey?"

"A moment's peace, sister," the man urged. "I am Hindreck, and this is Shalon, and we can tend to your injuries, if you have any."

Elyana bowed her head briefly in acknowledgment. "I am a fair healer, but some of my group are wounded. Illidian, would you take Hindreck to Aladel and Grellen? And have Cyrelle show him the dogs."

Illidian nodded once. "This way."

Hindreck headed off. Shalon remained, frowning.

"Did we hurt you personally?" Lisette asked her. "Killing the monster's more important than your customs."

"They're not customs," the woman retorted, "they're laws!" Her gaze turned once more to Elyana. "Do we traipse into Kyonin, then ask for your permission?"

"I'm not from Kyonin," Elyana said simply.

"So this is revenge," Lisette said to the druid, "for the elves not letting you into Kyonin?"

Shalon exploded with fury. "This isn't your affair! None of you should be here, not in the Wilewood. And no elves!"

In her weird way, the redhead was like one of those society matrons Lisette used to know in Cheliax, whose noses went all out of joint any time someone dared alter a color scheme from the prescribed ball decorations. She was a creature of orders and laws for their own sake and might not even understand the intent behind them.

Fortunately, they were saved the need for further comment when the fey kings turned and Snowlock called for attention.

Kilvor waited to one side, his hands folded over one another on the middle of his oaken staff.

Both kings spoke at once with the same words, their voices identical save that one was lush and vibrant, the other brittle and cold.

"Subjects, we kings have decided that this contest was a draw. All champions are to be released from their bargains with us, and new champions will be chosen. Former champions and their masters are guests of the Wilewood and are not to be interfered with, but must leave at their earliest convenience. So speak we, the kings of the Wilewood."

The two strange beings then dissolved once more into detritus, and the air was filled with the chirruping of insects.

The fey who had watched from the circle's edges, and the kings themselves, were gone. Somehow, that was more unsettling than anything else Lisette had witnessed this evening.

"Where's the summoner?" Elyana demanded of Kilvor.

"That's not your concern," Shalon snapped. She looked as though she planned more, but swifter than Lisette could draw breath, Elyana snatched the woman's collar and drew her close to the blade of her gleaming knife. Lisette hadn't even seen the elf pull it, and was stunned by both the speed and the sense that the elf had snapped. Until then she'd assumed Elyana was one of those who kept razor-sharp control, even when pushed to the edge.

"You damned well know it's my concern now, don't you?" Elyana asked.

Lisette laughed at the madness of the situation. She didn't know what would happen next, but she raised her pistol.

"Unhand her!" Kilvor roared. He hurried toward them, staff raised as if he meant to call down lightning.

Elyana shoved Shalon away and stood with narrowed eyes. "That thing's killed almost half my party. We had it wounded, and by the terms of the fey contract, it could not withdraw." Her voice rose to a roar. "And you set its master free! Where's the summoner now, Oaksteward?"

If looks could have killed, Elyana would have dropped dead from the venom in Shalon's eyes.

"King Woodlock has given him safe conduct to the western edge of the Wilewood," Kilvor declared, "and will not disclose to me where he will go. But I shall have all of the Oakstewards and other resources at my disposal watching for him."

"And us," Elyana said. "You will take us to the western edge of the Wilewood."

"That I cannot do. But I can I transport all elves to the western border of Sevenarches. Immediately."

"You're a damned fool," Elyana told him.

"I'm sorry you think so. You will keep your hands, and your weapons, from my people."

"Take us, then," Elyana said, not so much a request as an order.

"If that is what you wish."

"What I wish—" Elyana began, baring her teeth, and then fell silent. "What I wish does not bear repeating." She slammed her knife home in its sheath.

Chapter Thirteen
Helping Hands
Elyana

She had not meant to care. Not this time. Casualties had been certain. Yet she had not expected so many, and as if to drive the knife into the wound, she counted the bedrolls as they were spread that evening. So few were left.

A huddle of tents lay a few yards to the right. The Oakstewards had a blazing fire, and six of them now sat beside the dancing flames. A seventh, Shalon, stood apart, watching the expedition. Elyana could feel the woman's ire like a tremor through the earth.

The polite course of action would have been to turn away, but Elyana bared her teeth and stared harder. Sheer willpower had stayed her hand when the Oakstewards arrived. The monster had been weakening, and in a few more minutes she was sure they could have brought it down. Then Calvonis would have been hers.

But because of the high-handed Oakstewards, all the injuries and deaths had been for nothing.

The Oakstewards had used their magic to transport them to the crumbling walls of an old outpost just beyond the border of Sevenarches, where they'd erected this camp and fed her people, though Elyana had refused their aid for herself. The druids claimed they would deal with the summoner as he rode west from the Wilewood. Miles of open ground lay between the edge of the Wilewood and the western border of the Oaksteward's domain, and the druids assured her the summoner could not possibly escape their seasoned experts.

Elyana turned as Shalon finally looked away. She considered the camp. Drutha's dog, Emblid, now saddleless, lay near to but apart from Cyrelle's pack, somberly restive. Elyana's people had thrown down their bags along one of five long wall segments left of the old outpost, near what must once have been a flying buttress. One arch still rose grandly, breaking off in mid span.

She walked past the silent members of her group sitting beside the dying fire in the chill breeze. Fall would come in hard this year, with winter on its heels, and its fingers lay hands against the spines of her comrades. They were hunched close, those few who remained, where before they had been apart. Not even the elves had bothered with their tents.

Only Cyrelle sat alone, a few lance-lengths out, on an oddly shaped boulder, her hawk on her gloved wrist. She was feeding the animal little bits of dried flesh, which it leveraged with its little beak to better swallow.

"Balok seems hungry tonight," Elyana observed softly.

"It's been a long day," Cyrelle answered.

That it had. It was hard to believe they had come so far. That with the morning Drutha and Galarias and Karag had been alive. Back then, what seemed a hundred years ago, Calvonis had seemed their ally, and she would have risked her life to preserve him. Now there was no man in the world she would rather see dead.

Cyrelle reached into a little leather pouch and offered up another wet strand of meat to the hawk. "Do you ever wish we were like them?"

Elyana felt as though she had missed something. "Like who?"

"The animals. They just *are*. Balok here doesn't worry if some other bird's not really telling the truth, or is plotting against him. All he has to do is get enough food to eat."

"I suppose so," Elyana replied.

"What would that be like, do you think?"

Elyana reflected for only a moment. "Most people I know who live in the moment, the way Balok does, are evil."

Cyrelle looked up slowly.

"They don't care about anyone else, only what they need at that time."

"You think that's the way Calvonis is?"

Elyana shook her head. "No."

"So why do you think he's done all this?"

"I've seen his type before. They always believe they're special. Better than the rest of us by dint of their money, or knowledge, or race or sex. And they want everyone to know it."

"You think that's why he's killing all these people?"

"Oh, it's more complicated than that, but if you strip away the layers of justification, I can just about guarantee it. You heard him this evening. He's thrown in with the Razmiri. They think they've got a lock on the religious truth, and are damned well sure they can make everyone else listen up. At swordpoint."

"You aim to take on the Razmiri, too?"

Elyana caught the hint of rebuke in the huntswoman's tone, and looked down at that broad, homely face. "No. Just Calvonis. He's the only one I want."

Cyrelle nodded sagely. "You know it doesn't matter who kills the man, don't you? So long as he and the beast are dead?"

"I want to know why he's done this."

"I thought you just told me you figured that out."

Elyana nodded. "But I want the specifics. And I'll be damned if I want to give the druids the satisfaction . . ." she felt her anger gathering, and tightened her sword hand into a fist before knocking it against the pommel of her sword.

Cyrelle lowered her wrist and Balok hopped down onto a small brown blanket that the huntswoman had spread for him. He preened his feathers. She then stood, tall enough that she could levelly meet Elyana's gaze.

"Elyana, I like you. You know that. You're a fine ranger, and you're probably the best horse trainer I've ever met."

"But?" Elyana prompted.

"But I don't see how you've lasted as long as you have. How old are you, anyway? Never mind, it's not polite, I know. I've seen some young elves, and you aren't one of them. I figure you're at least a hundred and fifty."

Elyana watched as the woman sighed. Cyrelle's voice grew wistful. "My father used to tell me that anger is a fire that burns from within. You let it stoke you too quickly. Seems to me maybe you knew the deal we made with the fey was sour to start with, and maybe that's why you drew the knife on Shalon."

"I drew the knife to shut her up."

Cyrelle chuckled. "Well, she surely needed shutting up. But you've got to know it wasn't the proper way."

Elyana nodded slowly.

"So what if the Oakstewards get the summoner?" Cyrelle prompted. "So what if you never know why he's done all this? He'll be dead, and that's what all of us want."

Elyana knew the woman was right, but could scarce stomach the thought of someone else bringing Calvonis to justice.

"This may be better," Cyrelle pressed on. "If a force of these druids is mustered against Calvonis, who's already weak, what hope does he have? Who's to say how close we really were to killing the monster, or whether the fey really would have turned him over if we'd won?"

Elyana frowned. She'd been unwilling to admit this possibility to herself, but it had been a real one.

Cyrelle stepped closer, voice low. "I know you want to make sure Drelm's secure in his life here before you move on."

Elyana started. "How did you know that?

"It's easy. You've nothing holding you in Delgar but Drelm. And Lady Pharasma will come for him long before you even gray. I've had some elf friends before. I know how you think when you get close to us short-lived types. You aim to watch out for our futures."

Elyana sighed.

"You should be happy, then. The Oakstewards will kill the summoner. The monster will be dead, and us—look at us—we won't have to face it again. We're just about whipped, Elyana."

"We just need rest."

"We need some luck, not just some rest. How many times has Drelm almost died?" Cyrelle shook her head. "His number's about up. Let the druids get Calvonis. And then Drelm can get back to his little bird and raise a nest of hatchlings."

Elyana breathed out slowly. "That's what should be important. No—that's what *is* important." She didn't add that she still wanted to see the light go out from the summoner's eyes. Or that she wanted to beat the Oakstewards with their own staves.

"Well, get some rest. It's hard seeing those you're leading fall. It isn't easy, leading dogs *or* men."

Elyana nodded once more and composed herself. "Thank you, Cyrelle."

"No problem. You get some rest. The gods know you've earned it."

"Haven't we all." Elyana retreated to her bedroll, but though she was tired, she couldn't sleep. Somewhere in the darkness was the Wilewood, and somewhere west of it was the summoner. She envied the rest of her expedition as she heard their snores rising, and wondered if the real reason she couldn't let the matter go was because she didn't like to lose.

She was still staring up at the stars when a horse galloped in. Instantly Elyana was out of the bedroll and thrusting her feet into boots. Before she'd even buckled on her sword, she heard the Oaksteward sentry challenge the newcomer. Her keen eyesight picked him out in the darkness as he breathlessly threw himself off of his horse, asked for Kilvor, then hurried to the lead druid's tent. Most of the rest of the Oakstewards had retired to their own tents, although Shalon and two others stood watch.

Of Elyana's group, only Lisette seemed still to be awake, and she had crept up to Elyana's side to watch with her.

"What do you think that means?" the bounty hunter asked.

"Something about Calvonis," Elyana replied softly.

"You think they've lost him?"

It was nice to hear that possessive tone in someone else's voice. "I think we should find out. Because I'm not sure they're planning to tell us."

"What do you have in mind?"

"We're going to go listen in."

Lisette's mouth curled into a dangerous smile. "That suits me."

While the markswoman retreated to grab her gear, Elyana quickly took her own, then worked her way over to Drelm. She had all but completely pushed her worries about Lisette aside. They resurfaced briefly now, but with Lisette long since having proven herself, she ignored them.

Normally it was easy to wake the half-orc, but that night, merely touching his shoulder didn't do the trick. He was even more weary than Elyana had supposed, and she felt a pang of guilt at having to rouse him from his sleep. She shook him, harder. The snores faltered but did not abate.

Strange.

Elyana slid over to Illidian and found him even less responsive. By the time she'd moved on to Aladel she'd grown truly suspicious. Neither was dead, but their sleep was entirely too deep.

Lisette joined her at the second elf's shoulder. "What are you doing?"

"I can't rouse any of them," Elyana whispered.

"Do you think Calvonis cast a spell?"

Elyana had mulled that possibility over, but she had a deeper suspicion. "Did you eat any of the Oakstewards' food?"

"No." Lisette came to the same conclusion instantly. "You think the bastards drugged us?"

"Yes," Elyana said.

"Why?"

"Let's see if we can find out." Elyana pushed down the rage she felt building and motioned Lisette after her. Soon the two women were crawling slowly, expertly, through the grasses.

She passed only a few meters beyond Shalon and bit down a curse as the messenger stepped from the tent and made his way over to the Oakstewards' fire. In the three-foot-high grasses, she and Lisette were almost invisible, and the man didn't see them. What point in listening now, when the message had already been delivered?

Elyana almost gave up, but then she heard voices from inside.

She crawled slowly forward until she and Lisette were within a few feet of the tent, close enough to see the shifting shadow of a bearded man thrown upon the canvas. Kilvor, she thought, and recognized his voice.

". . . no further help," Kilvor was saying. "We managed to get the fey to assist us, briefly, but their attention wandered back to their seasonal ceremonies."

"You were our best hope for them," a second male voice said, although Elyana saw no other shadow. Some kind of communication spell?

"You cannot entice them?" the unfamiliar voice asked.

"With promises of what? They're back to playing their strange games in their wood. They have no reason to aid us."

"What about the little force you escorted?"

"They're bone weary," Kilvor said. "And I'm not sure how far to trust them. Their leader is . . . governed by her emotions."

Elyana's lip curled. She would show him emotions.

"Is there any sign of the plague among the elves?"

Plague? What had she stumbled upon now?

"Nothing," Kilvor assented. "I led them from our lands as swiftly as I was able. I've drugged enough of them so they'll be too tired to move for the next day, so we should be able to observe them through the danger period."

Elyana felt as though she'd been dealt a physical blow. They'd been exposed to some kind of plague and the Oaksteward's hadn't bothered to tell them?

"Do you have any idea where the summoner has gone?" Kilvor asked.

"We tracked him briefly as he left the Wilewood," the echoing voice responded. "But I am sorry, brother. He slipped away."

"If he has any sense," Kilvor said, "he'll ride for the border directly."

So the Oakstewards were not only liars, they were bunglers.

Behind her there was a rustle of grass, and then a thud. Kilvor and the other were still talking, but Elyana turned to find Shalon standing with her staff, looking down into the grasses a few feet off. She had found Lisette.

"I have my night eyes," she said, sternly. "And you won't be wriggling loose from that spell any time soon. I think we'd best have a word—"

Elyana did not reason. She shot to her feet and rushed. Never, she'd learned, give a spellcaster time to react.

The druid saw her a moment too late, stopping in mid-sentence and attempting to bring up her staff. The woman's breath left her body in an explosive gasp as Elyana slammed into her, and in a moment the elf wrestled her down into the grass. The druid, dazed, still managed to smack the back of Elyana's head with the staff. It was a good knock, but Elyana gritted her teeth and pushed her knife blade to the woman's throat.

"Whatever you try next might work," Elyana whispered, "but I guarantee you'll be bleeding anyway. A lot. So I suggest you start talking."

"You wouldn't kill me," Shalon said quietly. Defiantly. "I have weighed your heart."

"I don't know, druid. Your Kilvor says I'm emotionally unstable. What do you think? I understand there's a plague, and that you've drugged us to make sure we're well before we leave. What do you plan if we're not well?"

The woman's eyes flared. "You won't," she said, but now she sounded less certain.

"Do you really want to try me on that? Release Lisette."

"Her spell will fade in time."

Elyana pressed the blade tighter to the skin and felt it give, making a shallow cut. The druid flinched beneath her. "Talk."

"There's a plague in Sevenarches," Shalon said softly, "but it strikes only elves. It has no cure."

"And you've told no one?"

"We wish no one to become alarmed."

"Instead you just piss off everyone with your high-handedness."

The druid did not reply.

"And what do you do with those who sicken?" Elyana demanded.

"Make them as comfortable as possible."

"But you don't say anything? To their relatives, or friends?"

The woman didn't answer.

Elyana pulled back, yanked the woman's staff from her hand, and pitched it out into the grass.

"Get away from me," Elyana said, and climbed to her feet. Shalon stalked off to retrieve her staff. Elyana stepped to

Lisette, who lay facedown with grass wrapped about her ankles, arms, and waist.

The grass reached up for Elyana as she neared, but the elf made quick work of it, chopping the dark blades down to size while Lisette fought to her knees against the grasping vegetation. By the time Elyana had the bounty hunter extricated, Shalon had summoned Kilvor from the tent and returned. The druid regarded them sourly, his arms folded over his chest.

Elyana sheathed her sword. "So you sabotage my mission and drug my people when you say you'll heal them."

"It is necessary, for my people."

"We're on the border of your lands, druid. I need not obey you. I would move my camp, save my folk are apparently drugged. Tell me: how will you stop me from spreading word of this plague?"

Kilvor shot a look at Shalon, then considered Elyana. "I would prevail upon your good nature."

Elyana laughed shortly. "It strikes me that if you really wanted to do the right thing, you would warn people away rather than trying to suppress the information."

Kilvor sounded tired. "You presume reasonable people. Suppose that some come seeking a way to fight Kyonin, and export the plague? Suppose Kyonin were to investigate? There might be war—or worse, the spread of the plague."

"So you've decided for everyone else. If we were already exposed, did it not occur to you to give us a few more minutes to fight the summoner's beast?"

"My duty," Kilvor said, "is to keep peace between the fey and the rest of Sevenarches, and to escort all elves to the border. I do not make policy. I enforce it."

"You do as you're told," Elyana said, and almost spat. "A great deal of evil is done in this world by people who claim they merely do what they're told."

"A greater deal is done by those who will not follow the laws. Now, for your sake—for the sake of all elves—I think it best if you let us observe you for another twelve hours. But on your own head be it." Kilvor turned and ducked low as he cast the tent flap aside. Elyana saw no one else within, confirming her guess that earlier she'd been listening in on some kind of magical conference between him a distant colleague.

They were left with the glowering redhead. Blood still trickled from the wound upon Shalon's neck, and, seeing the track of Elyana's eyes, she lifted a finger there.

"You do this to those who try to shield you?" the woman said.

"You're lucky she didn't do worse," Lisette snapped.

The druid's mouth tightened, and she walked away.

Elyana stepped up to Lisette and they walked down the hillside toward their own camp.

Elyana stood looking down at her team in the bedrolls.

"What do you want to do?" Lisette asked.

From the edge in her voice Elyana knew the markswoman was still itching for a fight.

"What I want to do is different from what we can do," Elyana said. "A real healer could cure them."

"But you can't."

"No. So we two will have to trade watches."

Lisette nodded. "And how much do you want to tell the others?"

Furious as she was with the Oakstewards and their methods, she found herself understanding their reasoning, if not all of their actions. She mouthed a curse. "Let's just keep that between us. For now."

"Sure," Lisette answered. "For now."

Chapter Fourteen
Glory of Razmir
Drelm

Drelm dreamt of a misty lakeshore where he walked with his mother. She seemed impossibly tall and very sad, and when he tried to ask her why, she seemed not to hear, but clutched his hand tighter. He didn't see her face. He could never remember her face, even in dreams.

An otherworldly call came from somewhere out in the water, and he knew immediately that it was Daylah. As was the way with dreams, he found himself alone on the shore and fully grown, with his mother gone, and thought nothing of it. He called back to Daylah, who merely repeated his name, and then waded into the chill water and struck out with a strong if inexperienced stroke.

The calls grew louder, and the water darker. Drelm finally realized that he didn't know how to swim in black water, which was much more challenging than blue water, and was deciding to ask an especially wise-looking green-scaled fish about it when the creature's eyes glowed brilliantly and it began to shout his name. Drelm was surprised, for he had never heard such a loud fish before. The whole sea seemed to shake with the sound of its voice.

And then the fish's voice became that of Elyana, and Drelm opened his eyes to find his friend staring down at him with anxious eyes. Over her shoulder was a riot of stars, gleaming in the night sky. The ground shook beneath him.

"Rise up!" Elyana shouted. "The summoner's back!"

Drelm sat up. He wasn't entirely sure where he was, for his thoughts seemed strangely foggy. But his armor lay to his right, and he grabbed it in one massive hand and thrust it over his head as he sat up. Elyana stepped away, calling to Lisette. Dogs were barking.

Drelm asked Abadar for guidance and buckled on his weapons belt, then tore his battleaxe from its sheath. There was no time to don his boots.

It bothered him that he swayed as he stood. Lisette was still shouting at the unresponsive elves. Groggily, Drelm took in the lay of the land.

The beast seemed to have run straight for the high hill where the tents of the Oakstewards were a trampled mass of snapped spars and waving canvas, lying ruined like a flock of broken-backed birds slapped from the skies by the hand of an angry god. Three robed figures stood near the dying fire, their backs to one of the ruined walls, chanting and waving staffs at something that moved in the darkness. Drelm thought that the figure with them, the one with the sword, might have been the mercenary Grellen.

But the barking dogs weren't there, nor were the gunshots. They seemed to be off toward what Drelm suspected was the southwest, though he couldn't be sure.

And Elyana had disappeared. He hadn't seen her move away. He raised his voice, wondering why it quavered a little as he shouted. "Elyana!"

Strange—he was not usually so tired when he woke, even in the dead of night. The lust for battle normally roused him. "Elyana!"

"Here!" came the answering call. It seemed as though it rose from the direction of the barking dogs. Drelm launched into a staggering run. His gait was unsteady, and he thought that might be because he was barefoot. His soles were tough, though. Dimly, he was aware that the monster needed killing, but he was sure Elyana would know better what to do, and she might need help killing something else.

Some ten or twelve paces on he realized someone else was running at his side and glanced over to find the young sorcerer there, bleary-eyed, hair a wild corona, clutching the wand in two hands as if the thing were her salvation. Drelm noticed for the first time that the wand had a blunted tip, and wondered how it could possibly be useful for killing anything until he remembered it was for working magic.

This troubled him, for he knew that he should have known that without having to think so hard.

The dogs had surrounded a tall elm with bowed branches and now bayed at its base. One of their number lay dead. Two others shifted back and forth, the dead halfling's dog with them, and a third put forelegs to the bark and bayed.

Lisette and Elyana watched the upper branches, limned against the stars. The elf had her bow nocked, and the markswoman held her rifle.

"And what, exactly, are you planning to do?" A male voice called down from somewhere within the tree.

Calvonis.

Melias paused, breathing heavily, and Drelm felt her hand on his shoulder as she leaned there for balance.

"What are you planning?" Elyana called up.

"First, I'm going to watch the druids die."

"I don't mind that so much," Elyana said, which bothered Drelm. She launched an arrow into the tree.

Again came the laugh. Calvonis sounded amused. "Even if you come close, you cannot hurt me, elf. I thought you'd have learned that by now. I've been blessed by holy Razmir. I am one of his chosen."

"Chosen for what?" Elyana asked.

Lisette had stepped away now and was moving to the left even as Elyana let fly with another arrow.

"Surely you must be running out of those," the voice called down. "Running low on arrows, running low on dogs, running low on warriors. Yet I still live, and so does my angel. For I am blessed and I have heard the word!"

This last was almost a chant.

"And what do you reap," Elyana asked, "for sowing the word about your mad god?"

"In the here and now? Glory. And in the future, eternal life in the blessed paradise of Razmir, greatest of all gods."

Drelm growled deep in his throat. Razmir was a little god.

Calvonis carried on almost conversationally. "Your blasphemies do not trouble me, elf. For you are an insect. You toil and strive to make a difference, to save these other lives, but who lives and who dies is completely up to Razmir, and I am his agent upon Golarion."

There was a brilliant flare along the tree trunk. Drelm whirled, then saw Lisette dashing from the bole. A fire had begun in the trunk.

Calvonis laughed. "You think to flush me out with fire? I can summon my angel back at any time! How long do you think it will be before the fire even begins to trouble me? Your arrows and your stones cannot reach me. Nor your orc's axes. Yet I may destroy any of you any time I like."

The sorcerer had lifted the wand and was now muttering as she pointed it toward the sound of Calvonis's voice. She seemed to be repeating every few words he said.

"You're surely powerful," Elyana said. "I'll grant you that. And clever. But I still don't understand what your purpose is. You speak of angels, and being chosen, and the glory of Razmir. How do you honor Razmir through this madness? Are you a priest?"

Lisette's fire was now licking up the trunk of the tree, and a braid of smoke twisted through its branches.

"I am no priest. I am a disciple. I am like the scythe to the grain! Those who do not know the glory of Razmir will—"

Drelm happened to be looking right at the muttering sorcerer when the green bolt sped from the wand and into the treetop. It flared and defined a screen of energy and stopped the madman in mid-sentence. Melias muttered "glory of Razmir" once more, and a second bolt followed.

"He's got a magic shield," Drelm shouted.

"Glory of Razmir!" the little sorcerer shouted, and a third glowing green bolt of acid sped into the sky.

There was a sudden popping noise, and a strange, reptilian scent, and Drelm spun, a little unsteadily, to discover that the beast was there.

Most of it remained invisible, but there were splotches of blood across its scales, and ichor dripped down its face.

Drelm charged, even as the girl behind him continued to shout, "Glory of Razmir!"

The bolt of magical energy streamed past Drelm's shoulder as he ran and caught the beast in the same eye socket already dripping gore. It roared its pain, and Drelm roared his own fury and leapt to bring his axe down upon the eye ridge. A gunshot erupted beside him, and what must have been the eye exploded into ruin, rendered real and visible in its destruction.

The axe blade sank deep. Rather than prying it free, Drelm used the haft to scramble up the beast's face, and realized after he had done it that he had pushed off a fanged tooth while the monster screamed in pain. Something heavy whistled through the air just past his head, spraying him with blood. The tentacle? The odds were good that one of them would strike him. He hung on with one hand and smashed again and again into the ruined eye with his throwing axe. The creature shifted beneath him, crying in pain, the scales sizzling each time there was a cry of "Glory of Razmir!" and more of its face was revealed.

After six good blows, something whiplike grabbed Drelm about the leg and threw him to one side. Drelm, still woozy, managed to land with his hands out so that he ended in a drunken roll.

And it was then that Abadar smiled upon him, for there was a cry of dismay from above and the sound of crashing branches. Drelm looked up.

Later he would be told how Melias's wand blasts had worn through Calvonis's magical shield, and that Elyana and Lisette had been able to hit the still-invisible summoner via the sound of his voice and the visible movement of a branch shaking as he retreated from the main trunk of the tree. But Drelm knew nothing about any of that. He merely knew something unseen had dropped out of the tree before him, and saw from a patch of blood that seemed to show a shoulder and part of an arm—not to mention a decorative arrow fletching—that he was near a man.

Drelm threw himself toward this new target even before he realized it must be Calvonis. The summoner was already clambering to his feet, but Drelm seized hold of an ankle, then what must have been a belt.

He felt something sharp drive into his arm. A small blade, as invisible as its wielder. But Drelm only grunted and punched. He heard a sickening crack, and a groan, and the flow of blood defined part of a mouth, and lips. There was little trouble then in finding a neck, with both hands.

Again he felt the blade bite into his arm, and then he heard Elyana and Lisette as they grabbed the invisible summoner's arm. Elyana commanded Drelm to release his hold. This he was reluctant to do.

"Banish your monster," Drelm ordered, "or I'll crush your throat."

"He has, Drelm," Elyana said. "He's been begging you to release. Didn't you hear?"

Drelm grunted. All he'd heard was a sort of whispering noise. But he relinquished his hold on Calvonis's neck and stepped back.

"Drop your spell," Elyana demanded.

Suddenly, Calvonis was there, bloody and bruised. Lisette immediately flipped the man over and began to bind his hands behind him.

"Witch!" Calvonis shouted at Elyana. His voice was strangely distorted, probably because Drelm had broken his nose rather profoundly. It leaned heavily to the left.

"Lisette, let's frog-march this coward back to the camp."

"Coward!? I am no coward! I would like to see you—"

Lisette smacked the side of his face, then kicked the back of his head for good measure. "I don't plan to kill you before we get there, because I'd have to carry you then. But I bet you could walk with a few more holes in you. Do you want to find out?"

Calvonis didn't answer.

While Lisette stood guard, Elyana searched the summoner's belongings and patted him down, taking a number of items.

"You dare profane sacred articles of Razmir with your touch? Those were in the palm of the Living God himself!"

"Any god with you as a chosen messenger doesn't interest me much," Elyana replied.

"I'll bet this wand would melt your face clean off," Melias said matter-of-factly.

The summoner lapsed into sullen silence.

If Drelm had felt poorly dressed when he raced into the fray, the girl was even worse. Melias was barefoot as well, and wore only a light shift. The young woman pushed back locks of hair and sternly eyed the summoner, her wand at the ready.

"You came through at just the right time, Melias," Elyana told her as she pulled a leather satchel from Calvonis's shoulder pack. "Without you, we couldn't have brought him down."

Melias's lips turned up in a grim smile.

Elyana spoke on. "I'll see to it that you get a proper share. The one Venic was supposed to receive."

"I want no money." Melias's voice was soft, but final. "Just seeing him dead . . ."

"Vengeance doesn't put food on the table," Elyana told her. "I'll see you get paid."

Melias shook her head but made no more complaint.

Elyana recovered little of seeming interest—apart from the satchel, which seemed to hold paper and drawing utensils, she found only some jewelry and various weapons. Elyana set all of these aside without comment. "That will do for now. Go ahead, march him back. Melias, go with them. If he so much as twitches, blow his head off."

"With pleasure."

Lisette pushed the madman before her, one pistol to his back, her hand upon his wrists. Melias followed along on the left, wand at the ready.

Elyana then considered Drelm. "You look like hell."

"I've been worse."

"Don't I know it." The elf smiled at him. "I think you can last until we get back to camp. Let's gather up what I found on Calvonis, then I'll take a look. I want to make sure there's no one worse off."

As it turned out, the Oakstewards had taken the brunt of the action. Cyrelle and the elves had never fully awoken, so deeply had the drugs affected them. Fortunately, the fight had never reached them.

Five of the seven Oakstewards were dead, including Shalon, the redhead.

Before Calvonis had summoned the beast to defend him at the tree, the druids and Grellen had managed to inflict a great deal of damage on the beast. Grellen claimed he'd severed one of the tentacles and that the druids had blasted halfway through the other, which might have explained why the beast had been so slow about attacking Drelm.

So far as Drelm was concerned, the mission had worked out beautifully—and, more importantly, he would shortly return to wed the woman of his dreams. While Lisette led Calvonis over to speak with the druids, Elyana sat Drelm down on a log and saw to his wounds.

He watched her work, still unable to entirely shake the strange daze that had touched his thoughts. It was good to have such a friend, and he thanked Elyana as the torn skin on his forearm mended under her touch and there was nothing left of the dull ache but a faint tingle. She then touched his hand, turned it palm-up, and pressed a thin ring into it.

"What's this?"

She tapped the ring's edge. "One of the secrets to Calvonis's health."

Drelm brought it close for inspection, and he saw that it was carved with little flowing letters he didn't recognize. A small gem winked at its heart.

"It was made by elven hands, the gods know how long ago. It bestows health to its wearer. I've seen its like before. And," she continued with a smile, "it might just fit on your smallest finger."

Drelm grunted skeptically. "Why give this to me?"

"Because I've never seen anyone get wounded as often as you."

Drelm was no master at reading a woman's expressions, but there was something in her voice as she went on that gave him pause. "If I weren't always there to heal you, I think you'd long since be dead. Now neither of us need worry."

"I never worry," Drelm said, "because you're always there."

Elyana paused. "That may not always be true."

Most women were mysterious, but never Elyana. So why now? "What does that mean?"

Elyana shook her head.

"You never hide things from me."

She sighed. "You'll be settling down now, Drelm. You have a home."

"You also have a home," Drelm reminded her, and spoke on even as she shook her head. "Wherever I make my home is yours. But there's also the town, where you're revered. You shall be aunt to my children, and teach them to shoot, and ride."

"That would be something to see," Elyana said.

He felt a heaviness then, as if chains had suddenly been set upon his heart. "But you don't want to see it?"

"Now's not really a good time to talk about it." Elyana bent to open Calvonis's satchel. Drelm saw a paper that had been stowed in eelskin along with a compass, pen and ink, a ruler, and various other small metal implements he didn't recognize.

Elyana studied each of these, then unfolded the paper and examined it carefully in the light of the coals about the fire. Drelm wondered if she truly found something of interest there, or if she were simply changing the subject.

"What is that?" he asked, although he wasn't actually interested. He would rather be asking her why she thought she needed to leave Delgar. Why she needed to leave him.

"It's a map."

As Drelm worked the ring onto the last finger of his left hand he stepped around so that he could look over her shoulder. "A map of what?"

"The River Kingdoms. Here's the Sellen." Elyana put her finger to a long ribbon winding along near the bottom of the map. Drelm could make out shaded areas that were probably supposed to be forests, and dots that indicated settlements, beside cramped labels.

But there were other dots besides, with even tinier handwriting that Drelm couldn't make out. "What are those?"

Elyana's answer was tinged with disgust. "Looks like he's keeping track of his attacks. Look. Here's the date when he attacked Illidian's scouting party, and the number of dead."

Drelm couldn't quite read the tiny handwriting, but he let out a little whispered prayer to Abadar and put a finger on a string of letters near the attack point. "Is that—"

"Onderan's massacre. Onderan *was* working with him. Given Calvonis's spouting of Razmiri doctrine and the activation words on Onderan's wand, it seems even more obvious now. I'll bet Calvonis is the one who gave Onderan the wand and paid him."

"But why?" Drelm asked.

"I'm not entirely sure," Elyana answered. "But he's been busier than we realized. Look at all these sites he has marked off, both east and west of Delgar."

Drelm couldn't read many of the details, but he could count, and it seemed to him that there were at least fifty attack sites. "Is it some kind of pattern?"

"Not that I can see." She frowned and folded up the paper. "I think we'll have to show it to the druids."

"I thought you didn't trust them."

"I don't. But there may be something else here that only a magic-worker could notice."

Elyana looked up suddenly, and Drelm turned to find that Lisette had returned from the druid camp to join them. The markswoman was almost as quiet in the grass as Elyana.

"Sorry to interrupt," Lisette said, "but I think you need to get over here."

"What's going on?" Drelm asked, rising.

"Calvonis says he'll only talk to Elyana."

Drelm cracked his knuckles. "I think I could make him talk."

Lisette smirked. "I wish the druids would let you."

Elyana carefully refolded the map, then all three of them walked to the hill's height and the ruined tents where the Oakstewards were talking. They found the summoner seated cross-legged on the ground, hands bound in front of him, facing the fire. Kilvor and the balding druid, Hindreck, sat across from him, the flames at their back.

Calvonis grinned at Elyana. The druids, Drelm saw, had healed his nose and pulled Elyana's arrow from him, but they hadn't cleaned him up. Dried blood stained the summoner's face and shirt.

"There she is!" Calvonis said. "The icy warrior woman with the heart of gold. These two are idiots. But you, you have promise."

"Do I?" Elyana didn't sound especially interested.

"Oh, you do. You want answers? I have them for you. As many as you want. But first there's something you must do for me."

Chapter Fifteen
Fireside Tales
Lisette

Lisette had undergone rigorous training to divorce her emotions from her actions, but, as her master had constantly repeated, she'd only ever gotten good at pretending they were separate. That had engendered many a sharp rebuke over the years she had worked with the Black Coil. She knew the master was dead wrong—she had functioned quite ably under his tutelage and continued to do so, no matter his sharp words.

So often had he critiqued her that she could imagine his words even in new situations. And this one time he would have been right. There was the half-orc, her target, painted red where the fire touched him and clawed by darkness where it did not.

Yet because she let her emotions hold too much power, she wanted even more to blast the cocky summoner.

She tried never to waste money killing things that couldn't earn her pay. She'd already won her fee by helping catch Calvonis, so now she knew her time was best spent finding a way to plug the sanctimonious half-orc.

She'd missed a fine chance at a shot at him in the midst of the battle because it might have raised suspicions. By now everyone had seen her shooting with such precision that it would take a fantastic melee to be able to explain a stray, half-orc-slaying bullet. She now fumed that there might be no other opportunity.

Calvonis leered up at the tall, spare figure beside the half-orc. Elyana's weight was planted on her left foot, hand resting easily on the deceptively ornamental pommel of her magnificent longsword. Most weapons with such intricate filigree were to be hung as decoration in the halls of lords, but Elyana's blade was entirely functional.

"Don't you want to hear my conditions?" Calvonis asked.

There was no immediate answer. The firelight shifted, highlighting now one corner of Elyana's high cheekbones, now a smudge of dirt along her brow where she had pushed back her hair with a soiled hand.

"A few hours back," Elyana told him, "I was still very curious. But do you know what? Now I'm bored. You bore me, Calvonis." She fingered her hilt. "I'm thinking I could drive this sword through you before anyone could stop me and then we could all get some sleep."

Calvonis laughed. "You're bluffing."

"Am I?"

Lisette, expert though she was at reading subtle emotional cues, couldn't tell. She would have guessed that Elyana remained curious, but it might be that her opinion had shifted.

"He is a prisoner," Hindreck interjected. "We do not countenance the mistreatment of prisoners."

Lisette smirked. Hindreck was too stolid to be playing along with Elyana's interrogation, which would only magnify the summoner's concerns. If Hindreck thought

Elyana's threats were real, it would better convince Calvonis and make him more likely to talk.

Then again, Elyana might not be bluffing. The elf was a little more challenging to gauge than Lisette had first suspected.

Elyana turned her head toward the druid. "We caught him. I have as much right to him as you do."

"Isn't there some sort of Kyonin code for prisoner conduct?" Hindreck asked.

A slow, satisfied smile spread across Elyana's face. "I wasn't raised in Kyonin."

"She's footloose and wild," Calvonis said. "A traveler who makes her own way, carving her path with reckless abandon and the sword of her fathers." He giggled.

Elyana shifted ever so slightly. "So which is the real Calvonis? The madman foaming here? The Razmiri prophet shouting at us from the tree? Or the canny man who played the part of a grieving husband? And," Elyana added slowly, "I think you'd best remind me why I should care."

Calvonis shifted in his bonds, slowly raised a finger to scratch some of the dried blood from the side of his nose. "I'm not the only agent of change."

"I know," Elyana replied.

Both druids seemed caught off guard by that pronouncement, and stared suddenly at Elyana.

"I suspect you've known that for a while." Gone was the madman. Now Calvonis sounded completely reasonable. "But there's more to it. Don't you want to know the plan?"

Elyana patted her sword hilt. "Curiosity gets me into a lot of trouble. It seems to me that, as facile as you are with the truth, you'd tell me just about anything. Kilvor, what's your plan for him?"

The older druid's eyes gleamed in the firelight. "We mean to transport him to Sevenarches. We can learn the truth there before he's tried, found guilty, and hung. His ashes will be mingled with the earth so that some use will come from him."

That was the first thing Lisette had heard from Kilvor that she actually liked.

"Do you mean you can compel the truth from him?" Elyana asked.

Lisette didn't think she imagined the hint of pleasure in Kilvor's answer. "Through one means or another."

"I won't respond to spells," Calvonis said. "Or violence."

"Oh, I imagine you will," Elyana countered. "I'm just wondering if it's worth the trouble. I'm not welcome in Sevenarches, you see, and I'd like to see the moment they string you up. I want you dead. So . . . because I can't go there, I might just have to end things myself. I could take your head in one blow. Tell me, Kilvor—you're a master healer. How are you at putting people together when their heads have come off?"

"I've had little practice," Kilvor admitted.

Drelm laughed heartily.

Elyana slapped the side of her sword. "Calvonis, you'd best get interesting really fast. I'll probably just let the druids have you. But if you irritate me, I'll kill you. It's up to you."

Calvonis pondered only for a moment. Lisette had the sense that this conversation wasn't going as he had planned. "I'd like to live."

"Guess again."

"I think you're bluffing," Calvonis said slowly. "I can tell you things that will help you, now. You can learn them later, surely, but then it will be too late."

"We can make no deals with you," Kilvor said. "But we can offer you the chance to make your peace with your god."

Calvonis laughed at that. "I *am* at peace with my god, little man."

"He doesn't call the orders," Elyana said. "I do."

"Now wait a moment—" Kilvor said, but Calvonis paid him no heed.

"I see that," the summoner responded. "And why you haven't carved a country for yourself out of this mess of the River Kingdoms, I'll never know."

"A country," Elyana said. "Why would I want the bother?"

"Surely you're not ignorant of the possibilities."

"Are you suggesting we discuss philosophy, Calvonis? Or trade career advice?"

Calvonis smiled.

"You have limited time," Elyana went on. "Say your piece so I know whether I walk away, or drive a sword through you."

"We have a base, in the wilderness. I can take you there."

"For an ambush," Elyana suggested.

"No," Calvonis said quickly. "I had planned to weaken you, then lure you there, after I had called my allies. They're waiting. I can show you the way. But if you wait until you compel me to speak, they will have drifted off. And they will cause as much havoc as I have."

"Why have you done this?" There was a wheedling note in Hindreck's voice. "You wish to bring people to the altars of your god . . . by killing them?"

The druid was such a fool. "How stupid are you?" Lisette asked. "They've sent these agents into the River Kingdoms to stir up trouble. Those who welcome the Razmiri church into their lives will be spared. It's nothing but a protection racket."

"If you like," Calvonis said. "But it's already working. And it will work regardless of anything you say. The faithful will say that you malign our holy god and blaspheme because you will not see his light."

Hindreck sighed in disgust.

"So you lie for your god," Drelm said. He had been silent throughout the discussion, and it was startling to have him suddenly weigh in. "You bring violence, then say he protects those you do not harm. Because you harm only those who do not worship your god."

"Yes! Even the half-orc can be taught, it seems. My god spoke to me and sent me forth to punish—"

"A god you would betray." Drelm touched Elyana's shoulder. "Kill him. His faith is true; he would not betray his people. This is some trick."

"You're right," Elyana said.

"No," Calvonis said, and lifted bound hands as if to ward off a blow.

"I'll have him draw a map," Kilvor declared ominously, "and we'll send forth our followers to scout it. If we find he speaks the truth, I'll speak on Calvonis's behalf. To commute his sentence to a life of servitude."

Calvonis's gaze settled for a long while on Kilvor before shifting again to Elyana.

"He has a map." Not taking her eyes from Calvonis, Elyana removed a browned sheet of parchment paper from inside her vest and slowly unfolded it. She passed it over to Kilvor.

"What do you think of that?" Calvonis asked with a smirk.

Lisette's curiosity was piqued. "What's on it?"

"Everyone he's killed, or been involved in killing."

"I do so like to keep track of these things," Calvonis said. But Lisette felt like she'd seen something different in his eye then. He was nervous.

She looked back at the druids, now carefully examining the paper, and slid over beside them. Disappointingly, between the dim light and the way they hunched over the parchment, she saw only the suggestion of some landforms, a twisting line that was surely the Sellen River, and a whole lot of handwriting she was too far away to clearly discern.

She returned to Elyana's side. "He's worried about something on that map."

"I'm certain you're right." Elyana still hadn't ceased looking at Calvonis. "Take a good long look at it, Kilvor. And meanwhile, Calvonis can tell us all about his allies. The ones who are going to ambush us."

"But we have no agreement," Calvonis protested.

"I haven't killed you yet," Elyana pointed out. "Keep talking and I'll see if I remain kindly disposed."

"There are four," Calvonis said, betraying very little reluctance. "Two sisters. One studied with druids from the east, and the other is a witch. They are very accomplished, and devoted to Razmir. Then there is Tyaval, the Cleanser of Razmir, the Shepherd of Wolves."

"What's that mean?" Drelm prodded.

Calvonis chuckled. "You think Cyrelle is powerful? Wait until you come up against his beasts."

"What sort of beasts?"

"Wolves. But such wolves as you find in nightmares."

"Who else?" Elyana said.

"Why Elyana, you don't sound impressed. Should I start making up details?"

Lisette heard the druids talking in low tones behind her. She couldn't quite make out what they were saying, but Hindreck sounded excited.

"Sounds like they spotted it, Calvonis," Lisette told him, and he pretended nonchalance.

"Maybe they did and maybe they didn't," Elyana said, and a crafty look came into the summoner's eyes.

"Did you find it, Elyana?"

Elyana smiled.

"What did you see?" he asked.

Lisette surprised herself in her eagerness to hear the truth. But she said nothing.

"You didn't see it," Calvonis suggested. "You're bluffing."

Elyana's smile broadened. "Not knowing maddens you. I like that."

Lisette laughed. She was growing to enjoy the elf.

"The fourth member of this band of yours," Elyana prompted.

"We are the Five Fingers of Razmir," Calvonis said. "The fifth of us is a high priest of Razmir himself, and a mighty warrior. He needs no magic or monsters, for his blessing is so great he need only wield his sword to slay his enemies in whatever form he finds them."

"I shall look forward to crossing swords with him," Drelm said.

Calvonis laughed. "You won't stand a chance."

"You're trying to intimidate Drelm?" Lisette asked, then chuckled. "You're even dumber than I thought."

Annoyance flitted across the summoner's face, but he relaxed as Kilvor and Hindreck set down the map. Kilvor stepped up to Elyana and handed the paper back to her.

"What did you find?" she asked.

Calvonis cut in quickly. "Do you ask because you don't know, or because you test them?"

When Elyana didn't answer, he smiled. "Oh, you are so clever, Elyana."

"There are patterns there," Hindreck said, "but we don't know what they mean. The summoner planned some kind of magic."

"For the glory of Razmir," Calvonis said. "Blessed be his name, blessed be the dirt that bears his boots."

"What are you up to?" Drelm growled, but Elyana threw up a restraining hand. It never failed to amaze Lisette how tight a control the elf had on the half-orc.

"I'd ask much the same thing," Hindreck said. He would, of course, because he wasn't very bright.

"No," Elyana said, quickly. "Just have him show us where this ambush spot is."

"But what of my reward?" Calvonis asked. "What do you promise me to betray the other fingers of the hand?"

"Elyana," Kilvor said slowly, "I think we should have him draw the map. Do not let him touch that one."

The elf cocked an eyebrow at the druid.

"We must remain cautious."

Elyana nodded. "Give him a life of labor with your people. For the map."

"I'm not sure I can do that."

Elyana crooked one finger toward Kilvor, and he and Hindreck stepped to the other side of the fire. Lisette dearly wished to listen in to that, but she remained, looking down upon Calvonis.

The summoner smiled up at her.

"What is it you like so much about Razmir, anyway?" Lisette asked. "What sort of god needs humans to cheat for him?"

"I am an instrument of his divine will. You cannot understand."

"She's right," Drelm grunted. "You make calamities. A real god would make them himself. Razmir is weak."

Lisette laughed gleefully. Drelm's barb had hit home, for Calvonis's face twisted in fury.

"It's you who are weak, orc-blood! You and your Abadar! Does your god speak to you? Does your god send you forth to punish?"

Drelm's answer was calm. "Abadar teaches so that men may make their own choices. The wise follow him. But he doesn't send forth murderers when his will isn't obeyed."

"You're no man," Calvonis said. "How dare you even name yourself one! How were you fathered? Some green-skilled filth catch a fat farmer's wife too slow to run? Is that how it was?"

Drelm should have snarled and launched forward to throttle him then. Calvonis wanted it. Lisette, watching the half-orc, saw the anger pass over him like a wave. His face remained almost frighteningly blank; the tension instead crossed him in a slow straightening and roll of his shoulders.

Calvonis saw it too, and tried further. "How many orcs got her, Drelm? Did you ever wonder?"

Lisette didn't like the half-orc, but even she felt her gorge rising at this. Slowly, deliberately, Drelm put his hand to his weapons belt.

"Or maybe—maybe she's the one who crawled off to the greenskins and begged for it. Just like that whore you're going to marry did."

"Don't do it, Drelm," Lisette hissed.

Drelm opened his mouth. And then he chuckled. The chuckle grew into a rolling laugh.

Lisette could scarcely believe it. Neither, apparently, could Calvonis.

Drelm grinned down at Calvonis. "You think I've never heard such things? That I could look like this, and never encounter such vile words? Abadar be praised, I heard worse things from children, and you're a fool if you thought to goad me with them. The teachings of Abadar showed me patience. Your god seems to have taught you nothing but foolishness."

"My god is a warrior god," Calvonis said. "I see now I underestimated you. I but tested you—"

"Shove it, Calvonis," Lisette said, and considered the dull-looking half-orc beside her.

Drelm reached out and put a hand on her shoulder. "He is good only for killing," he said. "But I will do it when I wish, not when he wishes."

Lisette nodded in understanding, and Drelm removed his hand.

Elyana returned with Kilvor and Hindreck. "How are things here?"

"I'm getting to know everyone better," Calvonis said.

"He wants to die," Lisette told Elyana. "He tried everything he could to get Drelm mad enough to kill him."

"It must be hard to fail at so much," Elyana said. "Kilvor's agreed. You get to draw us a map. It seems like I'm too distracting for you, so Drelm will watch."

"And I'm to be spared?"

"You will be spared," Kilvor said. "So long as you speak the truth."

Drelm snorted at that.

"Am I to draw with my hands tied?"

"You'll make do," Kilvor replied sternly.

The Oaksteward had more sense in him than Lisette would have guessed.

"I will watch him carefully," Drelm promised.

Elyana started back, and Lisette fell in step beside her.

"So," she said quietly as they departed, "what was all that about?"

"Kilvor doesn't have the strength to use one of his transport spells again, not tonight, so he can't send Calvonis away. But he can still contact other Oakstewards. One of them is going to come here in the morning."

"And?"

"And compel some answers from the summoner."

"Then what? Do you really think that there's a fortress out there where there's more like him?"

"It's hard to say. I think it's certain that there are more Razmiri out there doing . . . this." Elyana stopped outside the light of their own campfire and considered the horizon. A low-hanging cloud was a dark blot under the stars.

"And you're thinking about going after the fortress, aren't you?"

Elyana nodded slowly. "We've stopped the summoner, but unless we stop his group, then the problem isn't really over." The elf considered her. "But none of you signed on for that. We've lost so many already, and—"

"I'll go," Lisette said. She almost felt guilty when she saw Elyana smile faintly. Another battle was one more chance to see Drelm get killed. "Do you think the others will agree?"

"I'm certain the elves will join us. Maybe Grellen. I don't know about Cyrelle. I'll speak to them come dawn."

Elyana eyed her for a moment, then nodded. "Thank you, Lisette."

The gratitude struck Lisette oddly, and she found herself wandering back toward where Illidian and Aladel still lay. It should not have mattered to her that Elyana had thanked her. It should not have mattered at all.

Aladel slept facing east, Illidian facing west, away from one another. She crouched down beside the crippled captain.

His good arm was tucked under his head like a pillow, and his half limb hung out from the blankets, obscene and strange. Even still, he remained the most beautiful creature she had ever seen, and as she sank down beside him she desired once more to know his lips upon hers, to feel his arm around her. She tried to pass it off as lust, but at some level she knew she desired company, and this wounded, driven creature was perhaps the only one with whom she could pretend, for a little while, that only the present need trouble her.

She reached out to brush a stray lock of Illidian's hair from his forehead and was surprised to see him shift his head, as if in reaction. Well, the drug the druids had given him would have to wear off at some point. Lisette bent down and kissed the nape of his neck. When he spoke softly, as if in a dream, she smiled to herself and slid beneath his blankets to continue nibbling that same patch of skin.

She took her time with him, pressing her body against his, and soon he was responding, in a slow and foggy way. She helped him remove his leggings, and pulled off her own, then slid slowly onto him. She didn't care that others might hear their low moans or sighs; darkness still covered all.

When they were through, she lay content with him, his good arm across her, her hair against the stump of his arm.

"Do you never need rest?" Illidian asked. His voice was groggy, but he was alert, and she wondered if sex were the best way to counter any drug used upon a man. Aladel still lay motionless nearby, and she didn't think he feigned sleep from politeness.

"I needed you more," she said, attempting to be playful and then realizing it was true. Her expression hardened but Illidian seemed not to notice.

"I was dreaming that there had been a battle," he went on, "and that many years had passed, but I slept on, and on, and there was nothing left here but the grass and stone and me, beneath the blanket."

He played with her hair, and she found that she liked it.

Yet his tone grew bitter. "Do you know, even when I dream, now, I have but one hand."

"There was a battle," she told him. "We fought and captured the summoner."

He stopped stroking her hair immediately. Even his breathing halted. She felt the intensity of his gaze even without being able to see his eyes. He tried a short, soft laugh. "That's a strange jest." A note of disapproval. "And I don't really think it's funny."

"I'm not joking." She regretted saying anything at all to him. Hadn't she simply planned to feel his arm about her? "The summoner attacked the camp. While the druids and Grellen held off the monster, Elyana and I—and Drelm and Melias—found the summoner in the tree. We captured him. He's drawing a map for the druids right now. He claims that there are more like him out there, and that he was going to lure us to them."

Illidian breathed at last, deeply. "All this happened, and I did not wake?"

"The druids laced our food with something. To help our healing." She wondered at the lie, until she realized it was because she'd already upset him enough. She didn't care one way or another if the druids' stupid secret was kept. "Those of us who ate only a little, or none, roused more swiftly. You and Aladel didn't wake at all."

Illidian cursed and sat up, then fumbled for his false arm. She reached up for him. "What's the rush?"

"The summoner," he hissed.

For all that he hurried, Illidian was precise. He even allowed her to help attach the false arm as he pulled on his outer tunic. Swiftly, stiffly, he finished the rest of his dressing on his own, asking quietly for additional details, which she supplied resignedly.

"What are you planning to do?" she asked him. The sun was still down, but she could sense it stirring, for there was an expectation in the air, a stillness as though the dawn held its breath and the night spirits flitted nervously for their deep caves.

"I shall find out when I arrive." He stood and buckled his sword belt with a snap that rang of finality.

Lisette quickly threw on her own gear, urging Illidian to wait. But the elf stalked off, and she was forced to hurry after with only her breeks and weapons belt fastened.

"Crazy elf—Illidian! What are you doing?"

But he strode on, faster than she. Too late, she realized the mistake was having allowed herself to feel resentful as he dressed, like a slattern fallen in love with her customer. If she'd dressed at the same time . . .

She had just pulled on her boots when she heard the first scream, and was dashing forward by the time the second, shorter one, died abruptly.

Chapter Sixteen
Death Blow
Elyana

Elyana's eyes snapped open at the sound of the scream. She felt the lack of sleep acutely even as she threw herself out of her covers and grabbed her sword. Dressed only in a loose leather jerkin and pants, she ran at full speed with her sheathed sword, arriving at the druids' campfire in time to find a weird tableau.

Everyone stood before the fire but Calvonis. Hindreck was shouting at Illidian, who held a bloodstained sword. Lisette actually looked shocked: her hair was mussed and her eyes wide. Drelm stared down at Kilvor, and Kilvor was bent beside Calvonis, who leaked a copious amount of blood from two brutal head wounds. As Elyana stepped closer, she observed that one blow had scored nearly through the middle of the summoner's head. Another appeared to have taken off his ear and some surrounding flesh.

Both wounds bled prodigiously, but there was no helping Calvonis. His eyes were relaxed and unfocused, and he reeked of voided bowels and bladder.

"There's nothing I can do for him," Kilvor said.

"What about the druid who's arriving this morning?" Elyana asked. "Can't he resurrect him?"

"Let him rot in Hell!" Illidian shouted.

Elyana had no patience for the elf's nonsense. "Get him out of here," she snapped. Lisette put a hand to Illidian's arm and tried pulling on him, but the elf stormed off on his own. After a moment Lisette followed.

"Kilvor?" Elyana prompted.

"It is not . . . our place," Kilvor said, rising. "My order does not interfere with the natural course—"

"Oh gods—that's all you do!" She felt her lips twist in disgust. "The only thing different is that you impose *your* order."

"You're wrong. I will not alter what's come before. What's done is done."

Elyana cursed and glared over at Drelm. Why hadn't he done anything?

"Forgive me, Elyana," the half-orc pleaded.

She could not answer.

He hung his head, shame rendering him uncharacteristically loquacious. "I was watching the summoner while the elf argued with the druids. There was a whole lot of talking, and I thought Calvonis might try something. I was a lot more worried about him taking advantage of the distraction than . . . I failed. I'm sorry."

She knew that this admission hurt him more than a sword blow, yet she couldn't quite stay her tongue. "Illidian had a sword, Drelm, and you didn't see the attack coming?"

"He was faster than I supposed."

"Captain Drelm did all he could," Kilvor said. "He diverted the first blow so it only struck the Razmiri's ear. But Illidian is nimble."

Elyana frowned. Sighed. "Alright, Drelm. Did Calvonis at least finish the map?"

"He was nearing completion," Kilvor told her, and pointed at a piece of paper lying near the hands, still roped together. One of them clutched a broken stylus.

Elyana considered bending down to lift the paper, then decided against it.

"What's on it?"

"Essentially, there's a wilderness base. A small, hidden fort a few hours east, in Tymon. I don't think we need the map—I can send scouts to find it based on this information."

"Scouts?" Elyana asked.

"I'm a druid, Elyana." Kilvor actually sounded amused. "Many birds and beasts are my allies."

Elyana stared down at the pitiful-looking dead thing below her. It was so much easier to hate when your enemies were alive. "He was lying, Kilvor. Drelm was right. Calvonis believed too fervently to betray his people. He agreed too easily."

"Then we just need to be cleverer than him. If he thought to ambush us, then we will thoroughly know the area. And we will bring reinforcements. Some are already on their way from Sevenarches, and should reach us come the dawn. And I've sent word to our contacts at Tymon. They will meet us there."

"Us?" Elyana prompted.

"I had assumed you would want to go."

Elyana nodded slowly.

"Yes," Drelm said.

"And Lisette has volunteered," Elyana said. "But I'll have to check with the others. They're all volunteers, and what they were paid to do has been done." A thought suddenly occurred to her and she considered Kilvor carefully. "Don't you need to check the elves for your plague?"

"If any of you had it, we would know by now," Kilvor replied grimly.

"You do realize you're wanting us to work with people who drugged our food."

"I explained why that was necessary."

"What?" Drelm asked.

Neither answered him.

"You surely have. You Oakstewards are big on talking and deciding what the right thing is. I'd like to point out that if Lisette and I had eaten your drugged food we'd all be dead now."

Kilvor sighed. "You're right about that," he admitted. "And I apologize. It would surely be easier to work with your allies if you didn't mention that."

"I'll speak with them," Elyana said reluctantly. "I damned well wish that I'd gotten better sleep. Come on, Drelm."

As they moved off, there was a hint of color on the horizon. Gods, how much sleep had she actually gotten last night? Not nearly enough for her to be on her game and risking her life against untested foes.

"I apologize, Elyana," Drelm said.

"Don't. Illidian is fast. And I think we all discount him a little because he's only got that one arm. I'd forgotten how . . . crazy he is."

The grass was cool under her toes as she walked.

"He was practically begging me to kill him," Drelm said, "but screamed like a little girl when Illidian did it."

"Maybe he only meant for you to try to kill him. Maybe he meant some kind of distraction. Maybe he didn't want to give up any more information."

"I'm glad he's dead," Drelm said, and Elyana couldn't help but agree.

Elyana put the rest of her gear on quickly, then went first to Illidian. When offered the chance to kill allies of the summoner, he agreed with only a nod. Elyana didn't press him for an apology, or point out that his actions were likely to cause greater problems. He was bitter and a little mad, and she had always known it and should never have forgotten it.

Grellen and Melias, whom she found holding hands at the breakfast fire, looked at one another before pledging they'd bring down the whole of the band that had set this plan in motion. Elyana went next to Cyrelle, who was kneeling by one of her hounds. The animal sat patiently while she examined its right front paw.

"Cyrelle," Elyana said gently, then knelt to rub behind the ears of Drutha's dog, Emblid, who promptly sat and banged his tail against the grass.

The huntswoman turned, swaying a little. She must have drunk deeply of the drugged wine. "I don't know what's wrong with me this morning," she said with a little laugh. "I can't shake the sleep fog."

Elyana remembered the great gusto with which the woman had devoured food the night previous. She rubbed Emblid behind the ears.

"I can't believe I slept through the fight, though."

"Neither can Illidian or Aladel," Elyana told her. "It was over swiftly, though. I took your hounds away from the monster. They're the ones who found Calvonis."

"That's what Grellen said. Thank you." She released her hound's paw and told the animal to relax. It sniffed the air before trotting off.

"There's something else I want to talk to you about," Elyana went on.

"I figure you want to go after whoever else is involved, don't you? Lisette said something about it already."

"That's right."

"I've lost so many animals. That's hard going."

"I know."

Emblid let his tongue loll out, then fell on his side, legs folded in. Elyana smiled to herself and leaned in to scratch his belly. "Are you going to be able to find a home for him?"

"He's not the kind of dog I usually work with," Cyrelle admitted. "But Emblid's superbly trained. We should probably write Drutha's village and see if someone in the family wants him. If not, I'll be glad to have him." Her voice grew soft, almost wistful. "I think I may be about done with this kind of thing myself. I want some land of my own, but not somewhere out in the wilderness. Someplace where I can raise my dogs and sell them to folk who need good hunting and tracking hounds."

"A larger city," Elyana guessed.

"Right. There just aren't enough steady customers out here in the Kingdoms. And I'm tired of living wild all the time. It'd be nice to have someone else do some cooking. To have someone else mend the clothes."

"So you're looking for a wealthy tailor to settle down with. Who can cook."

Cyrelle stared hard at her a moment, then chuckled. "You think the druids have one of them handy?"

"It can't hurt to ask."

"You're alright, Elyana. I don't think I'm going."

Elyana stood. She'd guessed as much before she even broached the subject. "I want you to know—I gave your advice a lot of thought last night."

"I'm glad I could help."

"Thank you, Cyrelle. For everything."

By the time she finished talking with Cyrelle, Aladel was waiting to speak with her.

"I suppose you've heard something about all this already," Elyana asked.

Aladel didn't answer this. He said only: "Walk with me," and turned from the camp. A half-dozen riders were cresting the hill toward them, four wearing the oak tree tabard of the Sevenarches guard force, and Elyana watched for a moment, tense until she saw that Kilvor recognized and welcomed them.

They walked south of the camp toward the burned-out tree.

"You're being awfully mysterious," Elyana said.

"And you're rightfully wary," Aladel replied. "I want you to put aside your assumptions, though, Elyana, and pretend with me."

"I'm in little mood for games, Aladel."

"But you trust my judgment. I've seen it. Trust me now."

His look was peculiarly intent, and she nodded, once.

"Pretend that you work for the Kyonin border patrol, and one of your officers has lost two commands while following some kind of beast. Miraculously, he survives each attack. Would you be suspicious?"

"There are a lot of incompetent officers."

"True enough. But not, usually, among Kyonin's rangers."

Elyana agreed with a nod.

"Then Illidian lost a third, Elyana. You saw it happen."

"Wait a moment. I thought he'd only lost one command prior."

"He had divided his first command to investigate some strange tracks. His squad went one way, and the other got sent straight into a massacre. Then he lost almost all of a larger patrol sent to follow up. *Then* he came on across the river."

Elyana halted, and for the first time in a long while, she studied Aladel closely. On the surface, he didn't look so different from other elves, although there was a certain ease of manner when you saw him among other races. That was to be expected from an elf that'd been out wandering in the world.

Or from a spy.

"Do you know why Kyonin sent only a small force with Illidian on this expedition, Elyana? It's because we suspected his involvement. We feared he was leading the patrols to slaughter."

They reached the tree, and the scent of the burned wood was almost pleasant. "If you doubted him," Elyana asked, "why not compel answers from him with a spell? In my experience, if Kyonin's leaders want something, they make it happen."

"I suggested that very thing. But Illidian's family has powerful connections. And then there was the loss of his arm, which certainly seemed to leave him in the clear. After all, who would deliberately do that to themselves?"

"Right. So why are you telling me this? You can't still suspect him. His blood cousin died, too. Are you saying he pretended grief about all of this?"

"He killed Calvonis. Before Calvonis could be forced to talk."

She couldn't believe it. "You really think he's been pretending all this? I was there when he was wounded. When he lost his arm, and when our camp was attacked. Either time he could have died if a healer wasn't on hand. Or if I'd been a moment too late."

Aladel nodded. "And he and Calvonis had to have known you were there, and who you were. Everyone along the border knows about Elyana Sadrastis. As long as you were left alive, you could heal him. And among all those injuries you weren't wounded either time. It's as if they wanted to make sure you lived, to heal people."

She shook her head. "That doesn't make any sense. My magic is extremely limited. Any spellcaster would know that. Suppose I'd already used mine up for the day? It seems a stupid risk just to get us to trust Illidian."

"I think getting him wounded was more to remove any of the border patrol's lingering suspicions."

She couldn't believe it. Her gaze drifted back up to the camp. The shadow of one ruined wall stretched down the hill, cast by the upper half of the rising sun. "There are all kinds of holes in your theory, Aladel."

"Think about it, Elyana: Calvonis wanted us to get to certain places. He never wanted *everyone* dead. He could have killed the people he trapped in the pit instead of dropping the dead dwarf on them."

"There had to be survivors," Elyana agreed, "to spread fear. We've been over that."

Aladel shook his head once more. His manner had begun to irritate her. "There are some spells that require blood."

"I know that," Elyana snapped.

"And there are some spells that require a certain sort of blood."

"I've heard the tales, Aladel. Children. Virgins. Certain family lines. Get to the point."

"Heroes," Aladel finished.

And at that Elyana froze.

"Where better to find heroes than in the Kyonin border patrol?" Aladel said. "Unless perhaps you arrange to summon the best and brightest in all the River Kingdoms?"

"Gods. Blood for what, though?"

"I don't know yet. They want nothing good, you can be sure. Remember Hindreck saying it was in some kind of a pattern, but he didn't recognize it?"

She did, but she still couldn't accept Aladel's theory. "What would compel Illidian to kill his own people? His own cousin? Subject himself to the pain of that amputation?"

"There are healers gifted enough to restore that arm, Elyana. You know that as well as I. It's temporary. And it's a dramatic show. He refused transfer to Iadara to see it tended, saying he deserved the wound."

"That sounds like something he'd say."

Elyana turned from the elf and looked once more toward the camp, where one of the newcomers was leading his horse toward the rest of the herd. Another, a slim feminine figure, seemed to be looking down at them.

Aladel seemed almost to read her mind. "Calvonis was an inspired actor as well. Razmiri are known for that kind of thing."

She shook her head. "You're saying that they deliberately led us to all these places so that blood would be shed."

"Yes."

"What about our fight at the fey court?"

"What of it?"

"Think back. Did Calvonis and Illidian want blood shed there as well?"

"They must have."

"But there we were winning. And I daresay that we would have won but for one thing."

Aladel mulled that over only for a moment, and when he supplied his answer, his eyebrows were lowered in worry. "The Oakstewards."

"They're the ones who stopped the fight, not Illidian. He's innocent, I'm sure of it."

"But the Oakstewards revere the natural order. They'd no sooner betray it for Razmir than—"

"Than a captain of the Kyonin border patrol?" Elyana cut in. A coldness crept through her. She pulled the map from her satchel and unfolded it quickly.

"What's that?"

"The map Calvonis kept of all his attacks."

She turned it the proper side up, then cursed at her foolishness. "Damn. Why didn't I see this?" She tapped at a marking on the paper.

"Is that our location?"

"It is. If Calvonis is just a loan loon tracking his kills, he *could* have sat in the tree and made notes on this paper while he sent his beast to the camp to assault us—but that seems too crazy even for him. Which means this mark was here already." She looked up. "The druids are in on it."

"What?" Aladel looked shocked.

"You just implied that this is some kind of huge ritual. Well, that means everything has to happen in a certain way. At a certain place, right? So these points—all save the battle with the fey, which you'll note isn't written in—had to be predetermined."

The color drained from Aladel's face. "Surely . . . surely the druids aren't involved. What about the attack last night?"

"All it would take is one traitor. The one who receives word that we're interfering with the fey and stops us from finishing off the monster. The one who suggests this place to transport us and survives the monster's next attack. The one who just waved in a half-dozen reinforcements."

Aladel made the name a curse. "Kilvor."

Chapter Seventeen
Changing Times
Drelm

Drelm didn't know why Elyana and Aladel walked so far from the camp, but it was not his place to question Elyana's actions, especially after he'd let her down so profoundly. Grellen had something in the stewpot by then, and it smelled very good, but he didn't really feel like he deserved to eat anything, so he wandered over to where Cyrelle sat with her dogs.

Drelm liked dogs. A well-trained dog was even better than a horse, and someday Drelm hoped to own a pack of them himself. If he wasn't putting all of his money into house fixtures and furniture, he'd surely be saving for one of Cyrelle's hounds.

He watched as the huntswoman fed them, then, at her suggestion, helped feed the hawk, letting the fragile but deadly creature sit on his wrist while he offered it little bits of meat.

He was reaching into the satchel for more to present to that sharp little beak when the fog rolled in.

"That's strange," Cyrelle said, rising.

Almost at the same moment he heard Elyana calling for him he heard the howl of wolves. Cyrelle's hounds were instantly on their feet, ears high, fur bristling. Drutha's dog, Emblid, searched this way and that, as if looking for his dead mistress.

"Up," Cyrelle told the hawk, and the animal beat its wings and lifted from Drelm's upraised arm.

"Grab weapons!" Drelm shouted. "Gather at the fire! Elyana!"

Even standing, he could no longer see through the fog. There was no sign of Elyana, and he prayed that Abadar would see her to safety, even though he knew his friend trusted her sword arm more than any god.

Around him rose the panicked shouting of his companions. The fog was so thick that he could see little beyond a few spear-lengths. There was no time even to seek the fire, and he told Cyrelle to ready, for he heard the growl of wolves approaching. He unlimbered his axe. He had not yet removed his armor, and Cyrelle, busy with her hounds, had not donned hers.

The woman was bent to grab her leather cuirass when the wolves, great gray beasts half again the size of Cyrelle's animals, loped into view.

Cyrelle's loyal animals rushed forward with Emblid, barking their fury.

Drelm went with them.

As a wolf bore down on Emblid, Drelm brought the axe through half its snarling face and yanked the weapon free as the beast sank on nerveless limbs.

From behind him, Melias screamed like some battle goddess, shouting again and again to the glory of Razmir.

One of the wolves grabbed a hound at the neck and bit down even as another of the brave animals attacked the wolf's flank. Drelm's axe whistled down and clove the wolf almost in two. Cyrelle was finally in armor then and came up to his side. The other wolves sped on, and Cyrelle urged her hounds after, leaving only Emblid and Cyrelle's lead dog, its ruff matted with blood. It growled, clambered to its feet, and came with them.

There was the sound now of shouted incantations, and the clang of swords, and, oddly, laughter.

"Witchery," Drelm spat. "Calvonis said there were witches, and druids."

"Then let's hunt them," Cyrelle suggested.

He liked the woman's determination, and they jogged off together, following the dogs through the fog. There was an explosion immediately on their right and, a moment after, the smell of gun smoke and a whimper.

A figure resolved itself into Lisette, with another wolf at her feet. She carried a smoking rifle.

"We're hunting wizards," Drelm told her, and the woman grinned and fell in step.

Someone rode past on their right, but the fog was so dense Drelm saw only the suggestion of a dark shape and nothing more. Lisette, lagging slightly behind, did not fire, probably because the target was uncertain even for her.

He sensed the end of the fog a moment before he reached it, and wondered if its edge would be watched.

Drelm glanced back to find Lisette trotting right on his heels, rifle leveled.

"Spell ends in about a foot," he told her. "You ready?"

She nodded once.

"Scouter's spotted something," Cyrelle said, then flinched, and cursed, her voice choked off with a sob. "Someone throwing spells. He's hurt bad."

"Now," Drelm said, and leapt forward. No better time to attack a caster than right after they worked magic.

Lisette charged out of the mist, dropped to one knee and blasted off a shot at a trio of gray-backed wolves starting up from a downed dog. The brown-clad man in the robe beside the wolves was probably the graver threat, but the wolves would reach them sooner, so Drelm charged. His axe caught one in mid-leap. The blow bit deep, but the wolf's speed and weight tore the battleaxe from his hand. The animal hit the ground with a thud, kicking its legs feebly.

The third wolf was a few steps behind the first two. Lisette was tugging at one of her pistols, but could not possibly clear it in time, so Drelm threw himself at the beast and both fell.

It buried fangs in his shoulder and sharp claws dug furrows in his tabard and screeched against his scale mail. Drelm roared at the wolf and the pain, pressing with the full weight of his body. One gauntleted hand pushed back the beast's great maw while the other tightened around its neck.

Cyrelle stepped up and with a savage shout drove her sword through the wolf's neck. The creature reflexively let go and Drelm rolled away.

The druid continued his charge.

"Is that one of the Oakstewards?" Cyrelle asked.

"Not for much longer." Lisette stepped to her side and aimed her pistol

Drelm heard the shot as he leapt over to the wolf and grabbed his battleaxe.

But if Lisette hit, the bullet left the man unfazed. His cloak seemed to flow like water about him. Drelm saw it had become a part of his skin, like a furry layer. His face, too, changed, enlarging and widening, and he dropped suddenly onto four legs, transformed fully into a great brown bear.

Lisette cursed. "I'll reload! Keep him busy!"

Drelm rushed to meet the beast. Just before impact he veered right, reaching one-handed with his weapon. The blade bit into one flank, but the bear-man swatted him sideways, shredding tabard, armor, and the skin beneath.

Drelm hit the ground on his shoulder and rolled back to his feet. The bear slowed, turned, and came forward on two legs, growling. The half-orc had a brief respite to grab the bloody axe, then the battle began in earnest.

The bear towered over him and could swipe with either of its great paws with stunning force. Then, too, there was the huge maw, open and ready to snap. Drelm, though, had his axe, wielded with such cunning it was like an extension of his own body. He and the bear feinted and swiped and dodged each other's blows, partners in a lethal dance.

Drelm heard the rush of hooves and, from the corner of his eye, saw Cyrelle cut down by one of the Oaksteward rangers. Her remaining hound and Emblid cast themselves savagely at the forelegs of her assailant's mount, and then the moment was lost to him as he and the bear pivoted. Some part of Drelm knew then that the Oaksteward reinforcements were all in league with the summoner, but he had no time to dwell upon the information.

He ducked a slice with a massive paw that would have laid open his head, then drove his axe deep into the creature's chest. There was a satisfying crunch and a welter of blood. The resulting backhand set him staggering, and he lost hold of his weapon.

Partly stunned, he still managed to grab one of his throwing axes. He gained a quick impression now of the rest of the battle. There was Lisette, loading her smoking rifle. Cyrelle was down, but so was her attacker's horse, and one of their attackers lay across the dying beast with his skull blown open. Cyrelle's hound stood guard over her motionless body; Emblid, though, was dancing around the feet of the bear, barking furiously. The other hounds lay mixed in among the dead wolves.

Drelm shook his head to clear the spots of blackness that danced in his vision, then launched his axe. Almost at the same moment, Lisette fired her rifle. Brains and gore sprayed forth from the bear's head, and it swayed for a moment before toppling heavily to the side.

Drelm grunted in satisfaction and ripped his second throwing axe from his belt.

"That was my brother," said a woman's voice beside him.

He whirled, but there was no one to see, only a smell of sage and a faint perfume. He swung out with his axe and heard only a cackle. "I have something for you, half-orc," the voice said.

Drelm snarled his defiance, but a strange sickness seized him at the same time a slim woman in a tattered skirt appeared nearby. His throwing axe slipped from fingers suddenly no more nimble than sausages. He heard another cackle and the rage that always lay within him broke free from his control.

Gone was his governing intellect. Gone was any semblance of sanity. He felt his body changing. His teeth elongated into fangs and his tusks transformed into savage, dagger-length protrusions. His fingernails warped into hardened talons.

He had not even the reason left to charge toward the magic-worker who had cast the spell. He was angry, and something was calling his name and waving a smoking stick.

Drelm roared and ran at her.

Chapter Eighteen
Lucky Shot
Lisette

Lisette didn't believe in luck. Success was a matter of being well trained, well prepared, and flexible so that when something fell right into your hands you took advantage of it.

The moment the fog dropped, she'd thought about offing Drelm. No one would have seen. But she'd been reluctant to do that for the same reason that the mayor hadn't wanted her to kill the captain before the monster died. He was simply too good in a fight, and there was no telling what exactly they were up against. She'd been tempted to blast him two or three times as they moved up through the fog, but then she'd seen the druid—the Oaksteward?—and knew things had suddenly gotten a lot, lot weirder. There was no telling who was on her side then, except for Drelm and Cyrelle. And then Cyrelle dropped. All she could tell for sure about what was going on within the fog was that Melias was still blasting things, because the girl kept shouting about Razmir.

Then a woman appeared out of nowhere and worked magic on Drelm, and now the captain was eyeing her like dinner. It was the chance she'd been waiting for.

Lisette didn't want to take it.

"Drelm," she shouted. "Damn your eyes! Snap out of it—"

He screamed and leapt at her.

She had a pistol in either hand, and there was no hope for it. She fired the right a split second before the left so that the kick of the weapons wouldn't throw off her aim.

It was near point-blank range, and the half-orc fell back with a spray of blood as two holes punched through his armor. Her sight of the wound was obscured by the billow of powder smoke.

She tossed down the pistols and wrenched her sword free. Drutha's brave dog came hurrying over, barking at the witch. But Lisette knew even as she lifted the blade that she'd taken too long. She saw the sly smile on the woman's bony face and the sparkle of rings on long fingers as dry lips spoke twisted words. There was still a gap of six paces left between them when the cold fingers of sleep dragged her down, and as Lisette staggered she threw her sword. She was asleep before she knew whether she'd struck.

Chapter Nineteen
Truth of the Matter
Elyana

The fog dropped moments after she and Aladel began their run. Elyana shouted for the rest of her band to take up arms, and Aladel cried a warning about the Oakstewards. Yet even as they spoke there came the sounds of spells being cast, and the howl of wolves.

The ground shook under hoofbeats as she and Aladel crossed into the fog, so thick Elyana couldn't see more than a few paces. Sound, too, was strangely distorted by the unnatural mists.

Elyana pulled off her bow, strung before she'd begun her sprint, and nocked an arrow in the direction she thought the rider approached from. "Friend or foe?" she shouted.

There was no answer other than the sound of oncoming hooves. She let fly, once, then again.

"How can you see?" Aladel asked. He stood beside her, arrow nocked.

"I don't need to see." As she launched the third arrow a horse reared out of the darkness and a figure on its back paused with raised sword, then slumped from the saddle. She raced to grab the animal's halter, willing it to calm as Aladel pulled the corpse's foot from the stirrup.

"One of the new arrivals," Aladel told her.

She made soothing sounds to the horse, a chestnut stallion with a white blaze. She spared a brief glance for its former rider as she vaulted into the saddle. A warrior dressed in the colors of the Sevenarches. Two arrows stood out from his chest, one high, one low, and the blood had ruined his pretty tabard.

The pop of Lisette's guns and Drelm's distinctive battle roar rose on the wind. As Elyana leaned down to offer Aladel a hand she heard Melias cry "Glory of Razmir!" and a resulting scream of pain. She wondered if Kilvor had expected this level of resistance.

Elyana urged the horse forward and searched the gloom. "Why didn't they just kill us all last night, while we slept?"

"Maybe they couldn't until the rest of their people arrived," Aladel pointed out. "Or maybe last night was to eliminate opposition, and this morning was for the ritual."

"Pray then that they need more than blood," Elyana said darkly, "because plenty of it will spill." She urged the animal forward, straining for sight of something, anything, in the rolling walls that surrounded them.

Kilvor hailed from the fog before them. "Who's out there?"

"Flank left," Elyana whispered to Aladel, then the two dropped silently from the horse. She slapped the horse's hindquarters, and it stamped forward with a snort.

From up ahead came a cry of surprise and a flash of lightning. The horse cried out in alarm

She arrived a moment before Aladel to discover Kilvor turned away from her, standing beside the body of

Hindreck. Judging by the parallel furrows in the ground that led to the younger druid's boots, the elder had been dragging him.

Kilvor was completely unaware of her approach, and stared off toward the sound of the horse galloping away through the grasses. His head snapped to the left as Aladel emerged from the fog, and the druid lifted a hand just as Elyana closed from behind and slammed her sword hilt against the side of his head.

Kilvor groaned, wobbled, turned toward her and reached out with grasping fingers. She saw his lips working.

It would have been very nice to hold the sword to his throat and demand explanation, or troop movements, or any number of useful things, but she was tired of wizards and druids and tricks and so she drove the blade deep into his chest. The only thing that rose from Kilvor's lips then was blood. His hands clawed at her blade as she drove it deeper. He sagged.

She pulled the blade out and let go of him. He dropped to the ground with a dull thud, twitching, eyes already glazed.

Aladel looked at her in surprise.

"Make sure he's dead," she said, then bent to Hindreck.

The younger druid wasn't dead, only unconscious.

"It would have been nice to question him," Aladel pointed out.

"Maybe." From out in the fog there were still calls of "Glory of Razmir" and an occasional wolf cry. "We'd best . . ."

She fell silent as she heard the steady thud, as of something heavy moving out there in the gloom. The sound was unfamiliar, but the shift of the ground was identical to the vibration made by Calvonis's creature. Aladel must have recognized it too, for he looked up in surprise, one hand holding a large black amulet he'd wrested from Kilvor's cloak. Elyana motioned him forward, rammed her bloody sword into its sheath, then grabbed Hindreck's arms. Aladel quirked an eyebrow at her but swiftly bent to grab the druid's legs, then the two lifted him and backed away from Kilvor even as a monstrous form reared up, obscured by fog. She saw a huge, lizardlike head and heard the voice of a woman.

"This is the place," the woman's voice said. "Kilvor?"

"Disperse the fog," snapped a familiar voice, and Elyana tensed at the sound. Calvonis?

She bit back a curse. Of course. She had seen Calvonis die, but magic could bring men back from beyond.

She set Hindreck down and shrugged the strung bow from her shoulder. She had but five arrows left, and if she had her way, she'd drive each of them through the summoner's head.

"They're still fighting out there," the woman's voice said. "I'm not dropping the fog until we have a living body for each of Drolgug's mouths. We've got the woman, he's got Hindreck. You go—"

"Shut up," Calvonis snapped. "Don't you see? They've killed Kilvor."

"Well, use his own amulet on him, then," the woman's voice said crossly. "We need him."

While Elyana quietly put an arrow to her string, Aladel slid silently into the fog.

"Idiot," Calvonis snapped. "Someone's close. Velandril smells it."

There was no mistaking the swish of boots through the tall grasses. The other speaker stepped close enough for Elyana to perceive her shape in the fog. She was tall, very slim. As she bent to look at Kilvor, her back was exposed.

It was too fine a shot to miss, and Elyana took it.

The stone-tipped arrow drove into the back of her skull. The woman threw back her arms, spine arching impossibly far, then collapsed.

"Elyana!" Calvonis spat.

The monster rushed out of the fog and a tentacle reached for her. It was scarred, nicked, and oozing black blood, but even as she rolled clear she was astonished that something so awful could be touched with such beauty. The clean portions of the limb were formed all of different swirled shades of blue, inlaid with lines of sparkling gold, like some elaborate mosaic on a mansion floor. The head loomed then, first just a blot of darkness, then a knobbed and scaled visage, vaguely draconic, its scintillating azure scales hacked and scored with injuries. One eye had been shot away and was nothing now but a gaping wound. It was as fine a place as any for an arrow, but she could not pause to fire, for the beast's mouth was opening.

Elyana dashed beneath the tentacle and dodged past a stump of a ruined column. She heard the deep cough and the sizzle of the grassland behind her as the beast launched a gout of acid. The ground shook as the monster turned to follow.

Melias shouted from somewhere. Gone was the hesitant, mousy young woman. Her voice now was confident, certain. "Glory of Razmir!"

The monster roared.

"Melias!" Calvonis called. Elyana guessed he must either be at the side or the top of his monster. "How you ever survived this long—"

"Glory of Razmir!" Melias called, then shouted in pain that was quickly strangled.

Elyana knew instantly the monster had grabbed her with its tentacle. She had meant to wait and time her moment, but she'd be damned if she'd let another of the expedition die. Not while she still breathed.

She launched herself from behind the pillar.

The monster had turned to seek Melias and she now confronted its shell-like back and a long blue tail, curled up toward its monstrous back legs. Calvonis sat astride the thing at the height of the shell, though he was draped now in a spare robe. His hair was still matted with blood from the injuries that had killed him.

At the same moment Elyana launched the arrows at the back of his head, Aladel lunged out of the fog and drove his blade deep into the beast's right front leg. It howled in pain.

The arrows rebounded from Calvonis without ever reaching him. His cursed shield was up again. How many spells could he possibly have left?

The monster pivoted to face Aladel, still bearing Melias in its remaining tentacle. The girl struggled weakly, though both arms were pinned to her sides. Aladel retreated, and there was no scream when the beast spit acid after him, so she assumed he'd dodged clear.

Maybe she couldn't hit the summoner, but she could damned well hit the tentacle. Wind swift, Elyana cast two more shafts, plunging one after the other into the scarred area she'd noted earlier, halfway along the length of the limb. The beast hissed in pain and dropped Melias, who landed with a groan.

"You're only delaying the inevitable," Calvonis cried. "Hide in the fog if you like! I will kill you—"

The monster turned to face her, sweeping the tentacle like a battering ram. She grabbed her final arrow, nocked, let fly, then threw herself in the air, arching her back to pass above the swatting limb, clearing it so close that her trailing hair brushed against one of its golden veins.

At the same moment she struck the earth the arrow sank deep into the creature's eye socket. She looked up, watching her bow bounce once as it hit the ground.

And then, with a miserable, muted cry of anguish, the monster vanished. Elyana did not think it intentional, else Calvonis would not have plummeted suddenly to the ground with a bone-jarring thump.

Elyana was sore. Fatigue ate at her very being. Yet she fought down the first instinct, to reach for her sword, and scrambled over to Melias, still groaning upon the grass. The girl's eyes met Elyana's dully as the elf plucked the wand from the hand that grasped it tightly.

Calvonis was already climbing to his knees, and Aladel was hammering at the summoner's unseen shield with his sword.

The summoner's eyes widened as Elyana advanced and aimed the wand at him. "Glory of Razmir!" she cried, and the spherical shape of the magic shield was suddenly delineated by a splotch of green energy. Elyana repeated the call once, twice, as a wide-eyed Calvonis fumbled, searching the pockets of his robe.

And then the shield was down. The acid still sizzled in the grass surrounding Calvonis, who first tried backing from Elyana, then found himself arrested by the point of Aladel's sword.

He raised his open palms, slowly, and Elyana studied his face and the fine brown hair, clotted with his own blood and brains. Presumably the organ had regenerated all the ruined parts that still flecked his skin. She raised the wand.

"There is much I can tell you," Calvonis said. "I can be very, very valuable."

"Oh, I think I've figured it out. You were going to call something up, and use it for the glory of your mad god. I don't really care what it was, or what you were after."

"It's a lot more complicated than that," Calvonis said with a knowing smile.

"I'm sure it is. Everything you say is a lie, Calvonis. So give me one truth I can test."

He actually looked relieved. "Name it."

"That amulet of resurrection we found on Kilvor. How do I use it?"

He laughed. "The same way you activate that wand." Then he tried to make a jest. "You going to test it on Kilvor?"

"Oh, I'm guessing you've killed someone I cared about out there, or I'd have more allies joining me by now." She aimed the wand.

"I thought you said you were going to give me a test!"

"Glory of Razmir," Elyana answered.

He only screamed once, because she had aimed very carefully.

Aladel practically leapt from the smoking body, then shouted at her. "I thought you were playing with him!"

"No." Elyana looked down at the corpse. "That really was the only thing I wanted out of him, and probably the only true words he would have spoken, because he thought I'd test it immediately." She turned away from the staring elf and the mutilated body, and walked to the wounded girl. "Let's see to her, then look for the rest of our friends."

Chapter Twenty
The Calm Before
Drelm

The fog was gone when Drelm opened his eyes, and the sun was up. The warmth kissed his skin and he sucked in the fresh air, cool with the breath of winter.

The last thing he truly remembered was the sorcerer, witch, or druid—Drelm didn't know what she'd been and didn't care—throwing a spell upon him. After that all had been a blur of rage and pain. And now he was here, peacefully lying in the grass.

Was he a prisoner? What had happened to Elyana and the others?

He sat up and instinctively reached out to his right. His axe was there, and so he knew even as his eyes took in the scene that Elyana was alive and well, and that she had tended him, for only she would have known to put the weapon in comforting reach.

The sun shined down from a pale blue sky and wind brushed the tips of the long green grass. In the wreck of the camp, Elyana and Aladel stood talking with three brown-robed strangers. More Oakstewards? A few yards to the right were armored men he didn't know, assaulting the ground with heavy shovels, and near them were what he briefly took for a pile of rags, then understood as bodies.

"Tymon," said Lisette beside him, and he turned to consider the markswoman.

She sat on a log just on his left, a pistol resting in the palm of her hands. In the bright light the bore of the weapon took on a beautiful cherry glow.

"Warriors from Tymon and some real Oakstewards turned up a while back," she said. "Hindreck sent for them. He wasn't in on it."

"In on what?" Drelm asked.

"Remember how I said that this whole thing was a protection racket?"

"Yes." The summoner had meant to draw people to his god by causing fear and chaos, and then keep the beast and other attacks away from the newly converted followers.

"Turns out there was more to it." Lisette sounded tired. "The summoner was setting up a huge summoning ritual. It looks like they were going to call something in from the Outer Planes, which is why he was making sure blood was spilled in specific places, sometimes at specific times. At least that's what these new druids think."

Drelm wasn't entirely sure he wanted to know, but he couldn't help wondering. "What was he going to call up?"

"Nobody knows. Elyana killed Kilvor and Calvonis both."

"Kilvor was—wait, did you say Calvonis?"

Lisette smiled thinly. "The druid was in on it. Seems even some of them can be bought for the right price—in this case, probably that Razmiri amulet he used to bring Calvonis back." She seemed to recognize Drelm's growing confusion, because she hurriedly changed the subject.

"Anyway, he resurrected Calvonis when the rest of the summoner's allies turned up disguised as reinforcements. Their original plan was to drug us last night so we'd be nice and quiet for a big dawn ceremony. But Elyana and Grellen and I didn't go under, and Kilvor didn't want to play his hand too soon, so he waited—"

"But Calvonis is dead?" Drelm asked. He wanted to be sure of that.

"Twice." Lisette flashed a death's-head grin.

Her eyes turned briefly toward where Hindreck sat hunched with Melias and Illidian and Cyrelle, drinking beside a fire. Drelm knew a sudden pang of hunger, as if the sight of the food had awakened his stomach.

"Hindreck thinks some of the spells Kilvor was throwing against the monster last night were probably thrown against Shalon. The redhead."

Drelm grunted. "So Kilvor was a traitor?"

"Kilvor," Lisette said, turning the pistol over in her hand, "was helping to drag four of us to the middle of the field where we were going to be used in a ceremony. That little piece that turned you into a monster was carting me. Whatever they were going to conjure up had to have blood from a living host."

Wizards, summoners, and sorcerers. Drelm didn't much care for any of them. "Casualties?"

"Grellen didn't make it," Lisette answered slowly. "It was the damnedest thing. Cyrelle and Illidian and Grellen were all of 'em deader than dirt. You were close to death too, incidentally."

Drelm blinked.

"I shot you," she went on, "when you attacked me. You remember that?"

Drelm shook his head.

"I've been sitting here watching your body finish healing itself for the last hour. Elyana said it was the ring she gave you."

Curious. But since he was clearly fine, he was more concerned with other matters. "You said the others were all dead. And they're alive right over there."

"Right. Like I said, Kilvor's amulet brings people back from the dead, remember? He used it to pull back Calvonis. Well, Elyana used it on the first two of us she found. But when she got to Grellen . . . the thing was out of power. Makes you think, doesn't it? I mean, if she'd gone left instead of right she probably would have found Grellen before Illidian."

"Grellen was a good fighter," Drelm said. "And brave."

"But not lucky. You need luck, too."

"Even luck runs out."

"So it does." She shook her head and looked at the gun again. "So," she said slowly, "it's all over. You get to go home now and have a happy ending."

Something in the way she said that sounded strange to Drelm, but he didn't understand why. She was probably weary, or sad because she had liked Grellen. In any case, it wasn't his place to pry, though he did think of a polite inquiry. "What are you going to do?"

She stared at him as if in shock, then fell suddenly to cold, cutting laughter. She set down the gun, pulled her battered hat from her head and rested with her hands on her knees, still laughing. At some point the hat's feather had been lost.

"What?"

She finished with a few final chuckles, then pushed hair from her eyes. "Nothing. It's just that you asked a fine, fine question. I don't know the answer yet." She paused, then added, "I have some choices to make."

That was like a woman, to keep talking even when she didn't really want to say anything. All the women he knew but Elyana were like that. "Elyana is leaving," he said.

The way Lisette looked up and stared, he knew that she'd misunderstood him.

"After my wedding," Drelm went on. "She thinks that she doesn't belong in Delgar."

Lisette sounded curious. "Where's she going?"

"She didn't say."

Lisette was quiet for a time, apart from the sounds of her adjusting her hat. In the end, she snorted and tossed it into the grass. "Damned thing's ruined." She looked him in the eye. "Elyana doesn't belong in Delgar. She's bigger than that place."

"She's welcome there. Avelis is a good man, and honors her."

Lisette let out a strange noise, almost as though something were caught in her throat, but when he turned to look at her she coughed briefly and waved off his concern.

"You could stay, too," Drelm offered. "Delgar will grow. There will be bandits, and raiders, and I will need steady hands to keep it safe."

"You want me to serve in Delgar?"

"If you like. You need not be a guard. Elyana serves the town, but holds no rank. You could be like that. You remind me of her," he added, "in some ways."

"What ways are those?" She sounded . . . unguarded. Often there was a wary, world-weary note to her voice, as if she were always holding something back.

Drelm shrugged. He thought it obvious. "You are both swift but deadly. Stealthy. Good in a fight. Reliable. It is hard to find trustworthy people. I am sure Lord Avelis would welcome you."

"I'm not so sure of that." She sounded wryly amused. She stood, then bent over to grab her hat and pistol. She pushed the former onto her head with a look of distaste and thrust the latter through her belt, where its twin already hung. "Let's see if there's any wine left."

"I'm hungry," Drelm said.

"Let's see about getting some food in you, then."

He liked that plan, and was soon sitting with all the surviving comrades of the road but Aladel and Elyana. All were silent, tired. Melias's eyes were red-rimmed. Yet travelers found strength in each other's company, even if they did not speak.

After a little time, Elyana and Aladel—his black cloak cast off—strode up to their campfire. Drelm moved aside and indicated a space beside him, but Elyana did not yet sit.

"The Oakstewards are going to be able to send us back to Delgar, soon," she announced. "But I think I want to wait for nightfall so we can have a chance to rest. And there's another matter."

Drelm saw that her eyes were bloodshot, and her shirt and breeks were streaked with dirt and blood. "The outpost," he offered.

Elyana seemed to see him for the first time, and gave him a sad smile. "Glad to see you up and around. No, Drelm. Our allies from Tymon already checked out that outpost, and it was abandoned. Maybe that's where Calvonis's allies were before they attacked us this morning. It's hard to know. There've been so many lies . . ." She shook her head. "No, I'm talking about the Razmiri temple in Delgar."

Drelm growled in sudden realization.

"We can't be sure that any other Razmiri were in league," Elyana said quickly. "So I don't mean to wander in and start slaughtering. But I think it best we escort any of their priests to the village edge before word of our return leaks out. I don't expect any of you to help," she added, "because that's out of—"

"Of course we'll help," Illidian said sharply.

"I'd like to come," Hindreck said, and Drelm studied the chubby druid as he spoke on. "As penance or my brother's betrayal. He should not have interfered in political matters."

"Political matters," Cyrelle repeated with a snort.

The druid didn't acknowledge her comments. "You might need me against a priest. But don't you need your mayor's approval before you start throwing people out of your settlement?"

"I am the guard captain," Drelm said with pride, "and act with the mayor's full blessing."

"In more ways than one, I hear," Cyrelle said, then laughed at her own rude humor, adding, "or at least you will pretty soon."

Drelm frowned at that, but many of the others smiled, so he judged that the comment had been offered in good humor.

Everyone else spoke up then, saying that they, too, wanted to be there for this final act. Elyana stressed again that they shouldn't wander in with swords bared, although she thanked them for their support.

"Still, someone should inform the mayor." Lisette set down the wine sack and wiped her lips with the back of her hand. "When we arrive, why don't I run to tell him, and I can summon Demid and the rest of the guard in case you need backup?"

Drelm thought that good sense, and was further evidence of why someone of Lisette's intelligence would be welcome in Delgar on a permanent basis.

"Well said," Elyana agreed, and then, after a few more details were sorted out, walked back to converse again with the trio of druids. Aladel followed.

"She's got a shadow now," Illidian said, eyeing his comrade.

Aladel seemed an alright sort, for an elf.

"I wonder if she's planning to do a little unwinding this evening with her new friend," Cyrelle said to Drelm with a smile. Drelm liked the huntswoman, but she tended toward a sort of coarseness that the half-orc didn't approve of. He stared hard at her.

"Oh, what are you looking at?" Cyrelle asked him. "Everyone needs a good ride now and then, to clean out the pipes. Death comes for all of us sooner or later, and then you'll regret those chances you didn't take."

Drelm finished chewing the deer jerky, swallowed, then lifted the filthy remnant of his tabard between thumb and forefinger.

"You might as well throw that out," Illidian told him.

"It's the only tabard I have with me," Drelm said. "And if I'm to present myself as a guardsman of Delgar tonight, I must wear it." He wondered if there was a stream nearby where he might rub out the worst of the stains.

Illidian's eyebrows rose delicately. "Your ethics are commendable, Captain."

"Wouldn't you do the same," Drelm asked, "if you reported for duty in Kyonin?"

Illidian smiled sadly. "Perhaps I would. I'm not sure, now." The captain had changed into a clean blue shirt, and his false appendage protruded from its half-length sleeve.

"What's changed?" Drelm asked him.

"I've lost three commands, Captain. And my arm. I can still use my bow, after a fashion, and my skill will improve with practice. But I think my days as a border guard are finished. I'll have to find something else, and I don't know what it will be.

"You don't have to return," Lisette said.

Illidian shook his head. "I must report all that has transpired."

"Aladel could do that," Lisette said casually, as if it were perfectly appropriate for an officer to walk away from his post without notice.

"And where would I go?"

"You might go with Elyana," Drelm suggested.

"To Delgar?" Illidian asked.

"She's not staying anymore," Drelm told him.

"Really? Why not?"

Drelm wasn't sure, but as he turned the problem over in his mind, he thought back to Baron Stelan and Renar and how she had grown sad to see them aging. He frowned. "Because she is tired of outliving her friends," he managed finally.

"You should feel blessed for every friend you have," Melias said.

Apart from an occasional please or thank you, these were the first words the girl had spoken since Drelm had joined the meal, and he was surprised to hear from her. The young sorcerer sat with her knees hugged to her chest.

"Wisely said," Hindreck told her.

"Where are you going to go, girl?" Cyrelle asked, not unkindly.

It was a long time before she replied. "I don't know. The monster killed my family and smashed our home. My brother is dead. All I have are the belongings I packed with me."

"You can buy new things when the mayor pays you," Drelm reminded her.

"That's not what's really bothering her, Drelm," Cyrelle said. "Melias, you can come with me if you want. It's rough living, but there's space for you till you figure out what you want to do."

Drelm understood then, and nodded in sympathy. "I'm sure the lord mayor would provide the same," he said. "I'll speak to him."

"The Oakstewards are grateful for your help as well," Hindreck ventured, cautiously. "I'm certain you would be welcome in Sevenarches."

"You are all very kind." A sad smile ghosted across the girl's lips.

"I know things have been bad." Cyrelle's gaze was intent. "You lost a long line of people, and someone you were getting fond of in another way. But you won through, Melias. You've got courage. Someday this pain will be a dull ache."

"Do you think?" Illidian asked. "I'm forever stuck with my reminder. And even if I seek out a healer with the magic to regrow my limb, how do I ever forget the loss of those who served with me?"

"They have spells for that," Lisette offered.

Illidian laughed bitterly. "So I should push the memories of my friends from my thoughts?"

"I was mostly joking." Lisette sounded annoyed. "But if you can't remember them, they can't hurt you."

"If I don't remember them," Illidian said, "who will?"

"To forget your friends dishonors them," Drelm said simply.

Illidian watched the half-orc in silence for a moment. "I grow to like you more and more, Captain."

"What are you going to do now, Lisette?" Cyrelle asked. "You have plans for the money?"

"I did. I'll probably put it toward the purchase of a new musket, although I don't know if I can buy one outright. I may have to hire a craftsman to try and make one off of this plan. It won't be cheap."

"How will you find a new . . . assistant?" Illidian asked.

"If you know any capable volunteers, tell me." Lisette studied Illidian as if she waited for something, but he didn't speak.

A fine idea had come to Drelm. "Illidian," he said, "you could come to Delgar, like Lisette."

"I'm not staying in Delgar." There was a vicious edge to Lisette's response. "You really think you're going to get your happy ending?" She sounded as if she thought he was stupid, which puzzled Drelm.

"What's gotten into you?" Cyrelle demanded.

Lisette laughed bitterly. "Do you think *any* of us will get a happy ending? Look at us. Like as not you'll die alone with your animals."

Cyrelle's thick brows drew together.

"Elyana and I are veterans of so many fights we can't even form proper attachments. And the girl over there—she's scarred for life now, with home, family, brother, lover, all dead. What's the best that can happen to her? And Illidian. Talk about scars."

"And me?" Drelm asked quietly. "You didn't say what was wrong with me."

Lisette laughed shortly. Her hair hung wildly about her face and there was a mad gleam in her eyes. "You've the best chance of all of us." She climbed to her feet, steadied her hand on her gun belt, and stepped away. "It's the damnedest thing," she muttered as she walked off toward their bedrolls.

"Don't let her bother you," Cyrelle told Drelm.

"I won't," he assured her.

"What do you suppose that's all about?" Hindreck scratched his beard.

"Some of us have scars that are more obvious than others," Illidian answered.

Drelm wasn't entirely sure what he meant, but he did know that some kept their problems quiet, which he respected. Something was troubling the bounty hunter. He supposed that she'd talk about it if she wanted advice. Otherwise, it was really none of his business.

Chapter Twenty-One
Errands in the Night
Lisette

She should have stuck to the strategy she and Kerrigan had adopted upon her departure from the Black Coil. She would only hunt the men and women identified as criminals by established governments.

If Kerrigan had lived, all sorts of things would be different, of course. If he'd been with her, he would surely have discouraged her from the deal with Avelis, no matter how good the money was.

Misfortune had dogged her since that meeting. It wasn't just that the trip had been unpleasant; she'd dealt with much unpleasantness over the years to get close to targets. It was the loss of Karag. Surely she could train someone else to load her weapons, but would any new assistant be so excellent at disposing of other problems as Karag had been? Would anyone respect her privacy so well, and so easily stand to fight when the enemies swarmed in?

As she closed her eyes that morning, trying to find the rest her body craved, she wished more and more that she had understood, sooner, that Karag had been more than an assistant. Maybe not quite a full partner, but someone that she might at least have consulted. For Karag had been right about the mission. If she'd taken the simple step of speaking with him about the mayor's offer, he would have talked sense, and they would even now be on their way to Andoran and some better opportunity. But she'd kept him at arm's length, maybe because, after Kerrigan, she didn't want anyone really close.

Now Karag was worm food, so he couldn't tell her he'd been right to be suspicious. It's not as though she could complain to Avelis that Drelm had been wearing a magic ring she hadn't known about. A clever assassin wouldn't have let that stop her.

More bothersome, when she'd finally tried to kill him she hadn't wanted to pull the trigger. Assassins didn't *like* their targets. She'd gotten her emotions involved, just as the master had always complained.

Lisette didn't go out of her way to pray to any gods, because she figured if she ignored them they might be more inclined to ignore her. But she was starting to feel that they'd had it out for her on this one. It was funny, really, to present her with the perfect moment to slay the half-orc and then make it impossible to do so. The ring had been a marvelous touch.

More and more she was thinking that she'd simply slide out of Delgar after collecting those heads Karag had preserved for her. Just disappear, and count the whole thing as a loss, and herself as lucky it hadn't gone even more wrong. She wouldn't run to the mayor. She'd retrieve the chest she'd paid the innkeeper to store, and leave town on whatever horse or boat she could find. Avelis could kill Drelm himself. She'd keep the half payment because she figured she'd more than earned it, but she wouldn't bother with the rest, seeing as how she hadn't finished the job.

And Illidian . . . he could go sulk in Kyonin. She shouldn't even have considered the possibility, however briefly, that he might accompany her, and she was furious with herself for making the desire so patently obvious. Actors and poets had nothing on elves as far as brooding self-involvement went.

Tired as she was, she managed to drift off despite her worries, and the gods were kind, for it passed dreamlessly.

On waking, she even felt moderately well rested. But she was still in no mood to eat with the others, who acted injured that she wouldn't laugh and joke and talk further of the future. It was with great relief that she packed her gear at sunset and lined up with the surviving expedition members in front of the ash tree. Elyana had told the druids that an ash stood on Delgar's outskirts, and that, apparently, was enough for the parchment-skinned Oaksteward to work his magic.

After much chanting the old man touched the tree, bowing his head to the old wood as though it were a high noble, then motioned Elyana toward the tree.

Elyana stepped up first, putting a hand to the bark. Her fingers passed through. The elven woman glanced back at the line of them, offered an encouraging smile, and then the tree rippled as she moved into it, like passing through a curtain. Drelm went next.

And then it was Lisette's turn. Once she had moved into the tree (or was it through? She was a little uncertain about the specifics) there was a moment of almost breathless darkness and the smells of moist earth, distant cook fires, and the half-orc's oiled chain. Another step, and she stood beside him and Elyana outside the darkened bulk of Delgar. She moved aside, looking with her comrades at the avenues of the village, carefully planned by the man the two of them revered. The man who actively planned to kill his own guard captain.

A few lights flickered in the windows of homes, and music rolled out from a tavern farther down the street, but on the whole the place was nothing like the bustling town it had been when they departed. It still smelled of the river, and fish.

"It's better," Drelm said quietly, "without all the strangers."

Melias came through the tree next, then Hindreck, and, whimpering, Cyrelle's dogs, their tails slung low.

It was time to act. Lisette shrugged off her reluctance with her bedroll and camping gear and set the equipment beside the tree. With any luck, she'd shortly be back with a horse and off on her way.

She slipped her rifle over her shoulder as Aladel and Illidian came through.

"I'm headed for the mayor," she said softly. "Wish me luck."

"May Abadar guide your steps," Drelm said solemnly.

She offered only a sad smile in answer. Briefly, her mind touched again upon the idea that she might leave some kind of note for them, a warning, so they'd know what Avelis really planned. But that wasn't her lookout. Karag might've argued that she owed them her life, but the way she figured things, they'd all risked their lives for one another plenty of times. Nothing was owed anybody, lest you count the money from Avelis. The mission was over.

She hurried away, hand to the strap that kept the rifle to her shoulder, and soon she was in among the shadows and moving down a little side alley. The keen-eyed elves might well be wondering why she darted to the east rather than heading straight north toward the city center and Delgar's tower. Presumably they would think she thought to move without being seen. But while that was true, this was the faster way to the home of Madame Celene.

She knew she didn't have long. How long could it possibly take for Elyana and the others to clear out a Razmiri temple? Likely there would only be one or two priests, and maybe some guards. There might be some shouting, but the Razmiri couldn't possibly have so many powerful clerics that they'd send them to remote outposts in the River Kingdoms. The odds were fair to good that the local priest would have little or no magic.

In all, it would probably take no more than fifteen minutes to speak to the Razmiri and get them moving. Perhaps another fifteen would pass before someone from the expedition encountered the local guardsmen, or even the mayor himself, at which point Elyana would start wondering where Lisette was and why she hadn't spoken with them.

As Lisette rounded the corner, jogging for the narrow wood-frame house near the end of the street, she began to realize how trapped she truly was. Even supposing she got out of town in time, Elyana could, and probably would, track her. If for no other reason than because she left so mysteriously.

Unless she left a note.

Lisette slowed as she neared the door to Madame Celene's, and got her breathing under control as she headed up the steps to the small wooden porch.

She wouldn't have to be specific. All it would take would be a letter saying that she hated goodbyes, or something to that effect.

Lisette reached the sturdy door and knocked gently upon it, and after a brief delay she detected the flare of a lantern through cracks in the wood. An eye slot slid open.

"Who is it?" Madame Celene asked. Her voice was taut, as if with worry.

"One of your boarders. Lisette Demonde."

"Oh." Madame Celene sounded surprised. The eye slot slid shut. "Just a moment," Celene said, her voice muffled.

But it was more than a moment, and Lisette soon found herself knocking a second time.

The door opened as she lowered her hand.

Stuffy little Madame Celene clutched a shawl over her stooped shoulders with one hand and held a lantern in the other. Muscles clearly unaccustomed to a smile strained into one. "Sorry," she said. "I needed to take the kettle off. My goodness. So you're back! Does that mean the monster's dead?"

"The monster's dead," Lisette affirmed. "I need access to my belongings."

"Well, of course. Our prayers have been answered, then," she said, leading the way to the cellar door.

The space beneath the home was small and cramped and, thankfully, the woman did not follow her down when Lisette went to unlock the chest.

The two grisly mementos of her most recent bounty-hunting expedition were still stored in their eelskin sack inside. Celene stared down at her from the height of the stairs, but could not see within.

Lisette pocketed her lock, cinched up the bag, and lifted it free. "I wonder if I might purchase a piece of paper to write a note."

"Of course."

The bag in hand, Lisette pretended nonchalance as she followed the woman into the front room of the house, which was a cramped receiving room complete with a desk and ledger.

"But the monster really is dead?" Celene asked.

"It won't bother anyone ever again."

Madame Celene tore a piece of paper from the ledger and cleared her throat as she pushed it across the dark desk, along with an inkwell and pen. "That will be three silvers for keeping things in my storage chest. I'll let you have the paper as a gift, for your service to the village."

Lisette had met bookies and highwaymen more generous than this woman. "Kind of you."

As Lisette set the bag at her feet she heard the two heads thunk lightly together and grinned at the thought of Madame Celene having no idea what lay so close beside her. She tapped the desk, staring at the parchment. There was no time to delay; why, then, couldn't she put her thoughts together?

For some reason, some part of her still wanted to warn Elyana and Drelm about Avelis.

She cursed under her breath. What to say, though? How much time had passed?

In the end, the words just flowed out of her.

Elyana,

I left this evening rather than bring the city guard. Wish it didn't have to be that way.

Don't trust the mayor. He tried to hire me to kill Drelm.

It would have to do. She folded the paper, then reached into the lantern, broke off the candle—eliciting a gasp of disapproval from Celene—and dripped hot wax all along the seal.

Lisette then plopped down four silvers and held out the letter and the candle.

Celene took them both with a sniff of disapproval.

"This is for Elyana Sadrastis. Give it to her when she comes looking for me. But only her, no one else."

"As you say," Celene said, looking down her nose. Apparently someone who broke candles ranked about as highly in the old woman's esteem as a sweat stain, hero or otherwise.

"It's been great being here," Lisette said, then swung up the proof of her bounty and hurried out the door.

Maybe if she hadn't been in such of a hurry, she might have noticed the two men before they stepped out of the shadows.

She halted on the edge of the porch as they came up, thick fellows pushing back cloaks to better reach their sword hilts

"You're Lisette Demonde, ain't you?" the one on the left asked.

"Who are you?"

"Friends of the mayor," said the dark figure on the right. His diction was far more precise, his manner cultivated.

Behind her she heard Celene latching the door tight.

"He don't like loose ends," said the first speaker

"Terribly sorry about that," the second said. "Terribly."

So Celene had been told to watch for her. Clever. Her nephew had probably been sent to find these two, which was the real reason Celene had been so long about answering. If Lisette hadn't been so preoccupied, she would probably have been a lot more suspicious. She forced a pleasant note into her voice. "You boys must have been waiting a long time."

"Weren't no big thing," the large man on the left said. "We had rooms in the home, like. Easy money, waiting on you."

"What did the mayor offer?" Lisette asked.

The polite one cleared his throat. "Now, in your line of work, you know it's bad form to discuss contracts."

"Or to talk too much."

Lisette tossed the bag of heads at the dumb one and, by reflex, he fumbled to catch it.

The other had a knife ready, but the startled cries of his friend delayed him just a moment.

A moment was all Lisette required. She drew her gun in a flash, drew back the hammer, and pulled the trigger.

Her assailant was rushing the steps when the blast caught him. The flash from the gun illuminated the scene as she blew off his chin, and he dropped screaming.

His big partner rushed the porch, sword out. There was no time to pull her second pistol, so she leapt over the dying man.

The larger man was hampered by the clutching hands of his dying companion, who tore at his pant leg. He cursed at her and came on.

But Lisette had gained the moment she needed. One moment, one bullet. At point-blank range, with dry powder, she couldn't miss, and didn't.

The big man grunted as the bullet took him in the chest, but the rest of his body didn't realize he was dead. He thrust. Swift as Lisette was, the blow grazed her ribs.

She bit back a cry as she hopped away and felt her side. The giant crumpled in on himself, as if bowing to her, then lay in the dirt. Elsewhere, up and down the street, candles flared to life in windows. Voices called out in surprise.

It just couldn't get much worse. Lisette's hands came away wet from where she pressed them to her side. Damn. It stung like blazes. No time to bandage, now, and her medical supplies were back with the tree in any case.

She shoved both smoking pistols back through her belt and scooped up the bag before speeding into the darkness, free hand clutching to her side.

She owed Celene, but there was no time. Not when there was a more important target. Lisette had planned no claim against Avelis before, not when she hadn't come through. Now he owed her, and she planned to take payment in blood or money, whichever came easier.

Chapter Twenty-Two
Blood and Dust
Elyana

In larger cities the temple district might stretch on for blocks, or there might be temples to various gods scattered randomly throughout the streets. Delgar was so small that there were only two buildings that could be classified as temples. The goddess Calistria was worshiped by all those who thrived on trickery, hoped to punish those who'd wronged them, and liked a good roll in the hay, which meant practically everyone. She remained as popular in Delgar as she had ever been throughout the River Kingdoms, and her temple was the oldest by a year, and the largest, though it was little more than a converted cabin rumored to once have been a whorehouse. Calistria, Elyana suspected, probably didn't mind.

More recent was the stone shrine beside it, erected at Drelm's behest, to Abadar.

Most recent of all was the temple to Razmir. It too was wood, but the Razmiri had spared no expense and covered it first in plaster, then painted it with brilliant gold and reds and hauled in stone steps that led to the wide doors opening to its interior.

Elyana and the others paused just beyond those doors. As she directed Cyrelle, Aladel, and Melias to scout the building's rear, she couldn't help overhearing the prayer from within.

"Sounds like a full house," Drelm said, frowning.

She didn't remember any exits on the building's right side, opposite from where she'd sent the others toward the back, but she wished to leave as little to chance as possible. "Make sure there are no north-side exits," she told him, and Drelm hurried into the darkness.

The Razmiri priest, she supposed, was haranguing the crowd. Hindreck stepped up to her shoulder, turning his ear toward the door.

"Pray," the voice cried. "Pray with all of your fervor, all of your heart, and ask Razmir for protection. It is his to give. His is the will."

"His is the will," a chorus of voices repeated.

"What a strange religion," Hindreck muttered.

"Aren't they all?" Elyana asked.

"His is the way!" The priest cried.

"His is the way," his followers repeated.

Drelm came trotting back up from the darkness. "No exits on the north."

"Right. You ready for this?"

Illidian had been strangely silent since Lisette had hurried off, and when he spoke, his savage eagerness was startling. "I am more than ready," he promised darkly.

"Pray then for Razmir to shield you!" the priest shouted. "Pray that he might guide all your people to his loving embrace. For there is safety with Razmir."

Drelm growled low in his throat.

Elyana was putting her hand to the doors when she heard the gunshot. She froze. A week ago she wouldn't have recognized that popping noise.

It seemed to have come from the northwest, near the city's outskirts.

"That was a gun," Illidian said, but she silenced him with a raised hand, for she thought she'd heard a shout.

Then there came a second gunshot.

"Drelm, you handle this. Illidian, back him up."

"But—" Illidian started to object.

"Stay with Drelm!" Elyana snapped. She was already running.

It had taken longer than she wished to drop their heavier gear and divvy up roles, but then she'd taken it slow because she wanted to give Lisette time enough to reach the city guard post and the mayor. Much as she wanted the Razmiri out of the city, she wanted the mayor involved, lest she or Drelm be accused of overstepping their authority.

Now she wondered both if she'd waited too long and what it was that Lisette was doing at the wrong end of the city. Surely no other guns had come to Delgar in the intervening days.

Her long legs carried her quickly through the streets. Tired as she was, she was breathing heavily by the time she rounded the corner and found the crowd gathered outside the tall stone building that was the widow Celene's home and boarding house.

A throng of some dozen were there with lanterns, and Madame Celene herself watched timidly from the porch. Everyone else crowded around something in the street. Elyana didn't see the bodies until she had pushed her way through.

At sight of her the crowd fell silent, and her examination of the scene was disrupted and delayed by glad cries. At any other time she would have been delighted to be so well received, but she offered only a distracted smile at the questions.

"The monster's dead," she said, "and Drelm and I are returned."

At mention of the captain a number of the people brightened further. Not even in Stelan's lands, where he had first risen to a position of leadership, had he been so well regarded. A small woman then lay into her with a whole set of questions, and Miklos the tanner chimed in, asking for details. As other queries thundered around her she held out her hands.

"Silence, please. What happened here?"

They told her how they'd heard the shots and the scream. A few had seen a shadowy struggle at the door of Celene's home, then someone had run into the darkness.

More and more people gathered, and Elyana asked them to step back. They'd probably already made a muddle of the tracks.

"Which way did the figure go?" Elyana asked.

Miklos pointed south, and Elyana slipped quickly past the crowd, searching the ground. A few steps farther on, beyond the crowd's prints, she discovered a drop of blood and the leather-soled shoes she knew by shape for Lisette's.

So she'd been wounded. Elyana turned quickly back, her eyes raking over the bodies. It was easy to recognize Lisette's handiwork. One of the victims, the one with the ghastly face wound, was still groaning feebly.

"Get him to a healer," Elyana snapped. "And hurry."

Miklos snapped to work then. Calling two burly men to aid him, he lifted the fellow up. A child of no more than eight picked up the blood-and-dirt-crusted thing Elyana now recognized as what was left of the man's jaw and trotted after. At sight of that, one of the women turned and vomited in the street, and a few others looked noticeably pale.

Lisette was wounded, and probably in need of help. But there was much here that Elyana didn't understand. She turned to Madame Celene. She had never been especially fond of the old woman, but she'd never before been suspicious of her.

"Did you see what happened here?"

"Not really," Celene said thickly. "It was very dark."

"Any idea why Lisette Demonde was on your doorstep?"

"She roomed with me. She'd come back to gather something."

"Something?"

"A bag. I don't know what it was."

"Her nephew ran over to my tavern," said a voice behind her, "and got those two. The dead one and the dying one."

Elyana glanced back to find the red-bearded owner of The Roisterer's Inn glaring at Celene.

"They've been staying at her place the last couple days," he continued.

Celene blinked nervously then, and hemmed and hawed until Elyana advanced upon her.

She shrank back.

"I'm tired right now," Elyana said, "and I don't have much patience. I suggest you start with the truth and save me some time."

"They showed up right after she left," Celene said. "They took rooms, and made sure I always knew where they were going. They were good tenants."

"Model, I'm sure," Elyana said dryly. "Get to the point."

"Well, they told me they were waiting for Ms. Demonde to return, and to notify them as soon as she did. I didn't know they were going to attack her!"

"Of course not. Did you mention them to Lisette?"

Again Celene hemmed and hawed.

"Because they paid you not to mention them."

"They didn't say why," Celene said primly.

This was taking entirely too long. Elyana fought down the urge to shake Celene, partly because she knew it was the wrong way to handle an old woman, but mostly because people were watching. "Alright then. I think I've got enough grounds to run you out of town. I'll just send for the mayor—"

Celene's eyes bulged. "No! I didn't do anything wrong!"

"Sounds to me like you did." Elyana glanced at the crowd behind her, and saw their hardened looks. Celene would find no sympathy from them.

"There anything else I need to know? Something I can tell the mayor to help your case?"

Celene glanced frantically between Elyana and the grumbling folk behind her. "There was a letter," she blurted out.

"A letter?" Elyana prompted. Gods, the woman was slow.

"Lisette wrote a letter. Said to give it to you if you turned up."

"Then give it to me!"

"I can't!"

Elyana stepped even closer, towering over the woman. It took tremendous willpower not to take her by the shoulders. "Why not?"

Celene's face drained of all color. "I burned it," she whispered, then licked dry lips. "I . . . I was afraid about what it said."

"You read the letter?"

She nodded. "I was going to reseal it until I saw . . ."

Elyana lowered her voice. "I'm only going to ask once. Tell me, very quietly, what it said."

Again the woman gulped. Her breath smelled of sour apples and disease, and Elyana held her breath lest she breathe in more as Celene whispered her answer.

At the words, Elyana's brows rose in astonishment, and she pulled away. Celene cried out, shielding her face with one arm as though she expected Elyana to strike her.

But the elf's mind was already racing on, trying to reason through what she'd been told.

"What's happened?" the innkeeper called.

"Let her be," Elyana answered distractedly, then gently lifted the lantern from his wife's outstretched fingers. "Don't follow," she said, and used the lantern to pursue the tracks into the darkness. She was pretty sure she knew where they'd lead, and she was afraid she'd find something very bad when she reached their end.

Chapter Twenty-Three

The Temple and the Cleric

Drelm

Drelm pushed the temple doors open with such force that they slammed into the walls to either side.

The congregation sat in pews facing the altar where the masked Razmiri priest stood on a little platform. Two acolytes, broad-shouldered fellows in dark robes with deep hoods, stood behind him with bowed heads. The man faltered as Drelm stood on the threshold, then spoke on, asking the assembled to continue praying to Razmir for safety and protection.

Those at the rear of the temple turned to see who had made such noise, frowning in disapproval, then stopped short as Drelm advanced down the central aisle. More and more began to mutter, and word spread through them faster than fire in dry summer grass: Drelm had returned.

Hindreck and Illidian followed.

Finally, so many in the congregation were distracted from their prayer that the priest stopped his speech and addressed Drelm.

"May I help you, my child?"

It was only then that Drelm realized who sat in that front row nearest the aisle, for Daylah turned suddenly, her face lighting in wonder, then climbed to her feet and threw herself into Drelm's arms.

"Praise Razmir!" she said into his shoulder. "I knew it! I knew you would return to me."

When had she turned to this god? "Razmir had very much to do with it," Drelm said, "but not in the way you think." He put her aside, as gently as he was able, ignoring the curious, hurt look in her eyes. "The beast is dead," he told her, then addressed the congregation, louder. "We have killed the beast!"

The temple erupted into cheers of joy, and the priest cried out, clapping, "Razmir be praised!"

"The beast was sent by priests of Razmir," Drelm shouted, and the cheers floundered and clapping came awkwardly to an end.

"Surely," the priest began, then his iron mask turned as Illidian and Hindreck advanced from left and right. Hindreck looked none too pleased, but Illidian's face was bright with vicious joy. The two acolytes cast their robes aside and put hands to revealed sword hilts.

Drelm would let the others take care of the priests. It was time to explain. He faced the worshipers. "The priests sent the thing against those who would not worship their god, and protected those who did. They've tricked you."

"You blaspheme!" The priest cried.

Drelm turned to him in time to see a corona of blue energy come to the priest's fingertips as he raised them. "You mock Razmir in his own temple! My god's wrath is swift and terrible!"

His fingers flexed, and lightning sparked and hummed in a blue arc and struck the half-orc.

Drelm gritted his teeth against the numbing burn and shook his head to clear the spots from his eyes as he charged. The eyes behind the iron Razmiri mask widened in fear.

About him he heard the scream of those who watched, and Daylah's was especially cutting. He did not like to hear her worried.

The priest's cloaked acolytes raised swords as Hindreck and Illidian rushed forward. Drelm heard the druid chanting and the elf laughing in mad pleasure as swords clanged, but he did not see what they did.

He caught the lead priest by the throat and lifted him from the ground, the axe ready in his right hand.

"It is you who blaspheme," he snapped. "Yours is a false god."

While the fellow wriggled Drelm cast down his axe and tore free the mask. It clanged against the planked floor. The face of the man beneath was utterly ordinary: middle-aged, pockmarked, with a brown mustache and beard going to gray.

"Tell them," Drelm cried. "Did your so-called god send the beast? Give them the truth!"

The priest writhed for a long time, prying with his hands against the gloved fingers that seemed of iron. Finally, he gasped, "Yes!"

Drelm released him, and the priest crumpled to the floor planks, gasping and massaging his throat.

"Depart this land," Drelm commanded. "Depart this temple, and crawl back to your little god."

The priest climbed to his feet, stumbling down the aisle toward the front door, gasping as if he had run a span of miles. He reeled out the door. Illidian had killed the other acolyte, as Drelm might have guessed. The second knelt, quivering, before Hindreck.

"Send him away," Drelm commanded the druid.

Drelm took up his battleaxe as the moaning acolyte stumbled after his master, then considered the crowd. "Let the taint of Razmir's name be banished. Henceforth, this building shall be a temple to Abadar, where we can all contemplate justice and balance in his name."

Drelm spoke on. In the past, words had sometimes been difficult for him. This day, though, they came easily. He knew precisely what must be said. "There are some who say Abadar is god only to the wealthy, or that he means to pave the nations of the world so there's no land that does not quiver under the tread of empire. They profane his teachings! Laws and wisdom must be carried forward to all the lands. Thus will you prosper, so long as you strive always for balance."

Drelm felt then as though a weight had been lifted from him. For a moment, he breathed more clearly than he had ever breathed, and the aches and pain in his body eased. He stood blinking, looking at the familiar faces that stared back at him. He gazed then upon his axe, and at a strange gleam upon the gauntlet of his left hand. Until that moment, it had always been plain, yet now he saw it had been emblazoned with a golden key: the symbol of Abadar.

A miracle. The touch of Abadar's glory. Flabbergasted, he held it up to catch the light, letting the assembly look upon it.

Another might have sought to make further speeches, for he could tell that the crowd still waited upon his word. Yet he had no idea what to say.

"Daylah," he suggested at last, "let us go see your father."

Chapter Twenty-Four
Reckoning
Lisette

She saw no lights in the fortress and tower complex apart from those borne by the guard at the open postern gate. The building she knew for the mayor's residence betrayed light through a number of shuttered first-floor windows.

The best way forward now was to bluff her way in through the front. As she started up the steps to the house's porch she was surprised by a figure that rose from a sitting position.

"Lisette Demonde?" the figure asked, and she knew him immediately for the Brevic guard, Demid. His cheer did not sound forced. "It is you! But where are Drelm and Elyana? What's happened? Did you kill the beast?"

She didn't trust him; she was in no mood to trust anyone. Yet she sensed that his enthusiasm and interest were real, and she could play that to her advantage. "They're fine. And we killed the beast. I've got an urgent message for the mayor. Drelm and Elyana are at the Razmiri temple.

The Razmiri were behind all of it. You'd better get there and help them."

"The Razmiri?" Even as he asked the question, Demid hurried down the steps, his silver boot heels glinting in the candlelight. "I wish to hear it all," he said as he dashed off.

He'd hear more than he wished, very soon.

Lisette had forgotten to ask him to unlock the door, but she found it came open at her touch. The Brevan might be seasoned, but he trusted too easily.

She stepped into a sitting room where a stout older woman was folding sheets by candlelight. The lady turned in surprise.

"Message for the mayor," Lisette said, with a smile.

But the woman's expression didn't change, and Lisette realized the woman's gaze had tracked to Lisette's side. The bloodstain across her blouse was larger than she'd expected.

"It's worse than it looks," Lisette said easily, hoping that it was. "Where's the mayor?"

The maid directed her to another door with a shaking finger.

Lisette walked past, pushed open the door, and found Avelis behind a desk, studying a sheet of paper. A chandelier with a dozen candles was suspended above his head. He didn't look up until Lisette closed the door.

Avelis's handsome face froze in astonishment.

"I met some friends of yours," Lisette said, "outside Madame Celene's."

Avelis tried a smile, first. "You sound upset. I think there might have been some misunderstanding. Why don't you let me—" he started to rise.

Lisette leveled the rifle and pulled back the hammer. "There's been a misunderstanding, alright. I want the rest of the gems."

He raised empty palms. "I don't have them with me. Truly. You're a professional—is it really good form to come to my house? Doesn't that make this whole thing—"

He was stalling. Everyone wanted more time from her today. "Shut up. I'm likely to pass out soon, from blood loss. Maybe you're counting on that. Count on this: I'll shoot you before I drop. I want what I'm owed. And I'm owed double, seeing as how you tried to have me killed." She stepped closer, rifle still rock-steady. "I'm going to watch, and you're going to pull money out of that desk. You pull anything else out, and you'll die."

"You won't be able to leave Delgar alive if you shoot me."

Lisette laughed. "But I'll die satisfied."

The mayor opened a drawer and felt around inside. She stepped around to his side, her back to the timber wall. She was thankful to be able to lean on it for support, for she felt faint. "You've got the whole town fooled. Even Elyana, and she's no easy mark. What are you, really? A thief? A murderer?"

"Murderers don't raise children."

"Some third son who ran off with the family riches? I'm getting closer, aren't I? And where's your wife? Did she run with you, or run away?"

He pulled a small canvas sack from the drawer and set it, slowly, on top of the papers before him. "It was nothing like that."

"Are those the gems?"

The door opened behind her and a woman screamed.

Avelis was a hair faster than Lisette; her reflexes had slowed. He sprang out of the chair and knocked the barrel aside. Her shot blasted into the wall and the maid in the doorway screamed again. Gun smoke billowed in their faces and Lisette breathed in the acrid stink.

Before Avelis could press his advantage, she smacked him in the temple with the gun barrel and retreated around the desk.

The mayor grabbed a sword from the wall behind him and vaulted after.

She threw the rifle at him. Whatever he really was, he was out of practice as a warrior, no matter how fit he looked. He fumbled and stumbled and tripped over the gun, enough that she had time to draw her sword, though she could not hold off a gasp of pain as she did so.

"Go find help, Kandren," Avelis said, and Lisette heard a choked sob and retreating footsteps behind her. Avelis directed his sword toward her and came forward with a professional stance. "You'll never get away now. And no one will believe anything you say."

"Drelm's still alive," she told him, noting with pleasure the fire that lit in the back of his eye.

The mayor lunged in a fury.

Lisette deflected his blow, and the two that followed, astonished by her own weakness. In the old days she would have had a dagger up her sleeve, blinding powder ready. She had none of those things, now. Had she gotten careless, or old? Cocky?

"What did you possibly hope to do?" Avelis asked. "No one will believe you. And you'll be dead in any case. I know the sword. I studied with the finest fencing masters in Andoran."

"Elyana knows," she said. "I left a letter for her. She may be reading it now."

The mayor drove forward recklessly.

Lisette nicked his side and kicked a vase into his way, but her strength had ebbed almost completely. For all his posturing and his trim, athletic shape, she knew she could normally take Avelis, even on a bad day. The problem was that she was bleeding to death. She managed only a partial parry of a blow to her heart and his sword found her side.

She gasped, and nerveless fingers released their hold on her sword as she sank against the walls. As she dropped she spotted that bag of gems on the desk. Damned gems.

He advanced, swishing the sword in the air so that blood drops sprayed.

Lisette thought then of the knife in her left boot. It was agony to move her leg closer; each movement felt like she was ripping every muscle in her side.

"Where is this letter?" Avelis asked. "Tell me, and I'll spare you!" He pointed the sword tip at her throat.

"Go screw yourself."

"I gave your assassins poison," Avelis said, "to wipe upon their blades. I'm surprised it hasn't struck you yet. But I have the antidote. A wise man never handles poisons without an antidote. I'll give it to you if you tell me where the letter is."

She was too weak at that moment to tell him to screw himself again, but she thought her look conveyed the sentiment, because he pulled his sword back. She raised her chin so the strike would be quick. She thought of Kerrigan's broad, smiling face and his scarred brown hands, stained with black powder. Avelis swung.

Another blade interposed, his strike clanging against it.

Lisette turned her head and found Elyana in the room's doorway, weapon extended. The elf trapped the mayor's blade and forced him back as she advanced, eyes narrowed.

Avelis somehow managed to look relieved and stunned at the same time. "Elyana—it's wonderful to see you—"

Elyana's tone was short. Unlike Avelis, she didn't lower her blade. "What are you doing?"

"She got my letter," Lisette said, her voice little more than a whisper. "She knows."

"Set aside your blade, Mayor," Elyana instructed. "Lisette needs tending."

"I will not. This woman has tried to kill me. She is a member of the Black Coil—"

"And how do you know that?" Elyana asked

The mayor was stopped short by that simple question. "It's . . . I've made inquiries. It's complicated, Elyana. You'd understand if you'd—"

"Drop the weapon. Now. And step away."

The mayor released the sword, and it rang dully against the carpet thrown over the floor planks.

"Stand over there. In the doorway."

"She's bleeding to death," the mayor said. "It's probably too late."

Lisette thought the bastard was probably right. Elyana came around to her injured side so that she might see the wound and the mayor at the same time. She lay down her blade as she knelt.

"Summon a healer," she said as she ripped open Lisette's shirt fabric.

Avelis sounded like a petulant child. "I will not!"

She thought that Elyana tried to mask her reaction, but it was clear enough to see, as the elf studied her wounds, that it wasn't good.

"I've drained all my energies, Lisette," Elyana said simply. "I have no healing magic left this night."

She tried a laugh, but it was painful. "He tried to hire . . ." She coughed, and tasted blood.

"I believe you."

Lisette was very weary, now. There were things that had mattered to her very much, only a short while ago, that didn't seem to matter at all anymore. "Tell Drelm," she said, "enjoy . . . happy ending."

Chapter Twenty-Five

Farewells

Elyana

She knew it was only a matter of moments, then. She would sit next to her comrade while her life faded, and then she would decide what to do about the mayor.

Someone heavy had come into the house; she heard the footfalls, and a moment later recognized the distinctive jangle of Drelm's gear. The mayor stared at him in dread as he pushed through.

Something about Drelm had changed. Elyana thought she saw a peculiar, faraway look in her friend's face, and there was a curious sense of wisdom and sorrow there she'd never seen before.

The half-orc drove his axe through the carpet and into the floor, then knelt down on Lisette's other side.

She understood then what he must plan to do.

"Your ring can't help her, Drelm," she told him. "It can only heal damage taken while the ring is worn."

"I'm not giving her the ring," Drelm answered. He set his hand to Lisette's side, and a faint red glow arose from his fingertips, as though he had been touched with roses and cinnamon.

Elyana watched in astonishment as Lisette breathed in deeply, and the bloody holes in her side sealed from within. There was a faint lingering radiance, and an afterglow of warm light, and then the woman was fumbling disbelievingly at the site of her wounds.

"How . . ." was all Lisette managed. Elyana was wondering much the same thing. She would have asked her friend, but Drelm was rising to address the mayor.

"Your heart is torn," the half-orc told him. "By two mistresses: love and hate. You must seek absolution."

"From you?" the mayor spat. "Who led my son to his death? Who would taint my family's blood with that of orc?"

"He was fine with it while the boy lived," Lisette remarked to Elyana. "As long as he had an heir—a *human* heir—to pass the town on to, he was willing to give the girl as payment for Delgar's safety."

There were more footfalls from within the home, and as Elyana rose she saw Demid and Daylah arrive. Their faces were both fixed in strange, rapturous expressions.

The mayor sidestepped so he could address his daughter and keep his eyes upon the rest of them. "You shouldn't be here."

"Why did you hire her to kill Drelm?" Elyana asked.

"He killed my boy." The mayor's face twisted in anger. "You're so blind to it! Don't you see?"

"Your own grief blinded you," Elyana said wearily.

Daylah's brow furrowed, and she looked first to Elyana, then to Drelm for some kind of confirmation before finally turning to Avelis. "Father, is this true?"

All could see the answer in his glare.

"What about all those fine words?" Elyana asked. "Of a future where we could live as one. Together, no matter our origins or station. You meant them. I saw it in your eyes."

"We all did," Demid added quietly from the doorway.

Avelis struggled. "My child will not marry a monster."

"He's no monster, but a man," Daylah said, and went to take the man's arm. "The noblest one I know."

"Let us past," Drelm said, and moved for the door. Daylah walked at his side, her cheeks streaked with tears.

"You don't understand!" Avelis said. "It's so much more involved than any of you realize!"

Elyana bent to offer Lisette a hand, but whirled at a flurry of movement behind her.

It had happened in a heartbeat, and was already resolved, the figures falling from the action they'd taken. There was Avelis, halfway toward Daylah's back, a knife in his hand. But he was sagging, for Demid's sword had plunged through the mayor's chest.

Avelis landed a foot from Drelm's axe, clutching his bleeding side.

Demid pulled the blade out. His eyes were haunted. "I didn't mean—I just wanted to—"

Elyana shushed him as Daylah rushed past and threw herself down beside her father. "Drelm! Please, Drelm, save him!"

The half-orc turned on his heel and reentered the room.

"No!" Avelis cried. His voice shook with fury even as blood drained from his face. "He will not touch me! I will not look on a world . . . where you . . ."

He fell silent.

"Drelm, Please!" Daylah sobbed. "Save him! Please!"

"I don't have that power," Drelm said simply.

This morning you didn't have any powers at all, Elyana thought, but those were questions for another time.

The girl's head fell, and she sobbed as she draped herself over her father's body.

"I'm sorry," Drelm told her.

That night the expedition survivors gathered in the tower's hall for a strange and muted celebration. When they learned what had happened to the mayor, to a one they announced that they didn't wish to remain for his funeral. Elyana, acting as the city's ruler—for no other stepped forward—paid each of them promptly.

A few toasts were raised, and directions were exchanged among those who thought they might find their way to visit someday. Cyrelle made her farewells then, saying she'd be off before the dawn, and Melias said she'd be going with her. The huntswoman promised she'd turn Drutha's dog over to the halfling's relatives if they came to claim him. Drelm left next, saying he needed to go look in on Daylah, and the others all filed out of the hall where they'd first made their plans to fight the beast. All save Aladel, who waited for her beside the doorway as the servants came in to lower the wagon wheel and snuff the candles.

"I'll be leaving in the morning myself," he said. "I must make my report to Kyonin." His gaze then was level and direct. "If you're here when I return, I'd like to take some time to get to know you better. Over candlelight, firelight, or beneath the stars. Whatever you prefer."

She laughed gently.

"I think we're of a kind," Aladel continued.

"You have your charms," she admitted. "But you may well miss me. You can always seek me on the road."

"Which one?"

"Wherever the wind takes me."

He laughed. "You leave me a fair challenge!"

"Every courtship is a challenge, isn't it, Aladel?"

He laughed, then bowed to her and pressed her fingers to his lips. "I hope that we one day meet again, fair cousin."

With that, he walked from the keep and out into the night.

She woke early herself to brush and saddle Calda, who'd led all of the horses back to Delgar without any incident apart from something that had come out of the water after them. Despite the magic that allowed her to speak to the animal, the horse hadn't really remembered the details, only that the entire herd had gotten away.

Elyana expected there to be more goodbyes come the morning, so she wasn't surprised by the sound of footsteps in the dark stable, only by the person she saw when she looked up.

Daylah.

The young woman's hair was disheveled, though some attempt had been made to push it into place. Her eyes were red-rimmed.

The two stared at each other for a long moment, and then Daylah glided forward so that she stood in the lantern light. It burnished her locks with a hint of scarlet.

"Drelm said that you would be leaving," she said.

"Yes."

"He didn't think you'd ride out this morning."

"But you did?"

She smiled sadly. "Drelm sometimes believes what he hopes rather than what he expects."

Elyana hadn't realized the young woman was quite so perceptive.

"Do you know, I was just a little jealous of you at first," Daylah continued. "I knew there really was nothing between you two but friendship, but you still had something that he and I don't have."

"I don't know what you mean."

Daylah seemed reluctant to explain, but she cleared her throat. "Well, I have many friends. But how many of them would risk their life for me? It seems like there ought to be another word for *that* kind of friend. He trusts you in a different way than he trusts me."

"I am his sister. You are to be his wife. Of course it's different. But we're both family to him." As she finished, she saw Daylah's expression cloud.

"Family isn't always what it seems to be."

"Your father loved you," Elyana pointed out.

"I know. Among all that he did, I can hold onto that. But there's a lot I don't understand. Maybe I never will. Did he really believe all those things he was saying about living in harmony and working together? Were those the lies, and all that hatred for Drelm the real truth?"

Elyana hesitated, wanting to choose her answer with care. "Grief," she said at last, "can twist a person into strange shapes. I think your father wanted to believe what he said, even if he still carried hate."

"He fooled me."

"He fooled himself. He did a lot of fine things too, Daylah. Delgar wouldn't be so well ordered without him."

"Or without you, and Drelm. I think you two brought out the best in him."

"Maybe. I think there was good in there along with the bad."

"And it's easy to be good when good things are happening." She frowned solemnly. "I really didn't come to talk of my father, though. I wanted to thank you for being such a fine friend to Drelm. And I hope you know that, if you choose to return, you'll find another friend beside him."

Elyana smiled. "I think I knew that already. It was kind of you to come, Daylah. I want you to know . . ." she hesitated, and found that the words came only with difficulty. "How delighted I am that Drelm has someone else who can see who he really is, and not what he appears to be."

"You're sure that you can't stay for the ceremony?"

She shook her head.

"I thought I should ask." Daylah stepped forward, awkwardly extending her arms, and Elyana embraced her.

"I'm glad he found you," Elyana told her.

"Likewise."

After Daylah left, Elyana finished grooming Calda. She was cinching her saddle when Lisette and Illidian arrived. They looked surprised to see her.

"What are you doing?" Illidian asked.

"Readying to go," Elyana answered. "Just like you."

"But I . . ." Lisette fell silent, shook her head.

"The border guard can manage without me, I think," Illidian said. "I had a long talk with Aladel, and he'll turn over my resignation."

"We're traveling together," Lisette added. Elyana thought she detected a blush to her cheeks.

"I'd heard you two had a fight," she said.

Illidian glanced at Lisette. "A misunderstanding. I'm learning to be . . . flexible."

"Where are you headed?" Elyana asked.

"There's a bounty to claim, I gather," Illidian said. "And some gold to deliver to Karag's cousin. But then I think we might look into a real estate venture."

This utterly surprised Elyana. "Real estate?"

He laughed. "There are some mansions Lisette fancies, over in Andoran."

"He's beautiful *and* rich," Lisette said.

Elyana laughed.

"Thank you, Elyana," Illidian told her, then bowed his head formally. "We wouldn't have succeeded without you. Should the time come when you need me, I will come."

She bowed her head in acknowledgment.

"I owe you my thanks as well," Lisette said. "You reminded me . . ." Her voice dropped off, and she shook her head before finishing the thought. "Anyway, what Illidian said. It was good working with you. Let's do it again some time."

"Sure," Elyana said, though she didn't expect she'd see either again. "Lisette, when did you know you weren't going to kill him?"

The bounty hunter froze only for a moment, then glanced sidelong at Illidian. She didn't waste time asking how Elyana had deduced the truth, or figured out that the mayor hadn't just tried to kill her to cover up a rejected offer. "I've been wondering that myself. Some time before I actually shot him." She laughed shortly. "When I finally had the chance to do what I thought I wanted, I hesitated, and it gave the witch enough time to level me after I took him out. I'm glad I didn't . . ."

Again she glanced nervously at Illidian.

"I grew fond of him myself," the former captain said, so simply Elyana knew that he, too, must have deduced the truth. "You have good taste in friends, Elyana."

"So I see. I'm sorry for any harsh words I might have shared with you, Illidian."

"It's all passed now," he said carelessly. "The sun rises on a new day, and I ride forth with a friend."

She raised her hand to them, and they moved off toward the elf's horses.

She was leading Calda from the stables when Demid rode up, Drelm walking at his side. The Brevan, like herself, was packed with bulging saddlebags, blanket, sword, and travel pack.

Drelm was once again wearing a clean tabard with an image of the tower.

"It's bad enough that you leave," Drelm told her. "But why must you take Demid?"

"He doesn't believe me," Demid told her. "I keep telling him it's my idea, not yours."

"I believe you," the half-orc countered. "I just think she could convince you otherwise. Who will be captain of my guards?"

"I killed your father-in-law," Demid said very quietly. "Daylah and I both know the truth of how it happened."

The Brevan shook his head. "It will always lie between your wife and me, Captain. Elyana and I will see these payments delivered to their recipients. And then I'm for the steppe."

The half-orc shook his head, reached into a pouch at his waist, and lifted up a small bag. "Here, then."

"What's this?" Demid accepted the canvas gingerly. "I need nothing."

"Open it," the captain ordered with the hint of a growl.

Demid did as he was bid, and Elyana saw the thrill of discovery light his eyes.

"Maybe now you can buy that land that you always spoke of," Elyana said. "For your horses." She and Drelm had decided to give him a cut of the gems they'd found among the mayor's belongings.

"And fine land it shall be, too," Demid said as he tied the bag shut. "Where did you get this, Captain?"

"The mayor's past . . . must be complex," Elyana explained.

"I'll talk with Elyana alone now," Drelm told Demid, who bowed his head to them both and guided his animal to the watering trough.

"I thought you were going to give that to him last night."

"I thought you would stay longer." Drelm removed his helm and put it in the crook of his arm. "You won't stay for the wedding?"

She shook her head.

The half-orc ran a hand through his hair and struggled then to speak. "Why do you really go, my friend?"

"You don't need me anymore, Drelm."

He grunted. "You're wrong. I have never had a better friend, and I never shall. A man needs friends."

"You will rule Delgar as mayor and priest, and it will prosper. You don't need someone else giving orders."

Drelm looked skeptical, but was enough of a pragmatist to recognize when an argument was lost. "I'd like it if you returned," he said, then sounded oddly vulnerable as he spoke on. "But don't promise if you won't do so."

"I will be back to visit," she said. "I promise."

He nodded, then turned his head and fiddled with his hand. Elyana didn't fully realize he was fumbling with his ring until he'd half removed it.

"That's yours, Drelm."

He extended it to her, held delicately between one thick finger and one broad thumb. "You'll need it more than I."

"Do you think?"

"I know."

Elyana took the thing, then set it to her hand in the place where she'd once worn a ring of shadows. Decades before, Baron Stelan had gifted her with the shadow ring, and she'd worn it for years, hoping it meant more than it ever had.

Now she accepted a different ring from a different man. The first had been from a lover who had become her friend, and had led the way to strange realms of darkness. The second was from a friend whom she loved, and would see her through to safety so long as it remained upon her finger.

"I will cherish it."

"As I cherish you," Drelm told her.

He looked surprised when she embraced him, then folded those large arms around her middle, and they stood together for a long while. She had never truly grown used to the scent of him, but had long since given up caring.

When they broke apart he was dabbing at his eyes, and she chose not to stare, for tears had misted her own vision.

She raised a hand to him, climbed into Calda's saddle, then whistled for attention. "Come, Demid!"

She rode for the tower's open gate, the Brevan following.

She looked back once, halfway down Delgar's dusty street, and saw a thick figure in a shining helm on the tower's gated wall, hand lifted in farewell. She drew Calda to a stop and returned the gesture, then waited for Demid to reach her. "I'll race you to the oak grove," she told him.

The Brevan grinned as she touched her heels to Calda's flanks. The horse sprang forward.

About the Author

Howard Andrew Jones is the author of two previous Pathfinder Tales: the novel *Plague of Shadows* and the short story "The Walkers from the Crypt," both starring Elyana. His creator-owned novel *The Desert of Souls* was honored on the Kirkus New and Notable Science Fiction list and the Locus Recommended Reading List, and was number four on Barnes & Noble's Best Fantasy Releases of 2011, as well as a finalist for the prestigious Compton Crook Award. Its characters of Dabir and Asim have since appeared in a sequel, *The Bones of the Old Ones*, and a collection of short stories, *The Waters of Eternity*.

When not helping run his small family farm or spending time with his wife and children, Howard has worked variously as a TV cameraman, a book editor, a recycling consultant, and a college writing instructor. He was instrumental in the rebirth of interest in Harold Lamb's historical fiction, and has assembled and edited eight collections of Lamb's work. He serves as the Managing Editor of *Black Gate* magazine and blogs regularly at **blackgate.com** as well as at **howardandrewjones.com**.

Acknowledgments

This novel would not exist without the thoughtful and helpful guidance of the talented James Sutter. Thank you, my friend!

Glossary

All Pathfinder Tales novels are set in the rich and vibrant world of the Pathfinder campaign setting. Below are explanations of several key terms used in this book. For more information on the world of Golarion and the strange monsters, people, and deities that make it their home, see *The Inner Sea World Guide*, or dive into the game and begin playing your own adventures with the *Pathfinder Roleplaying Game Core Rulebook* or the *Pathfinder Roleplaying Game Beginner Box*, all available at **paizo.com**. Those readers particularly interested in the River Kingdoms should check out *Pathfinder Campaign Setting: Guide to the River Kingdoms*, and fans of Elyana and Drelm can find their earlier adventures together in the novel *Plague of Shadows*.

Abadar: Master of the First Vault and the god of cities, wealth, merchants, and law.

Alchemists: Spellcasters whose magic takes the form of potions, explosives, and strange mutagens that modify their physiology.

Alkenstar: A nation famous for the production of guns and gunpowder.

Almas: Capital city of Andoran.
Andoran: Democratic and freedom-loving nation.
Andoren: Someone from Andoran; of or related to Andoran.
Black Coil: An assassin's guild that operates primarily in Cheliax.
Brevan: Someone from Brevoy.
Brevic: Of or pertaining to Brevoy.
Brevoy: A frigid northern nation famous for its duelists.
Calistria: Also known as the Savored Sting; the goddess of trickery, lust, and revenge.
Cheliax: A powerful devil-worshiping nation.
Chelish: Of or relating to the nation of Cheliax.
Cleric: A religious spellcaster whose magical powers are granted by his or her god.
Daggermark: The largest city in the River Kingdoms, infamous for its poisoners' and assassins' guilds.
Delgar: A small frontier town in the southern River Kingdoms, established relatively recently.
Demons: Evil denizens of the plane of the afterlife called the Abyss, who seek only to maim, ruin, and feed on mortal souls.
Druid: Someone who reveres nature and draws magical power from the boundless energy of the natural world.
Druma: A nation which views the accumulation of wealth as the highest possible goal.
Dwarves: Short, stocky humanoids who excel at physical labor, mining, and craftsmanship. Stalwart enemies of the orcs and other evil subterranean monsters.
Eagle Knights: Military order in Andoran devoted to spreading the virtues of justice, equality, and freedom.
Elven: Of or pertaining to elves; the language of elves.

Elves: Long-lived, beautiful humanoids identifiable by their pointed ears, lithe bodies, and pupils so large their eyes appear to be one color.

Fey: Magical creatures deeply tied to the natural world, such as dryads or pixies.

First World: The rough draft of existence, where nature is more powerful and volatile. Original home of fey creatures and gnomes.

Galt: A nation locked in perpetual bloody revolution.

Galtan: A person or thing from Galt.

Gnomes: Race of small humanoids with strange mindsets, originally from the First World.

Gralton: River Kingdoms town with a large concentration of Galtan refugees.

Gray Gardeners: The masked secret police of Galt, who dispense harsh revolutionary justice to those who cross them or the state.

God of the First Vault: Abadar.

Golarion: The planet on which the Pathfinder campaign setting focuses.

Half-Orcs: Bred from humans and orcs, members of this race have green or gray skin, brutish appearances, and short tempers, and are mistrusted by many societies.

Halflings: Race of humanoids known for their tiny stature, deft hands, and mischievous personalities.

Inner Sea: The vast sea whose northern and southern continents are the primary focus of the Pathfinder campaign setting.

Isger: Vassal nation of Cheliax.

Jovvox: Town in the River Kingdoms.

Kuthite: Worshiper of Zon-Kuthon; of or related to the worship of Zon-Kuthon.

Kyonin: An elven forest-kingdom that borders the River Kingdoms. The center of elven power in the Inner Sea region. Largely forbidden to non-elven travelers.

Lambreth: Small River Kingdom.

Livondar: The lord of Daggermark.

Mivon: Large River Kingdom famous for its duelists.

Oaksteward: Member of the druidic cabal that rules Sevenarches.

Orc: Race of bestial, warlike humanoids from deep underground who now roam the surface in barbaric bands. Almost universally hated by more civilized races.

Ranger: Someone specialized in surviving in a particular terrain; often employed as scouts, guides, hunters, and skirmishers.

Razmir: The self-proclaimed "living god" who rules the nation of Razmiran and constantly seeks to spread his power.

Razmiran: Nation bordering Kyonin and the southwestern River Kingdoms, whose ruler may or may not be a god.

Razmiri: Worshipers and subjects of Razmiran.

River Kingdoms: A region of small, feuding fiefdoms and bandit strongholds, where borders change frequently.

Riverfolk: People from the River Kingdoms.

Riverton: Southernmost town in the River Kingdoms.

Sail: A gold coin of Andoren minting.

Sellen River: Major river whose branches run throughout the River Kingdoms.

Sevenarches: River Kingdoms nation run by druids and closed to all elves.

Sorcerer: Someone who casts spells through natural ability rather than faith or study.

Summoner: A spellcaster who focuses primarily on calling a single, specific magical servant to do his or her bidding.

Taldan: Of or pertaining to Taldor; a citizen of Taldor.

Taldane: The common trade language of Golarion's Inner Sea region.

Taldor: A formerly glorious nation that has lost many of its holdings in recent years to neglect and decadence.

Tymon: City-state in the southwestern River Kingdoms, home to a famed gladiatorial college and arena.

Wand: A sticklike magic item imbued with the ability to cast a specific spell repeatedly.

Wilewood: A large forest in Sevenarches.

Witch: Spellcaster who draws magic from a pact made with an otherworldly power, using a familiar as a conduit.

Wizard: Someone who casts spells through careful study and rigorous scientific methods rather than faith or innate talent, recording the necessary incantations in a spellbook.

Wolf: A sliver coin of Andoren minting.

Wyvern: A brutish draconic creature not as intelligent or cunning as a true dragon.

Zon-Kuthon: The twisted god of envy, pain, darkness, and loss.

The race is on to free Lord Stelan from the grip of a wasting curse, and only Elyana, his old elven adventuring companion and former lover, has the wisdom and reflexes to save him. When the villain turns out to be another of their former companions, Elyana and a band of ragtag adventurers must set out on a perilous race across the revolution-wracked nation of Galt and the treacherous Five Kings Mountains, bound for the mysterious Vale of Shadows. But even if they can succeed in locating the key to Stelan's salvation in a lost valley of weird magic and nightmare beasts, the danger isn't over. For Elyana's companions may not all be what they seem.

From sword and sorcery icon Howard Andrew Jones comes a fantastic new adventure set in the award-winning world of the Pathfinder Roleplaying Game.

Plague of Shadows **print edition: $9.99**
ISBN: 978-1-60125-291-3

Plague of Shadows **ebook edition:**
ISBN: 978-1-60125-333-0

Plague of Shadows

Howard Andrew Jones

Gideon Gull leads a double life: one as a talented young bard at the Rhapsodic College, and the other as a student of the Shadow School, where Taldor's infamous Lion Blades are trained to be master spies. When a magical fog starts turning ordinary people into murderous mobs along the border between Taldor and Andoran, it's up to Gideon and a crew of his fellow performers to solve the mystery. But can a handful of entertainers really stop a brewing war?

From author Chris Willrich comes a new adventure of intrigue, espionage, and arcane mystery, set in the award-winning world of the Pathfinder Roleplaying Game.

The Dagger of Trust print edition: $9.99
ISBN: 978-1-60125-614-0

The Dagger of Trust ebook edition:
ISBN: 978-1-60125-615-7

The Dagger of Trust

Chris Willrich

After a century of imprisonment, demons have broken free of the wardstones surrounding the Worldwound. As fiends flood south into civilized lands, Count Varian Jeggare and his hellspawn bodyguard Radovan must search through the ruins of a fallen nation for the blasphemous text that opened the gate to the Abyss in the first place—and which might hold the key to closing it. In order to succeed, however, the heroes will need to join forces with pious crusaders, barbaric local warriors, and even one of the legendary god callers. It's a race against time as the companions fight their way across a broken land, facing off against fiends, monsters, and a vampire intent on becoming the god of blood—but will unearthing the dangerous book save the world, or destroy it completely?

From best-selling author Dave Gross comes a new adventure set against the backdrop of the Wrath of the Righteous Adventure Path in the award-winning world of the Pathfinder Roleplaying Game.

King of Chaos print edition: $9.99
ISBN: 978-1-60125-558-7

King of Chaos ebook edition:
ISBN: 978-1-60125-559-4

KING OF CHAOS

DAVE GROSS

In the war-torn lands of Molthune and Nirmathas, where rebels fight an endless war of secession against an oppressive military government, the constant fighting can make for strange alliances. Such is the case for the man known only as the Masked—the victim of a magical curse that forces him to hide his face—and an escaped halfling slave named Tantaerra. Thrown together by chance, the two fugitives find themselves conscripted by both sides of the conflict and forced to search for a magical artifact that could help shift the balance of power and end the bloodshed for good. But in order to survive, the thieves will first need to learn to the one thing none of their adventures have taught them: how to trust each other.

From *New York Times* best-selling author and legendary game designer Ed Greenwood comes a new adventure of magic, monsters, and unlikely friendships, set in the award-winning world of the Pathfinder Roleplaying Game.

The Wizard's Mask print edition: $9.99
ISBN: 978-1-60125-530-3

The Wizard's Mask ebook edition:
ISBN: 978-1-60125-531-0

The Wizard's Mask

Ed Greenwood

With strength, wit, rakish charm, and a talking sword named Hrym, Rodrick has all the makings of a classic hero—except for the conscience. Instead, he and Hrym live a high life as scoundrels, pulling cons and parting the weak from their gold. When a mysterious woman invites them along on a quest into the frozen north in pursuit of a legendary artifact, it seems like a prime opportunity to make some easy coin—especially if there's a chance for a double-cross. Along with a hooded priest and a half-elven tracker, the team sets forth into a land of witches, yetis, and ancient magic. As the miles wear on, however, Rodrick's companions begin acting steadily stranger, leading man and sword to wonder what exactly they've gotten themselves into . . .

From Hugo Award-winner Tim Pratt, author of *City of the Fallen Sky*, comes a bold new tale of ice, magic, and questionable morality set in the award-winning world of the Pathfinder Roleplaying Game.

Liar's Blade **print edition: $9.99**
ISBN: 978-1-60125-515-0

Liar's Blade **ebook edition:**
ISBN: 978-1-60125-516-7

Liar's Blade

Tim Pratt

Kagur is a warrior of the Blacklions, fierce and fearless hunters in the savage Realm of the Mammoth Lords. When her clan is slaughtered by a frost giant she considered her adopted brother, honor demands that she, the last surviving Blacklion, track down her old ally and take the tribe's revenge. Yet this is no normal betrayal, for the murderous giant has followed the whispers of a dark god down into the depths of the earth, into a primeval cavern forgotten by time. There, he will unleash forces capable of wiping all humans from the region—unless Kagur can stop him first.

From acclaimed author Richard Lee Byers comes a tale of bloody revenge and subterranean wonder, set in the award-winning world of the Pathfinder Roleplaying Game.

Called to Darkness **print edition: $9.99**
ISBN: 978-1-60125-465-8

Called to Darkness **ebook edition:**
ISBN: 978-1-60125-466-5

Called to Darkness

RICHARD LEE BYERS

A pirate captain of the Inner Sea, Torius Vin makes a living raiding wealthy merchant ships with his crew of loyal buccaneers. Few things matter more to Captain Torius than ill-gotten gold—but one of those is Celeste, his beautiful snake-bodied navigator. When a crafty courtesan offers the pirate crew a chance at the heist of a lifetime, it's time for both man and naga to hoist the black flag and lead the *Stargazer*'s crew of monsters and misfits to fame and fortune. But will stealing the legendary Star of Thumen chart the corsairs a course to untold riches—or send them all to a watery grave?

From noted author Chris A. Jackson comes a fantastical new adventure of high-seas combat set in the award-winning world of the Pathfinder Roleplaying Game.

Pirate's Honor print edition: $9.99
ISBN: 978-1-60125-523-5

Pirate's Honor ebook edition:
ISBN: 978-1-60125-524-1

PIRATE'S HONOR

CHRIS A. JACKSON

EXPLORE YOUR
WORLD!

paizo
PUBLISHING